Ira David Wood III is an award-winning actor, director, and playwright. He is the founder and current Executive Director of Theatre in the Park, located in Raleigh, North Carolina. He is the proud father of three children: Ira David Wood IV, Evan Rachel Wood, and Thomas Miller Wood. He and his wife, Ashley, remain proud to call North Carolina "home".

For Ira, Evan, Thomas and Jack.

"Truth and Beauty survive."

Ira David Wood III

THE RUSSIAN GALATEA

AUSTIN MACAULEY PUBLISHERS™

LONDON · CAMBRIDGE · NEW YORK · SHARJAH

A CIP catalogue record for this title is available from the British Library.

ISBN 9781528900867 (Paperback)
ISBN 9781528900874 (E-Book)

www.austinmacauley.com

First Published (2018)
Austin Macauley Publishers Ltd
25 Canada Square
Canary Wharf
London
E14 5LQ

The Russian Galatea began as a stage play and was simply titled *Galatea*. It premiered at Theatre in the Park, Raleigh, NC, in 1987, and was well received by audiences and critics alike.

"Galatea hits nerves . . . maybe because the symbolism of its core event—fairy tale gunned down by rationalized brutality—has only more import as the 20th century grinds on."

"The play opposes intellect and reason with violence and expediency: Sokolov's rational assignment, to prove that the Romanovs are dead, carried out for purposes of propaganda in the midst of rising chaos—chaos let loose by rationalism in the first place. As Sokolov proceeds, he finds a world becoming exponentially madder, with the truth (or Truth) becoming whatever one chooses to make it—like the mythological statue of the title."

"The viewer is drawn through all this by the inherent fascination of the subject and by a nicely developing mystery story structure. Using the device of having Sokolov double as narrator, speaking directly to the audience, the play captures interest and sustains it—through some scenes that are themselves assaults on senses and sensibilities."

"It is engrossing theater."

"Cause for celebration, indeed."

Jim Wise
The Durham Herald

"David Wood has written an enigmatic ending that satisfies both recorded history and the romantic desire to believe that Anastasia lives."

"Galatea comes alive for its audience as did the ancient statue."

Harry Hargrave
The News & Observer

"Galatea is a detective story about one dauntless investigator's obsession with finding out what really happened to Russian Tsar Nicholas II and his family. It is absolutely intriguing."

"Galatea is riveting…"

"…may well earn Wood his highest honors in his distinguished local career as actor, director and playwright."

"The opening night audience certainly found a good deal to cheer in Galatea—and rightly so."

Robert McDowell
The Raleigh Times

Because of the demands of being a husband, father, and grandfather—as well as my duties as Executive Director of a year-round theatre—expanding the original stage version of *Galatea* into novel form has taken a bit of time. A paragraph here, a paragraph there. Thankfully I was able to move, unhurried, through the world of my imagination as the novel slowly began to take shape and finally moved beyond the boundaries of a stage setting.

To the casts and crews of all productions of the theatre version, I remain so deeply grateful. When I decided to tackle this project, their talent and dedication to the work was a constant inspiration.

There are several other individuals without whose unique support and encouragement, I would never have been able to finally complete the task.

I am particularly grateful to Thomas Porter (who played Anatoly Yakimov in the second production of *Galatea*) for sharing some very useful reference books on the subject.

Hannah Nicholson Poteat, a friend and former English teacher, read my early manuscript and responded with words of encouragement that seemed like water in the desert to this writer. Her support came just when I needed it the most.

I am also especially indebted to another dear friend and fellow thespian, Stuart Marland. Not only is he an extremely talented actor, but his invaluable knowledge of the subject matter, along with his steady encouragement, observations, and suggestions, came at an especially pivotal time. Having visited Russia and even writing a play on the subject himself, his contributions were extremely useful and so deeply appreciated.

Though based on historical fact and the lives of real people, *The Russian Galatea* is finally a work of fiction.

Perhaps, like Nicholas Sokolov, I simply wanted to somehow reaffirm the belief that truth and beauty can indeed survive the most extreme cases of indifference and unimaginable cruelty. If that happens to be a belief you share as well, I hope you will find some gentle reassurance in this story.

Ira David Wood III

Preface

Nicholas Sokolov's Journal
Hotel du Bon Lafontaine—Paris, 1921

What I am about to tell you is a true story.

Chapter One

Sokolov's Journal—1919
*"Life is a warfare and a stranger's sojourn,
and after fame is oblivion."*

The place—Russian Siberia. February 7, 1919. My name is Nicholas Alexeyevich Sokolov. Called 'Nicky' by closest friends. Thirty-six years old. Born in Mokshane, near Penza in 1882, I now serve as an officer in the Russian White Army—at war with the Reds, Lenin's Bolsheviks. My official rank is that of Special Court Investigator.

We are obviously separated by time, you and I. It may be difficult for you to completely understand the historical backdrop against which this story unfolds.

We have a saying here: "It is easier to kill six Russians than to conquer one." During the first twelve months of the Great War with Germany, we managed to verify the chilling accuracy of that statement. Within the space of two years—1914 through 1915— our Russian Army was crushed in Eastern Prussia. We lost Poland, Lithuania, Courland; and suffered disasters in Galacia on an unbelievable scale.

Due to sheer incompetence, corruption and an abysmal lack of leadership, our number of casualties—wounded and prisoner— came to 3,800,000 men. By 1916, of the 15,000,000 soldiers that had been called into action, 8,000,000 were dead—over half the total. An inconceivable waste of life!

That is why the old Imperial Russia stood for everything I had come to despise. And no one man represented the pathetic inadequacy, political atrophy and sheer devastation of that time more than Nicholas Alexandrovich Romanov—the last Tsar of all the Russias—and at one time, supreme ruler of more than one hundred and twenty million people.

Standing only five feet, six inches tall, his official title was Nicholas II, Emperor and Autocrat of All the Russias. Born on May 6, 1868, he succeeded his father Alexander III as Tsar in 1894. In regal splendor, Nicholas and his wife, Alexandra of

Hesse, a German princess and granddaughter of Queen Victoria, were coronated in 1896. Russia has only barely managed to survive the twenty-three catastrophic years since. Nicholas abdicated his throne two years ago. It was, however, an act of final desperation that sadly came too late to save Russia from the inevitable.

Vladimir Illich Ulyanov (now known simply as Lenin) once explained that for revolution to succeed, two conditions had to be present: serious discontent among the masses and loss of confidence on the part of the rulers in their ability to react. By 1917, therefore, the possibility of rebellion couldn't have been more ideal. Lenin sensed the time was right.

As he so keenly predicted, Russia is now engulfed in ruthless civil war. Of course, Lenin prefers the term: revolution. Simply translated: we extricated our country from war with Germany in order to continue the wholesale slaughter among ourselves.

Against this merciless tapestry of fiery revolution and a bitter winter, I have today made my way to Ekaterinburg, Siberia—a once bustling outpost located on the eastern slope of the Ural Mountains. The region is currently occupied by our White Army, under the leadership of one Admiral Alexander Kolchak—Supreme Ruler of the White Government in Omsk—before whom I have been summoned to appear.

The large, low-slung house with thick walls and stone carvings outlining its two-story facade appeared through the cold gray mist like a forbidding apparition. It sat on the highest point of land in Ekaterinburg—49 Voznesensky Prospekt. Originally built atop the ruins of the first Voznesensky Church and its seventeenth-century cemetery, it was now surrounded on all sides by guardhouses and a rough wooden double palisade that was fourteen feet tall...so tall that only the top most portion of the second floor windows of the house could be seen from the street. On the left side of the roof of the house was an attic dormer window where a Maxim gun had once been positioned.

Opposite the house stood the Church of the Ascension—one of the few remaining religious edifices still standing in Ekaterinburg. Next to the church and directly across the street from the low-slung house with thick walls stood another two story building which served as the British Consulate.

Nicholas Sokolov, his back to Voznesensky Square and shielded against the bitter Siberian wind by his long grey military

13

overcoat, paused just inside the stockade's entrance to gaze about. The residence looming before him had obviously once been a handsome dwelling built by well to-do owners. Now however, it materialized in the frigid mist as an ominous specter conjuring nothing more than the faintest glimmer of happier days.

The deserted courtyard which spread before Sokolov's gaze was located at the northern end of the property which also included a two-story carriage house, a storage shed, a pergola overlooking the gardens, a bathhouse, and a small servant's cottage—all now in various stages of neglect and disrepair.

Undeterred, the eager Investigator, leaning into another sudden gust of frigid wind, slogged his way across the empty courtyard, which was now almost completely covered by mud, dead tree branches, and drifts of icy sludge. As he approached the main house, two armed soldiers standing guard on either side of the doorway came to attention. After climbing six granite steps and dutifully presenting his orders and identification papers to the two rather imposing sentries, Sokolov was allowed to enter through the thick double doors.

Once inside, he found himself in a dimly lit vestibule with only the scarcest of furnishings. Though it was quite obvious that the house must have once been well appointed and warmly decorated, the barren and disheveled interior that now greeted Sokolov was nothing more than a sad remnant of its former life.

The warmer air that greeted him here was thick, musty, and laced with faint traces of the aromas that always seem to infuse the shuttered rooms and heavy stillness of old houses—the pungent and combined scent of oil cloths, sweet soap, lye, kerosene, terpin-hydrate mixed with codeine, cod liver oil, paregoric, bees wax from melted candles, camphor, dying flowers mixed with barely detectable medicinal odors including cloves, cinnamon, lavender, bay rum, rosemary and peppermint. To the young Investigator, the convergence of these dissimilar scents, combined with the engulfing stillness and dim light, created an ambiance of heavy mournfulness—as if something once vibrant and alive had been violently wrenched from the very heart of the place. Closing the heavy doors behind him, Sokolov silently proceeded to a handsomely carved wooden staircase directly in front of him and ascended to the second floor.

Former Lord High Admiral Alexander Kolchak, forty-five years old and a national hero during the Russo-Japanese War, was sitting at a small wooden table in one of the upstairs rooms that served as a temporary field office. A muscular man, his short cropped hair was flecked with silver and his starched white shirt was rolled to the elbows. Hunched over a small mirror and basin of steaming hot water, he was shaving.

A recent coup d'état had resulted in Admiral Kolchak being proclaimed *'Supreme Ruler of Russia'*—a dubious title at best since other stubborn factions were also still jockeying for the ever-shifting positions of power. In September 1918, however, one particular gathering of representatives from these various and disassociated groups had actually managed to come together in Ufa to form an organization called the Directory. They placed Admiral Kolchak at the helm. In doing so, a man whose training had been based entirely on naval warfare was now in charge of a crucial military campaign on land. It obviously made sense to someone, but was unfortunately typical of the sort of strategy that currently guaranteed the White Army's eventual defeat in almost any military campaign it undertook.

It was clearly a case of too many cooks inevitably spoiling the broth. Even though all of the disparate groups making up the Directory were united in stoic opposition to Lenin's Bolsheviks, fervent conviction was finally no substitute for effective strategy. It was proving extremely difficult to mount what was needed most—a coordinated and decisive offensive. The clearest proof of which lay in the fact that by the end of 1917, Lenin's Bolsheviks had barely managed to gain control of Petrograd, Moscow and the territory between both cities. Two years later, however, they had become a formidable force to be reckoned with. Lenin had actually found his greatest ally in the confusing disarray of his opposing forces.

Despite the fact that no Allied nation had yet recognized Admiral Kolchak's government as legitimate, on this particular February morning in Ekaterinburg, as Nicholas Sokolov prepared to meet his Supreme Commander face to face, the White Army's progress actually seemed commendable. Kolchak's greatest military strength in the region was undoubtedly coming from the Czech Legion, a force of about thirty-thousand former members of the Russian army, deserters from the Austro-Hungarian army or ex-prisoners of war. Though this group appeared ragtag to most observers, they had recently managed to rout the Bolsheviks and were now in control of most of the Trans-Siberian Railroad from Lake Baikal to the Ural Mountains—an area which included Ekaterinburg.

Sokolov entered the small upstairs room, came to formal attention facing the seated Admiral and extended the hand which held his official papers and identification.

"Court Investigator Sokolov reporting as ordered."

Kolchak glanced up briefly then resumed his grooming ritual.

"You're Sokolov?" he replied with a rather disinterested shrug. "Not quite what I expected."

Still in smart military fashion, the young Investigator stepped forward and placed his official documents on the table near Kolchak's shaving basin.

"I believe, Sir, you will find that my papers are quite in order."

Kolchak merely smirked, dipped his straight razor into the basin of steaming water and continued shaving. "You wouldn't be standing here if they weren't," he replied. "This is Russian Siberia, Investigator Sokolov. Even Jesus Christ would have difficulty bringing off His Second Coming without proper papers."

It was Sokolov's turn to smile. "With all due respect, I doubt He could do it even then."

"Oh?"

"The Son of God chooses Siberia as the site of his Second Coming? Even with proper papers, who'd ever believe Him?"

The Admiral shifted an exacting gaze to Sokolov, then leaned back in his chair. "The Son of God in Siberia," he chuckled, tossing his straight razor into the steaming basin of water. "I like that!" Kolchak's head tilted slightly. "I was referring to your preeminence, actually. You've quite an impressive reputation as a legal investigator. Photographic memory as well. Studied law at Kharkov in the Ukraine. I suppose I was expecting someone…else."

Reaching for a nearby bottle of vodka, Kolchak poured two drinks. Handing one of them to Sokolov, he continued jauntily. "At ease, Court Investigator Sokolov. Have some vodka! Good for you in cold like this. Doesn't make you any warmer, of course. It's just that, after a bottle or two, you won't give a damn if you're freezing!"

Sokolov took the small glass of vodka but dutifully waited to drink until the Admiral raised his own glass. Ignoring the opportunity, Kolchak rose from the table, drying his face with a hand towel. "So! You've only just arrived?"

"By train this morning."

This was true, but only partially. Sokolov had, in fact, walked fifty frozen miles through disputed territory in order to reach the rail line. The journey had been an arduous one to say the least.

"The trains are running?" the Admiral sniffed indifferently. "Imagine that!"

Kolchak's demeanor still seemed amiable enough as he strolled to a nearby window in order to peer into the courtyard below. In the cold and muddy Voznesensky Prospek that stretched beyond the imposing stockade fence, one of Ekaterinburg's few remaining electric street cars, its bell clanging noisily, slowly rattled past.

"The trains are running two days behind schedule," Sokolov added softly.

"Only two?" Kolchak turned from the window with a look of pleasant surprise. "Damned encouraging!"

The young Investigator was still politely awaiting the Admiral's first sip of vodka. Having been reminded of his treacherous journey to reach Ekaterinburg, he was more than ready for a drink. Kolchak, unfortunately, didn't seem to be in any apparent hurry to oblige. After rolling down his sleeves, buttoning his cuffs, and adjusting his necktie, he merely ambled back to Sokolov.

"On the other hand," the Admiral continued, "it's only been a year since Russia adopted the Gregorian calendar. We're too accustomed to being twelve days behind the rest of humanity. Only took one world war and a revolution to bring us to our senses. Russia may not be fast, Investigator, but by God, we're sure!"

Kolchak raised his glass at last and took a healthy swallow. Immensely relieved, Sokolov eagerly followed his host's example.

"We've finally arrived!" Kolchak groused, depositing his half-empty glass on the table and grabbing his military jacket which had been casually draped over the back of his chair. "Our White Army against Lenin's Reds. Civil War! Revolution! We've made it to the modern age. Why fight the Germans when we can simply brawl among ourselves? White armies, Red armies. What the hell's the difference? We're all Russians! At least, we were."

Kolchak slipped on his jacket and began to button the double-breasted front. Sokolov couldn't help but notice the jacket's breast. It was studded with medals.

"Tell me," Kolchak continued, gesturing nonchalantly around the room. "What do you think of this house?"

"This house?" The abruptness of the shift in conversation caught Sokolov slightly off balance. "Adequate, I suppose."

Kolchak's piercing eyes snapped back to Sokolov. "Adequate. Now there's a word," he boomed with another broad grin. Lifting the glass to his lips once more, Kolchak downed the rest of his vodka in one gulp. Once more, Sokolov happily obeyed the Admiral's example.

Reaching again for the bottle, Kolchak poured another generous round into Sokolov's glass. "Describes the place very well," he continued. "Built between 1875 and '79 they tell me. Twenty-one rooms. Belongs to a local merchant by the name of Ipatiev. We're borrowing it for a time."

Pouring still more vodka into his own glass, the Admiral blithely continued his elaboration. "Beautiful views from up here." He beckoned for Sokolov to join him at one of the room's windows. "Highest point of land in the area," he announced ceremoniously, pointing out a lake, public gardens and the distant rooftops of the town to the obliging Investigator.

"A year and a half ago it was borrowed by the Red Army. Lenin's Bolsheviks. They built the high wooden stockade outside and put up the ten guard houses you see down there. Turned it into something of a fortress really. Rooms on the ground floor below us were converted into more guardrooms and offices. Up here, living quarters. Adequate place for you, while you're here." Kolchak draped a congenial arm around Sokolov's shoulder. "You see, I have a little job for you."

This announcement was hardly a surprise to Sokolov. He knew he hadn't traveled hundreds of difficult and dangerous miles through decimated countryside in order to reach Ekaterinburg on a whim. Silently, he took a sip of vodka, delaying long enough for the Admiral to expound further on the assignment. It was promptly obvious, however, that Kolchak had not finished reminiscing. Taking another swig of his own drink, the Admiral perched nonchalantly on the edge of the wooden table that served as his office desk.

"So, Nicholai Alexeyevich Sokolov. Here you are! Ekaterinburg, Siberia. A long way from Moscow. Beautiful Moscow!" Kolchak suddenly turned to the young Investigator with a look that seemed edged with genuine regard. "Moscow is still beautiful? Yes?"

Sokolov smiled and nodded. "Very."

"Well, that's something of a consolation," the Admiral sighed with wistful relief. "Spent most of my youth there. God, those were carefree days!"

Kolchak withdrew a cigar from his jacket pocket and bit off its tip. Turning to Sokolov, he continued. "Do you smoke?"

"Cigarettes...occasionally," the Investigator admitted.

"Well, have one if you wish. We don't stand on much ceremony here."

Kolchak watched in deliberate silence as the Investigator obligingly dug into his jacket's breast pocket and, after a bit of awkward fumbling, withdrew a single crumpled cigarette, yellowed with age. Sokolov thoughtfully regarded the small battered relic between his fingers before becoming aware of the Admiral's gaze.

"You spend most of your time in Petrograd, don't you?" Kolchak observed wryly.

Thinking he'd just detected a slight trace of disdain in the Admiral's voice, Sokolov promptly returned the yellowed cigarette to his breast pocket.

"Yes, actually," he responded warily, "how did you know?"

Kolchak spread his arms in a grand gesture of dramatic delight. "Because you, my friend, have the unmistakable air of an intellectual!"

Sokolov's controlled reaction was one of muted puzzlement. The Admiral, obviously buoyed by the Investigator's lack of response, continued almost gleefully. "A singular lack of humor. You see life in terms of reasons! Hardly room for laughter there." With a sudden afterthought, Kolchak added with a grin, "Probably why I've never met a happy intellectual."

The Investigator rebounded with a query of his own. "And you never find yourself in need of reasons?"

"One of the benefits of my position," Kolchak chuckled. "When I need reasons, I appoint commissions. Amazing things, commissions. Provide whatever reasons I might possibly require...should reason ever achieve some sort of special preeminence in any of this." The Admiral's grin suddenly vanished. He leaned close to Sokolov and continued squarely, "Do you know that I could draw my revolver right now, and shoot you dead in this desolate little room for no reason whatsoever? But, give me one good commission made up of four or five paper-pushing bureaucrats, and I'll hand the world at least dozen rational and compelling reasons for your totally senseless murder. What's more, they'll be typed out in triplicate and bound in handsome, leather folders. Hell! I'd probably end up getting a medal for my trouble...which would be quite inconsiderable, I assure you."

Kolchak paused to light his cigar. After a few contented puffs, he concluded thoughtfully.

"The Son of God in Siberia? With one of my commissions, He just might make it!" The Admiral, once more awaiting Sokolov's response, jauntily thumped the tip of his cigar on the rim of a nearby ashtray.

The young Investigator considered his next words carefully. "The United States President, James Garfield, once said: 'A war that has no idea behind it is simply brutality.'"

"Yes," Kolchak fired back without a moment's hesitation. "Tell me; did he say that before or after they shot him?" The Admiral's unyielding gaze remained fixed on Sokolov. "Garfield was assassinated, I believe."

Concerned that his frankness had possibly been perceived as overstepping the boundary of rank, Sokolov attempted to backtrack. "I mean no disrespect," he offered with a slight but deferential bow.

"None taken," the Admiral shrugged, discharging the Investigator's apology with a dismissive wave of his hand. "Go on."

Sokolov decided to adopt a more guarded posture none-the-less "It's just that..." His voice trailed off for a moment before he finally squared his shoulders and continued with remodeled purpose. "Why would a man choose to pass through life without reasons? How does such a man view his world?"

Kolchak was clearly anticipating the question.

"Unconditionally" was his self-assured reply. "You intellectuals don't seem to handle that very well."

The Admiral let several seconds of silence elapse before continuing with purposeful earnestness. "Tell me something," he began. "Do you know the real difference between life and death?"

The abruptness of the query again caught Sokolov off guard. "Physically or philosophically?" It was the best response he could muster.

"There," the Admiral exclaimed, jabbing a finger into the startled Investigator's chest. "Exactly my point! You're searching so earnestly for deeper philosophical meanings, you've distorted the simple question. Intellectuals will never admit that some answers in this life...some people..." Kolchak patted his chest several times for emphasis. "Some people simply are!" With a slight flourish, the Admiral poured Sokolov yet another vodka. "Ah, yes," he went on, shifting once more into an almost wistful tone of voice. "Petrograd. Hell, I knew it when we still called it St. Petersburg. I was born there. The Maryinsky Theatre. Glinka, Rimsky Korsakov, Borodin, Mussorgsky and Tchaikovsky. Where you first read Dostoevsky and Tolstoy."

The stunned expression that transformed Sokolov's face wasn't caused by surprise as much as bewilderment at Kolchak's persistence in belaboring the obvious point.

"Don't look so astonished," the Admiral advised, pursing his lips indulgently in order to exhale another puff of cigar smoke. "Everyone reads Dostoevsky in Petrograd. At least they used to. Tell me, what do they read now?"

"Now?" Sokolov tried vainly to resist the slight trace of sarcasm now creeping into his own voice. "They don't read books in Petrograd. They burn them. Firewood is scarce, you see. They burn their books to keep warm."

As if completely unimpressed, Kolchak merely chucked to himself as he idly thumbed through the pages of one of the few books on his desk.

"You don't seem very surprised," Sokolov observed.

"Why should I be?" the Admiral shrugged with disarming nonchalance. "The Arts are expendable. They're always the first to go. Still, damned intriguing. Russians burning books in Petrograd. So—what, finally, has Dostoevsky done for the revolution? He's kept us warm!" Kolchak laughed heartily and downed his glass of vodka before once more assuming an air of solemnity. "They tell me you have a photographic memory," he said, squinting at Sokolov for a moment before concluding, "is that true?"

The Investigator was deliberately ambiguous. "I tend to recall things. Details."

Kolchak lifted a leather bound book from his desk, intentionally covering its front cover with his hand. "Suppose I asked you to tell me the title of this book...the one I thumbed through just a moment ago," he smiled. "Could you do that?"

It was Sokolov's turn to savor the moment. He returned Kolchak's smile with one of his own. "It was a Russian translation of *The Art of War*."

The Admiral's self-confidence seemed instantly diminished. He lifted his hand from the book's cover and studied it in curious silence for only an instant. Glancing back up at Sokolov with a smile that now seemed slightly forced, he replied, "Well, I'll be damned."

Nicholas Sokolov had long ago come to the point of dismissing such exercises as nothing more than parlor games, but this particular moment's triumph was simply too gratifying to abandon hastily. "One of the earliest known compilations on the subject of war and strategy," he continued deliberately. "Written in 4 BC by the Chinese author known as Sun-Tzu."

The ensuing dramatic pause belonged to Sokolov and he knew it. Kolchak sullenly studied the young investigator in calculated silence before gently returning the book to its place on his desk.

"Damned impressive," he finally admitted. "A photographic memory and a keen appreciation of history all rolled into one."

Shaking his head, the Admiral dissolved into laughter once more before suddenly realizing that Sokolov was not making the mandatory effort to validate his superior's attempt at humor. The Investigator, hands clasped firmly behind his back, was simply facing Kolchak in stony silence.

The Admiral's demeanor shifted at once. His body visibly stiffened as his brow furled ever so slightly. Then, almost as quickly, the outward agitation appeared to fade away. He was suddenly gazing at Sokolov with an air of almost childlike curiosity.

"You don't find that terribly amusing, do you?"

Sokolov never flinched. "I find very few things in Russia that amuse me anymore."

"Pity," Kolchak sighed, turning his back to Sokolov in order to once more face the windows in the room. "I couldn't imagine going through all this without being able to laugh at something!" The Admiral quietly puffed on his cigar for a moment before turning back to Sokolov. "I remember once…during the war…coming face to face with a German soldier. Both of us, in the wrong place at the wrong time. We rounded the corner of a stone wall, you see, and just came face to face. His weapon was at the ready. Mine wasn't. All he had to have done was pull the trigger. But you see, when we rounded the corner and saw each other, we simply froze. Frightening thing to suddenly see Death only an inch or so from your nose. I did the only thing a man could do in that situation. Lost control of my bowels! Could've heard it in Minsk! For a moment, we just stood there transfixed. And then, I couldn't help it… I started to laugh. It all suddenly seemed so ridiculously funny. What's even crazier is that the German obviously thought so too because, all at once, he was laughing louder than I. Two young men at war with each other, standing face to face in a battle zone, laughing our heads off! Saved my life though. A sense of humor. I've never forgotten."

"I doubt the German has either," Sokolov volunteered with a forced smile. "Something to tell his grandchildren."

The Admiral cocked his head to one side and grinned. "The German? He was laughing so hard he could hardly raise his rifle. So I raised mine. Shot him right between his eyes. Dead before he hit the ground. I stepped forward and looked down at his face. Not much left. A bit of nose and mouth. But... Do you know? All of the mouth that was left was still grinning. Only man I've ever seen who literally died laughing!"

Kolchak, bellowing with sudden laughter, strode jauntily to Sokolov and stopped directly in front of him, their faces only inches apart. The Admiral squinted at the Investigator with genuine amusement.

"You know?" he finally admitted, "I think I like you, Nicholas Sokolov. You're a bookworm, of course; but a rather particular bookworm. You have unusual ideas."

Sokolov managed a slight smile, but it quickly vanished under the weight of the Admiral's next verbal assault.

"You think me crude and barbaric," Kolchak observed. "A man who requires no reasons."

Sokolov attempted a reply in modest protest, but the Admiral, lifting his hand in a gesture for silence, continued deliberately. "We're complete opposites, you and I. And yet, like this house, I believe we'll both prove...adequate. Precisely why I've chosen you for this particular assignment."

There it was again, that tantalizing mention of an assignment. The good Admiral was dangling it like a carrot in front of a hungry mule and he knew it. Sokolov decided it was time to cut to the heart of the matter.

"What assignment?"

Kolchak's demeanor softened at once. Shrugging his shoulders, he replied almost indifferently. "I want you to find out what happened to Nicholas Alexandrovich Romanov and his family. We want to know what happened to the last Tsar of Russia."

Nicholas Sokolov actually staggered backward several steps in numb disbelief. He could manage only two words: "He's...dead."

23

Kolchak's eyes brightened immediately. "Oh, really? How do you know?"

Still struggling to regain his wits, Sokolov nervously cleared his throat before attempting to authenticate his last statement. "Lenin said so himself. He announced it at a public meeting of the presidium's Central Executive Council in Moscow. Pravda even reported it."

"Ah," Kolchak beamed, "Lenin said so! I see. You're obviously referring to the same Lenin who also declared that 'a war with Austria would be a splendid little thing for the revolution.' This from a man whose cry of 'Peace' brought him to power."

Kolchak paused briefly to pour himself another glass of vodka. "Of course, I'm only a rank amateur at this sort of thing," he resumed, "but it does occur to me that there still remains a nagging little question of proof. Or do you think we should all just pack up and go home satisfied…because Lenin said so?"

Sokolov's brain was still reeling. "Are you saying the Tsar is alive?"

Kolchak deliberately paused to savor a sip of his vodka before continuing. When he did speak again his eyes, glowing like stoked coals, bored into Sokolov.

"If you were Lenin, would you have permitted him to live?" Needing no reply, Kolchak simply barreled ahead. "Of course the Tsar is dead! Quite probably his entire family along with him. I believe he's dead because, given the time and circumstances, there's no way he could've survived. I believe he's dead because the civilized world is no longer able to contain such monarchs. In fact, I'd believe the Tsar is dead for any number of reasons. But never in a million years would I ever believe the Tsar was dead based solely upon the value of Lenin's personal assurance!"

Sokolov could do nothing but follow the Admiral's lead. "What is it you want me to do?"

"Prove it," Kolchak responded almost daintily. "Prove to me that the Tsar and his entire family were butchered by the Bolsheviks. That not even one survived. Any questions?"

Questions? Was the Admiral serious? Sokolov could think of hundreds of questions. Which of them should he select? Where to begin?

Sokolov turned to the Admiral with a hastily assumed and somewhat forced demeanor of professional coolness.

"It would be most helpful," he began as deliberately as possible, "if I could visit the scene of the crime as soon as possible."

There; he'd done it. A hurried defense to be sure, but at least he'd managed a slight reprieve. Unfortunately, the lull was more temporary than he anticipated.

"Scene of the crime?" Kolchak repeated Sokolov's words with feigned astonishment. "In that case, take a look around you. This house stands in a part of town once known as Ascension Square. The Bolsheviks rechristened it. We're now occupying a plot of ground known as The Square of National Vengeance. This is the scene of the crime, Investigator. The Ipatiev House is last place the Romanovs were seen alive. 'Adequate.' Damn good word!"

To describe Nicholas Sokolov as 'dumbstruck' would be an understatement.

Kolchak retrieved a large folder from his desk and deftly passed it off to Sokolov. "Here you are. All we have to go on, I'm afraid. A few names, letters, telegrams, hearsay. A beginning, at least."

On top of the folder, which was bound with a faded burgundy ribbon, was a small framed photograph of a young girl. Kolchak lightly tapped the glass with his index finger. "This photograph, for instance. One of the Tsar's daughters. The youngest, I believe. Pretty thing." Sokolov glanced at the photograph, but was forced to return his attention to the Admiral almost as quickly. "The Imperial family spent the last seventy-eight days of their lives in Ekaterinburg and yet there's precious little to show for it. That makes it a rather intriguing mystery, as far as mysteries go," Kolchak shrugged. "Nicholas Alexandrovich Romanov—a military man as well as an intellectual. Twice blessed. No sense of humor, though, and look what it cost him."

Kolchak, his cigar clinched firmly between grinning teeth, strode to the door of his temporary office and swung it open. The meeting had obviously come to an end. Sokolov, clutching the bundle and photograph under his arm, obediently responded by coming to attention and saluting before heading to the doorway himself. If nothing else, he intended to manage a dignified exit. The Admiral's final admonition, however, dashed those hopes on the spot.

"One last piece of advice," Kolchak concluded softly as if dispensing the most confidential information he possessed, "nothing will be what it seems. Never believe what you hear.

Believe only half of what you see. Suspect even what you hold to be fundamentally true. And with a great deal of luck, you just may survive all this. But the truth is, I'd doubt that too. Nothing personal. Politics."

Obeying a rather clear indication, Sokolov dutifully stepped into the hallway before turning back to face the Admiral.

Kolchak, poised in the doorway of the room, grinned one last time. "Good luck, Nicholai Alexeyevich Sokolov."

Then, as the recently proclaimed 'Supreme Ruler of Russia' swung the door shut in Sokolov's face, he added with a chuckled aside: "Luck. Yes; you're going to need a great deal of that."

Chapter Two

Local Newspaper Announcement
By Filipp Goloshchyokin,
Boshevik War Commissar
in charge of the family's incarceration in Ekaterinburg

"All those under arrest will be held as hostages, and the slightest attempt at counter-revolutionary action in the town will result in the summary execution of the hostages."

The Ipatiev House—Later That Same Day

Still considering the heady weight of Kolchak's challenge, Nicholas Sokolov decided to occupy the late afternoon by making a solitary inspection of the dwelling that was to be his living quarters for the remainder of his stay in Ekaterinburg. This was not merely an idle attempt to pass the time, however. Aside from a rather healthy dose of curiosity, he also felt an urgent need to somehow regain his bearings, ground himself, and try to determine just where and how he would formally begin the investigation. Without a clear plan of action, he always felt ineffective and listless.

At least he brought an impressive professional title to the task at hand: Investigating Magistrate for Cases of Special Importance of the Omsk Tribunal. His philosophy, on the other hand, remained what it had always been: intelligent conclusions come from intelligent choices. On the first page of his journal, he had scribbled the Latin phrase: *Amat Victoria Curam* (Victory Loves Careful Preparation.) Quite simply it meant that his professional decisions were always formed in methodical stages by means of logical deduction and measured progression. The process had served him well and, as a consequence, he never varied the routine. Of course this approach always meant tireless leg work at the outset in order to assemble the necessary bits and pieces of seemingly disjointed information. Uncovering clues. Organizing facts and discovering evidence. This was how it was done; how

27

Sokolov always preferred to advance. Randomness was loathsome. The restless vessel that harbored his brilliant sixth sense always required an anchor.

Sokolov paused in the doorway of an empty upstairs room in the Ipatiev House and took a deep breath. He wanted to clear his head in order to assimilate the first impressions of his new surroundings. Most people only *look* at such things. Not Nicholas Sokolov. It was never what he looked at, but always what he *saw*...details he always gleaned by visually absorbing a particular scene and then mentally cataloging everything within it. What, after all, is the gift of 'photographic memory' if not the singular ability to imbue consciousness with added dimension? To *see* and then to *remember*. That was the key. It was this exclusive ability that made Sokolov unique. His inner eye, like a camera, was continually capturing and 'printing' mental 'photographs' that could be recalled when needed.

Cameras have single lenses. In that sense, Sokolov was no different. Though very few people were aware of the fact, Nicholas Sokolov had only one eye—the left one. His right eye was artificial and made of glass. The match was so good, it was almost impossible to tell the difference. The few acquaintances who did know often observed that 'Nicky' could actually see more with one eye than most would ever behold with two. As for himself, Sokolov considered his infirmity to be an attribute in many ways. Myopic vision afforded him the opportunity to deal with fewer peripheral distractions. A narrower line of vision actually meant that his focus was keener and more easily directed. When, for instance, he studied small handheld things, it was almost as if he was peering at them through a microscope. When he gazed at more distant objects, it was as though he saw them through a telescope. Lacking depth of field additionally meant that everything he saw was displayed on a single flat plane...as if viewing a photograph.

Objects were not near or far in the same way they are envisaged by those with normal sight. Depth perception often assigns psychological significance to things based on their proximity to the viewer. A flattened image of the world therefore made it easier for Sokolov to assign conscious significance on a more dispassionate basis. The irony of it all, however, was not lost on those who knew him. This unusual man who possessed the ability to see more than anyone else was, in reality, half blind.

From the Diary of Tsar Nicholas II
Ekaterinburg, Siberia—1918

The house is fine, clean. We have been assigned four rooms: a corner bedroom, a lavatory, next door a dining room with windows onto a little garden and a view of a low-lying part of town, and finally, a spacious hall with arches in place of doors... A very high wooden fence has been built around the house... A chain of sentries has been posted there and in the little garden too.

The late afternoon light was already beginning to fade as Sokolov continued his solitary exploration of the empty rooms on the second floor of the Ipatiev House. All of the inner guards and outer sentries had hastily departed earlier in the day, as soon as Admiral Kolchak's automobile and armed escort pulled out of the muddy courtyard and chugged through the open gates of the wooden stockade. Since Kolchak's main headquarters was located in Omsk, the Investigator assumed that the Admiral would be returning there to oversee the White Army's progress and ground plans.

At any rate, there was no one left inside the Ipatiev House now but Sokolov and the few household servants who were preparing supper in the kitchen one floor below. His solitary tour of the upper floor of the Ipatiev House was noiseless but for the echo of his own footsteps—louder here, softer there—and the rhythmic rise and fall of the glacial outside wind.

At the northwestern end of the central corridor on the main floor was a lavatory, its linoleum covered floor stained and cracked from the constant drip of exposed pipes. The room also contained a large enamel tub, stove and copper steam boiler to heat the water. To reach the lavatory, Sokolov observed that the Romanovs had to pass through a drawing room and an anteroom—or through the dining room, main hall, kitchen and a secondary hallway.

The upstairs floor was covered in wide pine boards and various threadbare Persian rugs. The walls in the dim hallway were hung with a subtly striped wallpaper.

Reaching the end of the upstairs corridor, the Investigator came at last to a southeastern corner room. He paused only briefly in the open doorway before stepping inside.

Compared to the rest of the rooms on the second floor, this particular room could be referred to as spacious. Sokolov assumed it had once served as Ipatiev's own master bedroom. There were four windows, two of which looked out onto Ascension Lane, a dirt road that accessed the house from one direction and came to a dead end on the other. This had been the last road traveled by the Romanovs; the one that brought them to the Ipatiev House—a road they would not live to use again.

The second pair of windows in the room had a partial view of the church's bell tower which stood directly across the other access road known as Ascension Avenue. The church itself was almost completely obscured by the high stockade fence surrounding the house, so Sokolov returned his attention to the room's silent and musty interior. The walls were covered with pale yellow wallpaper upon which had been painted a freeform frieze of flowers whose once-rich colors had long since faded.

The room's worn and battered furnishings consisted of a rug, two beds, a couch, a baize covered table, a bronze lamp complete with a handmade lamp shade, a single empty bookcase between the two sets of windows, a card table, an armoire, and a washbasin on a cracked marble counter.

Sokolov imagined that the room must've been stifling during the summer months. The only source of ventilation would have been a fortochka located in one of the walls. All other windows had been sealed shut during the Romanov's confinement. Trying to open them or to attempt to glance outside would've been strictly forbidden.

As Sokolov continued to survey the room in studied silence, he couldn't help but recall the lines of a poem written by Nikolai Nekrasov, one of his own countrymen:

"You will live a glorious life...
And you'll die a glorious death!
Your declining days will pass
Peacefully like some Arcadian idyll:
Under Sicily's charming skies,
In the fragrant shade of trees,
Contemplating crimson suns
As they sink into the azure sea
Casting shining rays of gold..."

Nicholas Romanov's time in the Ipatiev House was far from an Arcadian idyll, and the sun's crimson rays were never allowed to grace the shadows of this desolate room. There were also many words that might have more accurately described the Tsar's death. 'Glorious' was not one of them.

As his gaze focused on the two beds in the room, Sokolov couldn't help but wonder whether or not Nicholas and Alexandra had slept in the same bed on their last night together? Did they, with some unconscious sense of impending doom, drift off to sleep holding each other close in what would be their last embrace? And if they did, who would ever know? More importantly, who would ever care?

Suddenly, something else in the room caught Sokolov's eye— a vanity and mirror with two electric lamps on each side was situated in the dimmest corner of the room.

Approaching the vanity, Sokolov tried the switch on one of the lamps. Nothing. He didn't waste time on the second lamp. As his eye became more accustomed to the dimness of the room, he noticed that a single item remained on the table...a small glass jar of cold cream. Picking it up for closer inspection, he immediately noticed that something had been inscribed on the top of the round lid. Holding it so it could better catch the light, the Investigator was stunned to make out the words: "*Court Pharmacy to His Excellency.*"

Nicholas Sokolov was holding a personal item once owned by the last Tsaritsa of Russia.

From a Letter to Nicholas II
Written by his wife, Empress Alexandra

This is the first time in my life I have no idea how to act. Until now God has shown me the way. Right now tho' I cannot hear His instructions.

His hand trembling ever so slightly, Sokolov carefully returned the tiny jar to its original place on the dust-coated table, turned and hurried out of the room.

#

Sokolov's Journal
Ekaterinburg, 1919

There is an old Russian folk saying: "Without God the world cannot be; without the Tsar the earth cannot hold."

As the setting sun finally dipped below the darkening gray horizon, Sokolov was quietly surveying his own living quarters. Admiral Kolchak had assigned the Investigator one of the fourteen rooms on the ground floor of the Ipatiev House. It wasn't large, but did have a small wood-burning stove which provided a degree of welcomed warmth. The pine floor was almost completely covered by a large, if somewhat faded, Persian rug. The room also contained a small bed, dressing table, a single desk and two chairs. Electricity in the town had become sporadic at best, so reliable illumination in the house was most often provided by candles and kerosene lamps.

Adequate.

Sokolov sat alone at the desk with his back to the glowing stove, having decided to finally inspect the parcel given to him by Admiral Kolchak. With studied care, he began to methodically withdraw, separate, and arrange the curious contents on his desktop.

Sokolov's Journal
Ekaterinburg, 1919

I began with what we knew were facts. One: the Tsar's document of abdication was signed and dated March 15, 1917. The Ides of March.

Fact Number Two: by April of 1918, he and, we assume, the rest of his family, were transferred from Tobolsk, Siberia, where they had been kept as virtual prisoners, to this house in Ekaterinburg. The royal family included the Tsar, Nicholas Romanov; (50) his wife, Alexandra (46); their son, Alexeis (13); their four daughters, Olga (22), Tatiana (21), Marie (19) and Anastasia (17).

The third and last fact is simply that on the evening of July 16, 1918—seventy-eight days after their transfer here—Nicholas Romanov, last Tsar of all the Russias, disappeared completely from the face of the earth. Without a trace, a single clue...perhaps without even a cry.

The Bolshevik leadership—located 889 miles to the west of Ekaterinburg—may have been initially unsure when it came to deciding the fate of the Romanovs. Their confusion, however, was never shared by Ilych Lenin. Sokolov suspected that the ultimate fate of the Imperial family—whatever his investigation might prove it to be—had been sanctioned and directed by Moscow from the very beginning. It was well known that Leon Trotsky, the Bolshevik's temperamental commissar for war, had lobbied hard for a public trial with himself as prosecutor. He wanted the proceedings broadcast throughout the country via radio. Lenin, who had little patience for sound and fury when it signified nothing, quietly vetoed the idea. He had other plans.

"Ilych [Lenin] believed that we shouldn't leave the Whites a live banner to rally around, especially under the present difficult circumstances...the decision was not only expedient but necessary. The severity of this summary justice showed the world that we would continue to fight on mercilessly, stopping at nothing. The execution of the Tsar's family was needed not only to frighten, horrify and dishearten the enemy, but also in order to shake up their own ranks to show that there was no turning back, that ahead lay either complete victory or complete ruin... This Lenin sensed well."

Leon Trotsky

Three months prior to the alleged execution of the Romanovs, Soviet Russia had signed the Treaty of Brest Litovsk with Imperial Germany. (Interestingly enough, the document contained a stipulation that no harm was to come to the Romanovs.) Peace, at least on one front, had seemingly been achieved—but at a stupefying price. Lenin had agreed to hand over one-third of European Russia and all of the western Ukraine to German occupation. Though the act stunned millions of disbelieving Russians, Lenin knew the outcome would be well worth the price. The reasoning was simple enough: Russia couldn't fight two wars at once. Lenin needed Germany out of the picture in order for the Bolsheviks to be able to focus their full attention on defeating Kolchak's White Army. What few knew, however, was that Lenin had been paid 1,000,000 British pounds sterling for signing the treaty. The money had changed hands for one reason: Tsar Nicholas II and Tsarina Alexandra were directly related to the British House of Saxe-Coburg-Gotha by virtue of the fact that both were first cousins of King George V of Britain. As fate would have it, the Tsar and Tsarina were also blood relations of Kaiser Wilhelm of Germany. As such, the captive Romanovs had now become helpless pawns in an ongoing game of Tug-O-War between Britain and Germany. (In order to hide the annoying fact that the British royals were related to the German royals, the nomenclature had simply been changed in 1917 from the House of Saxe-Coburg-Gotha to the House of Windsor.)

Russia's civil war was sending shock waves across Europe. The monarchies of Britain and Germany were nervously following the Romanov's tragic fall in the fervent hope that Russia's political turmoil would not set a trend. Initially, King George V had offered safe haven to the deposed Romanovs, but was forced to quietly rescind the invitation because of negative reaction on behalf of the British public. Whatever King George could do to help his royal cousin had to be done in strictest secrecy.

Because of this, only a very select group of individuals would ever be aware of just how deeply involved the House of Windsor had been in any number of classified negotiations and rescue plans regarding the Romanovs. In no time at all, Britain's finest secret agents were moving in and out of Ekaterinburg on a regular basis.

Lenin was, of course, desperately scrambling to appear in complete control of the ever-changing events that were shattering and reshaping Russia at breakneck speed, but he was rather like a man running downhill in front of a huge rolling bolder, while bellowing with some bravado that it was he who was directing its course.

Light a fire under a pot of water and it will eventually come to a boil. The question is, of course, how long it will take for the water to reach its boiling point. The answer depends on many variables.

Only six weeks before all hell had broken loose, an exiled Lenin, languishing fretfully in Switzerland, had moaned, "We who are old will never live to see the revolution!" Now, he was strutting and crowing like a proud rooster in a barnyard.

With the Treaty of Brest-Litovsk signed and Germany seemingly pacified, Lenin and his anxious Bolsheviks could at last turn their undivided attention to Russia's civil war. Still, when needed, he was certainly not averse to using the captive Romanovs as bargaining chips for his own purposes.

Should Kaiser Wilhelm ever entertain second thoughts about his country's pact with Russia, Lenin could always remind him that he still held the life of Empress Alexandra in his hands—a German princess who was also Kaiser Wilhelm's first cousin. As long as she was alive, Alexandra remained another invaluable chess piece in Lenin's devious game of treachery, extortion, and lust for power.

It was most especially for this reason that Moscow exerted meticulous control of all publicly released information concerning the bloody events in Ekaterinburg. On July 20, newspapers in Moscow and St. Petersburg carried headlines declaring:

"EX-TSAR SHOT AT EKATERINBURG! DEATH OF NICHOLAS ROMANOV!"

Nicholas Sokolov, in his own detailed review of these press releases, noted that the official execution announcement, as dutifully printed in Pravda and Izvestia, carefully omitted any mention of Nicholas's wife, son or daughters. As far as the public knew at the time, the Tsar had been the only casualty. Lenin obviously wanted the world to believe that Alexandra and her children remained alive. But were they?

When pressed, Georgy Chicherin, head of Lenin's Foreign Commissariat, serenely assured the anxious German envoy that Alexandra and the children were indeed safe and very much alive. This exercise in deception actually continued for some months— the German government routinely pressing for information and Moscow continually issuing deft assurances. Karl Radek, head of the European Department of the Bolshevik Foreign commissariat, even blithely informed the German counselor that it might be possible for the survivors—Alexandra and her children—to be granted freedom 'on humanitarian grounds'. Nurturing false hope was a card the Bolsheviks always played extremely well.

Still, it inevitably proved a flimsy charade at best—a house built of the most unstable playing cards imaginable. British Military Intelligence was, on an almost daily basis, fielding ominous reports that the Empress and all five of her children had most probably been murdered along with the Tsar. Germany, growing understandably suspicious of Lenin's empty assurances, began to ask for proof that the Empress was alive. Bolshevik protestations to the contrary were growing thinner by the day, and verifiable information was scarce at best. The number of foreign intelligence agents now ensconced in Ekaterinburg had grown considerably. What's more, they moved about with unusual freedom. Had Lenin's forces remained in control of the area, the espionage would have become considerably more difficult. As fate would have it, however, on July 25—a mere eight days after having finally announced the Ipatiev House massacre to the public-at-large—Bolshevik resistance totally collapsed as Czech armies, under the command of Admiral Kolchak, rolled into Ekaterinburg. The Ipatiev House was quickly discovered and the rest, as they say, was fast becoming official Russian history—all of which was clearly apparent to Nicholas Sokolov. The young Investigator was also aware of one other troublesome teaser: the truth and official history do not always peacefully coexist.

The Bolsheviks, of course, considered the life and wellbeing of Nicholas II as non-issues and had behaved accordingly since his arrest. It was a sad but undeniable fact that even before the ink of his signature had dried on the document of abdication, the last Tsar of Russia had already become expendable—one body more in an ever-growing mountain of corpses. The reasons, though undeniably cold and indifferent, were purely political. In the end, they were finally accepted by his supporters and detractors alike as unfortunate but inevitable. Some even managed to attribute the end of the monarchy to divine retribution. It was, after all, much less troublesome to devalue the fate of the Romanovs by fostering the twisted but handy notion that God, in His infinite and unknowable wisdom, was about to sanctify the dark and terrible storm that everyone seemed to know was coming.

There were, of course, a precious few who found it a bit more difficult to so easily trivialize the human qualities that had come together in this one diminutive and hapless man.

Count Paul von Benckendorff, for one, summed up his own personal impressions of Nicholas Alexandrovich Romanov, by writing the following:

"To the end of his life, he lacked balance, nor could he grasp the principles that are necessary for the conduct of so great an Empire. Hence his indecision, his limitations, and the fluctuations which lasted throughout his reign. He was very intelligent, understood things at once, and was very quick, but he did not know how to reconcile decisions with fundamental political principles, which he entirely lacked."

Sadly, therefore, whatever personal virtues Nicholas II did possess—loving husband, doting father—finally counted for nothing in the larger scheme of things. In the last analysis, the ultimate fate of empires and those who rule them are always finally determined by colder and more dispassionate concerns.

> *"They curse at him from every side,*
> *And only when they see his corpse*
> *They'll understand how much he did,*
> *And that in hate, he was yet full of love!"*

Nikolai Nekrasov

Sifting through the various contents of the curious parcel given to him by Admiral Kolchak, Sokolov suddenly noticed a particular piece of crumpled paper folded in half—a telegram. Once unfolded, the Investigator recognized at once that the body of the message was written in some sort of code. The time and date noted on the paper, which was not coded, read *"17 July 1918–9 p.m."* If authentic, this telegram had been wired from Ekaterinburg not even twenty-four hours after the alleged execution of the Imperial family! The author's name was listed as Alexander Beloborodov, chairman of the Ural Regional Soviet. Sokolov was immediately captivated, however, by the fact that the telegram was addressed to Nicholas Gorbunov—Lenin's personal secretary.

The Investigator carefully placed the unfolded telegram on his desk in order to more meticulously inspect the placement of the juxtaposed letters that formed the body of the short coded message. Within several minutes, he had identified the code—a polyalphabetic substitution system. Not particularly sophisticated.

With pencil in hand, Sokolov began to scribble down a series of letters on a clean piece of paper placed next to the telegram. He then worked his way through a relatively simple process of elimination, marking out certain letters and assigning new meaning to other letters in the alphabet. A few minutes more and the freshly deciphered message had been revealed:

> *"Inform Sverdlov [Chairman of the Central Committee]*
> *family suffered same fate as head.*
> *Officially family will die in evacuation."*

Sokolov crossed his arms over his chest, leaned back in his chair and sighed thoughtfully. As he silently continued to ponder the telegram's curious wording his gaze shifted to another nearby scrap of paper…a yellowed Ural Worker newspaper clipping which bore the headlines:

"EXECUTION OF NICHOLAS, THE BLOODY CROWNED MURDERER SHOT WITHOUT BOURGEOIS FORMALITIES BUT IN ACCORDANCE WITH OUR NEW DEMOCRATIC PRINCIPLES"

More words reporting only the death of the Tsar. As he continued to study the yellowed clipping, the Investigator instinctively withdrew the crumpled cigarette from his jacket pocket and idly rolled it back and forth between his fingers. He was feeling a nasty habit coming on.

In the midst of so much interconnected intrigue, there was also another bit of historical trivia, small and coincidental, that Sokolov, silently pondering the contents of the freshly decoded telegram, couldn't help but recall: centuries earlier when news reached the twenty-two-year-old Mikhail Fyodorovich that he had been unanimously elected by the national assembly to be the first Romanov Tsar, the messengers had finally found him at the Ipatiev Monastery in Siberia where he and his mother had taken refuge. How odd that the name 'Ipatiev' should be once more entwined with that of the Romanovs in such an ultimately ironic fashion. It was as if a great circle of life was finally completing itself.

Sokolov's thoughts were interrupted by a soft knock on the door of his room.

"Come."

The door slowly opened and two shabby household servants quietly entered—a middle-aged woman with stooped shoulders and a worn face accompanied by a girl in her late teens who walked with a slight limp. Both wore tattered overcoats and fingerless gloves. Their hair was hidden beneath ragged scarves that completely covered their heads, and their bodies were stooped from countless hours of heavy labor.

Sokolov smiled and stood obligingly.

"Your luggage and bed linens," the old woman announced huskily. She kept her head bowed in a continual posture of deference that clearly bespoke a lifetime of demeaning servitude.

"Thank you," the Investigator replied, politely indicating a corner of the room to the younger girl carrying his luggage. She obediently placed the two worn leather suitcases side by side on the floor while the old woman began to put fresh linens on the bed.

Sokolov, hands clasped behind his back in studied silence, remained near the wood stove, warming himself as he observed the two servants go about their silent duties.

Having placed the Investigator's suitcases as instructed, the servant girl—her head still bowed and her gaze on the floor—stood and casually brushed back a lock of hair from her dirty forehead.

"You are servants here?" Sokolov inquired.

"We are," the woman nodded as she continued her duties in the room.

"For how long?" the Investigator asked.

"Almost a year."

"Then you weren't here when this house was occupied by the Red Army," Sokolov noted.

The old woman turned slightly and motioned to the peasant girl who, after a slight curtsey in obedience, quietly exited the room.

"No one from the village was here then," the woman resumed, smoothing out the bedspread with her rough hands. "No one was allowed."

"The house was well guarded?" Sokolov inquired.

"There were four machine gun emplacements that I recall," the woman replied, "one in the bell tower of the Voznesensky Cathedral. It was aimed toward the house; a second was in the basement window facing the street; a third one guarded the balcony overlooking the garden at the back of the house; and a fourth was located in the attic overlooking the intersection, just above the tsar and tsarina's bedroom."

The old woman paused in her duties to indicate the window of the room. "The Reds also built the wall outside," she sighed as if the conversation was one she had endured more than once, and was weary of it.

"Do you know why?" Sokolov asked.

The old woman hobbled to the wood stove, pried open the iron grate and stoked the burning wood with a poker. A wave of welcomed heat immediately began to fill the room.

"Why do people ever build walls?" she sniffed with obvious disdain, shutting the grate again and replacing the iron poker.

His interest instantly piqued, Sokolov slipped the crumpled cigarette back into his jacket pocket and crossed his arms over his chest once more—a gesture he often made when intrigued by some particular subject of discussion.

"Do you know who they kept here in this house for eleven weeks while the Reds occupied the town?" he asked.

"I know who they say was here," the old woman answered drily. "Nicholas Romanov. The Tsar and his family."

"Do they also say what happened to them while they were here?"

The old woman slowly proceeded to the desk and lit the kerosene lamp. "Doesn't matter what they say," she finally responded with a shrug and a voice slightly above a whisper. "No one really knows."

"What do you think happened?" the Investigator continued to gently press.

"It isn't what I think. It's what I hope."

"And what is that?"

"That they are with the saints now...beyond suffering. That's all."

Her duties in the room completed, the old woman hobbled towards the exit. Pausing in the doorway, she turned back to Sokolov.

"Anything else?" she asked, sliding her gloved hands into the deep pockets of her ragged overcoat.

"Your name," Sokolov smiled warmly.

"Kolya," the old woman answered with a slight nod of her head. "Natalya Kolya."

The Investigator squared his shoulders and bowed slightly. "I am Nicholas Sokolov."

"Yes," the old woman sniffed as she turned to leave the room, "I know."

The door swung shut behind her and Sokolov was once again alone.

Sokolov's Journal
Ekaterinburg, 1919

Founded by Peter the Great in 1723 as a gateway to assist in furthering the colonization of Siberia, this town, built on the banks of the Iset River, was initially named after Peter's wife, Ekaterina. Whatever promise the town once possessed has long since faded. Its greatest distinction now is to be known as the setting for the

40

final epilogue to 304 years of Romanov rule in Russia—the last place the Imperial family knew on this earth.

There was one overriding reason for the choice of locale—the dethroned Autocrat of All the Russias had to be made to taste the bitterness and dreariness of exile...made to experience the icy blasts of that House of Dead Souls to which he and his ancestors had banished so many Russians. Siberia. Temperatures have been measured here as low as ninety degrees below zero. A long way from the warmth of the Winter Palace. A very long way.

And Admiral Kolchak—a man who says he has no use for reason or intellect. How does he demonstrate it? In the course of several minutes, he quotes from literature and Lenin, demonstrates more than a passing familiarity with Dostoevsky, and is able to name every major theatre and artist Russia has ever produced. And then...to give me a room in the very house where the Romanovs were murdered. He thought it would have an effect on me.

The bastard was right.

Chapter Three

It was well past midnight and the Ipatiev House was dark and silent. Outside, the brutal Siberian wind still rose and fell in sporadic gusts, relentlessly battering all obstacles in its path. Having barricaded themselves as best they could against the merciless winter's cold, the town's inhabitants—citizens and occupiers—slept.

In his own dim room, now illuminated only by a faint glow from the wood stove, Nicholas Sokolov, his body sprawled on the small bed, tossed fitfully as he sank deeper into a haunting world of vivid but confusing dreams.

His uneasy slumber was eventually soothed by the imagined sound of distant music rising gradually amid faint echoing laughter and sporadic applause. A haunting waltz was being played somewhere far away by an unseen orchestra. Through a shimmering mist which now began to gather and swirl before his imagined gaze, blurred images slowly began to materialize and intertwine. Beautiful. Intoxicating.

Sokolov's body, seemingly weightless now, began to experience the dreamy sensation of actually being lifted from his bed. Suspended in air like a ghost, he felt as though he was suddenly being transported through empty rooms and solid walls—drifting inextricably toward the sound of that haunting music.

As the engulfing mist suddenly began to recede and dissolve, he found himself standing at the far end of an enormous, semi-

42

transparent and ornately luxurious ballroom. As the blurred shapes moving within the rising light slowly came into sharper focus, Sokolov realized that the images were those of people in formal attire—military uniforms bedecked with silk sashes and golden medals, handsome tuxedoes, magnificent and bejeweled ball gowns—catching the glittering light from a thousand crystal chandeliers. And everyone was waltzing. Smiling couples in what appeared to be an endless procession of courtly splendor, dipped and swirled past Sokolov—apparently unaware of his presence among them. The Investigator was extremely grateful for this fact when he suddenly remembered that his own evening attire consisted of nothing but shirtsleeves, khaki field pants and felt boots—the clothes he was wearing when he had fallen into bed.

What was this place and who were the proud people who filled the shimmering dream room with such joyous dancing and laughter? Why had he been transported here?

Sokolov could do nothing but absorb the magnificent vision in silent reverence. With slow and measured steps, he eventually began to venture further into the glittering space, maneuvering invisibly among the waltzing couples who continued to swirl endlessly around him.

And then, through the warm golden hue that seemed to infuse the entire ballroom, his gaze suddenly fixed itself upon an amazing tableau that now seemed to be revealing itself through the dissipating mist.

At the far end of the huge room, sitting in gilded thrones on a raised dais adorned with flowers and potted palms, sat Nicholas Romanov, the former Tsar of Russia and his wife, Empress Alexandra. Behind them in a semicircle were also gathered their beautiful children: Alexei, Olga, Tatiana, Marie and Anastasia.

The Imperial family appeared to be serenely observing the room's twirling waltzers, smiling in approval and nodding occasionally at someone in the crowd. They appeared to Sokolov as he had so often seen them pictured in books or paintings—distant, benevolent, aloof and even somewhat benign.

The Investigator recalled the words of Aleksandr Kerensky, Minister of Justice in the Provisional Government, the man responsible for the safety of the Tsar while the family had been held in Tsarkoe Selo before being transferred to Ekaterinburg. Kerensky described Nicholas as being *"a pleasant, somewhat ordinary colonel of the guards, very ordinary except for a pair of wonderful blue eyes."*

Sokolov could see those same eyes clearly from where he stood now. Luminescent, he thought, but also somewhat melancholy.

The dream children appeared young—certainly younger than when they were being held as captives in the Ipatiev House. Obviously enchanted by the spectacle of so many waltzing couples spinning in such graceful array before their eyes, they smiled and frequently pressed their heads together in order to share some whispered aside. The girls, respectfully mindful of their demeanor in public, were as discreet as possible when giggles proved impossible to contain. Alexei, trying earnestly to imitate his father, would occasionally glance at his sisters with a feigned expression of disfavor until his own smile betrayed truer sentiments.

This, then, was 'Bloody Nicholas' and his family. Here at long last was the tyrant who had provoked so much contempt from so many, the blundering military leader responsible for plunging a mighty nation into a catastrophic civil war. Here was the one man Sokolov blamed for all of it, the wellspring of his own private bitterness and personal dissolution. Nicholas Romanov, the anti-Semitic, anti-democratic despot of Russia...a spoiled, aloof, and indifferent tyrant directly responsible for the persecution and massacre of millions of his hapless subjects. As for Sokolov, his opinion of the royal family had long ago shaped itself into a noble hatred—a bitter contempt without blush.

Yet, as he continued his cautious advance toward the Imperial family, still holding them fast in his gaze, the Investigator found himself strangely devoid of the very emotions he expected to feel. The righteous indignation and almost uncontrollable rage nurtured for so many years and for so many justifiable reasons seemed actually diminished if not inexplicably absent altogether. Instead, he found himself experiencing nothing more than a cryptic sense of professional detachment and a strange sort of unaffected curiosity. Perhaps, he thought, it was all due to his sensation of being invisible within the dream itself. As such, he wasn't there to confront anyone. No; his sole reason for having been transported to this place, as he now began to realize, was simply to observe. Any subsequent judgments on his part would, after all, be formed in methodical stages and by means of logical progression at a later time. How, though, could he possibly reconcile any impression collected in a dream? Wasn't this, after all, being created by his own subconscious mind?

For some curious reason, as he gazed at the ghostly figures of the Imperial family, the Investigator found himself recalling something Empress Alexandra had written in one of her husband's diaries:

> *"When this life ends, we shall meet again in another world*
> *and remain together always."*

Here, perhaps, was that other world at last, a mystical place in which father, mother, son, and daughters were to exist forever alive, happy, together—and for reasons he could not yet consciously fathom, Nicholas Sokolov was being allowed to experience it all.

Sokolov had traversed almost half the length of the glittering ballroom now. The beautiful waltzers still twirled around him in all of their regal splendor, but the sound of music seemed to fade as his concentration increased. He began to intentionally focus on each individual of the royal family with measured awareness.

He was finally drawn to the youngest of the daughters, Grand Duchess Anastasia Nikolaevna—the girl in the faded photograph singled out by Admiral Kolchak. This Anastasia, however, was not the young woman of seventeen who had so violently perished with her family in Ekaterinburg. Here, in Sokolov's dream, she was allowed to appear forever unfinished—eternally possessing the innocent happiness that belongs to those who are young—and which is, in turn, their priceless gift to the harsher and more judgmental world of Men. Her beautiful blue-gray eyes betrayed her joy, and her captivating smile bore unalterable witness to the absolute pleasure that obviously filled her soul. It seemed to Sokolov that this fresh-faced child stood out from all the rest. There was something about her countenance that held her apart—a perceptible radiance. For the moment, the Investigator was content to attribute the difference to her youthfulness, yet he knew there was much more to it than that. Intriguing, he concluded, while at the same time accepting the fact that this moment was about nothing more than first impressions. Solving the mystery that was Anastasia would have to wait for another time.

The sound in the grand ballroom, still teeming with joyous movement and life, suddenly began to fade into absolute silence. Sokolov was still transfixed on the young Anastasia when her expression instantly changed from joy to one of apprehension. It was as if she had heard something. Before Sokolov could react,

Anastasia's fearful gaze shifted to him. She was obviously aware of his presence! She could actually see him standing alone on the dance floor and he staggered slightly at the realization.

Then, he became aware of it...a faint noise inside his head. Anastasia must've heard it too, for it seemed that she was suddenly attempting to 'speak' to Sokolov with apprehensive eyes, urgently warning him of some approaching menace.

Nicholas Sokolov, jolted back into the threatening present, immediately bolted upright in his bed as the ballroom vanished completely along with Anastasia, the Imperial family and the teaming crowd of people. He was in his room in the Ipatiev House, engulfed by darkness and dread.

That sound again! He searched the dimness of the room until he finally located its source. In a flickering shaft of light from the wood stove, Sokolov could see that the latch on his door was moving. Someone on the other side of the door was trying to enter the room!

Instinctively, the Investigator's right hand swiftly slid underneath his pillow, retrieving the pistol he had placed there. In another second, he was on his feet, aiming the loaded Mauser directly at the doorway.

Another faint clicking sound. The door was slowly creeping open. As it did, the dim but unmistakable silhouette of a man came into view. Sokolov's finger tightened ever so slightly on the trigger and his body tensed in apprehensive readiness. With a silent movement, the intruder glided over the threshold and paused in the darkness at the foot of the Investigator's bed.

The flame from a cigarette lighter in the intruder's hand flickered suddenly and the room brightened enough for each man to see the other. The shadowy figure gasped, threw his hands into the air and shrieked, "God save Holy Russia!"

Still aiming the pistol in his right hand, Sokolov quickly located a box of matches with his left hand and lit the bedside candle. The room exploded with light.

There, just inside the doorway, stood a man in his late twenties dressed rather formally whose ashen face and trembling body told the Investigator he had nothing to fear.

"Sorry," Sokolov replied softly, "reflex."

The intruder relaxed only slightly. His hands remained raised in obvious surrender. "And a very sad comment on the times, I must say," he stammered plaintively. "Sad, but necessary for survival I suppose."

Sokolov allowed his body to relax a bit more and slowly lowered the barrel of the Mauser. Following suit, the stranger carefully lowered his own arms. It was only then that the Investigator noticed the intruder's trembling hands held two tin cups and a bottle of champagne.

With a sudden and almost jaunty air, the man crossed to Sokolov's desk in the middle of the room. Depositing the two tin cups and the bottle of champagne there, he drew himself into a formal pose, clicked his heals together smartly and gave the Investigator a sharp but slight bow from the waist.

"My name is Boris Gorev," he began while glibly manipulating the bottle of champagne in an effort to pry off the cork with pale feverish fingers. "And you are Nicholas Sokolov, here to find out what happened to the Tsar."

The cork finally released itself from the bottle with a loud pop and Gorev beamed in satisfied triumph. Observing Sokolov's lack of reaction, he continued with an even more determined tone of glib finesse. "You'll also find, and rather quickly, there are no secrets here. Well, of course, he's dead…and his family along with him. Right here in this house, so they say. Nasty business!" Gorev, having given the cork a dainty sniff, began pouring champagne into the two tin cups. "Well, whoever did it was very thorough, let me tell you. Not a trace left behind! As if the earth simply opened up and swallowed the lot. But then, of course, there is the little room in the basement. If only walls could talk! You have seen the room in the basement? No? Well, you will—because I hear you're very good at what you do."

The intruder offered the Investigator one of the cups filled with champagne. Sokolov took it numbly. Gorev giggled appreciatively and raised his own cup in the form of a toast.

"Symbol of modern Russia, dear boy. Champagne in a tin cup. Cheers!"

Gorev lifted the cup to his lips, closed his eyes and took a sip. "Excellent," he exclaimed with overacted delight before taking a seat in Sokolov's desk chair. With a white handkerchief daintily plucked from his coat pocket, Gorev dabbed at his pencil-thin mustache.

"Ah, yes," he smiled. "Be sure not to miss the South wall of the basement room. A line from a poem has been mysteriously carved into the plaster there. It reads: *'On the same night, Belsatzar was killed by his slaves.'* Absolutely intriguing, don't you think?"

Gorev paused to enjoy another sip of champagne. Sokolov decided to take advantage of the temporary lull.

"Who are you?"

Gorev smiled. "Let's just say...a friend."

"Let's just say that isn't good enough," the Investigator responded dryly.

"Certain you won't try the champagne?" Gorev practically cooed. "Crystal glasses are absolutely impossible these days of course; but I did, at least, manage to have the tin cups monogrammed. I do think one should partake of the finer things as often as possible. After all, tin cups aside, what could possibly be rarer than champagne in Russia?"

Placing his untouched cup of champagne on the table in front of Gorev, the Investigator delivered his answer in two words: "The truth."

"Ah, yes," Gorev sighed. "You're one of those. A seeker of Truth. But whose truth? Yours or...theirs?"

"I was unaware," Sokolov replied brusquely, "that more than one truth existed."

"Really?" Gorev giggled once more, shaking his head. "And where have you been these last few years, dear boy? In a vacuum?"

"In Moscow actually."

"Practically the same thing," Gorev smirked. "Moscow! Tell me; how much does the Truth cost in Moscow these days? I hear God Himself will swear on a Bible if the price is right."

"In that case, God is quite safe," Sokolov replied. "There are no Bibles left in Moscow."

"Well, there is the Gospel according to Lenin," Gorev chuckled after another sip of champagne. "But then, I suppose God could swear by that all he wished, couldn't He?"

"Somehow I can't quite imagine God swearing by Lenin."

"Depends on how badly God wants to back a winner," Gorev grinned. "Lenin will win this civil war, you know. He has a marvelous sense of timing. And, in case you hadn't noticed, the time is...right."

For a split second, Nicholas Sokolov regretted putting his pistol away. Gorev's pretentiousness was grating on what little patience the groggy Investigator possessed. Still, he decided to see what bits of additional information might be revealed even in the midst of such extraneous banality.

"Considering the fact," Sokolov replied, "that our army's advances are pushing the Reds back on all three fronts, I'd rather say that time is what you make of it."

Another annoying giggle from the seated Gorev. "Spoken like a true man of purpose, fresh from a round of pseudo-intellectual bantering with the good Admiral. How does he put it? 'When I need reasons, I appoint commissions.' Dear boy, you can't imagine the mileage he's managed to get off that!"

"You seem to know the Admiral rather well."

"As well as one can ever know a man who has no need of reasons," Gorev sighed. "Just between us, I often refer to the good Admiral as King of the Skoptzies."

"I beg your pardon?"

"Never heard of the Skoptzies?" Gorev gasped in mock astonishment. "Russian religious fanatics who, like our dear Admiral Kolchak, live by the Bible verse: *'Blessed are the barren.'* As fanatics will, of course, they've naturally managed to take their credo to the extreme. Self-castration. The operations are performed by both men and women using razors, pieces of glass, sharpened bone...whatever's handy when the mood strikes. The removal of the testicles is rather like one's inaugural encounter with the good Admiral, wouldn't you say? Both events are known as the 'first purification'. The second, as you will soon discover, is a bit more demanding. Those willing to remove their penises as well are awarded the honor of 'Bearers of the Imperial Seal'—and I'd be rather cautious if I were you. Kolchak has a desk drawer full of those little medals."

Sokolov couldn't resist. "Tell me; do you speak from observation or experience. You did say there were no secrets here."

"Touché," Gorev replied. "In that case, I would answer by saying there are definite advantages to walking lightly through this world. You see, I long ago determined that the difference between a corpse with testicles and one without was not all that exhilarating. It's enough to survive; and, if I may say so, that's something I've managed rather well."

Gorev stood and pulled his slim body erect. "To uncover the Truth is really not all that difficult, Sir. It's what we do with Truth, once uncovered, that poses such a problem."

Deflecting the remark with professional ease, Sokolov simply observed: "It would appear you've found a way around all that."

"That's because I know a secret," Boris Gorev smiled mysteriously. "The only Truth is that there is no real Truth. Nothing and no one exists beyond self. That's all we know or can possibly be certain of. Since that is so, our only aim in life is to please ourselves...the only way we know...the only way we can."

Nicholas Sokolov had reached the limit of his patience. "Interesting," he observed. "I've encountered only one other man in my life who embraced that same philosophy."

"Really? Who?"

"Nicholas Romanov."

Sokolov's reply struck Boris Gorev in the face like a glove. His pompous sneer abruptly vanished and, for a second, he glared at the Investigator in silent defiance. Then, just as suddenly, the anger dissolved and his reliable—if somewhat defensive—air of cool condescension returned to take its place.

"They say Truth and good champagne have one thing in common," he concluded smugly. "One should know when one has had enough...of either."

With a ceremonious click of his polished heels, Boris Gorev gathered the tin cups along with his bottle of champagne, bowed slightly and abruptly exited the room.

Chapter Four

"Vse obychno"
(Everything is the same.)

The hastily retreating Gorev almost collided with the old woman, Natalya Kolya, who was about to enter Sokolov's room carrying a lighted kerosene lamp. Gorev barreled past her in a huff, but the old woman, completely unruffled by the theatrics of his exit, merely sidestepped the potential collision and continued silently into the room. Blandly, she placed the lamp on Sokolov's desk and turned to leave.

Sokolov's voice stopped her. "Interesting fellow," he commented softly.

"If you say so," the old woman replied with a slight shrug of her stooped shoulders.

"He doesn't impress you?" Sokolov asked, stepping closer to the wood stove in order to warm himself.

"I suppose he might," the old woman replied, "if I gave him much thought. I don't give him much thought."

Kolya shuffled to the doorway and turned back to the Investigator. "Will that be all, Sir?"

"Actually, there is something else."

"Yes?"

"There's a basement room in this house?"

For the first time since he encountered the old woman, the Investigator noticed that her weathered face actually betrayed the slightest hint of an emotional reaction.

"Why do you ask," she replied.

Sokolov took a step forward. "Boris Gorev suggested I might want to have a look at it. What do you think?"

Her face once again losing all hint of expression, Kolya rubbed her gloved hands together for generated warmth. "With your permission," she sighed heavily, "I am not encouraged to think. I will take you to the room if you wish. I am encouraged to do what I'm told."

Sokolov smiled. "You don't mince words, do you, Babushka?"

The old woman turned toward the empty doorway. With a slight tilt of her kerchiefed head, obviously indicating Boris Gorev, she flatly replied, "I leave mincing to those with the talent for it."

In a world where life was cheap, Natalya Kolya was an unmistakable survivor. She refused to waste first-class attention on second-class causes. As a household servant, the old woman had long ago learned to go about her duties unnoticed by those around her. It was a talent that obviously served her well...almost like a cloak of invisibility that she could don whenever it was needed— which meant that she had most certainly seen things, overheard conversations, and knew secrets.

An aura of invincibility may have once belonged to the Russian nobility, but their servants possessed an even greater weapon—the air of invisibility. In the end, the power gleaned by peasants from a thousand gathered secrets proved to be the deadliest chink in the armor of the aristocrats.

To a man in Sokolov's profession, menial servants such as Natalya Kolya often proved to be extremely invaluable sources of information. If there were secret rooms in the Ipatiev House, Sokolov understood, without question, that this old woman not only knew where they were, she also most assuredly held the keys.

The Investigator smiled again. He couldn't help himself or the immediate fondness he was beginning to feel for this shrewd old bird who quietly held her ground in front of him. Admiral Kolchak had warned 'nothing will be what it seems', but Sokolov didn't feel it was the case here. There was an absence of extraneous agenda about Kolya that seemed almost refreshing. Her honesty was spontaneous, blunt and unaffected—useful currency in such precarious times—and she was obviously not about to squander it carelessly. Sokolov actually looked forward to getting to know her better, but the hour was growing late and there was more pressing business he needed to conclude.

"I believe," he announced gently, "I'll see that room in the basement now."

Still betraying no reaction whatsoever, Kolya nodded and obediently retrieved the kerosene lamp from the desk. "As you wish," she answered, and silently led Sokolov from the room.

As he stepped into the hallway, the looming darkness of the silent house swallowed him almost immediately. His only point of reference now became the soft illumination from Kolya's lamp that bobbed steadily ahead of him.

As the old woman led him further along the first floor corridor, he felt the air around him suddenly undergo a dramatic change. This was no figment of his imagination. The air in that dim corridor literally became colder, sending a sudden shiver throughout his entire being. It was as if he could feel the undeniable presence of someone else in the narrow passage—someone or something hovering close to him in the unmistakable chill of that ghostly darkness.

He couldn't help but recall childhood tales of such manifestations—places in old houses said to be inhabited by spirits of the dead—where temperatures would inexplicably drop, indicating the presence of troubled phantoms not of this world. The Russian people absolutely believed in such occurrences, and had long since accepted the fact that the living shared their world with other things. Things unseen...unknown...unknowable.

Empress Alexandra's haunting words floated back to Sokolov in the chilling hush of that spectral corridor:

"When this life ends, we shall meet again in another world and remain together always."

This time, however, the loving assurance of the Tsarina's vow was suddenly overshadowed by another more unsettling interpretation.

Slowly rounding a corner in that dark hallway, the Investigator allowed his imagination to wander. He actually tried to imagine the terrifying horror of suddenly coming face to face with the reanimated corpses of the Romanovs. He even perversely conjured their ghastly shapes in the darkness ahead—yellow eyes glaring from hollow sockets around which bloody and rotting flesh transformed once human faces into hideously putrid masks of Death. Even as he shook himself free from the specters of an overreaching imagination, the creatures lunged forward in a desperate attempt to reach him before their decomposing bodies melted away completely into thin air.

But then, as all dreamers do in the midst of such nightmares, Sokolov ordained himself fully awake and stepped back once more into the clearer realm of the living—an act never intended to suggest that restless phantoms are not able to inhabit our world; it merely signifies that for a time at least, we no longer wish to admit their presence.

In a moment, Solokov and the old woman were outside with a star-filled sky above them. In another moment, they had reentered the house and were once more descending even deeper into the darkness.

Kolya, bobbing in the flickering light ahead of him, continued to lead Nicholas Sokolov downward—ever downward into the musty shadows of that silent place—winding to the left, then shifting to the right once they had finally made their way below ground. One cautious step after another...further into the subterranean gloom. Turning. Descending into the dank and hidden depths of the mysterious Ipatiev House.

No sound except for their barely perceptible footsteps and the icy wind rising and falling outside...that mournful howling, distant but ever-present reminder of what lay beyond the sheltering walls of that empty house.

Finally, in the inky blackness at the top of a solitary stair landing, Kolya abruptly halted and reverently passed the kerosene lamp to Sokolov. With a solemn tilt of her head, she indicated twenty-three more steps below which led to a single doorway. Twenty-six steps—one step for every year of Nicholas Romanov's tragic reign as the last Tsar of all the Russias.

Sokolov took the lamp and stoically proceeded the rest of the way alone. Kolya watched him cautiously descend until he was finally swallowed by the enveloping darkness.

Reaching the bottom of the stairs, he dutifully pried the double doors apart, pushed them open, and stepped apprehensively into the thick gloom of that foreboding basement room.

#

Sokolov's Journal
Ekaterinburg, 1919

Death leaves its own aura—unmistakable. I've experienced it before. Never just this way. It was only a room—twenty-five by twenty-one feet. Adequate. Empty. No furniture. Nothing tangible. A floor of yellow painted pine boards. Plaster walls covered with cream and beige striped paper. A vaulted ceiling from which hung the room's only electric light. A heavy iron grill covered a single window.

One wall—the far wall as you entered, still bore marks of great violence. Large pieces of plaster blown away. Bullets do that. I counted twenty small holes in that wall alone. Also deep scars in the floor. Bayonets. If someone is lying prone and you're standing over them, stabbing downward—over and over. Do you know what dread is to someone like me? Finding a room such as this. Normally, you turn up something at any crime scene. Dried blood, bits of flesh or fingernail—a single strand of hair. Something usually manages to escape the perpetrator's notice in the passion—the emotion—of the moment. Not here. Not in this room. Every scar in the floor, every bullet hole in those walls had been scrubbed clean. White-washed. Totally and completely...sanitized. And yet, in some unspeakable way, this room will never be truly clean; nor will it ever be totally devoid of everything. Something remains. Some undeniable presence is—and always will be—part of that space and alive forever within its walls.

Sokolov's feverish writing was interrupted when Natalya Kolya unexpectedly reentered his room. This time, she carried a bottle of vodka on a tray.

As she placed the bottle and a glass on his table, a small piece of folded paper slipped noiselessly from her hand, softly landing next to the Sokolov's open journal.

"I've been thinking about something you said," Kolya observed with downcast eyes as she turned to leave the room. "Boris Gorev, a very interesting man."

A moment later, the old woman had melted into the darkness of the hallway.

Sokolov's Journal
Ekaterinburg, 1919

I noticed the single piece of crumpled paper even before she left the room. She had taken great pains to write it clearly. One word. A single name:

Demidova.

The first piece of a puzzle is always the hardest. Did you know that? The more pieces in place, the easier the challenge becomes.
Demidova. I had heard the name before. But where?

The realization came like a sudden sharp pain in his temple—a flash of electrical energy streaking through his brain. He winced as the mental photograph began to take shape before his inner eye.

He instantly knew he had seen the name before—glanced it earlier in the day—on a single piece of paper contained in the parcel presented to him by Admiral Kolchak. The connection was immediately clear.

Besides the Romanovs allegedly executed in the basement room of the Ipatiev House, there was a list of others who also supposedly perished with them: *"Doctor Eugene Sergéyvich Botkin, English teacher Alexei Yegorvich Trupp, Cook Ivan Mikhailovich Kharitonov, and girl servant Anna Stepanovna Demidova."*

Anna Demidova—maid to Empress Alexandra! The Investigator's rapid process of association had now completed itself. As quickly as it had come upon him, the pain in his head subsided.

"Occasionally," Sokolov thought to himself as he rearranged the file folders on his desk, "God smiles."

One more possible connection. Another piece of the puzzle. But why, Sokolov asked himself, had Natalya Kolya associated Demidova's name with Gorev's? What secret door did this strange key unlock? There was only one way to uncover the answer.

Chapter Five

"The execution of the tsar's family was needed not only in order to frighten, horrify and dishearten the enemy, but also in order to shake up our own ranks to show that there was no turning back, that ahead lay either complete victory or complete ruin."

Leon Trotsky

As dawn broke over Ekaterinburg, Nicholas Sokolov was just completing one more detailed review of the materials given to him by Admiral Kolchak. It had taken all night and his good eye burned from weariness. His brain and lungs craved a bit of fresh air, and his stiff body ached as much from lack of exercise as from the morning's chill. Throwing his heavy military overcoat around his shoulders, Sokolov made his way to the front door of the Ipatiev House and out into the cold, muddy courtyard. A blast of icy wind instantly revived his senses, forcing him to tug the overcoat tighter around his shoulders as he began to pace back and forth in the morning sunlight.

This part of the world had been quite a different place when the Romanovs were being held in Ekaterinburg only a year earlier. It was summer then, and the air must have been heavy with the sweet scent of trees, vines and flowers. Insects buzzed and darted from blossom to blossom in the late afternoons of June and July. The Tsar and his son, during one hour each day when the family was allowed outside to exercise, were most often seen wearing field caps and khaki military shirts bound at the waist by leather military belts. Their trousers were wrinkled and their boots scuffed. In short, there was no longer anything in their appearance that visibly connected them to the faraway splendors of St. Petersburg or the summer palace at Tsarkoe Selo. Here they performed subservient tasks—chopping wood, cleaning their own rooms, tending to a small garden next to the house. And yet, oddly enough, the Tsar seemed to quite enjoy these daily activities. Existing photographs of the family inevitably show him smiling contentedly.

As Sokolov continued to pace the empty courtyard, he recalled finding a different photograph in his collection—another face that seemed to glare back at him from the not-so-distant past. It was the face of Jacob Mikhailovich Yurovsky, commandant of the Ipatiev House during the Tsar's confinement. It was Yurovsky who, according to all reports, planned and carried out the execution of the Romanovs in the basement room of the house. It was Yurovsky who had also overseen the mutilation and disposal of the corpses.

Sokolov had spent several unpleasant hours studying Yurovsky's photograph, trying intently to decipher what clues to his personality might possibly lie behind his facial features. The Investigator was curious to learn as much as possible about the man who was capable of coldly carrying out the systematic murder of an entire family—father, mother and children—in cold blood. Not only had Yurovsky planned the slaughter, he had taken part in it. Literally as well as figuratively, the blood of the Romanovs was on his hands.

In the photograph, which is still in existence today, Yurovsky's mouth is obscured by a thick mustache and heavy goatee. Perhaps that was why the eyes seem his most arresting facial feature. To Sokolov, they seemed to glower with a steady intensity that seemed unquestionably sinister and almost hypnotic.

It is often said that the eyes are the windows of the soul. If that is so, Jacob Yurovsky's eyes should've been a clear warning to anyone who was ever caught up in his gaze. Filled with smoldering covetousness and an inextinguishable hatred, those burning eyes glared back at Sokolov from the photograph as they must have stared so often at the Romanovs—like a lone killer wolf gazing at a herd of unsuspecting sheep.

Born of June 19, 1878, in the Siberian city of Tomsk, Russia, Jacob Yurovsky was the eighth of ten children born to Mikhail Yurovsky, a glazier, and his wife Ester Moiseevna, a seamstress. His life was a story of hardship, disenchantment, and bitterness. Arrested several times over the years, Yurovsky had eventually become a devoted Marxist. It was a convenient way to lash back at anyone who appeared to be enjoying a better life.

Of particular interest to Nicholas Sokolov was the fact that Yurovsky had once been a photographer and had plied his trade in Ekaterinburg. Photographers generally see the world in terms of composition. They will spend an inordinate amount of time and energy trying to find just the right angle in order to capture a subject, an object or a landscape. In doing so, they compose the photograph to satisfy a personal sense of esthetics and balance.

In Sokolov's opinion, Jacob Yurovsky fitted that description perfectly. His dossier even suggested to Sokolov that one of the reasons the Imperial family and their entourage had allowed themselves to be so obediently arranged in such neat rows against the far wall of the basement room only moments before they were gunned down was because Yurovsky had told them that Moscow wanted a photograph taken for identification purposes. Under this ruse, he was reportedly able to specifically arrange his victims so that the Tsar and Tsarista, along with Alexei, were seated on the front row as easy targets. The daughters reportedly formed a second row and the servants made up the third.

According to all accounts, Yurovsky had sullenly observed the Imperial family on a daily basis during their captivity. He was always there, lurking in the background, silently watching everything that went on. It was almost as if he was forever consuming the Romanovs with his cold, dark eyes. He viewed them going about all of their daily routines both inside and outside the house. Stripped of their humanity, denied even the most rudimentary acts of common kindness, and pitifully unaware of their impending fate, the Romanovs must have seemed to Jacob Yurovsky nothing more than animated corpses.

As Nicholas Sokolov now stood alone in that deserted courtyard, he tried to imagine what Yurovsky might have observed during the short time the Romanovs were allowed outside for their daily exercise.

On such summer afternoons, while her husband and children must have enjoyed the hour allotted to them for exercise in that tiny Ipatiev garden, Alexandra had almost certainly busied herself with needlepoint. Alexei, not in good health, must have slumped in a wicker chair next to his mother, playing idly with a small toy battleship, while one of the family's dogs, Jemmy, probably rolled happily in the summer grass nearby.

Complaints from the Imperial family had been few, particularly in the beginning. No matter how trivial, the assigned work—whatever it happened to be—was still a welcomed break in routine, enabling the Romanovs to pass the lethargic hours, days and months that had come to define their confinement.

During the warm summer evenings, the Tsar would often read to the family. Occasionally, the daughters would even present an entertainment—a play for which they costumed themselves and in which they acted out all the roles, garnering laughter and happy applause from the small assembled group that always watched so appreciatively—a captive audience in the truest sense of the word.

Moments such as these broke the tedious monotony and, if only briefly, provided a welcomed reprieve from the harsher realities that now began to envelop the Imperial family and their small entourage. It was the gnawing uncertainty that eventually frayed nerves, sobered daydreams, shortened tempers, and fanned the embers of apprehension that were always smoldering just below the surface of everything.

Sokolov recalled the words of Edmund Walsh, a reporter, who described the Imperial family's confinement:

"It was the unending monotony, the drab Siberian monotony that oppressed, together with the almost complete absence of news. Toward the end, the prisoners were allowed but five minutes in the garden each day—the ex-Tsar maintained that astonishing external calm and passivity which characterized his whole life. His health did not seem to weaken, nor did his hair whiten. During the few minutes allowed for exercise in the open air, he carried Alexei in his arms, as the boy was unable to walk, and marched stolidly up and down until his precious five minutes were over. But the Empress never left the porch; she aged visibly, her health failed, and gray hairs appeared."

Lost in these silent thoughts, Nicholas Sokolov continued to stroll the gently sloping courtyard of the Ipatiev House. Dates, names, places, and countless written depositions had been crowding his weary brain and he needed this reprieve before plunging back into it all again. It was a relief to let his mind wander now in an attempt to simply absorb the sights and sounds of a new day. It was also a way to finally begin to assimilate, as dispassionately as possible, all he had gleaned from the long night's steady labor.

Upon further inspection, it seemed to him that the high wooden stockade, still silhouetted in the light of early morning, appeared to coil around the property like a huge serpent—a boa constrictor whose lethal embrace had relentlessly tightened around its helpless victims. Struggle was inevitably futile against such a slow and agonizing end. Sokolov wondered if this was what the Tsar had finally realized as well—instilling within him a sense of fatal acquiescence to what he knew would most certainly overcome them all—finally bringing the life they had shared together to an even more tragic end.

The glittering world the Romanovs had once known—along with its grandeur and way of life—was over. Even if escape or rescue seemed at times remotely possible, there could still be no going back to what once had been. The past was irretrievable. That much was certain, and any thought to the contrary was a fool's dream. Nicholas had to have known this—and that knowledge, according to so many accounts, had somehow transformed the benign little man whose rule had once seemed so vast and absolute.

As he ambled silently about the courtyard, Sokolov recalled the words of Father Storozhev, a priest who had visited the Ipatiev House twice in order to conduct religious services for the Imperial family while they were prisoners in Ekaterinburg. As he had departed the grounds for the last time on July 14, 1918, the priest had said of the Romanovs:

*"Something has happened to them there.
They seem to be some other people."*

Happier seasons would return to this place. They always did—always would. Sokolov also knew that governments would rise and fall in ages yet to be. Rulers would come and go. Still, he felt he had no claim on the future. He often said that after his own death, he would be no one's special memory. It was history that truly captivated him, filled his daydreams, and shaped his vision of the swirling present. It was, after all, the past that had taught him the most profound lessons of his life. It seemed only natural, therefore, that he so often contemplated the lives of others who had gone before—those whose stories had shaped the present even as they had once struggled inexorably toward the unknown and unknowable future. History had been determined by the course those few previous lives had taken. For better or worse, their mark on the past was indelible. Their continuing influence on the present, undeniable. And though he was drawn to a thousand yesterdays like a moth to a candle's flame, how mournful it inevitably seemed to Sokolov that the people who had delighted in other seasons, the human beings who had been such vital instruments of those mighty governments and sprawling nations, all who once were so much a part of another time and place—those people, once gone, were gone forever.

The past and all those who inhabit it must eventually dissolve and melt away. So will we in our time. Nothing finally endures but eyes that stare back at us from faded photographs; eyes inclined to whisper their stories whenever hearts are truly willing to listen.

Chapter Six

Belsatzar ward in selbiger Nacht
Von seinen Knechten umgebracht

Heinrich Heine

The dining room of the Ipatiev House was where Nicholas Sokolov decided to conduct his first official interrogation, scheduled to begin at ten o'clock that morning. The room was lit by sunlight from two tall windows, one of which opened onto a covered balcony connected to the terrace below by a narrow, exterior staircase. Since the room had once been used by Ipatiev and his wife to entertain, it showed signs of once being well appointed. It still boasted large oak doors, a parquet floor, carved oak wainscot, and crimson-and-gold patterned wallpaper. On one wall, a large pier glass mirror still dominated the marble mantel and nearby sideboard. An expensive, four-light brass-and-crystal chandelier hung from the ceiling in the center of the room.

Underneath this fixture, the room's long mahogany table, stripped bare long ago, was set up with two chairs, one at either end. Sokolov sat in one chair, his back to the two large windows. In the single chair at the table's far end sat the nattily dressed and smugly dignified Boris Gorev whose composure was now obviously a bit ruffled because of having to squint in the bright sunlight which poured into the room from the windows directly behind Sokolov.

The Investigator began softly but formally. "Citizen Gorev, do you know why you have been summoned?"

"A matter of business, naturally," Gorev responded coldly. "On matters of business, one is always summoned. On matters of pleasure, one is merely extended a kind invitation."

Gorev's dossier was open on the table in front of him, but Sokolov hardly referred to it. "You are a resident of Tyumen. Son of a former treasurer of the Holy Synod. During the war, you were an officer of a machine-gun regiment. Stationed in Petrograd. Son-in-law of Gregory Rasputin."

63

From the open folder in front of him, Sokolov withdrew a photograph of a strange monk with long hair and beard. He regarded it briefly.

"Gregory Rasputin. I saw him once, the *starets*. Amazing man."

Grigori Yefimovich Rasputin—the man in the photograph—once known throughout Russia as 'the mad monk', had been an infamous character during the turbulent months leading up to the Revolution. Born between 1864 and 1865 in the village of Pokrovskoe, his early life had been spent creating a name for himself by employing a mysterious power to heal the sick and sometimes predict the future. Despite the fact that he could barely read, he still managed to acquire unprecedented power on the sheer basis of his personal charisma. Some called it 'evil genius'. Whispered rumors of his 13-inch penis only fanned the salacious flames of public revulsion and private curiosity.

He had arrived in St. Petersburg in 1905. Two years later, he managed a meeting with the Tsar and Tsarina. The audience was granted because of the possibility, however slight, that this *strannik* might prove to be a healer for their son, Alexei, who was known to be frequently ill.

In fact, the boy's disease was hemophilia, a rare bleeding disorder in which the blood doesn't clot normally. Internal bleeding, particularly in the joints, was a real danger, and there was no known cure. Alexei would sometimes lie in excruciating pain for hours after only the slightest injury. The young Tsarvich's hereditary condition—actually widespread among European royalty—had been caused by a single mutated gene passed on to his mother from Queen Victoria. And though it was nothing Alexandra could have prevented, she never truly forgave herself.

To the joyous relief of Nicholas and Alexandra, however, Rasputin did seem to be the miraculous answer to their prayers. Alexei's illness, though never cured, did at least seem controlled by the 'mad monk's' reassuring and amazing powers. From that moment on, Rasputin's place in court was guaranteed. "It may seem profane to mention Jesus Christ in any connection with Rasputin," recalled one Englishman who met him, "but for all I know God may choose odd vessels to do his work."

In 1915, Rasputin persuaded the Tsar to leave St. Petersburg for the front in order to personally take command of the Russian troops fighting in World War I. It was a tragic misstep. Alexandra was left 'in charge' with Rasputin as her principal adviser. Rumors of a sexual relationship between the 'mad monk' and the Empress were inevitable.

Whatever the actual truth, Alexandra's growing dependence on Rasputin became the final straw for a small but particularly malcontent group of Russian nobles. Two of these men—Prince Felix Yusupov and Duke Dmitri—finally succeeded in murdering Rasputin on December 16, 1916. It reportedly took three bullets and enough poison to kill several men to finally bring the 'mad monk' down.

Though no one had definitive proof, it was highly probable that a member of the British Secret Service, Major Oswald Raynor, actually delivered the coup de grace—a single bullet to the center of Rasputin's forehead as he lay dying in Yusupov's snowy courtyard.

Either way, there was no doubt that relatives of the royal family had been involved in the murder. This fact alone had terrible import for the Romanovs.

Before his death—and seemingly even in anticipation of it— Rasputin had sent a chilling letter to Nicholas II which read in part:

I write and leave behind me this letter at St. Petersburg. I feel that I shall leave life before January 1... If I am killed by common assassins, and especially by my brothers the Russian peasants, you Tsar of Russia, have nothing to fear, remain on your throne of govern, and you, Russian Tsar, will have nothing to fear for your children, they will reign for hundreds of years in Russia... If it was your relations who have wrought my death, then no one in the family, that is to say, none of your children or relations, will remain alive for more than two years. They will be killed by the Russian people... You must reflect and act prudently. Think of your safety and tell your relations that I have paid for them with my blood. I shall be killed. I am no longer among the living.

Pray, pray, be strong, and think of your blessed family.

Grigory

As the stoic Boris Gorev, sitting in Sokolov's interrogation room, gazed intently at the photograph of his infamous father-in-law, it was difficult to decipher whether or not he was the least bit troubled by any of these dark memories.

"Is this why I've been summoned?" Gorev finally sniffed in an attempt to convey the impression that he was already tiring of the proceedings.

Undeterred, Sokolov continued steadily. "Does the name 'Demidova' mean anything to you?"

Ignoring the question completely, Gorev responded with one of his own. "Am I being formally charged with some crime?"

"For the moment," Sokolov replied, "you're simply being asked a question. The name 'Demidova', does it mean anything to you?"

"Not that I recall."

Sokolov's next question caught Gorev by surprise. "Where did you learn to speak German?"

"I beg your pardon?"

"You mentioned an inscription on a wall of the basement room in this house," Sokolov explained. "I've seen it. *'On the same night, Belsatzar was killed by his slaves.'* A quotation from the twenty-first stanza of the poem *Belshazzar* by Heinrich Heine. You failed, however, to mention the fact that it was written in German. You were able to read it."

It took the jolted Gorev several moments to muster his response, "I also read and speak French. Is that a crime in Russia these days? You've obviously seen my dossier. I studied in Berlin."

"Yes," Sokolov nodded, jotting down several perfunctory notes. Then, withdrawing another piece of paper from the folder, he continued his steady probing. "One other thing; in addition to the German inscription and a reverse swastika, I also discovered an additional group of letters carved into the base of that same wall." Sokolov held the paper up so that Gorev could clearly see the rubbing imprinted on it. Four letters: *V, S, Y,* and *L.*

"I don't suppose you have any idea what they represent or what significance the letters might have?"

"None at all," Gorev answered leaning forward in order to more closely examine the paper in Sokolov's hand. "It's the first I've heard about additional carvings in that room."

Sokolov slid his chair back from the table and stood. "Do you visit Siberia often?"

"Nein," Gorev smirked, settling back into his own chair with a self-satisfied air.

Sokolov strolled alongside the table, casually closing the distance between himself and Boris Gorev.

"My information indicates that you visited Siberia once in August of 1917 and again in October that same year. Two trips in three months to a place most Russians would be quite content never to see at all."

"My father-in-law had property in Pokrovskoe," Gorev answered curtly. "My wife, Maria, and I stayed there."

Nicholas Sokolov halted next to Gorev and leaned against the edge of the table. He regarded his adversary for a moment before continuing. "Son-in-law of Gregory Rasputin," his soft voice broke the silence with an easy observation. "Quite a connection in the old days."

Gorev visibly blanched. "I suppose so. I really don't recall."

"You're too modest," Sokolov insisted with undaunted purpose. "Isn't it true that you knew the Imperial family...quite well in fact?"

"I had occasion to be in their presence...as did many others."

Reaching into his tunic pocket, Sokolov carefully withdrew the small silver framed photograph given to him by Admiral Kolchak and placed it on the table in front of Boris Gorev. "Tell me; which of the daughters is she?"

Gorev's gaze shifted to the photograph and he tilted his head slightly to one side. "Ah," he answered with only the slightest hint of pleasant recognition, "the 'little mockingbird'. The youngest. Anastasia. I should think this was taken in the Crimea. Spring of 1912, most probably."

Gorev took the photograph from the table and held it gently in his hands for closer study. "Grand Duchess Anastasia Nikolaevna," he smiled finally. "Witty, vivacious, impertinent child. Called 'little mockingbird' because of her extraordinary ability to mimic foreign languages and accents...a talent that caused the Tsar some occasional public embarrassment, I must admit. Still, as I recall, he took it all rather well. He loved his children."

Sokolov took the photograph from Gorev and carefully returned it to his tunic pocket. Hands behind his back, the Investigator then continued his casual stroll around the table's parameter.

"I saw the Tsar once...from a great distance," the Investigator mused aloud. "But then again, that is how, I suppose, he always saw us. Only from a distance. I often wonder what might've been avoided had he looked a bit more closely."

Gorev leaned back in his chair and crossed his arms with a growing sense of self-assurance. "The Tsar was Supreme Ruler of millions of people...one-sixth of the earth's surface. Rather difficult to see all of that closely, wouldn't you say?"

Sokolov pivoted in order to face Gorev directly. "Then was he, in your opinion, a competent leader?"

Gorev, his smugness tapering slightly, stroked his heavily waxed mustache with his index finger. "When they brought him the news of this father's death in 1894," he replied rigidly, "do you know the first words out of his mouth? 'I am not prepared to be Tsar. I never wanted to be one. I know nothing of the business of ruling. What is going to happen to me and to all of Russia?'"

"Then he was not a competent leader?"

"I never said that."

"I assume you do have an opinion."

This was obviously the one question Gorev had been waiting for. "Pardon me, Investigator," he interjected. "I was not aware the Russian people were still permitted personal opinions."

Sokolov was equally prepared with an answer. "To have them, yes; to express them, occasionally."

Gorev's voice was reacquiring its icy edge. "And this is one of those occasions?" he sneered. "Why? What aristocrat are you punishing this week?"

"Something to remember about occasions such as this," Sokolov cautioned softly, "because they are so rare, it's never very wise to take undue advantage of them."

"In that case, what good are they?" Gorev snapped back in a flash of petulant anger. Then, as if having possibly reconsidered the abruptness of his response, his entire countenance softened markedly. "Oh, they were right," he smiled demurely, "you are quite good at what you do."

Gorev concluded with a slight sigh of resignation. "Mlle. Demidova was a maid to Empress Alexandra. I knew her. She had an apartment in Tobolsk."

"In August of 1917?" Sokolov asked.

"The Imperial family was being held in Tobolsk," Gorev explained, his patience obviously beginning to wane once more. "Demidova was in attendance to the Empress Alexandra. It therefore stands to reason that her apartment was also in Tobolsk. And yes, I visited the area twice during the Tsar's detainment there."

Gorev withdrew a pocket watch from his vest and glanced at it as if to signal that he had no further time to invest in such unproductive deliberation. "Is there anything else you wish to know, Investigator?"

"Only one thing," Sokolov replied simply. "Why you never completed your mission. Why didn't you try to rescue the Romanovs? That's obviously what you were sent here to do."

Gorev's only response was to quietly slide the gold watch back into his vest pocket.

Sokolov continued to press. "There were, of course, many other groups and organizations in the vicinity who, at one time or another, plotted to rescue the Tsar and his family. They all had one thing in common: a ridiculous lack of leadership...clarity of purpose. Every group but one. Yours."

Gorev could manage only one sputtered word in rebuttal, "Absurd."

"Oh, quite the contrary," Sokolov assured him with a disarming smile. "After all, you managed what no other group could. You actually made contact with the Empress through her maid, Mlle. Demidova. You had her smuggle notes of cryptic encouragement to the imprisoned Empress. 'Gregory's family and his friends are active.' Through Mlle. Demidova you even passed along money to the Imperial family. How much did they finally receive? How much did you keep for yourself?"

Though it was obvious that Gorev was floundering, he still struggled to reclaim some bit of solid footing. "I have no idea what you are talking about."

"Access," Sokolov fired back deliberately. "You had access to the Romanovs and I have access to the records of your contacts. You were clever, not tidy. You left a paper trail a mile wide from Moscow to Tobolsk. So, please, don't patronize me. Youth and total ignorance don't necessarily go hand in hand."

Sokolov paused for a moment in order to rein in the emotion that was creeping into his own voice. His strategy, after all, was to retain a composed veneer while prodding Gorev into being the one to finally lose control.

Reaching into a nearby dossier, the Investigator withdrew a crumpled letter that had been smuggled out of the Ipatiev House during the Romanov's captivity. Written in French on June 27th, the hastily penned communiqué's author had been either Olga or Nicholas himself—since they were the only two family members who were fluent in the language. Sokolov had memorized the letter's contents in any case, and now recited the words to Gorev:

"We spent an anxious night and stayed awake fully dressed. This was because, a few days ago, we received two letters, one after another, which informed us that we should prepare to be rescued by some people devoted to us. But the days passed and nothing happened, only waiting and the uncertainty were torture."

Sokolov let the crumpled paper slip from his hands and float easily to the surface of the table. Idly tapping the yellowed paper with his index finger for emphasis, he shifted his withering gaze once more to Gorev.

"The Imperial family must've had such faith in you," he continued. "In those final days, letters such as these were their last glimmer of hope. How they must've clung to thoughts of you! The rumor was that, at one time, you had actually employed three hundred faithful officers, disguised in the vicinity, and awaiting your signal. Three hundred! And yet you did nothing. Why? The situation was far from hopeless at that point. It wasn't leadership you lacked. It wasn't money. What was it? Simple courage?"

His mission accomplished, Sokolov calmly returned to his chair to quietly await the anticipated eruption.

"Very well," Gorev replied, straining to contain his growing indignation. "Let us both speak frankly." The veins in his neck were bulging now. Trembling slightly, Gorev seemed to be suddenly over enunciating—almost spitting his words.

"The day after the butchery took place in the basement room of this house, there was a train at the Ekaterinburg station, its windows painted black. For two days it sat there, waiting to take the executioners away once their job was done. Windows painted black so no one could see the faces of men who were able to murder defenseless women and children!"

Gorev suddenly shoved the chair back with considerable force and bolted to his feet. His face was flushed with undisguised rage. "How dare you pretend to speak to me of courage or the lack of it!" he bellowed. "What do you or those about you know of courage? White armies, Red armies! I make no distinctions. You have no names, no identities! You're fearful men—all of you. Your governments, philosophies, your precious wars and revolutions—all based on fear! Your only hope is to make the world around you more fearful than you are. And at that, dear boy, you are fast becoming masters."

Heaving for breath, Gorev stood at the end of the long table glaring at Sokolov, his trembling hands gripping the table's edge as if he was about to literally wrench part of it away.

From his vantage point, Sokolov took deliberate time to let the moment play out. Gorev had clearly lost the battle of containment, but the truth was that Sokolov was now having to suppress his own emotions.

"Citizen Gorev," he managed as calmly as his voice permitted, "I have asked for your cooperation in a matter of importance to our central government. That's actually all you need to know, isn't it?"

Gorev may have expended the brunt of his tantrum, but not his aggravation at the effrontery. "I'm afraid not," he seethed. "You see, I require something your central government seems unable to provide—a reason." His words were steeped in a condescending tone he could no longer control.

In order to reclaim some bit of lost poise, however, he sat once more and paused for a moment before resuming his haughty air and peevish monologue.

"I'm quite sorry to be such a problem," he began anew, "but civilized men have a tendency, in times such as these, to behave in just this manner. Starving peasants may rush to embrace your empty promises of a better life. Men of intellect? Never. When you and your government are able to offer more convincing reasons, you might begin to see some of the changes you long for. Not until."

His harangue at last concluded, Gorev snatched a white handkerchief from his coat pocket and dabbed his moist forehead. His face was still flushed with something akin to righteous indignation, but it appeared to Sokolov that the initial pique had been expended. This was indeed fortunate for Gorev, though he was obviously well beyond grasping the fact. The simple truth was that he would have paid dearly for any further histrionics.

"You may not believe this," the Investigator replied, slightly shifting his body's posture in the chair, "but I actually have considerable regard for opposing opinions. Not all of us are quite the barbarians you seem to think. Some of us indeed appreciate the fact that there are those among you who do need reasons and therefore ask...or, as in your case...demand them."

"And you have one?" Gorev sneered incredulously, "A reason powerful enough to convince me?"

Sokolov slid his chair back from the table and slowly stood.

"That," he replied, gathering his body into a fully upright posture, "I shall leave up to you."

The Investigator stepped around the edge of the table and casually made his way to Gorev. At the same time, he discreetly unsnapped the leather cover of his holster. His next soft command to Gorev consisted of only three words, "Open your mouth."

The seated Gorev pivoted brusquely to more fully confront the advancing Investigator. What he faced instead was the barrel of Sokolov's drawn Mauser hovering steadily only an inch from his nose. In another second, as all color completely drained from his face, Gorev underwent what could best be described as a radical attitude adjustment.

Sokolov, now towering over the stunned Gorev, softly repeated his command. "Open your mouth."

This time, Gorev numbly obeyed only to feel the cold, hard barrel of the pistol slide instantly between his parted lips.

Sokolov then delivered his second order, "Close."

Gorev's trembling lips obediently tightened around the barrel of the Mauser.

Sokolov's voice was still soft but lethal. "Now, citizen Gorev, I shall attempt to appeal to your intellect with one, and only one, reason. You will tell me everything you know about the imprisonment of the Imperial family in Ekaterinburg or I will most assuredly pull this trigger. Do we completely understand each other?"

Gorev, rigid as a block of Arctic ice, could only nod his head. He did so very carefully.

"I had a feeling we might," Sokolov smiled wanly as he slowly withdrew the gun barrel from Gorev's mouth. The action permitted a fuller response on Gorev's part which he undertook by instantly bending forward in his chair and gagging uncontrollably for almost a full minute.

"Amazing thing, the power of reason," Sokolov mused aloud as he slid his Mauser back into its holster. The Investigator then strode back to his chair at the other side of the table and sat down. Rifling through a stack of papers before him, he paused long enough to glance up at Boris Gorev. "We'll continue this discussion tomorrow afternoon, during which time I shall expect to be astounded by your astute memory recall and generous cooperation. That will be convenient, I trust?"

Gorev, dabbing the corners of his pursed lips with his handkerchief, rose shakily to his feet and obediently stumbled to the doorway of the room. Before exiting, however, he turned back to Sokolov.

"A bit of advice, Investigator," he managed hoarsely. "I should be very careful, if I were you. There are forces at work here about which you know nothing; '...more things in Heaven and earth than are dreamt of in your philosophy'."

On the verge of retching again, Gorev wheeled around and, fumbling to retain balance as well as some semblance of dignity, hurriedly staggered through the doorway.

Sokolov's Journal
Ekaterinburg, 1919

"Free cheese can be found only in a mousetrap."

For a long while after he left, I sat alone in that empty room. I honestly don't know what I detested more—that man or my behavior in his presence.

Boris Gorev grew rich on the suffering of the Imperial family. He waved hope like a banner in the wind before them and in the end, like his promises, melted away into nothingness. He bullied and cajoled. What's more, he got everything he wanted.

I've never had to actually pull the trigger to end a man's life. That fact does not upset me unduly. Harsh times, harsh measures; and you must eventually deal with the feelings of guilt and remorse that accompany such actions. This, I was completely prepared for. What I was unprepared for was the total absence of what I expected to feel. There was no remorse or guilt. There were, instead, only feelings of great satisfaction and pleasure.

Chapter Seven

Ekaterinburg's weathered depot was all but deserted later that same afternoon. His curiosity piqued by Gorev's mention of a mysterious train car with its windows painted black, Sokolov decided to inspect the area in an effort to confirm the accuracy of such strange information.

It didn't take long to locate several depot employees who'd been on duty during that same time period a year earlier, and both men immediately confirmed Gorev's claim. A train had indeed arrived several days prior to July 16, 1918, and had departed a day or two later. The workers had no trouble recalling the incident because the windows on two of the train cars appeared to have been painted over. One of the depot workers even pointed out the spot on the distant side tracks where the train car had been left.

Sokolov strolled the side tracks to the place indicated by the workman. There, he found a length of rusted siding where a waiting train could certainly have been positioned.

The area, abandoned now, was littered with debris—a silent testament to the economic instability of the region. It was also clear to Sokolov that the inactivity in and around the railroad yard was not due to a temporary lull. If the rail system was the life blood of Russia, the country was fast becoming anemic—a condition that spoke volumes about the White Army's inability to secure an area it had recently conquered and now occupied. But that, Sokolov reminded himself, was always a fundamental wartime challenge. Conquering a region or even a nation was one thing, occupation was quite another. History has repeatedly demonstrated that victories are often claimed prematurely when strategic planning for successful occupation has taken low priority.

Those forced to learn this lesson the hard way have always paid dearly for the gift of hindsight.

Venturing still further down the empty tracks, Sokolov caught a wisp of smoke in his nostrils. Curious to locate its source, he followed the acrid scent until it led to a small makeshift clearing where a shelter constructed of tree limbs and assorted debris came into view.

A family—father, mother and two children wrapped in ragged blankets—huddled there around a small fire for warmth. A rusty canister of watery broth was the only thing simmering on the glowing coals.

More remnants of humanity than actual human beings, the family numbly acknowledged Sokolov's presence with nothing more than dull stares from yellow, unblinking eyes sunk deep into drawn, gray faces. It was as if he was gazing at a group of animated corpses who were still numbly going about their vain attempts to cling to life. He wanted to turn away...avert his gaze, but something more powerful than self-consciousness held the young Investigator transfixed at the sight before him.

The many records of wholesale slaughter and the reports of thousands who simply froze to death were one thing, but they didn't truly register until you had seen just one example...and for Sokolov, this was it. The scene was certainly not an unfamiliar one, but for that moment in time, it was suddenly as though he was able to see it all for the first time, and grim truth, which will not be denied, at last began to sear his consciousness with heartbreaking clarity.

These people and millions more like them were the pitiful result of Russia's long years of turmoil, struggle and empty promises of better life. One saw them everywhere. Initially, they had merely inhabited the edges of civilization. No more. Now they filled shabby villages and roamed city streets in plain view—drawing out what was left of their pitiful lives. Finding shelter whenever possible and endlessly scavenging for scraps of rotting food, they trudged the muddy roads of Russia in endless lines, relentlessly plodding onward to unreachable destinations. They died by the thousands in ditches, fields and bleak alleyways along the way—their frozen twisted bodies merely serving to mark the hopeless path for others who followed them. Starvation, disease, exposure, murder, rape, suicide—statistics. Convenient labels. Numbers to be tallied in someone's bureaucratic ledger book. Nothing more. The countless frozen bodies would finally dissolve beneath the winter snows. By the time spring came again, there would be nothing left to mark the fact that they had ever existed.

Was this, Sokolov wondered, the ultimate tragedy? That human beings such as these were forced to suffer so unbelievably only to finally be swallowed up by the land that bore them? Or did the real catastrophe lie in the fact that they had been born into such a twisted and forbidding world to begin with, forced to trudge through their tortured time on the earth while shouldering such misery?

Sokolov knew only too well that to question his government's philosophy was to question the very foundation of an entire belief system—even in such a bleak environment of utter disillusionment. The truth was obvious enough. It wasn't War that was the answer; it was justice. Sokolov had dedicated his life to the quest. He had even known fleeting moments of brief accomplishment. Why then this nagging doubt—this secret and unspeakable notion that justice was finally unattainable?

Even Gorev had warned that there were unseen forces at work. "More things in heaven and earth than are dreamt of in your philosophy." Secrecy and world domination. The eternal struggle for power. Religious belief or religious discipline? Preconceptions of Hell. Manipulating the masses. These were the darker forces at play. In time, a few of the many monstrous crimes would come to light—shocking truths that would bewilder ordinary men for ages yet to be. The only possible consolation in Sokolov's microscopic view of this one isolated instance was the pathetic thought that, at least by morning, the suffering would be over for a few hundred more nameless souls. Nothing more.

There were other notions he could claim in order to bolster some false sense of moral fortitude. Collateral damage. Acceptable losses. Spoils of war. The here-and-now. Whatever the meager attempt at justification, it was simply too much for Sokolov to consider at this point in time. Besides, he knew it would only be an exercise in utter futility.

"Go out to the Volga: hear whose moan
Rises over Russia's greatest river? In our land,
This moan is called a song—
It's the boatmen straining in their traces!
Volga! Volga! In the spring your torrents
Cannot flood the fields as much
As our people's awful pain

Floods our land—
Where you are there's moaning—O, my people!"

Nikolai Nekoosa

As Sokolov stood alone on that abandoned side track, gazing at the ragged family huddled around their small campfire, a sense of profound hopelessness overtook his entire being. The price of his wisdom had always been such deep and unforgiving sorrow.

At last, there was nothing he could do but turn his back on the pitiful tableau and make his way back to the Ipatiev House. There, he fell into bed, where mercifully bereft of dreams, he slept straight through the long cold Siberian night.

"It isn't a question of Russia at all, gentlemen. I spit on Russia... This is merely one phase through which we must pass on the way to a world revolution."

Lenin

With dawn's first light, Nicholas Sokolov roused himself from a deep sleep with a renewed sense of determination. Even as Natalya Kolya served him hot breakfast tea, he was already immersing himself in a methodical review of all records pertaining to the Romanov case.

As the documents were sorted, they were placed in corresponding folders which were then carefully arranged on Sokolov's desk. Before slipping each piece of paper into its proper folder, the Investigator paused only as long as it might take someone else to snap a photograph, in order to imbed a mental image of the document in his brain. He worked rapidly but carefully. As he slipped one page into its corresponding folder with his left hand, he was retrieving another document with his right hand. The piece of paper was then held motionless before his intense gaze for no more than ten seconds. Each time his eye blinked, it was as though the shutter of a camera had been triggered.

In some miraculous way, the image of each page...an exact duplicate of each piece of paper...was being captured and processed in the recesses of the young Investigator's amazing mind. To recall a document, he merely had to concentrate—as though retrieving it from his own mental filing cabinet—a technique that usually took only a matter of seconds. Amazingly, there were times he didn't even have to consciously focus on the process at all. Occasionally something 'clicked' and everything else happened spontaneously.

After several hours of steady work, Sokolov pushed the chair away from the table, stood and strolled to the window of his room. Gazing out onto the frigid courtyard, he stretched, yawned, and shook his head several times hoping to ward off the drowsiness of the late morning's routine.

That was the moment it flashed inside his head—a single name on a list...one out of many in his files. The spontaneous recall seemed cryptic for only several moments before a mental image of the document's corresponding folder had been recalled and Sokolov was actually clutching the piece of paper in his hands. On it was a list of people known to have had access to the Ipatiev House during the Romanov's imprisonment. The name in question appeared as fifth from the bottom in a column of over forty names:

"Yakimov. First name, Anatoly. Twenty-two years old. Soldier in the Red Army. Stationed as a sentry—the Ipatiev House. On duty night of execution."

Sokolov was somewhat puzzled. Why had he unconsciously flagged the name of Anatoly Yakimov? The answer materialized even as he began to ponder the question. The name was a duplicate. It had appeared on more than one document in more than one folder. Such instances occasionally made for important connections—one more piece added to the complex puzzle of names, dates, and occurrences.

The young Investigator stood next to the table littered with folders. His eye carefully roamed the stacks of dossiers until he recalled a single piece of paper that had been included in the bundle given to him by Admiral Kolchak—a seemingly innocuous list of local Bolshevik prisoners currently being held in Ekaterinburg. Sokolov had seen Yakimov's name there—on that same list!

He hastily retrieved the piece of paper and located the name 'Anatoly Yakimov' almost at once. This was an astounding discovery! Anatoly Yakimov, one of the young men stationed at the Ipatiev House during the time of the Romanov's captivity, was possibly still alive and being held as a prisoner in Ekaterinburg!

Within two hours, special orders had been issued and the young prisoner had been plucked from a group of fifty men being held in a nearby prison encampment, loaded onto a muddy lorry and driven to the frigid courtyard of the Ipatiev House.

Sokolov discreetly observed Yakimov's arrival from a window in one of the empty upstairs rooms.

The young prisoner—petrified at what he was possibly about to undergo—was brusquely herded into the house. Two burly soldiers, prodding him with rifle butts, propelled the frightened youth down a long, dim corridor and into what had now been designated as the interrogation room.

This was not the room in which Sokolov had first interrogated Boris Gorev. The long dining room table seemed somehow too opulent for the task at hand. An empty side room on the ground floor had been chosen instead, and only a few pieces of furniture were going to be needed. Everything had been carefully selected and arranged by Sokolov to produce the desired psychological effect.

Upstairs, the young Investigator carefully adjusted his uniform while gazing at his reflection in a cloudy mirror hanging on one of the room's bare walls. He was calm and unhurried—intentionally delaying his entrance for additional dramatic impact.

Downstairs, Yakimov was shoved onto a single wooden stool which had been placed at the far end of the sparsely furnished room. At the other end of the room was Sokolov's single desk and chair. Aside from that, the room was completely bare yet intimidating. As previously instructed and without a word, the two soldiers who had served as the prisoner's military escort, turned and left the room.

Sokolov waited at least five minutes after observing Yakimov's arrival before making his way to the ground floor. His shoulders were squared and his professional bearing displayed just the right touch of detached austerity as he reached the room's doorway. This demeanor was not only professionally appropriate, it was indispensable to the entire process which was about to take place.

The prisoner waiting inside—Anatoly Yakimov—was a terrified young man with very little formal education—early twenties, pale skin, blue eyes, dirty blond hair hidden by a ragged forage cap—and a face that resembled, though vaguely now, someone who might have once served as a model for a Raphael painting. Though appearing much older than he actually was, in his eyes, nose and lips one could still discern traces of androgynous sensuality. Clothed in a long military overcoat which covered his tattered prison uniform, Yakimov was gaunt from months of mistreatment and undernourishment. Since he had been told nothing about where he was going or what to expect once he arrived, he was also extremely apprehensive. Still, he could do nothing but wait in the empty silence of that room, consumed with dreadful anticipation.

Taking a deep breath in the musty corridor just outside the door, Nicholas Sokolov steadied himself, quietly turned the knob, entered the room and purposefully strode to his desk.

Still trembling with fear, Anatoly Yakimov, struggled to his feet and stood in what could be assumed was an attempt at military attention. Aware of this fact, but never once making eye contact with the prisoner, Sokolov took his usual position of authority behind the desk, deposited Yakimov's dossier, and only then turned, with an air of professional nonchalance, to face his first challenge of the day.

The Investigator had made a few additional preparations in order to command the psychological high ground. The legs of Yakimov's wooden stool had been shortened on purpose. Through deft manipulation and simple positioning of body height, the Investigator had now achieved his first goal: he had become the symbolic schoolmaster and Yakimov, his subservient pupil. The pistol also strapped to the belt of Sokolov's military tunic was more than enough subliminal reinforcement.

Nicholai Alexeyevich Sokolov's first word was an order—not harshly barked in anger but issued softly with just the slightest hint of empathetic intent. "Sit."

Yakimov, struggling to support himself on unsteady legs, thankfully obeyed. Sokolov's next goal was to establish a relationship grounded in fundamental reciprocity. He needed Yakimov's cooperation and understood the importance of basing it on a simple foundation of trust. His methods, carefully honed during years of professional practice, were productive and dependable.

Additionally, he was firmly resolved at the outset of this all-important first encounter, not to forfeit a single point during the interrogation. So far, at least, Sokolov knew he was on solid footing. It was quite clear that his delayed entrance had elicited the desired effect, and he was ready to proceed with quiet command.

"You are Anatoly Alexandrovich Yakimov?"

The young prisoner nodded obediently.

"Born in 1887," Sokolov went on, recounting the young man's history from memory, "the son of a peasant, you were raised in Perm. Your father died when you were twelve, while you were attending Ekaterinburg Ecclesiastical Seminary School. You were a worker at the Zlokazov factory here in Ekaterinburg. Refused to join the Bolshevik Party. At the time of your capture by our forces, you were serving in the Red Army—and were stationed here in Ekaterinburg as a guard, yes? In this very house, in fact."

"Yes," Yakimov replied meekly, "except, I was never inside the House of Special Purpose. I was only a member of the outer guard."

Sokolov hesitated for a moment, trying not to betray any visible reaction. "What was it you just said? House of...what?" he asked as flatly as possible.

"*Dom osobogo naznacheniya.* House of Special Purpose," Yakimov repeated. "It's what they called this place. We assumed it was because the Romanovs were being kept here."

"House of Special Purpose," Sokolov intoned quietly. "Adequate. And how many guards did it take to secure such a special place?"

"There were sixteen men on the inside," Yakimov replied. "They slept in the basement, hallways and also in the commandant's office. Outside, in my detail, there were fifty-six men. There were ten guard posts, and those of us on the outside were ordered to patrol twice hourly day and night. By July of last year, the total number of guards must've been at least three hundred men."

"I see," Sokolov nodded. "So—as a member of the guard detail here, you must've had opportunity to observe the Imperial family—sometimes quite closely. Yes?"

Yakimov dodged the question slightly. "Sometimes."

Sokolov, deciding to shift the line of questioning, took several steps towards the cowering prisoner.

"May I see your hands?" he asked simply.

Yakimov glanced up in puzzlement.

"Your hands," Sokolov repeated calmly, "may I see them?"

With some difficulty, Yakimov again rose to his feet, removed his dirty gloves and dutifully extended both hands, palms down, towards Sokolov. Without a word, the Investigator took the young man's pale hands in his own. He turned them slowly in order to first observe the palms, then the back of the young man's hands again.

Eventually satisfied, Sokolov released Yakimov's hands and withdrew a pack of cigarettes from his tunic's breast pocket. Without a word, he held the pack towards Yakimov.

"Cigarette?"

"Thank you," the prisoner nodded. Sokolov silently passed the pack to Yakimov, who dutifully withdrew one cigarette and placed it between his lips. Striking a match, Sokolov lit the cigarette and watched as Yakimov deeply inhaled the smoke.

Snuffing the match and placing the pack of cigarettes back in his tunic pocket, Sokolov continued softly. "I'd be most grateful if you'd share with me any impressions you have regarding your time with the Imperial family. Think carefully. Does anything come to mind?"

"There was an old piano in the dining room," Yakimov replied. "In early May, the guards on the inside moved it into the commandant's office next door to the Romanovs' bedrooms. I thought it was such an unkind thing to do…and for no real reason except that they wanted the Imperial family to suffer as much as possible."

"Is there anything else you can recall?" Sokolov inquired.

"English," Yakimov replied with some enthusiasm.

"I beg your pardon?"

"English," Yakimov repeated again with a slight smile. "The royal family was forbidden to speak in English to one another."

"For what reason?" Sokolov inquired.

"Because none of us could speak English," Yakimov shrugged, "so no one but the royal family could understand what they would occasionally be saying to each other. That's why Russian was the only language the royal family was permitted to use."

"An interesting observation," Sokolov mused aloud.

"Yes," Yakimov nodded. "I was later told that while the family was in the basement moments before their deaths, Alexandra turned to her daughters and spoke to them in English. She was quickly reprimanded for doing so. I've always thought it was such a sad loss."

"What do you mean?" Sokolov asked.

"Since none of the guards could understand English, we'll never know what the Tsarina's final words to her daughters were."

"You think her words would've been significant?"

"If she knew they were to be her last words, yes."

"You are, of course, assuming that she knew they were about to die."

"Are you assuming that she didn't?" Yakimov asked simply.

Sokolov paused briefly to consider the question's significance. The truth was that he hadn't yet weighed the possibility of foreknowledge. The Romanovs could've gone peacefully into that basement room suspecting nothing more than what they had been told. They also could've knowingly gone to their fates like the stoic martyrs history would eventually declare them to be. Unfortunately, this was not the time to weigh the possibilities. Assessing the validity of Yakimov's observations would come later. This was a time for gathering information.

Sokolov took a brief pause before beginning a fresh line of questioning.

"When was the last time you saw the Romanovs alive?"

Again, there was no hesitation in Yakimov's reply. "July 16th—one year ago."

"You were on duty that day?"

"Outside. I was a sentry. After July 4th, the usual guards inside the house were all replaced with the secret police."

Once more in an attempt to betray little or no emotion, Sokolov paused deliberately. "You refer to the Bolshevik Cheka. Lenin's secret police. Officially known as the Extraordinary Commission for Combating Counterrevolution and Sabotage— yes? What were they like?"

"Cold-blooded killers," Yakimov replied disdainfully. "Most of them weren't even Russians. Five were prisoners of war from the Austro-Hungarian army. There was another man with blond hair who was occasionally with them too. I don't think he was a regular part of the detachment. Anyway, they were the ones who gave this place the name, House of Special Purpose. Their leader was a man named Jacob Yurovsky. He'd been a photographer here in Ekaterinburg before the war."

Sokolov took a moment to jot down a few written notations, then leaning against his desk and crossing his arms, he addressed the young prisoner once again. "Can you recall your memories of that day? July 16th?"

Once more, there was no hesitation on Yakimov's part. "I remember that morning...July 16th. Everything seemed normal...except that Yurovsky ordered Leonoid Sednev, the fourteen year-old kitchen boy, sent away from the house. But first...and this seemed strange...he took the boy's clothes, then sent him off in an old, borrowed uniform. Too large. I remember that; the uniform was too large."

"The uniform given to the kitchen boy?"

"We thought orders to transfer the family had finally come through. But no one told us anything. At four that afternoon, the Tsar and his four daughters went for their usual walk in the garden outside."

"This was a custom?"

"Every day for an hour. Then, at seven that evening, Yurovsky summoned all of the Cheka men into his room. After a few moments they came outside to those of us on guard and demanded that we give them our revolvers. We had no idea what had been planned. They collected twelve weapons in all and carried them back into the house. Still, nothing happened. The Imperial family went to bed at ten thirty. Usual time. The house was dark and quiet for a long while. Then, at midnight, a light came on in an upstairs bedroom window. I saw it from below...where I was positioned. I watched for a moment and suddenly Grand Duchess Anastasia appeared. She pressed her face to the window pane and gazed out into the darkness as if searching for something. Her hair had been cut short. I remember that. They cut all of the Imperial family's hair. That's why I noticed, that night at the window, a single strand of Anastasia's hair had come out of place and fallen slightly across her forehead. She brushed it back with her hand, but I remember this...and always thought it strange that I would recall it so clearly...she brushed the strand of hair back with the last finger of her right hand. Just the last finger. It seemed so...natural for the daughter of the Tsar. Then she disappeared from the window for the last time. Finally, the light went out. Time passed. I don't know how long. We knew what was happening."

"You heard the gunfire?" Sokolov asked.

"Not actually. They had parked a truck in the courtyard next to the house and were constantly revving the engine. It went on for at least fifteen minutes so you couldn't hear anything else. I think they did it to cover the sound of gunshots...and the terrible screams."

Silence engulfed the interrogation room for several moments as Sokolov, deep in thought, strolled to a window and gazed out into the frigid courtyard. He allowed even a bit more time to elapse before he finally turned back to Yakimov. "Do you remember anything that occurred after the truck stopped revving its engine?"

The young prisoner took a long drag off the cigarette as he considered Sokolov's question. "I was ordered to return to my room. I don't know what happened after I left my post. My guard duty was over at dawn. I only remember being very cold."

"You believe they were executed?"

"I never saw them again after that night."

"That isn't what I asked," Sokolov interrupted. "Do you believe they were executed?"

"I want to believe," Yakimov confessed with lowered head. "Death is sometimes a blessing."

"You never joined the Bolshevik Party," Sokolov observed. "Why?"

"I never thought it would make much of a difference," Yakimov sighed. Then, as if suddenly reciting a memorized passage from a book, the young prisoner began to elaborate. "I agree with many of their principals. I'm not ashamed to say so. I still think that there will be a good and just life only when there aren't any rich and poor, as there are now, and this will happen only when all of the people understand through education that such a life does not yet exist. I viewed Nicholas II as the number one capitalist, who always will be holding hands with the capitalists and not with the workers. For that reason, I didn't want a Tsar, and thought it was necessary to keep him under guard, imprisoned for the safety of the Revolution."

"I see," the Investigator nodded. Sokolov waited while Yakimov snubbed out the cigarette on the bottom of one of his tattered boots. Once this was done and a bit more silence had settled into the room, Yakimov's posture began to sag once more as he again resumed a more timid and self-conscious demeanor.

"That will be all for now," the Investigator concluded. "You've been a great help. I'll see that your cooperation does not go unrewarded."

The prisoner struggled to his feet. Hugging his military cap to his chest with both pale hands, he bowed obediently. "Thank you."

Reaching into the breast pocket of his tunic, Sokolov withdrew the pack of cigarettes and again held it out to Yakimov. "Here. Take these."

Anatoly Yakimov stared at the Investigator in disbelief. "Only one, if you please," he finally replied.

"Why not the whole pack?" Sokolov asked. "I give them to you."

Yakimov took several halting steps toward Sokolov before replying. "In the place I've just come from, they'd slit my throat for a pack of cigarettes. With your permission, I'll take only one and smoke it on my way back. You understand?"

Sokolov nodded and waited as Yakimov took a single cigarette from the pack and gently slipped it into the pocket of his muddy overcoat. The young prisoner then turned and shuffled to the doorway of the room. Once he reached the door, however, he turned back to Sokolov.

"Good-bye, Investigator," he said in a soft voice. "I hope you find whoever it is you're looking for."

Yakimov's parting words took Sokolov slightly off guard, and he glanced back at the prisoner with a quizzical expression tracing his face. "What makes you think I'm looking for someone?"

Yakimov shrugged slightly. "Nothing," he replied. "I suppose... I just assumed you were."

Without another word, Yakimov placed the tattered forage cap on his head, opened the door and, with a downcast gaze, shuffled out of the room.

Sokolov's Journal
Ekaterinburg, 1919

Why is it, I wonder, that God gives clearest vision only to dying men? A kitchen boy's clothes. Shorn hair. Two more pieces of the puzzle. But where do they fit?

Have you ever noticed something out of the corner of your eye? A shadow moving in the half-light of an empty room? And have you ever shifted your gaze to that moving shadow only to find it gone? I tell you this in all honesty—some of my best friends have been those shadows.

It was such an unconscious thing in the beginning. A shadow perhaps—but undeniable. I hardly noticed; and I confess to more than a bit of pride in usually being more astute. I remember being drawn into her eyes... eyes that peered sadly back to me from a torn and faded photograph. The same photograph Kolchak had singled out as if by accident. I should've suspected something then. But that's the nice thing about total ignorance; it's usually very sincere. What was it I felt?

Sympathy? I say without blemish that I have always hated the Romanovs and everything they have ever represented in this world. So...why, suddenly, this...difference? This tiny, nagging doubt?

That poor boy was right. I was looking for something. Something hidden, but just barely. One of those lost shadows. Obscured, you see, but not completely. Tantalizing. Something I hadn't planned to find. But what? A young girl's face in a lighted window? A piece of blood soaked clothing? Something.

Anything!

Chapter Eight

"With the saints give rest, O Christ, to the souls of your servants where there is neither pain, nor sorrow, nor suffering—but life everlasting."

It was inevitable that Nicholas Sokolov's quest (and his dogged determination) would eventually lead him to members of the city's local clergy. Ekaterinburg's resident priests and nuns had, after all, been privy to occasional firsthand information regarding the Imperial family's confinement in their city. Two priests in particular—Father Ivan Storozhev and his colleague Father Meledin—were living eyewitnesses by virtue of having been occasionally allowed inside the Ipatiev House to conduct religious services for the Romanovs. Besides the priests, a group of nuns from the Novo-Tikhvinsky Convent delivered milk, cream, and eggs each morning to 'The House of Special Purpose'. The nuns even managed to occasionally hide packs of cigarettes in their baskets for their chain-smoking *batushka-tsar*. Nicholas II preferred Benson & Hedges or the delicious Turkish cigarettes he often favored during happier times. In captivity, he had been forced to resign himself to cheap and unpleasant papirosy, small cardboard tubes stuffed with vile smelling makhorka tobacco enjoyed by the ordinary Russian population.

In truth, Nicholas II battled more than nicotine addiction while a prisoner in Ekaterinburg. Though very few knew of it, the Tsar had also developed a rather serious dependence on narcotics...albeit under the guise of following well intentioned medical advice. Before his abdication, he had often been administered a blend of henbane and hashish by a Tibetan doctor known as P.S. Badnaeu. This closely guarded regimen had been recommended by none other than Gregory Rasputin as a way to help Nicholas counter frequent bouts of stress and insomnia. As time passed, however, a few alarmed courtiers were of the private opinion that the Tsar's growing dependence on these 'treatments' had 'seriously affected his mental powers' to the point that affairs of state were often performed with 'callousness and complete insensibility to anything that befell him'.

Whatever his secret addictions may have been, the bare truth is that Nicholas II had been forced into a state of withdrawal and recovery that followed closely on the heels of his abdication. Once he became 'Citizen Romanov' most of the debilitating habits he may have once possessed were forced aside. It was therefore with an unusual degree of clear-headed sobriety that Nicholas II spent his seventy-eight days of captivity in the Ipatiev House.

The priests and nuns from Ekaterinburg who tended to the Imperial family's spiritual needs were blissfully unaware of these things, of course, and remained instead deeply impressed by the family's apparent spiritual strength and stoic resolve in the midst of so much anguish.

Of course, the nuns from the Novo-Tikhvinsky Convent had not been permitted to see the Romanovs at all during their daily visits. They were met at the stockade's main entrance by Yurovsky or one of the other guards who accepted the convent's daily donations of milk, cream and eggs.

While the priests were allowed to conduct religious services inside the Ipatiev House, they were not permitted to engage in idle conversation with members of the Imperial Family. Their impressions, therefore, were the result of eyewitness encounters filtered through a righteous desire to see all of God's children in the best possible light—especially those who had come to find their salvation through such Christ-like suffering. Coupled with this was the historically strong connection the 'batushka' Tsar had always shared with the Russian people...a tenacious spiritual bond that dated back hundreds of years.

As for Nicholas and Alexandra, they were both devoutly religious and seemed, at least in the last days of their captivity, to share a mutual reliance upon 'all of those obscure, emotional and visionary elements which find their highest expression in religious mysticism'. The Tsaritsa had always been drawn to miraculous and mysterious spiritual influences, and more often than not she found them in the miracles attributed to wandering Russian pilgrims and various 'holy men'.

"Such people speak more strongly to my mind and heart," she once said, "than the Church hierarchs who come to me in expensive silk vestments." Perhaps because of this, it was apparent to the priests who visited the Ipatiev House that the Romanovs, over time, had become less concerned with religious redemption and more focused upon the soul's preparation for that mysterious transition from one plane of existence to another.

Whatever the impressions of the local clergy, it was certainly important for Nicholas Sokolov to hear them firsthand. He therefore took it upon himself, on a particularly blustery afternoon, to pay a visit to the Ekaterininsky Cathedral on Glavny Prospekt where he was able to meet with Father Ivan Storozhev.

#

The pungent scent of incense and candle wax hung heavy in the air of the quiet sanctuary as Nicholas Sokolov and Father Storozhev sat together on a pew close to the church's altar. The two men, paying reverent deference to the sacred surroundings, were speaking in hushed tones.

It seemed to Sokolov that Father Storozhev was actually grateful—even eager—to finally unburden himself by sharing his personal recollections of the captive Romanovs. Perhaps this was because the priest still harbored some degree of guilt at not being able to more effectively minister to the spiritual needs of the Imperial family. Given the circumstances, of course, it appeared that Father Storozhev had certainly done all he possibly could have. Still in all, hindsight has a nasty habit of bringing even the strongest resolve into occasional question. It was Sokolov's definite impression that by sharing his recollections, Father Storozhev was seeking a sort of absolution through confession. Whatever the reason, the Investigator now felt gratefully confident that a good many blank spaces were about to be filled with vital eyewitness testimony.

"It was a beautiful Sunday morning," Father Storozhev began. "I was just preparing for the services when I heard a knock at the door. It was one of the guards from the Ipatiev House...a young man named Anatoly Yakimov. He told me that I had been summoned to conduct a liturgy for the Imperial family. I was surprised to say the least. Only the night before, I had been informed that my colleague, Father Meledin, had been chosen to conduct the service. For some reason, there had been a change of plans. I was told to be at the house by ten o'clock, so I hurried to the cathedral to gather the things I would need."

"Before that Sunday morning," Sokolov inquired, "how much time had elapsed since the Imperial family had last been allowed to celebrate mass?"

"At least three weeks," Father Storozhev replied. "It had been an agony for them, I'm sure."

"Do you know why the guards at the Ipatiev House suddenly decided to allow your visit?"

"I'm not sure," Father Storozhev sighed with a shrug of his shoulders. "I believe Dr. Botkin had actually made a written request for a priest to celebrate *obednista*."

"Liturgy without communion?" Sokolov mused aloud.

"That is correct," Father Storozhev nodded. "I was asked specifically for the *obednista* by the commandant, Jacob Yurovsky."

"Did you consider that unusual?"

"I was deeply troubled by the order," Father Storozhev replied. "I was fully expecting to perform the *obednya*, the full service with communion. The *obednista* is, after all, more commonly reserved for troops in the field...especially when time is of the essence. I thought it particularly cruel that the family was to be denied the sacrament of the Eucharist. It was, after all, their right as Christians. I was even bold enough to suggest that to the commandant himself."

"Yurovsky still refused?" Sokolov asked.

Father Storozhev nodded. "Perhaps it was all for the best."

"Why do you say that?" Sokolov inquired.

"Well," the priest explained, "it was clearly obvious that the Tsarista and Tsarevich were in poor health. Perhaps, in that case, a shorter ceremony was the best choice after all."

"Is there anything else you remember about the appearance of the Imperial family?"

"I thought the Tsar appeared calm and in rather good spirits. He was in military dress and had the cross of St. George pinned to his tunic."

"What, if anything, do you recall of the daughters?"

"They were plainly dressed and their hair had been cut short."

Father Storozhev suddenly raised his hand as if to signal a fresh thought. "The hair," he exclaimed. "Yes, I remember now. The Tsar's beard...it was very short as well. In all of the photographs of him, I've never seen his beard trimmed as short as it appeared that day."

"Your memories are very helpful," Sokolov responded with a reassuring smile. "Your attention to detail is commendable."

Sokolov then leaned toward the priest in continued earnestness. "Is there anything else you can recall ... something you might even consider to be insignificant?"

Father Storozhev thought for a moment. "The service took place in the sitting room," he continued. "I do remember being shocked at the appearance of Alexei and the Tarista. They both appeared to be sickly and quite pale. I say that because the Tarista had always seemed so majestic in my eyes. She still possessed her royal bearing, only it seemed to me...on that day at least...that she was forcing herself to play a part in which she had lost all interest."

"And the ceremony itself," Sokolov continued to probe with his usual quiet determination, "What are your recollections of the *obednya*?"

"It saddened me," Father Storozhev replied without hesitation. "The Imperial family didn't participate in the sung responses as they normally would have. Moreover, when Deacon Bulmirov began to recite the traditional prayer for the dead... '*With the saints give rest, O Christ, to the soul of your servant where there is neither pain, nor sorrow, nor suffering but life everlasting*' for some reason, he began to sing the words instead of simply reciting them."

"He sang the words? Sokolov repeated softly.

"Yes," Father Storozhev nodded. "And when he did, the Romanovs sank to their knees at once in reverent silence. It was a deeply emotional moment for everyone in that room...Commandant Yurovsky included. It was perhaps for that very reason that he allowed the Tsar and Tsaritsa to receive the sacramental bread from me as they and their servants came forward to kiss the cross. The daughters took the opportunity to whisper their thank-yous to me. As they passed, one by one, I saw tears in their eyes."

Father Storozhev paused to clear his throat and compose himself by wiping away a few tears of his own. Sokolov sat in respectful silence until he felt the priest was once more ready to continue.

"I'm curious," the Investigator softly began once more. "What were the reactions of the others in the room?"

"No one else was present," Father Storozhev shrugged, "except Yurovsky. He was always there...and always apart from the rest...silently observing everything. At one point, and for some reason known only to him, Yurovsky got up from his chair and entered the room. He then rearranged where members of the family were standing."

"You mean he adjusted their positions in the room," Sokolov asked for clarification. "He changed the places where they were standing in relation to each other?"

"It certainly seemed as if that was what he was doing," the priest replied.

"Well," Sokolov smiled, "he was once a photographer by trade...in more peaceful times, of course. Perhaps he had an eye for what he considered to be a more proper composition."

"I hadn't thought of that," the priest mused. "I suppose old habits do tend to persist, don't they?"

"You were speaking of the last service you conducted for the family," Sokolov interjected. "The *obednista*."

"Ah, yes," Father Storozhev nodded. "Well, when the service was over and I was changing out of my vestments, Yurovsky then turned to me privately and remarked in a solemn voice, 'Well, at least they've said their prayers and unburdened themselves.' Unexpected words from such a man...and uttered, I believe, in all sincerity."

"Did you respond to his remark?" Sokolov asked.

"Yes," Father Storozhev answered. "I suggested to him that those who believe in God's will always find their faith fortified through prayer. That's when Yurovsky fixed his dark eyes on me and said 'I have never discounted the power of religion.' Again, such unexpected sentiments! In truth, I think we both knew that the Romanovs had actually just taken part in their last rites...their *panikhida*. Of course, I'm assuming all of this in retrospect. In that moment, Yurovsky obviously knew that they were going to be killed. I, of course, had no idea."

"Do you think the family suspected anything? Anything at all?"

"Hard to say," the priest replied, thoughtfully stroking his long beard. "Still, something in me says perhaps they did. Yes, I believe they somehow knew the end was very near. As for me, I left the Ipatiev House that day with such a heavy heart...unable to shake such an unmistakable sense of impending doom. Now, of course, I understand why."

"Tell me," Sokolov asked, "do you remember how many religious services were conducted for the Imperial family during the entire seventy-eight days they were prisoners here?"

"In all?" Father Storozhev answered softly. "Five. No more than five."

Sokolov shifted his posture slightly and decided to begin a new line of questioning.

"What do you remember," he continued cautiously, "of the Tsar's youngest daughter?"

The priest's face immediately brightened with a warm smile of happy remembrance. "So very full of life," he replied. "Hopelessly stubborn, delightfully impertinent. From what I gathered, she undoubtedly held the record for mischievous deeds in the royal family."

Father Storozhev's happy expression suddenly transformed itself into one of undisguised curiosity. "Why do you ask specifically about Grand Duchess Anastasia?" he inquired.

Sokolov allowed deliberate silence to hopefully serve as a mindful reply.

Seemingly oblivious to nuance, however, or perhaps simply undeterred by subtlety of any kind, the priest continued to gaze intently at the young Investigator as if trying to somehow extract more meaning than the intended silence was meant to provide. What was immediately clear, however, was the fact that this was a subject that was obviously of considerable interest to both men.

Then, in an obvious attempt to further entice Sokolov, Father Storozhev continued blithely, "I'm sure we have all heard the rumors."

"Yes," the Investigator responded drily. "I'm sure we have."

Father Storozhev nodded but said nothing more in immediate response. In the resulting silence, both men simply studied each other in guarded anticipation. Sokolov, not wanting either of them to slip into the convenient roles of priest and postulant, resisted what he determined to be Father Storozhev's natural tendency to illicit confessions. He was instead hoping that his purposeful silence would induce the priest to be a bit more forthcoming with his own disclosures. It was a judicious strategy that produced immediate results.

"The railroad signalman from Perm," Father Storozhev suddenly exclaimed with undisguised eagerness. "The one called Maxim Grigoryev. Is it true…what he saw?"

Sokolov was at a complete loss, but did his immediate best to cover any outward reaction. This was a name he had no knowledge of, and obviously an incident about which he knew absolutely nothing. Still struggling to mask his own stunned reaction, the Investigator simply shrugged his shoulders at the priest's question.

"It is, I will admit, an interesting report," Sokolov responded as blandly as he could. "We are of course attempting to follow up all possible leads."

The Investigator then crossed his arms and shifted his posture slightly as if to better scrutinize Father Storozhev. "It would be helpful," Sokilov continued, "if you would relate to me the details you have heard...for purposes of comparison, naturally."

Father Storozhev considered for only a moment and then nodded his head in acquiescence. "Grigoryev says the incident occurred on the twenty-first of September last year. He is a railroad signalman, as you must know, and was working at Siding 37 on the railway line northwest of Perm."

"Yes, I am aware of that," Sokolov lied. "Please go on."

"Well, at around noon on that day," Father Storozhev continued, "someone told Grigoryev that soldiers of the Red Army had caught a daughter of the Tsar in the woods close by and had taken her to a sentry box near the siding. Well, naturally he ran over to see. According to him, it was a young girl, who appeared to be about 18 or 19 years old. She was sitting in the sentry box, near a wood stove. Grigoryev says she wasn't crying, but he could see that there were bloodstains on her blouse. She had no scarf on her head. Her hair was cropped and of a dark color. He also said there was blood on her face, bruises around her eyebrows, and she was cut around the lip."

Father Storozhev paused and gazed at the Investigator as if seeking permission to continue his intriguing story.

"Go on," Sokolov nodded.

"Grigoryev says the girl was detained at the sentry box for an hour before the Red Army fellows tossed an army coat and hood on her and dragged her away."

Sokolov took his time before asking the next question in order not to appear too agitated...which of course he was. Still, he did his best to assume an air of professional detachment.

"Did Maxim Grigoryev ever mention the girl's name? Did he say which daughter he thought she was?"

"Yes, of course," Father Storozhev replied with a confident nod of his head. "He was told in no uncertain terms that it was the Grand Duchess Anastasia."

The priest sighed and shook his head. "There have been so many rumors. One never truly knows what to believe."

"Yes," Sokolov agreed softly. "A great many rumors."

The Investigator's heart was pounding in his chest. This was stunning news which certainly seemed to confirm his own private theory. At least he now had an eyewitness account, secondhand though it was, from someone who had possibly seen evidence of a survivor. What's more, the sighting had occurred some time after the date of the alleged execution, and the girl had been identified to the exclusion of the other daughters.

"That is why I was curious," Father Storozhev continued almost apologetically. "When you mentioned the Grand Duchess Anastasia in particular I naturally assumed..." The priest's voice trailed off into intended silence once again.

"Of course," Sokolov replied. "I certainly understand."

"And Maxim Grigoryev's story," the priest inquired meekly, "just another rumor among many?"

Sokolov stood and slid his hands into the pockets of his overcoat. He considered silently for a moment, mostly for theatrical effect, before gazing back down at the priest.

"Too early to tell," he answered solemnly. "As I said, we're still in the process of gathering as much information as possible. And, as you must know, these things take time."

"Oh, absolutely," the priest agreed. "And time is so valuable in cases such as this. That is why I do hope I haven't wasted yours."

"Not at all," Sokolov concluded with a smile. "I appreciate your willingness to be of assistance in this very important matter."

Father Storozhev suddenly stood and faced Sokolov with his best expression of earnest sincerity.

"There is something else you should know," he whispered confidentially. "Forgive me for not mentioning it at the outset of our conversation. It's just that it is...well...a matter I wouldn't normally share with anyone else."

"Of course," the Investigator said with belabored sincerity. "Please continue."

"There is a woman," Father Storozhev confided softly. "Her name is Evdokiya Semenova. A cleaning woman by trade. Quite poor. Lives on the outskirts of Ekaterinburg. I have received word that she is very ill...with not much time left. I mention her to you because a year ago she and three other women who belonged to the Bolshevik's Union of Professional Housemaids were routinely assigned to clean the Ipatiev House."

"While the Romanovs were being held there?" Sokolov immediately inquired.

"Oh, yes," Father Storozhev nodded enthusiastically. "She has firsthand knowledge of the family as well as the conditions under which they lived during their captivity."

"Would it be possible for me to meet her," the Investigator inquired.

"I had actually planned to visit her today," the priest replied, "my horse and cart are just outside. You're quite welcome to accompany me if you'd like. As I said, she is quite ill and time is of the essence."

Sokolov immediately stepped into the aisle of the church. Glancing back at the priest, he bowed slightly from the waist.

"I would like very much to accompany you, Father," he smiled.

A few moments later, the two men emerged from the warm shadows of the Ekaterininsky Cathedral into the frigid chill of another gray Siberian afternoon.

#

Not quite an hour later, Sokolov and Father Storozhev stepped down from the priest's horse-drawn cart and quietly entered Evdokiya Semenova's shabby dwelling on the outskirts of Ekaterinburg. The priest led the way as they crossed the threshold and were silently ushered into a dimly lit room by an elderly relative. Father Storozhev raised his hand in solemn benediction and whispered a short blessing on the household. He then nodded to the relative who obediently led the two men to Semenova's bedside in a small adjoining room.

The old woman lying in the death bed before them was very thin and frail. Her shallow breaths were coming at longer and longer intervals. It was obvious to Sokolov that she had only hours of life left, perhaps less.

The Investigator remained in the shadows of the room as Father Storozhev silently approached the bedside. A kerosene lamp on the bedside table cast a steady light on half of the dying woman's face. Her features were delicate...almost childlike. Her skin was porcelain in color and so transparent that one could easily make out the veins and arteries that lined her exposed arms, neck and temples.

Taking a seat on the edge of the bed next to the old woman, Father Storozhev quietly took her hand in his and softly intoned a gentle prayer. Sokolov observed the proceedings with respectful curiosity. He had always been fascinated by the subject of death and how people chose to face their last moments. Evdokiya Semenova was no exception.

Father Storozhev leaned close to the dying woman's face and said softly, "There is someone with me who would like to meet you. Would you mind if he spoke with you for a moment?"

Semenova's eyes flickered open and widened with immediate comprehension, while a delicate smile traced her parched lips.

"Someone would like to meet me?" she repeated.

"Yes," replied the priest. "He came all the way with me just for that purpose. Isn't that wonderful?"

"Oh, yes," the old woman replied softly. "I would be happy to meet your friend."

Father Storozhev turned to Sokolov and nodded. He then stood and moved away from the bed. Sokolov stepped forward and slowly took a seat on the bedside next to the woman.

Semenova's eyes grew wider with anticipation and she reached for Sokolov's hand. The Investigator gently took the old woman's hand in his.

"My name is Nicholas," he said softly.

"My name is Evdokiya Semenova," the old woman smiled.

"Yes," Sokolov nodded. "And I understand you have a very interesting story to tell."

"Do I?" The old woman looked suddenly confused.

"Father Storozhev tells me that you actually met the Imperial family while they were here in Ekaterinburg."

Semenova's eyes brightened and she smiled again with childlike delight at the instant recollection of that special day in her life.

"You and a few other women were sent to the Ipatiev House on the morning of July 15th," Sokolov continued in a gentle attempt to jog the sick woman's memory.

"I remember," Semenova recalled with a happy expression that seemed to restore some bit of color to her pale cheeks. "We arrived at the Ipatiev House at ten-thirty that morning."

"Who were the other women who accompanied you?" Sokolov inquired. "Do you remember?"

"Mariya Starodumova, Vavara Dryagina...and another woman whose name I don't know. She was new to the Union of Professional Housemaids. I believe she was new to Ekaterinburg as well."

Sokolov took particular note of Semenova's last statement, and immediately suspected that this fourth unknown woman, newly arrived in Ekaterinburg, was most probably a spy...but for whose side? The Bolsheviks? The Monarchists? Perhaps even the British? With no name to go on, it would be practically impossible to ever be absolutely certain. For the moment, however, Semenova's memories were quite sufficient and foremost in Sokolov's mind. This pitifully ill woman and her companions, were, after all, the last Ekaterinburg civilians to see the Romanovs alive.

Evdokiya Semenova feebly reached for a glass of water which had been placed on her bedside table next to the carefully arranged religious icons. Seeing her faltering attempts, Sokolov retrieved the glass himself and carefully guided it into Semenova's trembling hands. For an instant, as he helped maneuver the glass of water into her delicate grasp, Sokolov's hand made the briefest contact with Semenova's. The pale flesh of the back of her hand brushed ever so lightly against the palm of his own—and the breath caught in his throat at the sensation.

The soft touch of a woman had become quite a foreign thing to Sokolov, and he was suddenly aware of the profound significance of that fact. The truth was that he no longer honestly knew how to comfortably respond to a woman's presence, much less to the sensation of her touch. The awkwardness he felt in the moment dissipated when he quickly realized that no response on his part was necessary. Semenova had been completely oblivious to the brief contact anyway. The sad realization that accompanied the moment belonged to Sokolov alone.

He silently helped Semenova guide the glass of water to her parched lips, after which she managed several deep swallows before passing the glass back to Sokolov with another sweet and appreciative smile.

"You were telling me about the wonderful day you met the Imperial family," Sokolov gently coached as he returned the glass to the bedside table.

"Yes," Semenova replied, "we had been sent to wash the floors."

"In the Ipatiev House?" the Investigator inquired for the sake of clarification. "All of the floors in the house?"

Semenova responded with a weak cough and a slight nod of her head. "They told us to begin with the rooms in the basement."

The sick woman's last statement was of particular interest to Sokolov.

"Can you tell me what you remember of those rooms in the basement?" he asked softly.

"Some of the guards had their beds in those rooms," Semenova recalled with a tinge of agitation. "They were very untidy. Sunflower seed shells everywhere, and there were a great many empty vodka bottles. Most of the guards in the basement rooms were foreigners...not Russians. I remember that very clearly. We cleaned the floors as quickly as we could because some of the men were still occupying those rooms...some sleeping fully dressed on their cots...some nursing their heads from the night before. They weren't in good humor...or certainly didn't seem to be. I remember telling my dear friend, Mariya, that it served them right. They were there to protect our *batushka-tsar* after all. What were they thinking...drinking themselves into such a state?"

"There was one particular room in the basement," Sokolov added. "One of two rooms located furthest into the hillside of the building. Do you happen to remember that room at all?"

Semenova thought again for a moment, her shifting gaze searching the ceiling of the dim room as if the answer she sought was hovering somewhere in the semidarkness above her. Then her misty eyes brightened once more in triumphant recollection.

"Yes," she finally replied. "I do remember that room! One single window and a vaulted ceiling. The stone walls, covered with plaster. Pretty striped wallpaper on top of it all."

"Pretty striped wallpaper," Sokolov repeated with an encouraging nod of his head, "yes, that's the one. Do you remember anything else about that room?"

With apparent difficulty, Semenova struggled with her thoughts for several moments before the rekindled memory seemed to take form. Again, she smiled proudly.

"The room had skirting boards," she beamed. "Yes. And the wooden floor was very plain...easy to wash down."

"Do you happen to remember whose room it was?" Sokolov asked.

Again Semenova paused to think. Even more minutes passed this time before her pale face finally brightened once more. "Kabanov!" she smiled proudly. "Mikhail Kabanov. Leader of the machine-gun squad stationed inside the house. I remember because there was a woman with him in the room that morning, and she wasn't supposed to be there. Of course we didn't know that when we opened the double doors and barged in, so we just went about our jobs. That was when, startled at our intrusion, the girl sat up in his bed...half naked...and pulled the sheets around her body. So embarrassed, poor thing. And of course Kabanov only laughed at her! But then, he told us we'd have to leave the room for a bit and finish washing the floor once the girl had gone. Of course, we did as we were told."

Semenova, suddenly remembering Father Storozhev's presence in the room, turned an embarrassed glance his way as if apologizing for the more lurid details of her story. When the priest merely smiled reassuringly, the happy expression returned to her pale face and she turned her gaze back to Sokolov.

"I will never forget that day," Semenova sighed. "The day I saw, in person, the Tsar and his family!"

Sokolov gazed down at the old woman's face, now filled with a beautiful expression of soft delight, and decided to reflect her joy with a gentle smile of his own.

"It was," Semenova went on, "the happiest moment of my life!"

"I would love very much to hear your recollections," Sokolov replied softly, hoping to gently prod her memory once more.

"Where to begin?" Semenova queried. "I was so full of girlish dreams in those days. I had so often pictured the Tsar and Tsaritsa in my mind...in all their royal finery. Vestments of shimmering gold. Crowns decked with precious stones. Before that day, in my eyes, the Tsar had been a god! A giant among men! And the Tsaritsa! A figure of living divinity, with a voice like a flute from paradise. Until that morning...when I finally saw them in the Ipatiev House. Eleven people trying to do their best in only eight rooms. I remember being greatly shocked to see Alexei, the young Tsarevich, lying on a simple cot. He was pale to such a degree that he seemed ghostly...his skin almost transparent. Only his eyes were alive and bright, looking at me from his bed with noticeable interest. He had on a white nightshirt and was covered to the waist with a blanket. Near the bed was a chair in which Alexandra Feodrovna sat. She appeared tired, possibly ill. I'm not sure. You could tell that she still possessed great height and bearing, which I would describe as stately, though it seemed to me she was somewhat annoyed by our presence. She never once acknowledged us...as if we weren't even there. And then...I saw him. The Tsar! He entered the room so very quietly. As he did, he glanced at me, smiled and nodded. It was only a moment, but he smiled at me. At me!"

Semenova grew silent for a moment as tears welled up in her eyes. It was as if her memory of that day was suddenly transporting her back in time...back to that one moment when her presence was acknowledged by the Tsar of all the Russias. Sokolov let her savor the moment as long as possible before he finally broke the silence.

"What specifically do you remember about the Tsar?"

"For a moment, I was frozen in disbelief," the old woman whispered. "Who wouldn't have been? But then, after a few moments more...as it all settled in my poor brain, I began to see him not as a god but as a man. And such a drab little man, so much smaller than his wife; and seemed much simpler than she. His graying hair was thin and he had a bald patch on the back of his head. His legs seemed too short for his body. His beard was trimmed. He wore a khaki field shirt, khaki pants, and high boots. On his breast, he wore an officer's Cross of St. George, but there were no epaulets."

The smile faded from Semenova's ashen face as she shook her head in lingering disappointment. "Not a god after all," she sighed sadly, "just a dull little man...smaller than most...bland and unassuming. All of them...ordinary people...and finally, like the rest of us, merely mortals."

For a few moments, the room remained in somber stillness. The window curtains had been drawn, but small rays of setting sunlight still occasionally managed to pierce the dimness of that quiet room. A gentle reminder of what possibly lay only a few shallow breaths away.

Sokolov and Father Storozhev exchanged brief glances of acknowledgement while Semenova, her bottom lip trembling slightly, simply gazed up at the ceiling of her little room. And then, miraculously, the warm smile slowly returned to the old woman's dry lips and her entire countenance brightened.

"But then," she beamed with childlike excitement, "I met the Tsar's four beautiful daughters! They were wearing dark skirts and simple white jackets, and had their hair cut short at the back. One of them even spoke to me! They were forbidden to do that. We were not allowed to speak to any of them and they were not allowed to speak to us. But that morning...while we scrubbed the floors in those upstairs rooms, Yurovsky left his place just outside the hallway door. Before that, he had been watching us like a hawk...but then he got up and walked down the hall...perhaps to the lavatory...I don't know. That's when one of the Grand Duchesses spoke to me."

"Do you remember which Grand Duchess it was?" Sokolov inquired softly.

"Grand Duchess Anastasia," was Semenova's immediate and unfaltering reply. "She actually got down on her knees next to me and began to scrub the floor with us. A Grand Duchess! Cleaning a floor like any other peasant girl! And she turned her face to me...the sweet face of a cherub...and whispered: 'It's all right. We enjoy this. In Tobolsk, we used to appreciate work of the hardest kind and undertook it with great pleasure.' And I don't know how I mustered the courage, but I spoke to her as well! 'Please God,' I whispered, 'you will not have to suffer under the yoke of these terrible monsters for much longer,' I said. 'Thank you, my dear, for your kind words,' she answered with a sad smile. 'We hold out great hope...' That is when Yurovsky suddenly returned to his place just outside the open hallway door and we didn't dare speak another word. It was strictly forbidden. But I will never forget those beautiful eyes or her sad but lovely smile. That day...which was to be the last day of their lives...will live in my heart forever. The next morning, we returned to the Ipatiev House to be paid for our work, but no one was there except for a few Red guards who were hurriedly packing to go to the front. They told us the house was empty...that everyone had been taken away. Perhaps, deep inside our souls, we knew what their words truly meant. If so, we never admitted it to each other. Still, I suppose my prayer to God was answered. At least the Grand Duchess and her family are no longer suffering...and that thought has made me happy all these months since that terrible day. Their suffering is at an end. The Romanovs, at last, are free."

Semenova's gaze was on Sokolov now...and it was one of profound happiness. After a few moments of extended silence, however, the Investigator became aware of the fact that the woman's eyes were no longer focused on him. Her expression of contentment was transforming itself into one of deeper peace.

In the next moment, as Sokolov watched in solemn reverence, Evdokiya Semenova—along with her life's happiest memories—slipped away...passing into Paradise on the breath of one last contented sigh.

#

As the horse-drawn cart steadily rattled its way back to Ekaterininsky Cathedral, Father Storozhev and Sokolov remained for a while in thoughtful silence. Semenova's story had touched them both, albeit in different ways.

"Have you ever heard of the Russian monk known as Abel?" Father Storozhev finally asked. Sokolov shook his head.

"His given name was Vasily Vasilyev..." the priest explained, "a humble man with an amazing gift of prophecy. For instance, he correctly predicted many events including the death of Empress Catherine the Great who died on the very day and hour predicted by Abel. Ten years before Napoleon's invasion of Russia, he predicted the date of the capture of Moscow. Emperor Pavel the First was assassinated by conspirators on the night of March 11, 1801, the exact date also predicted by Abel."

Not fully understanding why Father Storozhev had decided to share this particular story, Sokolov nodded and simply replied, "Interesting."

"Oh, there's much more to the tale," the priest smiled. "It seems that before Emperor Pavel was murdered, Abel reportedly told him about the future of the Russian Empire...a future that included the reign of Nicholas II. The prophecy was written down, placed in an envelope, and sealed personally by the Emperor himself. The inscription on the envelope read: 'To be opened by my descendant on the 100th anniversary of my death.' That descendant happened to be Nicholas Romanov."

Sokolov, his interest suddenly aroused, turned his gaze and full attention to the priest.

"In a small hall in the Gatchina Palace, near St. Petersburg..." Father Storozhev continued, "there once was a large box that contained that same sealed letter. On March 11, 1901, one hundred years after Pavel's death, Nicholas and Alexandra made a special trip to the palace. They had heard of the mysterious letter and were rather excited to know of its contents. After a memorial service for Emperor Pavel, the royal couple retired to a private chamber and opened the letter. They emerged from that room very thoughtful and somber, and spoke to no one about what they had learned. It was after that, however, that the emperor began to refer to 1918 as a year that could be fatal to him and the dynasty."

"What happened to Abel?" Sokolov asked.

"He died in 1841 and is buried behind the altar of the monastery church of St. Nicholas. None of his books of prophecy have been preserved, unfortunately, and his written prediction which was stored in that box and read by Nicholas and Alexandra, has long since disappeared."

A few more moments of thoughtful silence passed before Father Storozhev suddenly turned to the young Investigator.

"I wonder," the priest mused once more, "what my stories might be worth."

"I beg your pardon?" Sokolov replied.

"The stories of the Romanovs," Father Storozhev explained as he gazed into the distance. "What I've seen and heard. What I know of their last days. I wonder what they might be worth."

"To whom?" Sokolov asked.

"To anyone," the priest replied with a shrug. "A publisher, perhaps…or some news agency in England or America."

Father Storozhev turned once more to the young Investigator. "After all, there's obviously quite an interest in what has been unfolding here," he announced. "Oh yes, quite an interest. A tantalizing mystery to say the least. And I've been a party to some of it…one of the few people who actually saw the royal family while they were here. A witness to a rather extraordinary event in the history of Mother Russia, wouldn't you say? And so, I was wondering what my observations might be worth, you see, to the outside world."

Before Sokolov could reply, Father Storozhev continued. "I do have some talent as a writer. Perhaps a book of my recollections. Hypothetically assigning some worth to the information I possess, of course, what do you think?"

This time, the priest paused in actual expectation of an answer. Sokolov considered for a moment more.

"The question of value verses worth," he finally mused aloud, "is an interesting one, and has certainly been the subject of more than a few discussions. I suppose you would set a price on what you know based upon what you consider it to be worth. Price and worth are similar, of course, but then, you're not talking about either. Not really."

Father Storozhev's smile began to fade from his face, replaced by a look of polite but growing incomprehension.

"In any case," Sokolov continued with a disarming smile, "you're hardly discussing intrinsic worth at all. What you're really talking about is profit."

Father Storozhev's bottom jaw sagged under the sudden weight of belated comprehension.

"And if honesty had anything to do with what you were just saying," Sokolov continued, "your real question to me would be 'how much do I think you could profit from the murder of the Romanovs?' Well, quite a bit, actually. I suppose there are as many people who are willing to pay for such stories as there are people, like you, who are willing to squeeze some bit of profit from them. I'm sorry I don't have a more exonerating answer for you, Father; and I'd be less than honest if I told you I wasn't enjoying the obvious discomfort you're experiencing this very moment because of asking me such an idiotic question in the first place."

Sokolov let the full weight of his rebuke linger a moment longer in Father Storozhev's ears.

"Besides," the Investigator smiled once more in mock reassurance, "you're obviously a very enterprising man. Given a bit more time, I'm sure you'll find some way to assign an actual cash value to the life of Nicholas Romanov."

As usual, Sokolov's timing was exemplary. The horse-drawn cart, just arriving at its destination that very moment, was rattling to a stop in front of the Ekaterininsky Cathedral. Sokolov wasted no time in vacating his seat next to the stunned priest and was already making his way down the sidewalk when Father Storozhev finally regained the power of partial speech.

"I meant no disrespect," the hapless priest called out to the departing Investigator.

"No one ever does," Sokolov snapped back, tossing the words over his shoulder without so much as a backward glance.

It then suddenly occurred to the intrepid Investigator that no self-respecting priest would ever allow someone to part company without halfheartedly dispensing some well-worn platitude as a form of benediction. Father Storozhev was not about to disappoint. With quivering voice rising so as to achieve just the right dramatic effect, he called out once more to the departing Investigator.

"Take comfort, my son! God sees how much your heart is troubled!"

Sokolov stopped in his tracks and wheeled around to face the blundering priest.

"Really?" the Investigator replied coldly. "I suppose you have that on excellent authority?"

Father Storozhev, pulled himself to his feet in that rickety, horse-drawn cart, spread his arms in a self-righteous gesture of universal inclusion, and with what could best be described as artificial conviction, he intoned, "God lives here in this holy place!"

"In that case," Sokolov shot back, "I can only assume He's living incognito."

The Investigator, adjusting the thick collar of his overcoat against the freezing wind, gave the looming church one last bitter glance, then turned his smoldering gaze once more to the self-inflated priest.

"Do me a favor, Father," he concluded. "Throw open the windows and doors of your church and tell God that it's time to get back out here into the world He created. Otherwise mankind may eventually conclude that He could care less about what's going on outside those doors...or worse, that He never really lived inside a church in the first place."

Chapter Nine

"It is better to see once than to hear a hundred times."
Russian Proverb

Late that afternoon, Nicholas Sokolov decided to take a walk in the garden of the Ipatiev House. He wanted to see for himself the place, mentioned by Anatoly Yakimov, where the Romanovs had once been allowed to briefly stroll in the summer sunshine during their daily respite from the sweltering confines of the house.

The waning day was still relentlessly cold and overcast—so very unlike the summer months the Romanov's must have known during their captivity. Sokolov, shielded against the bitter weather by his heavy military overcoat and fur hat, silently crossed the courtyard and approached the old coach house. He was drawn there because of a huge padlock he had noticed on the double doors that fronted the building. He assumed there was a reason for such security and strolled around to the side of the building in order to peer inside through one of the small, dirty windows.

The interior of the silent coach house was shrouded in musty darkness. Sokolov used his gloved hand to wipe away some of the snow and frosty grime from one of the window panes in order to get a clearer view.

Curious. The central room of the building appeared to be filled with steamer trunks stacked one atop the other…huge trunks only partially visible because of several large canvas tarpaulins that halfway covered them as protection against the elements. A quick survey indicated that the trunks numbered over twenty. They practically filled the entire room. Sokolov concluded that they most probably belonged to the Ipatiev family. Since the Ipatievs had been given only hours to vacate the property before it was taken over, first by the Bolsheviks and then by Kolchak's White Army, the family's belongings had obviously been hurriedly packed, moved, and stored in the carriage house.

His idle curiosity satisfied, Sokolov returned to pace the icy courtyard for several more minutes before continuing around the house in order to locate the garden. It wasn't difficult to find. He entered the area by passing underneath the icy remains of an old wooden trellis entwined with the remains of bare, frozen vines. Linden, birch, and fir trees ringed the small patch of frozen ground. Not far from the trellis, he encountered what appeared to be an object half buried in a mound of muddy snow. Several sweeps of his gloved hand revealed a stone bench, weathered by the elements. Here, Sokolov imagined, the Empress probably sat, passing the time by reading or doing needle work. From this vantage point, her eyes could have easily roamed the entire garden, taking in the sight of her beloved son and daughters enjoying themselves in the afternoon sun. From here she also might have observed her husband as he busied himself with a bit of gardening. The sweet scent of flowers must have been thick in the warm humid air during those last days. The sprawling vines that most certainly crowned the trellis with blossoms and lush green leaves must have occasionally even afforded some bit of welcomed shade.

Clearing more snow and ice from the stone bench, Sokolov sat down and gazed about. He wanted—for his own particular reasons—to gain a better understanding of what the Romanovs must have experienced in this place, this small yet private oasis. Sokolov realized, however, that he was considering the garden in much the same way as one might view a corpse; he was only seeing the cold and lifeless shell of something that had once contained vibrant life and hope. Also like a corpse, the garden and all memories it once contained were now decomposing...melting back into the earth from whence everything had come. Odd, Sokolov thought to himself, that inanimate objects such as these— a battered trellis and garden bench—should be the things to survive long after the living, breathing bodies of those who created them had so sadly vanished without a trace. Peasant, king, wise man, fool...in time, all will go and be forgotten.

The cold wind rose and fell in mournful gusts as the early evening settled in and the heavy gray shadows lengthened. An hour rolled by and then another as Sokolov held silent vigil in that frozen place, seemingly oblivious to the passing time or the evening's stubborn chill. He knew that winters always seemed to foster thoughts of mortality. It was an inclination he had come to understand only too well. These visceral reactions were finally transformed into more heartening ones as the seasons rolled one into another. But thoughts—even happier ones—had a habit of colliding with memories; and memories never came without some customary regret.

A world at war was almost all Sokolov had ever known—and yet there were those few distant recollections of childhood, family, friends, and a place called home—that were always floating in the far recesses of his mind like distant echoes in some abandoned house—a once familiar place that used to contain so much love and happiness. Silent and empty now. Devoid of familiarity, of warmth, of everything. Like viewing what sometimes seemed to be the shell of his own life. And yet, as bittersweet as these reflections were, they were feelings Nicholas Sokolov had grown accustomed to over time.

The truth was that he rarely opened this hidden part of his heart. There were too many old wounds that had yet to heal—or so he preferred to believe. Real or imagined, the pain of remembrance became Sokolov's primary reason for not having to deal with recollections of his past, preferring instead to keep them all at a safe distance...unexplored...buried well below the surface...never in clear focus...as if refusing to let his eyes become accustomed to that particular Darkness. Remembering was anathema to him—and not simply because childhood days were gone forever. He certainly accepted the fact that youth was temporary. He knew too that the past would always continue to shape the present. It was simply that the ever-expanding distance between childish dreams and the realities of sober adulthood made it somehow easier to adjust to the inevitable—to finally accept the imposed order of things. On those very rare occasions when he did allow himself the brief luxury of remembrance, he was always reassured by the knowledge that the real world would always find a way back into his reveries. Acknowledging that fact had actually served him well in his professional life—and occasionally allowed him insights that others often failed to notice.

It was the present, however, that now gave him the most nagging regret. The reason was simple enough. Nicholas Sokolov never felt, labor though he might, that he had made a significant difference. That was all—and yet, it was everything.

In days such as these, it was an accepted fact that men like Kolchak and Lenin held sway. The others—men such as himself—always seemed to be swallowed by the overpowering abyss. The only chance for redemption lay in the attempt—no matter how vainglorious—to make the present a better place for those who inhabited it, and to instill a sense of hope in all who would follow.

Perhaps this was why Sokolov felt drawn to this cold, sad and desolate little garden next to the Ipatiev House. It was where he felt he truly belonged. Here, at least, he could be surrounded by other forgotten things. For reasons he was only beginning to fathom, Nicholas Sokolov shared a strange and yet reassuring kinship with ineffectual things.

His reverie was suddenly shattered by a sound that hurled him back into the present with amazing force.

"It is the faith within the fear that holds us to the life we curse."

Lines from a favorite poem entitled *Children of the Light.* Also the pet name Sokolov had chosen to bestow upon his group of closest friends during their time together as university classmates. How many nights under how many stars had they stood arm in arm, filled with a brave and communal sense of youthful purpose, reciting those same stirring words together— pledging the best within themselves to all future endeavors.

"So let us in ourselves revere the Self which is the Universe."

Sokolov could actually hear the words. Not inside his head. Instinctively, for the first time in years, he began to repeat them aloud as well:

"Let us, the Children of the Night, put off the cloak that hides the scar."

Another soft voice was now joining Sokolov's in perfect unison—rolling back to his ears like a gentle wave lapping at some familiar shore. It was a gentle voice he knew only too well. It belonged to the only person capable of still infusing his heart with such courageous sentiment:

"Let us be Children of the Light, and tell the ages what we are!"

Leaping to his feet, Sokolov spun around in joyous anticipation coupled with absolute disbelief. Not five feet away stood his best friend, Dmitri Volkov! They had known each other since childhood, attended the same university, and had even joined the White Army together. Separated by the war, it had been many months since they had last seen each other.

"Dmitri," Sokolov whispered softly, still not completely able to fully acknowledge the happy sight before him. "My God, I don't believe it."

His handsome friend, appearing even more dashing in his military uniform, riding boots, great coat and officer's cap, grinned broadly and flung open his arms with boyish abandon.

"Neither did I when I found out you were here."

Sokolov took a few disbelieving steps toward Dmitri as the reality began to settle in. With a burst of laughter that quickly transformed itself into joyous weeping, the two men fell into each other's arms. Burying their faces each into the shoulder of the other, they held that strong embrace until the physical contact was sufficient proof that the impossible had indeed occurred. This unforeseen reunion was certainly all but unimaginable, especially considering the chances of survival and the odds of locating each other among the millions who were embroiled in the endless fighting and dying—but they had done it. They had grown from boys to men in a world at war. They had survived. The exultant joy they shared in the dying light of that frozen dusk is a euphoria known only to those who have likewise beaten such odds—those who have looked Death in the face and seen it blink—those who have ridden together into the Valley of the Shadow and come through unscathed. It is a divine intoxication known to a fortunate few comrades who, despite the display of shining medals, marble monuments and marching bands, have come to understand that they were blessed by luck as much as courage. Theirs is a sacred and incommunicable bond that neither Time nor Death will ever be able to weaken or destroy.

His gloved hands cupping Dmitri's face, Sokolov attempted to give words to his utter amazement, but could muster none. He could only gaze into the eyes of the one friend he loved above all others, trying to say it all with a tearful smile.

Dmitri laughed and hugged his friend again. "And where else would I find you but in the middle of Siberia!"

"Where else?" Sokolov repeated, still struggling to overcome his tearful amazement. "The edge of the world. We might've known!"

Throwing an arm around Dmitri's shoulder, Sokolov led him back towards the Ipatiev House. Regarding the impressive structure that now loomed before them in semidarkness, Dmitri turned to his friend. "What're you doing in a place like this...besides burning the midnight oil?"

"I'm on holiday," Sokolov replied cheerily. "Can't you tell?"

Entering the cozy warmth of Sokolov's room at last, Dmitri quickly shed his overcoat even as he continued to goad his friend. "You wouldn't know what a holiday was," Dmitri chuckled knowingly as Sokolov poured two glasses of vodka.

Noticing the small framed photograph of Anastasia perched on the table, Dmitri strolled over and picked it up in order to observe the face more closely. "Then again," he smiled while carefully studying the young woman's face, "I could be wrong. Who is she?"

"No one," Sokolov replied with a shrug of his shoulders.

"A very lovely no one," Dmitri continued. "Incredible eyes. 'If I could write the beauty of your eyes, and in fresh numbers number all your graces, the age to come would say, this poet lies...'" Dmitri's gaze shifted from the faded photograph to his friend. "Sure you won't tell me?"

"Nothing to tell," Sokolov responded, casually reclaiming the photograph and replacing it with a glass of vodka. "Just a photograph," he countered as he carefully returned the keepsake to its place on the tabletop. "Part of the case I'm working on."

Sensing he'd hit a familiar wall, Dmitri strode to the wood stove to warm himself. The two men gladly raised their glasses in silent celebration of the moment and drank together for the first time in almost two years.

"And you?" Sokolov asked with sudden eagerness. "What on earth are you doing in Siberia?"

Allowing his muscular body to sink into a nearby chair, Dmitri draped a leg over one of its arms. Sokolov smiled at the sight, remembering that Volkov seldom touched the floor with both feet whenever he occupied a comfortable chair.

"Escorting a trainload of Bolshevik prisoners to some godforsaken corner of another frozen hell," Volkov sighed in soft reply. "They put me in charge at the last minute. Doesn't matter to those poor souls on the train. Most of them will be dead from the cold before we get to wherever we're going. And they'll be the lucky ones." Lifting the glass to his lips, Volkov downed the rest of his vodka before concluding. "Sounds callous as hell, but it's the truth."

Pouring his friend another drink, Sokolov could only nod in silent comprehension. "Still, better them than us," Volkov added quietly. "And never, in a million years, did I ever think I'd hear myself say something like that—much less believe it." With a heavy sigh, Volkov closed his eyes and titled his head back until it rested against the chair. "But then I think of those we've lost, and I don't really care anymore."

Sokolov was pouring himself another drink when Volkov suddenly leaned forward in the chair, his eyes open and bearing down on his friend. "You remember Sergé Tegleva?"

"Sergé?" Sokolov replied, smiling in immediate acknowledgement. "Of course I do! We were classmates at the University."

Dmitri's handsome face seemed suddenly set in stone, his dark brown eyes gazing not at Sokolov but at something beyond. "Murdered by the Bolsheviks in Tobolsk just over a year ago," he announced solemnly.

Sokolov was stunned. Though he had grown used to inhabiting a world ravaged by war in which days were measured by piles of fresh corpses, this sudden news of Sergé's death was singularly tragic. "Tobolsk?" the Investigator managed to stammer, "What was Sergé doing in Tobolsk?"

"Gathering information for us," Volkov replied, his gaze still riveted on something seemingly beyond the confines of the room. "Last October. All very secret, I understand. Someone betrayed him…and two other men who were with him. They were ambushed, dragged out into the town square and shot. All three. Lenin must pay very well."

Sokolov directed his sad gaze to the flickering light of the wood stove and sighed. "We're a long way from St. Petersburg, Dmitri."

Volkov nodded and once more settled back into the chair. "A very long way, old friend."

Both men allowed a bit of thoughtful silence to engulf the room until something suddenly clicked in Sokolov's brain.

"October, a year ago?" he asked, turning from the wood stove with a quizzical expression on his face. "In Tobolsk, you said?"

Dmitri opened his eyes slightly and turned his face to Sokolov. "Why? Does that mean anything?"

Recalling his most recent interrogation sessions and mentally fast-forwarding through seemingly disjointed bits of collected information, Sokolov made the mental connection in only a matter of seconds. "Someone I questioned today was visiting Tobolsk that same month."

"Coincidence?" Dmitri yawned.

"Most probably," Sokolov shrugged before turning once more to his friend. "Listen; do you have a place to stay?"

Eyes closed and hands folded comfortably across his stomach, Dmitri grinned. "Not as nice as this, but…"

"Well, you know you're more than welcome here," Sokolov offered.

"Thanks," Volkov replied, "but they prefer us being closer to the trains. Besides, there's hardly room for anything else in here." Dmitri chuckled as he indicated the stacks of dossiers littering the room. "Up to your ears in paperwork as usual."

Sokolov returned his friend's smile. "Some things never change."

"Who're you trying to find this time?" Dimitri casually inquired.

The Investigator glanced at the nearest stack of dossiers so neatly arranged on his desk, then back to his friend. "The Tsar and his family."

Volkov sat upright in the chair and gazed at Sokolov as if waiting for the punch line of a joke. Realizing it wasn't forthcoming, his jaw sagged slightly. "My God."

"No," Sokolov replied. "God would be a great deal easier to locate—I assure you."

Dmitri leaned forward in the chair, resting his arms on his knees as he peered quizzically at Sokolov.

"That must be why they assigned Strovka to my train," he mused quietly—speaking more to himself than to Sokolov.

"What do you mean?"

Volkov pondered the revelation again briefly, then continued: "One the prisoners on my train. Surely, they've told you about him."

"I don't know who you're talking about."

"Really?" Once more it seemed as if Volkov was continuing to think aloud. "Odd," he finally observed while slowly pouring himself another drink. "Someone in authority obviously knows he's on that train. They've certainly made arrangements for his special consideration."

Still musing out loud, Volkov pulled himself to his feet, and ambled over to Sokolov in order to pour his friend another drink as well. "And they had to have known we'd be coming through Ekaterinburg," Dmitri continued. "In fact, it seems to me they made certain of it. Doesn't make sense that no one's told you."

Sokolov was warming his hands over the wood stove. "I still don't follow," he replied. "What doesn't make sense?"

Volkov considered for several seconds more until it seemed he had finally reached some sort of private resolution. "Nicky," he said evenly while turning to face his friend, "there's a man on my train. A prisoner. They say he was one of the men who did it."

It had yet to register with Sokolov. "Did what?"

Dmitri squared his shoulders. "They say he's one of the men who shot the Tsar."

As the magnitude of Volkov's shocking disclosure began to instantly pound itself into Sokolov's dazed consciousness, he could only return his friend's gaze with nothing more than a blank expression.

"He's the only prisoner I've been denied permission to interrogate," Dmitri added, now pacing the room in growing animation. "Curious, wouldn't you say? The other prisoners seem very afraid of him. Of course, if he was a member of the Cheka, that would explain it. His name is Strovka. Karl Strovka."

Sokolov actually had to repeat the words aloud: "One of the men who shot the Tsar?"

"We've been ordered to place him in hospital," Dmitri concluded. "The official explanation is Typhus."

"One of the men who shot the Tsar," Sokolov repeated yet again. "But that's impossible."

The Investigator was already at his desk, hurriedly leafing through several folders while softly repeating the name, "Strovka." Suddenly, he froze. There it was…the same list of names in which he had first discovered Anatoly Yakimov's…a single sheet of paper revealing the identities and brief background information of all those known to have been members of the Bolshevik detachment stationed at the Ipatiev House during the Romanov's imprisonment. A list which obviously included the names of the actual executioners. If Dmitri's information was correct, this was a monumental discovery.

Sokolov hurriedly scanned the brief list of the suspected executioners: *Yurovsky, Nikulin, Medvedev, Kudrin, Kabanov, Netrebin, Tselms, Yermakov, Strekotin, Vaganov.* The name *'Karl Strovka'* was the last one listed in the short column. Oddly enough, a short paragraph following his name had been inked out. Next to the crudely redacted paragraph, one word had been hurriedly scribbled in: *'Deceased'*.

Without a word, Sokolov handed the piece of paper to his friend. It took only a moment for Dmitri to absorb the document's significance. Passing the paper back to Sokolov he slowly lifted his puzzled gaze to meet that of his friend.

This time it was Sokolov who spoke with studious intention. "You've got to get me in to see him, Dmitri. I don't care how you do it. It's absolutely vital that I speak with that man."

Volkov thought for a moment, then sighed deeply. "That's going to be difficult," he admitted. "I'll have to pull some strings."

"Whatever you have to do," his friend immediately declared. "Whatever it takes. It's that important." Sokolov kept his gaze on Volkov, expectantly awaiting a reply.

"All right," Dmitri concluded. "Come to the hospital first thing in the morning. I'll meet you there. Tell no one who you are or what your business is. Leave that to me." Retrieving his military overcoat and draping it around his broad shoulders, Volkov adjusted his military cap and turned to leave the room.

"Dmitri?" Sokolov's voice pulled Volkov back to once more face his friend. "Thank you. You've no idea what this could mean."

An expression of slight amusement brightened Volkov's face. "And I have the distinct feeling, Nicky, that I'm better off that way."

As the door closed behind his beloved friend, Nicholas Sokolov turned back to face the warm glow of the wood stove's dying fire. Slow-dancing shadows were performing flickering pirouettes along the walls of the room as the Investigator, deep in silent contemplation, sank back into his chair. Unconsciously, his hand had already slipped into the breast pocket of his military tunic to withdraw the crumpled cigarette he always kept there. There was, of course, a fresh pack which he also usually kept close by as well, but they were reserved for acquaintances and occasionally even bartered to potential confidants like Anatoly Yakimov. In both cases, the results usually proved beneficial. Idly rolling the yellow-papered remnant in his fingers, Sokolov fixed his gaze on something beyond the looming dullness of the silent room.

And there he remained, motionless and transfixed, for most of the night. As a new day finally dawned, so too did the realization that sleep had become yet another casualty of Russia's civil war.

Chapter Ten

From Sokolov's Finished Report

The Bolsheviks are human beings like other human beings, capable of the same weaknesses and the same mistakes. We must give them credit where it is due. They disposed of the bodies as carefully as possible. They lied cleverly. But the Bolsheviks could not help making some mistakes. And the point is that they overestimated the effectiveness of the precautions.

Late that night, it began to rain—an icy, ponderous downpour that lasted well into the next day. The gray dawn breaking over Ekaterinburg was still laced with dark cloud formations that moved with ominous slowness against an otherwise barren sky, making the heaviness of the morning seem all the more gloomy. Nude birch tree branches, pelted by the cold rain, swayed mournfully in the wind while the sound of faraway thunder, rolling like distant cannon fire across the frozen landscape, added a sort of funereal cadence that only underscored the bleakness of the day.

One person in Ekaterinburg, however, remained absolutely impervious to the soggy gloom. With the first gray light of dawn, Nicholas Sokolov roused himself from a fitful sleep. After shaving and dressing, he wolfed down a breakfast brought to his room by Natalya Kolya. While hurriedly devouring the plate of food and two large cups of hot tea, he simultaneously busied himself by reviewing several dossiers containing the few scattered bits of gathered information relating to the prisoner known as Strovka.

Sokolov knew that this was an unprecedented opportunity—not a time to contemplate the strange happenstance that seemingly brought Dmitri to Ekaterinburg; nor was it a suitable occasion to consider what part Kolchak might've played in routing Dmitri's train. Such nagging questions, though clearly worthy of more time and attention, seemed merely secondhand considerations when compared to the momentous development that now presented itself.

Sokolov, dressed as always for the unforgiving weather, paused one last moment in the foyer of the Ipatiev House to adjust his side holster containing the loaded Mauser pistol. He expressly wanted the firearm to be in plain sight today—a silent show of force should anyone need such a reminder.

Fastening his long overcoat, the Investigator snatched up his *Ushanka* fur hat, opened the front door and stepped out into the courtyard. A military automobile requisitioned earlier that morning was parked only a few feet away with the motor running. Dashing through the pouring rain, Sokolov opened the car door and quickly slid into the back seat. A nod to the driver and the automobile shifted into gear, made a slow half circle, and chugged out of the rain-drenched courtyard.

> *"After the fall of Ekaterinburg, I asked Sverdlov in passing,*
> *'Where is the Tsar?'*
> *'It's all over,' he answered. 'He's been shot.'*
> *'And where is his family?'*
> *'The family with him.'*
> *'All of them?' I asked, apparently with a touch of surprise.*
> *'All of them,' replied Yakov Sverdlov. 'What about it?'*
> *He was waiting to see my reaction. I made no reply.*
> *'And who made the decision?' I asked.*
> *'We decided it here. Ilyich [Lenin] believed that we shouldn't leave the Whites a live banner to rally around, especially under the present difficult circumstances.'"*

Leon Trotsky

The Ekaterinburg prison camp, located on the outskirts of the town, was a stark and forbidding place. The fence surrounding the camp was makeshift at best, but its shabbiness made little difference. The majority of prisoners confined to the area were simply too weak to pose any substantial threat. Escape, which in Siberia meant having to suffer the elements without proper shelter, clothing or food, was suicidal. When the infrequent trains did lumber into Ekaterinburg, it was usually to disgorge a new group of prisoners and then collect the pitifully emaciated few who had been moldering in disease ridden confinement for weeks, perhaps months. Prisoners would be endlessly shuffled from one place to the next until, finally, there was simply no one left to shuffle; at which point the slow process of elimination would merely begin again with a fresh batch of captives brought from still another senseless defeat.

The cold rain had tapered off slightly by the time Sokolov's automobile pulled up next to the gates of the camp. He disembarked and quickly sprinted to the guardhouse located next to the main entrance. Inside he found Volkov waiting for him. Their greeting was a silent one, but not without some bit of theatrical pomp intended to impress the camp's commander and several other soldiers who also happened to be occupying the guardhouse. Dmitri actually came to attention and bowed slightly when Sokolov entered. The Investigator completed the charade by returning Volkov's salute with nothing more than a condescending nod of his head. He had no idea what Dmitri had told the camp's commander or guards prior to his arrival, but whatever the concocted story, it was certainly producing the desired effect. When the Investigator strode into the room, the commander as well as the two armed soldiers leapt to their feet and immediately came to sharp military attention. Sokolov hesitated for a moment, fully expecting that someone in the room would demand to see his identification papers. It was clearly evident, however, that no such command was going to be made. The rear door of the guard house opened directly into the main yard of the camp. Seizing the initiative, Dmitri strode to the door of the guardhouse and pushed it open. A slight tilt of his head indicated that Sokolov should make immediate use of the exit.

Still maintaining their haughty silence for the benefit of any possible observers, the two men stepped outside and briskly strode toward a low wooden building, a former warehouse that now served as the prison camp's infirmary.

Because of the heavy rain, the snow blanketing the camp had mingled with the thick mud to create an icy brown slush that coated everything within view. Long wooden planks had been placed end to end along the ground from one building to the next in order to create passable walkways, but the mixture of ice and mud made them so slippery that anyone trying to navigate them had to have a very good sense of balance.

When they reached the entrance to the infirmary, Volkov turned to his friend.

"Once inside, you'll find yourself in a narrow corridor," Dmitri advised the Investigator in a low voice. "Strovka's cell is the last one on your right. The door is always unlocked."

Always unlocked? Sokolov nodded to his friend then, clearing his throat, turned the latch, pushed open the rough wooden outer door, and entered the building.

The putrid stench of excrement and gangrenous flesh immediately assaulted his senses. The empty corridor was thick with it and the dampness of the frigid air only intensified the obnoxiously acrid smell. Sokolov quickly withdrew a handkerchief from his coat pocket and placed it over his nose in an attempt to keep from gagging.

As he cautiously proceeded down the dimly lit corridor, he could hear raspy coughs and low, agonizing moans coming from the double row of closed rooms that served as cells for the sick and wounded prisoners. The door to one of the rooms was propped open and, as Sokolov passed, he glanced inside.

It appeared to be a makeshift surgical room complete with a long wooden counter that the Investigator assumed served as an operating table. Nearby, another small tabletop was littered with used surgical tools—knives, clamps, probes, and saws. Four buckets filled with dirty water sat next to one of the room's bare walls while an open wooden box in the far corner appeared to contain a tangled pile of contaminated bed linen. Dark spatter stains of dried blood were still visible on the planked floor which appeared to have been 'cleansed' by nothing more than an infrequent dousing of mucky water slung from one of the four rusty buckets. Thick leather straps dangling from both sides of the makeshift operating table were silent testament to the fact that the use of anesthesia was an obvious luxury here. The unsanitary condition of the room clearly indicated that being slated for surgery of any kind in this place was tantamount to a death sentence.

The other rooms lining the damp and shadowy corridor actually served as makeshift holding cells and were sealed from public view by heavy wooden doors that were locked shut from the outside. Sokolov was thankful for it. The dull chorus of pitiful moans and wheezing coughs that filled the empty corridor conjured up too many disturbing images. While the reality may not have been as horrid as what he imagined, Sokolov didn't care to test the presumption. The Investigator had come for one reason only.

Refortifying himself with that thought, he continued down the long gloomy corridor of the infirmary. There was, amid all the shuttered sounds of suffering, one compelling force which held him steady with quiet resolve. He was about to interrogate a man who, among a very select few, had helped to alter the course of history.

As he approached the last door on the right of the narrow corridor, Sokolov's steps slowed down and he swallowed hard. Lifting the handkerchief from his nose, he quickly wiped away the small beads of sweat that were suddenly forming on his forehead. His heart was pounding in his chest and he paused to take a measured breath before proceeding any further. It was vital that his demeanor, at least outwardly, appeared calm and controlled when he met the prisoner. Strovka was, after all, a professional killer with a honed ability to sense fear. The Investigator stuffed the handkerchief back into a pocket of his overcoat and pulled himself into the most erect posture he could manage. He squared his shoulders, took one more quick breath and reached for the door latch.

Karl Strovka, a large burly man with extremely short cropped dark hair, was sprawled on a small cot near the far wall of the musty room. A ragged blanket partially covered a hulking body which was clearly too large for the cell's wooden cot. When the door to the room swung open, and he turned his head to face Sokolov, the Investigator found himself gazing at a face that appeared almost mongoloid. A thick and protruding forehead jutted out above two puffy slits for eyes. Below a flat, broken nose, heavy jowls framed thick cracked lips that sagged at each corner, forming an almost permanent sneer. A huge right hand, dangling off the edge of the cot, clutched a half empty bottle of vodka. Below that, a tin plate resting on the dirty floor contained a small heap of chicken bones—remnants of the prisoner's generous morning meal.

Sokolov wondered what, if anything, the other prisoners had been given to eat or drink. The obviously well-fed man now glaring at him from beneath a warm blanket was clearly enjoying what Dmitri had referred to as 'special consideration'. Food, drink, warmth and an unlocked cell—the prisoner's comportment suggested he felt deserving of it all.

Nicholas Sokolov remained motionless in the open doorway as his good eye completed its adjustment to the dim light of the murky room. The hulking prisoner pulled himself into a sitting position on the cot and glared at the strange man gazing at him from the doorway.

"Who th' hell are you?" Strovka finally snarled in a low, graveling voice.

"You're Karl Strovka?" the Investigator asked softly.

"Who wants to know?"

Sokolov took a few steps into the shadowy room and closed the door behind him.

"They tell me you're dying," the Investigator bluntly observed.

"What the hell do they know?" Strovka scoffed in defiance. "I'll outlive 'em all; wait and see."

The prisoner's subsequent convulsive laughter quickly transformed itself into a dry, rasping cough. Hoisting the bottle of vodka to his lips, Strovka tilted back his head and took several deep gulps. His coughing spasm subsiding, the prisoner turned his cold gaze once more to Sokolov.

"Tell me," he began with a sudden air of almost childlike curiosity, "is there snow in Lys'va?" The huge man then cocked his head to one side in anticipation of an answer.

Sokolov had no idea what the question meant nor what prompted it in the first place. Before he could consider further, however, Strovka had recoiled and was once more loudly demanding, "Who th' hell are you?"

"My name is Nicholas Alexeyevich Sokolov. Special Court Investigator."

The prisoner's heavy brow arched noticeably. "I know you from somewhere?" he finally muttered.

"I know *you* from somewhere, Comrade Strovka," the Investigator replied. "The House of Special Purpose."

"That supposed to mean something to me?" Strovka asked with an indifferent shrug of his heavy shoulders.

"It should," the Investigator nodded. "One place in particular. A small room in the cellar."

"Ah," the huge man sneered. "And what did I do there? Rape your daughter or sleep with your wife?"

Sokolov quietly held his ground. "That's where you killed Nicholas Romanov."

The prisoner's grin faded abruptly.

"You were a member of the Bolshevik Cheka," the Investigator continued, "assigned to shoot the Tsar."

Karl Strovka's bottom jaw sagged slightly as his jowly face transformed itself into another quizzical expression. "Who told you that?" he demanded.

"Each of the other men in the room with you that night," Sokolov replied flatly.

The prisoner's eyes narrowed into even tighter slits and his yellow teeth splayed themselves in an evil grin. "You'll have to do better than that," he glowered triumphantly. "The other ten men? The ones who were in the room with me? They're all dead now. Nobody told you anything!"

"You just did." The Investigator's soft reply stopped Strovka cold and his grin transformed itself into an almost comical expression of complete bafflement.

Realizing the stupidity of his stumble, the prisoner's demeanor soured again. "Get out!" he growled with renewed ferocity.

Sokolov, still quietly dominating the center of the room, smiled slightly. "I thought, perhaps, you might tell me about it."

"Why?" the prisoner snapped. "So I can die with a clean conscience? Who told you I was going to die anyway?"

"No one," Sokolov answered. "I just know."

"And how do you know something like that?" the prisoner sneered.

The young Investigator's answer came without forethought or the slightest hesitation.

"Because I am Death, Comrade," he said simply. "Believe that."

The lethal significance of Sokolov's reply hung in the heavy silence of the room for several minutes as the stunned prisoner carefully considered his next move. He had been completely unprepared for the Investigator's chilling declaration and more than slightly taken aback at the unmistakable tone of self-assuredness in Sokolov's voice.

Strovka adjusted his heavy body on the small cot. When he spoke again, his attitude had undergone a definite modification.

"Got a cigarette?" he inquired almost sheepishly.

Sokolov remained stoic. "When you've told me what I've come to hear."

The prisoner considered briefly, then managed a slight smile. "The death of the Tsar for a smoke? Why not?" Leaning back against the dirty wall of his cell, Strovka crossed his heavy arms over his flabby chest and nodded. "The execution had a code name. It was called *trubochist*—'chimneysweep'. And yes; I was there. One of the men who did it. The last one alive as far as I know. There's always someone left alive."

Sokolov relaxed slightly but continued to hold the prisoner's gaze with his own. "What happened to the Romanovs on the night of July 16th?"

"They went to bed at 10:30," Strovka began. "Usual time. At midnight, Yurovsky, our leader, woke them up. Told 'em your

White Army was closing in so they should get dressed and come downstairs. I saw 'em as they came down the stairs from their rooms on the second floor. Nicholas came first, carrying his son, Alexei. They both wore military caps and the boy had his arms around his father's neck. He was sick, you know. Anastasia was next, holding a little dog. I think she called him Jemmy."

Excerpt from Sokolov's Investigative Notes
Ekaterinburg—1919

Anastasia Nikolaevna had a small dog, some kind of Japanese breed, very small, with long hair; its coloring was black and ginger; the black hair on the upper parts of the body, the reddish hair on the lower parts. Its tail was long and long-haired; also its ears were long. It had several distinctive features. Large, round eyes. Its teeth were bared and were always visible. Its tongue was very long and used to hang out of its mouth, I can't remember on which side. Its name was Jemmy; and it was so small that it was often carried. The whole family loved it, especially the Tsar.

"What about Joy and Ortino?" Sokolov asked as if the question was nothing more than a casual addendum to Strovka's initial observation.

Again, a look of complete bafflement transformed the prisoner's face.

"The Romanovs had three dogs in Ekaterinburg," the Investigator continued. "Besides Jemmy, there was an English spaniel named Joy and a French bulldog named Ortino. What do you think happened to them? I mean, why would the royal family bring only one of the dogs with them to the basement room, leaving the other two upstairs in the Ipatiev House?"

"Who th' hell knows?" Strovka finally exclaimed defensively, "Who th' hell ever knows when it comes to royals and how they choose to behave? Not me!"

Sokolov regarded the prisoner in much the same way a teacher regards a pupil who has just been caught lying. After a moment or two of enduring the Investigator's mute but accusatory expression, Strovka lowered his gaze and actually appeared to be sulking.

"Go on," Sokolov finally instructed the prisoner.

"Yurovsky told the family that they were being moved," Strovka continued, "because the White Army was closing in on the city. He asked them to dress and come downstairs. Not one of them spoke as they finally made their way down the stairs."

Strovka paused to stroke his chin in brief contemplation. "I've often wondered if they suspected anything," he began again. "Yurovsky led 'em into a small basement room with a heavy iron grill over the only window. He told them that he needed a photograph of the entire family in order to prove they were still alive. Imagine that! A photograph to prove they were alive! He positioned them as a photographer might do, quietly suggesting where each of them should stand. And all the time, he was lining them up to be shot. When they were all in the desired positions, Yurovsky asked them to wait in the room until the photograph had been taken and the automobiles arrived to take them away. The Tsar then asked for chairs for the Empress and his son. Yurovsky brought in three."

"Three chairs," Sokolov repeated. "And the daughters; where were they standing in the room?"

"Behind their mother," the huge man replied. "Against the far wall."

"Why did you cut their hair?" Sokolov inquired.

Strovka looked confused. "Who knows?" he shrugged indifferently.

Undeterred, Sokolov continued his questioning. "Who else was in the room?"

"Besides the girls? Dr. Botkin, the valet, the cook and the Empress's parlor maid."

"The parlor maid," Sokolov once more interrupted. "Do you remember her name?"

It seemed that when Sokolov's questions didn't follow what Karl Strovka considered to be a natural progression, he became slightly muddled.

"Was the maid's name Demidova?" the Investigator prompted with a tinge of impatience in his voice.

Strovka suddenly sat up straighter, his narrow eyes opening as wide as they could. "Demidova?" he blurted as if with sudden realization. "I'll be damned."

"What is it?" Sokolov demanded eagerly.

"You won't believe this," Strovka replied, "but…" He leaned closer to the Investigator as if to share a confidence. "We were never formally introduced."

Strovka fell back onto his soiled pillow in gales of hoarse laughter. "Our orders were to kill those people," he roared hysterically, "not to become socially acquainted."

Nicholas Sokolov waited for the laughter to subside completely before continuing. His stony silence and lack of response achieved the desired effect rather quickly. Strovka's laughter died away and he lifted himself once more into a sitting position on the cot.

"Is that what you did?" Sokolov continued solemnly. "You killed them all?"

Strovka couldn't resist the grin. "Well, I haven't seen the Imperial family lately; have you?"

The Investigator fully expected another convulsive fit of laughter, and was rather surprised when Strovka merely took a swig of vodka before continuing matter-of-factly.

"When Yurovsky left the room, he came out into the hallway, nodded to us and went back in. We followed, holding the revolvers behind our backs so they couldn't see them. Once in the room, we formed a line directly in front of the Romanovs. Yurovsky stepped forward and said something. Don't remember what it was. Don't think any of us heard. The Tsar did. He stood up and said one word. 'What...?' All he had time for. Yurovsky raised his pistol and fired. He was aiming right at the Tsar's chest when he pulled the trigger. Then all ten of us fired at him. He was the one we had come to kill after all. He remained standing until the last bullet hit him, then, with his dead eyes still wide open in frozen surprise, he just toppled forward and fell face down onto the wooden floor."

"What about the truck parked outside?" Sokolov asked. "The truck revving its engine during the gunfire?"

"I don't know about any truck outside," Strovka replied blandly. "I do remember an airplane circling overhead sometime during the early evening. That, we could hear. No other sound."

Strovka paused to take another swig of vodka. As an afterthought, he held the dirty bottle out to Sokolov.

The Investigator responded with nothing more than a quiet order, "Go on."

"Not much else to tell," Strovka replied, wiping the dirty sleeve of his prison uniform across his thick wet lips. "Once the Tsar fell, we turned our pistols on the others. Yurovsky had ordered the shots to be aimed at the victims' hearts. Each of us had been assigned one specific person in the room to shoot. The Empress had just enough time to make the sign of the cross. I remember that. She died from a bullet in the head. Marie and Anastasia crouched in one corner of the room with arms over their heads. The maid survived the first volley. Screaming and running back and forth along the wall, holding a pillow in front of her like a shield. We'd used all of our bullets, so two of the men had to stab her to death with their bayonets."

The Investigator's next question once more stalled the prisoner in mid-story. "How many times?"

Strovka faltered slightly as he glared at Sokolov in obvious confusion.

"How many times did you stab the maid?" the Investigator elaborated as simply as he could.

"Until she was dead," Strovka thundered in exasperation. "Who the hell knows how many times? Executions aren't like parlor games. You don't stand around keeping score!"

Sokolov's expression was one of ice. "I've never known a huntsman yet who didn't know how many shots it took to bag a trophy."

The prisoner's face was once more transformed by another grin. "Very good," he practically cooed before his smile vanished as quickly as it had appeared. "They stabbed her more than thirty times at least. It wasn't until later that we realized the women had sewn jewels into the bodices of their clothing. They were also wearing steel corset stays and the bullets were hitting them and bouncing off. I remember that Maria ran to the double doors behind her and tried to open them. One of the men shot her in the thigh and she fell. The screaming finally died away. There were a few more gunshots. Blood and urine began to cover the floor. The stench was awful. Then everything grew quiet. We opened the doors to let some of the smoke clear away. That's when we heard the sound of soft moans and whimpers. It was coming from the children! They were not only alive; they hadn't even been seriously wounded by the gunfire. I think that's what pushed everyone over the edge. Then men seemed to lose control. They rushed forward, screaming like crazy men, and began to finish the job with their bayonets and rifle butts. Yurovsky even killed the dog. Crushed its head with the butt of a rifle. Then everything was quiet once more. I remember it was still hard to see the bodies; there was so much smoke. Only one electric light hanging from the ceiling. Smell of gunpowder. God awful! Burned your eyes and lungs. When the smoke cleared a bit more, we couldn't believe our eyes. There sat the boy…Alexei, the Tsarevich…all by himself in one of the chairs."

"He was dying though, wasn't he?"

"No," Strovka answered blandly. "He was unhurt...still sitting there...upright in his chair...motionless...staring back at us with horrified, unblinking eyes. Yurovsky stepped forward and shoved the Tsarevich to the floor where he lay motionless for a moment or two. We stepped in to have a look. Just as we did, the boy moved his hand. With a soft whimper, he reached out and clutched his father's coat. Yurovsky kicked the Tsarevich in the head, lowered his pistol until it was only a few inches from the boy's ear and fired two shots."

Sokolov didn't speak for several minutes as, hands clasped tightly behind his back and with bowed head, he slowly paced the center of the dingy room in silent deliberation.

Finally, he stopped and turned his cold gaze to Karl Strovka. "Is that all?" he inquired as flatly as possible. "I ask, you see, because I'm a bit confused. You said there were eleven men in that basement. Eleven men; eleven executioners. Fourteen heavy military guns—six pistols and eight revolvers. Two Brownings, two American Colts, two Mausers, one Smith & Wesson and seven Nagants to be exact."

Strovka's jaw began to sag in utter astonishment as Sokolov continued to reel off his specific list of memorized details.

"You faced eleven unarmed and defenseless people," the Investigator continued, "in a room measuring twenty-five by twenty-one feet. Have you ever stopped to consider what those last few minutes must've been like for them? Never mind the Tsar and Tsarina. Have you ever wondered what it was like for their daughters? Imagine being one of them...forced to stand silently with your entire family during those final moments in that basement room. Imagine how you would have gasped in fright when those double doors opened and eleven ominous men strode into the room, their hands hidden behind their backs. Imagine watching with sudden horror as the guns appeared. Think of how you would have screamed in terrified disbelief as your mother and father are slaughtered before your eyes. And then, in the next horrifying moment, as the sight and smell of death began to crowd everything else from your senses, imagine seeing the cold eyes of those silent murderers turn slowly to you."

Sokolov paused for a moment and then leaned closer to the sullen prisoner.

"You opened fire on those people at point blank range," he began again in a low voice. "And you didn't stop until the guns were empty. An average of six shots apiece. That comes to at least one hundred and three bullets, one hundred and three possible hits. Yes? And as you said yourself, the Empress fell with only one shot through the head. If every man with a gun fired at the Tsar, that accounts for only a dozen bullets total. That left ninety-one bullets for the remaining victims in that room. A gracious plenty for nine people, wouldn't you say? That's why I'm curious, you see."

Suddenly exploding with terrible rage, Sokolov collared the prisoner and violently yanked his face close to his own. "How is it possible that you still had to bayonet one woman over thirty times and kick a dying boy unconscious before firing twice into the side of his head, you miserable son-of-a-bitch?"

Releasing the stunned prisoner, Sokolov paused a moment to let his anger subside a bit. When he felt more in control of his emotions, he concluded with one last apprehensive observation.

"Even after all of that, it still wasn't over...was it?"

Strovka took a moment to study the man looming over his bed. He'd just detected a chink in the Investigator's armor and fully intended to use that knowledge to his advantage.

"You're dying to know, aren't you?" he finally sneered. "Why can't you just come out and say it? A little professional pride getting in your way?"

Strovka could see that the young Investigator was cringing slightly. Instantly imbued with more confidence, he decided to press. Wrapping the filthy blanket around him like a toga, the prisoner hoisted himself off the cot and pulled himself to his full height in an attempt to loom over his adversary.

"Yes, there was one thing more to do," he seethed with obvious relish. "Seventy-two bullets, thirty bayonet thrusts and there was still one person left alive in that room!"

Strovka threw open his gigantic arms in an almost orgasmic gesture of sadistic ecstasy and bellowed, "The Grand Duchess...Anastasia!"

Nicholas Sokolov reacted like a wounded but deadly animal. The horrific sound that erupted from the pit of his soul was practically inhuman. Something between an unimaginable shriek of pain and a deafening roar of psychotic rage, it filled the small room with fearful intensity and traveled like the sonic wave of some terrible explosion, down the entire length of the infirmary's empty corridor.

Sokolov's ashen face had transformed itself as well. Convulsed by spasms of deforming anguish, it seemed completely drained of blood. His upper lip curled itself into a vicious snarl that bared his teeth like those of some savage animal.

Even as his body wheeled around to face the looming prisoner, Sokolov's hand was already yanking his Mauser from its holster. In another frightening instant, the barrel of the weapon was pointing directly at Karl Strovka's face.

The prisoner's reaction was instantaneous and came from nothing but sheer animal instinct.

"Do it!" Strovka bellowed defiantly as his right hand shot out, grabbing the barrel of Sokolov's Mauser. Instead of trying to wrestle the gun away, however, Strovka pulled the barrel toward his face until it pressed hard against his sweaty forehead.

"Go ahead; pull the trigger," the enraged prisoner kept shrieking over and over. "Kill me! What're you waiting for? Death is a giant against whom even the Tsars must draw weapons. So do it! Do it now! Give your sins to me, Investigator. I am your absolution!"

For several terrible moments, neither man dared to move. Strovka, his arms still spread wide in a dramatic display of audacious defiance, stood facing Nicholas Sokolov, who also remained frozen in place, his gun barrel still pressed firmly against Strovka's forehead.

As one second seemed to turn with agonizing slowness into the next, the room grew deathly still except for the gasping breaths both men were laboring to make. The shared adrenal rush had thankfully peaked, however, and was now beginning to subside along with some bit of the raging hostility.

Strovka was the first to relax his defensive posture. He slowly let his heavy arms lower until they rested at his sides. "You sorry sack of shit," he finally gasped hoarsely. "Can't do it, can you?"

Nicholas Sokolov stubbornly held his threatening pose, the Mauser still pressing firmly against Strovka's forehead; but he knew what Strovka understood perhaps from the beginning: he wasn't going to pull the trigger.

"Do you know why?" the hulking prisoner finally responded to Sokolov's unspoken question. "You can't pull that trigger because you can't kill yourself. You see, Comrade... I am you. You made me. I take your orders, do the things you don't have the stomach for. Caesar, Christ... I killed them all. I did it for people like you. Kill me, and there's no one left to hate or blame but yourself. No one to do your dirty work."

Strovka leaned forward for emphasis. "I know what I am," he concluded with a mocking sneer. "I've made my peace. What about you?"

The huge man pulled his forehead away from the barrel of the Mauser, turned his back on Sokolov and sank down on his small cot. He snatched up the bottle of vodka, took another long swig and only then turned to once more face his interrogator.

"So! What now, Comrade?" Strovka smirked with a bit of reclaimed impudence. "After all, it's better to be slapped with the truth than kissed with a lie."

Nicholas Sokolov allowed himself a deep and measured breath before slowly lowering his pistol. His face was ashen and covered with sweat. There was, however, no hint of subjugation in his posture. He had managed to regain control of his emotions and to pull himself back from the brink of what might have been a plunge into the terrible abyss of righteous madness.

True, he had come perilously close to that short leap into barbarism, but in the end, some bit of stubborn lucidity had finally prevailed. In that, he concluded, there was victory. Convoluted perhaps, but still a victory.

Sokolov wearily returned the Mauser to its holster and adjusted his overcoat. This done, he lifted his gaze to Strovka once more. "I want to know," he began deliberately, "what happened to the Grand Duchess Anastasia."

"Good for you," Strovka nodded blandly. "We thought it was finally over," he continued with a lethargic sigh. "That was when she moved. Opened her eyes...looked up at me. Ever had a dead girl open her eyes and look up at you? A bit...distracting."

"What happened then?" Sokolov asked with a tone of voice that somehow managed to project an abnormal sense of detachment.

"Don't have the slightest idea," Strovka replied with a disinterested shrug. "When she looked up at me, I left the room, stumbled outside and vomited. I'd had enough. After that...who knows?"

Nicholas Sokolov's brain was already conjuring the image of a document in his possession—a copy of Jacob Yurovsky's secret report setting forth his own recalled details of the Romanov's execution. The similarities between it and Strovka's story were clearly obvious.

According to Yurovsky:

"When the firing stopped, it turned out that the daughters, Alexandra Feodrovna and, it seems, Demidova and Alexei too, were alive. I think they had fallen from fear or maybe intentionally, and so they were alive. Then we proceeded to finish the shooting. (Previously I had suggested shooting at the heart to avoid a lot of blood.) Alexei remained sitting petrified. I killed him. They shot the daughters but did not kill them. Then Yermakov resorted to a bayonet, but that did not work either. Finally they killed them by shooting them in the head."

Sokolov, deep in unsettled thought, moved to the wall directly across from Strovka's cot and sagged against it.

"Think very carefully," he admonished the prisoner, crossing his arms over his chest. "When everything was over...when you were finished in that room...when they were finished...what happened to the bodies of the Romanovs? How did you dispose of the remains?"

"The bodies were wrapped in sheets," Strovka answered as though emotionally unconnected. "They were then taken to a truck outside the cellar room and driven to a predetermined place in the woods about six miles north of here. A local Bolshevik had picked out the site the day before the execution. God-awful place too—full of swamps, peat bogs, and abandoned mines."

"Do you remember the place?" Sokolov interrupted, "What did the site look like exactly?"

Strovka scratched his head and shrugged again. "An open mine shaft about seven hundred yards from the railroad crossing between the village of Koptiaki and the Upper Isetsk factory northwest of the village. I remember that. Damned hard job getting there too. Truck kept breaking down...getting mired in the mud."

"Go on."

"After stripping each body of its clothing, we crushed their faces with our rifle butts. The bodies were then cut into pieces with axes and saws. Fires were set. And, when that giant heap of bloody human body parts—chopped arms, legs and heads—was finally ready beside an open mine shaft, everything was drenched in petrol and sulfuric acid and set on fire. Took three days. All that was left after that...the ashes...were finally thrown into a rancid pool of water at the bottom of the shaft. I'd say it was probably thirty feet deep. Last of all, Yurovsky tossed several grenades into the pit in order to collapse the walls and cover everything forever.

I don't think he ever trusted the secrecy of that place. Eight days later, Ekaterinburg fell to your White army."

Strovka paused and stroked his flabby chin thoughtfully before finally concluding, "That's all I know."

Sokolov reflected on the concluding information for several moments before turning back to face Strovka. "All you've just told me is true?" he asked pointedly.

"Everything," the prisoner nodded, adjusting the ragged blanket so that it covered his bloated stomach and legs.

"You left nothing out? Not one detail?"

"I've told you everything I remember."

"You swear it?" Sokolov cautioned. "On your life?"

Karl Strovka smiled wryly. "On all I have left. One person was still alive when I left that basement room. That's all."

Sokolov turned and slowly walked to the doorway. Pausing there, with his back still to the prisoner, he concluded the formal interview with one more soft statement.

"In one of Empress Alexandra's last letters to the outside world," he began purposely, "she wrote these words: '*One by one, all earthly things slip away, houses and possessions ruined, friends vanished. One lives from day to day. We feel that a storm is approaching, but we also know that God is merciful. Our souls are at peace. I love my country with all its faults. Whatever happens will be God's will. Still, I feel old; oh, so old.*'"

Sokolov paused for a moment to compose himself. Though his back prevented the prisoner from seeing, the Investigator's good eye was brimming with tears.

"Today," he finally concluded hoarsely. "I think I understand what she meant."

"Nobody lives forever," Strovka chuckled before once more snatching the bottle of vodka from the floor and taking several long swallows.

"Who else knows what you've just told me?" Sokolov inquired.

"Besides you and me?" Strovka replied, wiping a bit of spittle from his lips. "Only God. And, if it's all the same to you, I'd rather keep it that way."

"Yes," Sokolov quietly sighed to himself. "So would I."

Strovka, lifting the dirty bottle again to his lips, hardly noticed the Investigator turn back to face him one last time. If he also caught a glimpse of the Mauser in Sokolov's raised hand, it didn't register on his face. There was hardly time.

The Investigator's first bullet sliced through the still air of the room, shattering Strovka's vodka bottle before continuing on to hit him directly between the eyes and explode through the back of his skull in a spray of blood, shattered bone and brain matter.

Strovka was dead before his head slammed back against the blood spattered pillow. The fixed and dilated eyes were still wide open and his mouth gaped wide in a frozen expression of complete shock that now became his death mask. The huge body heaved, twitched once, and was still.

Sokolov calmly took a single step forward and fired again. The second bullet splintered Strovka's lower jaw in another explosive spray of blood, tissue and small pieces of bone. The lifeless body jerked in an involuntary response to the force of the bullet's impact.

The Investigator took another step toward the lifeless prisoner and fired again. The third shot was lower, striking Strovka's huge torso near the heart. With each subsequent step toward the body, Nicholas Sokolov methodically squeezed off yet another round.

By the time Dmitri rushed into the room, Nicky was standing numbly over Strovka's bullet ridden corpse still repeatedly pulling the trigger of his empty pistol.

Chapter Eleven

Death answers before it is asked.
(Russian Proverb)

Another cold night had finally settled around Ekaterinburg like a heavy shroud. The freezing rain had finally subsided, but the ever present Siberian wind continued its low and mournful dirge into the wee morning hours. With the exception of light spilling into the frigid outside world from one window of the Ipatiev House, the rest of the landscape appeared dark and deserted.

Inside the house, Nicky and Dmitri, lounging in chairs pulled close to the warmth of the wood stove in Sokolov's room, had been drinking for most of the night. They were slumped side by side in a sort of vapid alcoholic stupor, gazing at the flickering firelight through the stove's iron grate. Neither one had spoken for quite some time.

"Galatea," Dmitri sighed softly, finally ending the heavy silence of the room.

It took a few moments for the word to register with Sokolov, who seemed to hear Dmitri's voice drift to his ears through some kind of thick and oppressive fog.

"I'm sorry," he finally murmured. "What did you say?"

"Galatea," Dmitri softly repeated the word. "A figure in Greek mythology. Pygmalion carved a statue of a woman from ivory. It was so beautiful that he fell in love with it. He called her Galatea."

Sokolov lifted his groggy head to gaze at his friend. "What happened to her?" he asked.

"Galatea?" Dmitri yawned. "One of the gods took pity on Pygmalion and breathed life into the statue."

Sokolov assumed, albeit disjointedly, that there was some logical connection between an hour's previous silence and his friend's sudden reference to Greek mythology, but his alcoholic stupor prevented any kind of sober resolution.

Though it might have been his initial objective some hours earlier, Nicholas Sokolov wasn't completely numb just yet. Three bottles of vodka hadn't been enough to achieve the desired effect, so he roused himself from his chair and staggered to a shelf in a far corner of the room where he knew two more bottles had been stored.

As he fumbled with bottles and glasses, his heavy tongue managed to give vent to a series of rambling thoughts.

"How extraordinary that must've been…" he declared, trying against all odds to keep his balance, "to have lived in an age when there were gods…and emotions like pity."

"If wishes were horses," Dmitri replied, "beggars would ride."

Managing a sad smile, Dmitri then leaned forward in his chair. "Russia has been at war all of our lives," he finally shrugged. "It's all we've ever known."

"Yes," Sokolov sighed. "So many bodies! Where will we ever bury them all?"

"In our hearts," Dmitri answered solemnly as though giving voice to a sacred promise.

The two men paused long enough to finish their glasses of vodka, thereby allowing the incommunicable sadness of the moment to play out in stoic silence. And yet, drunken remorse seemed such a feeble way to bestow some degree of sanctity to the memory of their fallen comrades. For the moment, however, it was all they had.

"We'll be left with three armies when this glorious revolution is finally over," Sokolov began again, struggling to open a fresh bottle. "An army of cripples, an army of mourners, and an army of thieves. And all of them, I'm afraid, will have come to fear life more than death."

The unsteady Investigator paused to gaze for a moment at the flickering flames dancing behind the grate of the wood stove.

"And who do we thank for this legacy?" he continued. "I mean, those who fought so valiantly to pass all of this along to us are dead themselves—most of them by the very thing they created."

"True," Dmitri replied, "but Peace isn't just the absence of war, Nicky. It also has to be a state of mind…a quality of the human heart. We're not there yet."

"Do you think we ever will be?" Sokolov wondered aloud as he finally succeeded in opening the bottle of vodka.

"No one's ever inherited a perfect world," Dmitri offered as Sokolov poured him a fresh drink. "Even if we had, we would've found a way to mar it somehow. Whatever it is, it's all we have. We make the best of it."

"How do we do that?" Sokolov blurted. "How do we make the best of war?"

The Investigator sank back into his chair and poured himself another drink before continuing.

"About four years ago, the Imperial Cabinet decided it was necessary to move the Tsar's Crown Jewels to Moscow—further inland than St. Petersburg. Safer. Nine huge strong boxes, packed with priceless gems, were secretly transported to a special vault in the Armory Hall of the Kremlin, while, just outside in the streets of Moscow, Russians were murdering each other for a single loaf of bread! That's war, Dmitri. Madness. And, dearest God, the tragedy of it all is that we're getting used to it."

"Feel better now?" Dmitri asked.

"I killed a man today," Sokolov's voice was suddenly choking with emotion.

"You killed something," Dmitri countered. "I don't know that I would call it a man."

"*It*? What would you call *it*, Dmitri?"

"Does it matter?" Dmitri replied, shifting slightly in his chair. "Nicky, this little bout of remorse is commendable, but it's also very temporary. Do yourself a favor and take it from someone who knows."

Sokolov leaned forward, glaring at his friend. "Let us be children of the Light," he said, choking back drunken but heartfelt tears, "and tell the ages what we are."

"A line from a pretty poem someone wrote after a nice hot meal and a few glasses of wine," Dmitri responded. "This is war."

"Then tell me you don't believe in that poem," Sokolov shot back with unconcealed anguish.

"Nicky…"

Before Dmitri could complete the sentence, Sokolov practically lunged at his friend, frantically grabbing hold of his broad shoulders.

"No," the Investigator cried emphatically, "I want to hear you say it! I want to hear you tell me you don't believe in those words!"

Dmitri silently considered his friend's demand for a moment longer before answering quietly. "The last words I utter…with my last breath on this earth…that will be what I believe."

Sokolov released his grip on Dmitri's shoulders and staggered backwards a few steps.

"If it helps you get through this," Volkov continued, "you might remind yourself that the man you executed today took part in the systematic murder of eleven people. He said so himself!"

"He was lying," Sokolov exploded. "None of it was true! Don't you understand? I've been sitting here half the night trying to convince myself that he was telling the truth. I can't!"

Volkov was stunned. "Why not?" he managed to stammer.

"What's Lys'va?" Sokolov immediately countered.

"Lys'va? Small village northeast of here. Why?"

"Strovka asked me if it was snowing in Lys'va," the Investigator explained. "Why would he want to know that?"

"You're grasping at straws, Nicky."

"Sometimes," Sokolov replied, "that's all you have!"

Dimitri gazed back at his friend in knowing silence. Sokolov sank down in his chair once more and leaned close to Dimitri as if sharing a confidence.

"Two young fish are swimming along in the Iset River," Sokolov began. "They pass an older fish and he calls out, 'How is the water today?' The two young fish swim a short distance further and suddenly one fish turns to the other and says, 'What the hell is water?' It's never the obvious, Dmitri. It's always some small, seemingly insignificant thing that's right in front your eyes. You just don't see it. By the way, Strovka wasn't captured by our forces. Did you know that? He turned himself in. Why?"

"What're you getting at?" Dmitri asked.

"'Is it snowing in Lys'va' wasn't a real question," Sokolov insisted vigorously. "It was some kind of code...a password. Strovka wanted to find out if I knew the right response! Instinct! Intuition. Never mind. Look."

Sokolov, suddenly imbued with fresh purpose, pulled himself to his feet and began to pace the room as he continued his animated if somewhat unsteady summation.

"The downstairs basement in this house..." he exclaimed, "the room the Romanovs supposedly died in was twenty-five by twenty-one feet. This small!" he protested, doing his drunken best to step off a rectangular shaped space much smaller than the dimensions of his own room. "Twenty-two people are supposed to have crammed themselves into that room," he went on. "Eleven victims and at least that many executioners. Twenty-two people in a room this small! And that doesn't even take into account the three chairs that Strovka said were brought in by Yurovsky. Fourteen pistols at that close range, and they still supposedly fired until the guns were empty. Imagine the noise that would've created. And yet, a boy on guard duty just outside this house, said he never heard gunshots or screams. How could that be? Why doesn't it make sense?"

All of Sokolov's private doubts were now literally spilling forth in a galvanizing stream of consciousness that seemed to take control of his entire being. Small details that had been lurking in the recesses of his mind were suddenly assuming shape, forming themselves into something approaching logical order. One disturbing thought gave life to another as the unsteady Investigator continued to make the necessary connections from previously disjointed ideas that had been seething in his brain for days. All he knew was that he couldn't stop himself now. The truth was simply this: Nicholas Sokolov possessed something of which he was no longer master.

"Yurovsky ordered that the shots were to be aimed at the victims' hearts," the Investigator continued with passionate emphasis, "but the position of the bullet holes in that basement wall are within two feet of the floor. What were victims doing? Kneeling? Making the sign of the cross before their deaths? I wonder, you see, because when I knelt on the floor in that room, the level of my heart was at least three and a half feet above floor level—a considerable discrepancy when body measurements are being accounted for. Other bullet holes indicate that additional shots were also fired into the victims after they had fallen to the floor. Even then, Yurovsky's men had to supposedly finish the job with bayonets. They were finally reduced to using their rifles as clubs! No! Too many inconsistencies. It's all wrong."

Sokolov strode to his seated friend and knelt down on one knee next to the chair. "And you, Dmitri," he asked with soft urgency. "Why were you...of all people...assigned to Strovka's train at the last minute? What are the odds? Was it coincidence that you were also ordered to stop here in Ekaterinburg? Or did someone assume we'd find each other and that you'd eventually tell me about 'one of the men who shot the Tsar'?"

His initial wave of exuberance fading now, Sokolov at last struggled to his feet and stumbled to a position in the center of the room. He bowed his head for a moment in silent reflection before finally concluding his summation.

"The execution of the Romanovs was not a minor event," he whispered softly. "If our White army dispatched three undercover agents to Tobolsk one year ago, how many others do you think we sent to Ekaterinburg during that same period? We most assuredly knew what was going on here. If we knew, and Lenin knew—and if that common knowledge was so vitally important to the balance of power in the rest of this civilized world—how many secret agents from other governments...other nations...were ordered here as well? Ekaterinburg must've been teaming with them! And if so, they were certainly privy to the accounts from people like Yakimov, Strovka, and Yurovsky—accounts that would've led them to the same conclusion I've finally reached."

Inhaling a deep breath, Sokolov paused to glance out of the window and into the empty darkness of that cold Siberian night. Turning back to his dearest friend, he finally gave words to his most troubling sentiment.

"What if," he finally heard himself utter, "the Romanovs weren't all killed that night? What if someone survived?"

"Everyone's heard the rumors," Dmitri managed to respond wearily.

It was Volkov's turn to stand. He'd been holding his vodka better than Sokolov, but was still a bit unsteady on his feet, affected not only by the alcohol but by his friend's sudden confession. He swayed for a moment, then finding his balance, fixed his eyes on Sokolov.

"Have you ever considered," he began slowly, "that, perhaps, it's best we never know the answer to that question?"

"No," Sokolov immediately exploded, "not once! Perhaps Man wasn't meant to know everything, Dmitri, but I do believe we were meant to try!"

"Pretty words," Volkov responded, staggering slightly towards Sokolov's desk. "But I know you, Nicky. This isn't just another investigation. It's become something more...something personal."

Dmitri grabbed the framed photograph of Anastasia and held it out at arm's length toward his friend. "You're becoming emotionally involved with the Romanovs...with *her*. What is it you want to do? Breathe life into your own Galatea?"

"She could already be alive," Sokolov insisted.

"What happens if you prove it?" Dmitri asked softly.

"What happens?" Sokolov countered. "Are you serious? We wave the survivors like banners in the wind to the rest of this godless world. That's what we do! We stand on the earth's highest summit to rage and bellow: 'No! You heartless bastards! You couldn't kill everything! Some bit of innocence and beauty survived! Some fragile shred of Truth still exists despite your mania for control!' That's what happens when I uncover the truth. And I will, Dmitri. As God is my witness…I will."

Volkov glared at his friend for a moment. Then, all at once, it seemed as if all emotion simply drained from his handsome face. He carefully placed the photograph of Anastasia back on Sokolov's desk, then turned once more to face his dearest friend.

"In that case, Nicky," he began with quiet resolve, "you're a colder son-of-a-bitch than those you hate or blame. If you really believe what you're saying, it means you care less about the Romanovs than they do. 'Wave them like a banner?' How noble, Nicky! What if a few of them did survive the first gun shots in that basement room? You think they'd survive the second volley? Or the third? Because the moment you breathe a word of what you believe to anyone else, they'll rush to join the hunt like dogs gone mad with the scent of a kill. And what if you're right? What difference will it make? Will it breathe life back into the dead? Restore the monarchy? Erase the bloody violence and mindless butchery from the past three hundred years? Wipe the pages clean? Is that what this is all about? Justice or revenge, which is it? You want the Romanovs alive for your reasons; they need the Romanovs dead for theirs. Consider the odds and make your choice. But, before you do…before you start pretending to be God with other people's lives… I want you to come with me."

"Where?" Sokolov stammered in total confusion.

"To see the Romanovs," Dmitri answered simply. "They're not far away…if what Strovka told you this morning is true. He said the remains of the Imperial family lie at the bottom of a mine shaft. According to the map, it's not far from here. That's where they are now, Nicky. Waiting for you. We can find them. So, let's go and see the Romanovs. Why not? Let's see what happens to people who're waved, like banners, to the rest of the world."

Dmitri faced Sokolov in silent but absolute determination. His blazing eyes gave witness to his resolve. "You have an automobile at your disposal outside," he said firmly. "I'll drive."

Taking several steps towards the doorway of the room Volkov suddenly snatched Sokolov's rabbit fur *Ushanka* hat from a nearby coat rack and angrily flung it at his friend, hitting him squarely in the chest.

"I said, let's go!"

Chapter Twelve

"We can achieve nothing unless we use terror."

Lenin

Once outside in the icy courtyard, Dmitri slid behind the wheel of the automobile and Sokolov reluctantly climbed into the passenger's seat. Moments later, the vehicle was rumbling out of the stockade gates and onto Voznesensky Prospekt. A right on Voznesensky Lane, then a left on Yakova Street. A mile west and the lumbering automobile turned onto Isetsky Road, past the racetrack, heading toward Versh-Isetsk.

It was a hazardous twelve mile drive from Ekaterinburg to their destination, a remote patch of snowy woods in a forest near the village of Koptiaki. Because both men were already drained from a full night of drinking and impassioned exchanges, the expedition was made in stony silence.

Sokolov remained slumped, rather petulantly, in the passenger seat of the automobile—still laboring to understand the urgent necessity of making such a risky trek in the dead of a Siberian winter's night. After all, he reasoned, the journey could've been accomplished—certainly with more ease—once day broke. He was still woozy from the vodka, a condition not improved upon by the constant jostling over bumps and muddy hollows in the winding, wet clay road.

The heavy darkness of the cold night seemed almost impenetrable. Snow was falling, and the headlights of the automobile illuminated barely enough of the road ahead to make continued progress possible.

Dmitri, stone-faced and determined, hunched forward in the driver's seat, gripping the steering wheel tightly with both of his gloved hands while squinting into the thick gloom ahead. The automobile, frequently encountering patches of treacherous ice and mud, veered dangerously close to either edge of the road. Dmitri fought the repeated hydroplanes by turning the wheels into the direction of the skid, then steering back towards clearer patches of red mud.

A mile and a half beyond Verkh-Osetsk, the automobile, skirting Upper Iset Pond, passed the Zlokazov factory before turning north-west. From the rear window, Sokolov could see the last remnants of Ekaterinburg's industrial suburb being swallowed by the encircling darkness behind them.

Finally, the automobile was forced to maneuver a particularly icy railroad crossing between Koptiaki and the Upper Isetsk factory to the northwest of the village. Here, near a clearing known as Pig's Meadow, Dmitri slowed the car, pulled to the side of the road and finally stopped the sputtering engine.

There was, however, still more distance to cover. From the point of that intersection, their final destination was supposedly located about seven hundred feet closer to the Upper Isetsk factory—one last snowy trek that had to be made on foot.

Dmitri climbed out of the car and retrieved a lantern from behind the driver's seat. As he lit it, Sokolov managed to disengage himself from the passenger's side and stumble out of the car into the freezing night air.

Despite the oppressive darkness and falling snow, the stars in the sky overhead seemed unusually bright. The beautiful glow, filtering through the bare branches of gently swaying treetops, produced a dim but welcomed radiance that softly burnished the surrounding wintry landscape. Somewhere in the distance, a lone wolf howled its mournful cry. The cold wind gusting through the clearing seemed almost refreshing to Sokolov as he shook himself alert in an attempt to get his bearings.

Before that could happen, however, he felt the sudden grip of Dmitri's strong and relentless hand on his arm, propelling him with some force towards of a patch of snow covered birch trees in the murky distance. His legs were already unsteady and the deep drifts of snow did little to contribute to his sense of balance. He frequently lost his footing and tumbled into the freezing slush several times only to feel once more the strong arms of his silent friend lifting and forcing his body ever onward through the deepening shadows. As he trudged through the knee-deep snow, Sokolov began inhaling deep drags of the frigid air, hoping his inebriated daze would somehow dissipate with each exhalation of alcoholic breath.

An unmistakable sense of increasing dread was beginning to churn in the pit of his stomach, however, as the two men plodded still deeper into the dark Koptiaki forest. Sokolov was actually startled at his growing apprehension over the possibility of actually seeing the place where the remains of the Romanovs were supposedly buried. Wasn't this, after all, what he had been summoned to Ekaterinburg to accomplish? Why else had he accepted Admiral Kolchak's taunting challenge?

"Prove it," Kolchak had taunted him. "Prove to me that the Tsar and his entire family were butchered by the Bolsheviks. That not even one survived."

If what Strovka said was true, this was the opportunity to do just that. Why, then, this sudden trepidation at the thought of achievement? Fear of the unknown? Whatever the cause, Sokolov was now gripped by a wave of tangible panic at the thought of what could possibly be awaiting him in the gloom beyond his limited vision. Had Dmitri's strong arms not occasionally held him upright, he would have collapsed on his knees in the snow.

Too late for that now. They had reached their destination—the Four Brothers Mine—so named because of four ancient pine trees growing close by. Dmitri, halting abruptly next to Sokolov, shoved the lighted lantern into his friend's trembling hand and pointed to a small clearing that lay just ahead in the gloom. Sokolov shook his head slowly from side to side, as if begging Dmitri for some sort of brief reprieve. It was not forthcoming. Volkov wrestled himself free of his friend's grasp and once more propelled Sokolov into the darkness ahead.

The Investigator had no choice but to steady himself as best he could and take several more faltering steps towards what now appeared to be a large and distinct shape in the snow covered ground just ahead. The glow from the lantern Sokolov held at arm's length, began to illuminate the surroundings, bringing the dark and foreboding area into clearer view.

The circular opening of a vertical shaft in the frozen ground suddenly appeared only a few yards ahead. Like a gaping wound in some bare patch of lifeless white flesh, it materialized through the icy mist before Sokolov's anxious gaze, causing him to halt in his tracks. That sense of dread was suddenly preventing him from going any further.

His heaving chest began to tighten and strain against convulsive spasms of sheer panic. His head was pounding, and though he struggled to control his equilibrium, his body was now swaying back and forth as he came dangerously close to losing consciousness.

The next moment's transformation was utterly unexplainable. As quickly as the terrible wave of nauseous fear had overtaken him, it suddenly subsided and vanished without a trace. The stupor and hazy vision had left him as well. Recovered strength instantly began to surge into his legs and upper torso, causing his body to pull itself completely upright. As the paralyzing anxiety transformed itself into a sense of calm assurance, his heart ceased to race uncontrollably—as if, inexplicably, Sokolov's entire being was suddenly at peace.

The Investigator pivoted to glance back at Volkov—now only a hazy silhouette against the distant backdrop of birch trees. Then, turning to face the pit once more, he began to calmly take his first determined step towards it.

As he drew nearer to the rim, the light from his lantern began to creep down the muddy embankment of the dark opening, spreading deeper into the murky depths of the pit with each purposeful step, pushing away still more of the heavy darkness within. Another mournful gust of wind rose, moved through the clearing and was gone. The night became instantly still and soundless.

As Sokolov's senses began to fully revive themselves, he realized that he was at last standing on the earthen rim of the Four Brothers Mine. For a moment, he could only peer into the vertical shaft—which, in the revealing lantern's light, now appeared to be only eight feet deep at most. Then slowly, as curiosity began to replace his sense of almost reverent awe, he slowly knelt in the snow and, placing the lantern on the frozen ground nearby, leaned forward in order to more closely examine the sight below.

Sokolov's Journal
Ekaterinburg—1919

I have no idea how long I stayed there in the bitter cold of that Russian night, gazing into that dark and silent pit like a surgeon peering into an open wound...probing its contents for answers, reasons, remedies.

I learned two things: the Dark doesn't give up its answers easily—and, when I left that place, something had changed. I had seen the end of Forever. And, from that moment on, whether in or around me—nothing was ever the same.

There's one other thing you should know. The next morning, at first light, I stood on a deserted platform at the lonely depot, watching Dmitri's train disappear into the cold, gray distance of that Siberian winter. He stood poised on the small platform of the last car, returning my gaze with his own warm but sad and peculiar smile. "Tell the ages what we are!" Those were his last words, I'm told, in front of a Bolshevik firing squad.

He was my friend.

Chapter Thirteen

**A group of workers from the Putilov factory,
stating their dismay at the Revolution:**

"Where is justice? Where are the results of the blood and lives of the fighters who fell in the revolution? Where is the new life? Where is the paradise like the green-red bird that so temptingly flew over our land and disappeared...as if to deceive."

The next day began a flurry of concentrated activity, overseen by Sokolov, that would last for several months. The Investigator's first directive was to immediately requisition a military detachment to begin excavation of the mine shaft in the Koptiaki woods. Armed guards were stationed around the perimeter of the forest clearing twenty-four hours a day. Within a week, all necessary equipment—vehicles, tools, wenches, lengths of chain, rope, railroad ties and lumber—had been collected and transported to that remote clearing in the woods. In addition, several rustic shelters were constructed near the pit itself. Photographs—existing to this day—show a determined Nicholas Sokolov, standing next to the pit, tirelessly directing the entire focus of the excavation.

Not surprisingly, the inhabitants of Ekaterinburg became intrigued with the activity at the Four Brothers Mine. In one sense, the excavation offered the local population a welcomed respite from the dreary news of war and the boredom of uneventful daily routines. Visitors to the site were therefore frequent but always kept at a careful distance by the guards.

The most distinguished visitor to the Four Brothers Mine was none other than Admiral Kolchak—arriving unannounced one mid-afternoon along with his sputtering motorcade and burly security detail in tow. The soldiers assigned to the excavation immediately stopped all work and came to attention. The Admiral, strolling the site with his entourage, acknowledged the gesture but motioned blandly for the men to return to their duties. The weather was frigid and Kolchak had long since forgone the usual public ceremonies. Why waste the energy? Words were now worthless when it came to rallying troops or restoring morale. Kolchak knew his men would continue to do his bidding. They would fight and die because war was all they had ever known. Peace had become the anomaly.

Sokolov spent a few moments bringing Kolchak up to date on the progress of the excavation work. The Admiral nodded once or twice at the summary and did seem interested enough in the progress that had been made...if only out of mild curiosity. When Kolchak had finally heard enough and trudged back to the sputtering motorcade with his entourage in tow, Sokolov did happen to notice a sullen Boris Gorev slumped petulantly in the backseat of Kolchak's waiting automobile—a sight that provided the Investigator his only bit of amusement in weeks.

The unpredictable Siberian weather was, as always, an unceasing problem. Whatever progress had been gained was often lost once more to the elements. Mounds of snow and ice at the site, trampled underfoot, inevitably became pools of thick sludge which constantly mired trucks and automobiles up to their axles. Mules, tethered to heavy chains, were brought in to pull vehicles free in order for the work to resume. The delays took precious time. When rains came, the pit rapidly filled with murky water that had to be constantly pumped out. Mudslides caused by the erosive run-off were also frequent, which meant that a previous day's work often had to be laboriously repeated. The military personnel assigned to the excavation detail were therefore being pushed to the point of exhaustion, and grumbling among the men was becoming intense. None of it, however, seemed to lessen Sokolov's resolve. He brooked no impedance from Man or Nature. In fact, the greater the hardship, the more focused his determination seemed to become.

Nothing underscored the ferocity of his singular resolve more than a particular incident which took place one afternoon at the site. As the men were laboring to remove more mud from the depths of the shaft, ominous storm clouds began to form above them. As the frigid wind also began to intensify, the work slowed down to a snail's pace as apprehensive eyes turned more frequently to the swaying treetops and darkening sky.

Suddenly, a blinding flash of lightning sliced through the clouds, immediately followed by a shattering explosion of thunder directly overhead. The work site, brilliantly illuminated for several seconds, returned almost immediately to its all too familiar dreariness as the ear-shattering thunder clap continued to reverberate through the surrounding forest. In dull anticipation of yet another impending downpour, the workers in the pit immediately threw down their shovels and trudged to ladders that would take them up to the relative safety of makeshift shelters on ground level. Before any of them could reach the surface, however, Sokolov, almost self-combusting with exasperation and rage, bounded from a nearby wooden shed. Eyes glaring wide and his mouth curling into an outraged snarl, he frantically pushed his way through the assembled workers and furiously clawed his way to the top of a large mound of earth and snow. There, as all eyes remained riveted in stunned disbelief, the enraged Investigator balled his right hand into an angry fist and raised it toward the churning sky in trembling defiance. Glaring heavenward, and with all mustered strength left to him, the exhausted man bellowed only one word: "No!"

Had it not been for the physical and emotional fatigue that gripped all those present, the moment would have been comical. To the uncluttered minds of these simple men, however, God had clearly been given two choices: strike the impertinent little man dead with another thunderbolt, or acquiesce to the command. The more religiously inclined in the assembly obediently braced themselves for what could only be considered a foregone conclusion. To the utter amazement of all, however, the wind instantly dissipated and the clouds actually seemed to roll back long enough for a single ray of sunlight to slice its way through the brewing gloom. This unbelievable moment couldn't have been more electrifying had the shaft of heavenly light actually fallen directly on Sokolov's head and shoulders. Audible gasps rose from the men, and a few even crossed themselves as the Investigator remained locked in that dramatic pose, like a makeshift Moses atop his very own Mt. Sinai—fist still raised high above his head in a gesture of frozen defiance.

Sokolov was, of course, as totally dumbfounded as anyone else—but instantly recognized a good public relations opportunity when he raged into one. He therefore decided to take full advantage of all benefits it might possibly provide. There was no need to wait long. Within hours, the citizens of Ekaterinburg were predictably abuzz with various and often embellished accounts of the irascible little man who had dared shake a fist in God's face while bellowing his now famous command—an edict to which God had undeniably complied.

Needless to say, there was no more grumbling among the men assigned to the excavation detail. After all, if God was willing to follow Sokolov's directives, who were they to take issue with any of the Investigator's subsequent mandates. Besides, they knew that exceptions were not the general rule. Given a choice, they surmised, Heaven still seemed very much inclined toward Divine retribution.

And so it was that the mysterious pit reluctantly began to give up its secrets. Each individual discovery, no matter how seemingly insignificant, was treated with the kind of delicate care typically bestowed upon artifacts collected during Egyptian archeological expeditions.

The recovered items were meticulously catalogued by Sokolov in his still existent notes:

"The body of the dog, Jemmy. A human finger—apparently from a middle-aged man—most probably Dr. Botkin's. Pieces of human bone; two pieces of human skin. A set of artificial teeth—again Dr. Botkin's. A belt buckle which had been exposed to extreme heat—most probably belonging to the Tsar.

Another belt buckle of brass with the Imperial crest—belonging to the Tsarevich. Six pairs of corset steels as well as clasps, side bones, hooks for laces and fasteners—(of particular interest to Sokolov). Shoe buckles; an earring of pearl, platinum, and gold—Alexandra's favorite earrings; a jubilee badge of a Lancer regiment with diamonds and sapphires—worn by Alexandra on a bracelet; pieces of burned fabric—most probably from the Tsarvich's overcoat (another point of interest to the Investigator); his knapsack, and a pocket case owned by Nicholas that held his wife's portrait. Fragments of jewels: diamonds, emeralds, rubies, sapphires, pearls, almandines and topazes."

As tedious days melted into even more tedious weeks, one question became foremost in Sokolov's mind: why wasn't there more recovered evidence of human remains? Bodies, even when professionally cremated, require a considerable amount of time and effort before they are completely reduced to ash. The majority of items recovered from the pit, however, consisted of clothing and belongings which had supposedly been stripped from the bodies before they were destroyed—items easily consumed by burning. Remnants least resistant to the elements had still managed to survive. On the other hand, the small pieces of bone so far unearthed (forty-two in all) would hardly fill a small glass jar. Additionally, not one human tooth had been unearthed; and, as the Investigator knew only too well, teeth are hardly ever destroyed by burning. Even taking into consideration Strovka's suggestion of cremation followed by the use of lye, there should still have been more evidence...more signs of human remains hidden somewhere in the murky depths of that forbidding pit. If they were there, Sokolov was determined to uncover them.

One bit of evidence had been particularly unsettling—the body of the dog, Jemmy. It was in an amazing state of preservation that couldn't be solely ascribed to having been frozen in the depths of the pit. The dog's body, in fact, was not frozen when it was unearthed, and yet seemed unusually fresh—as though its death had been recent. Additionally confusing was the fact that Strovka told the Investigator that Yurovsky had crushed the dog's head with a rifle butt—and yet the head of the dog's carcass found in the pit was completely intact. The evidence was inconsistent with the testimony. Important pieces of the puzzle didn't seem to fit. Why? Evidence was supposed to solve mysteries, not obscure the truth with even more nagging questions.

It was for reasons such as these that, after weeks of grueling labor in often adverse conditions, Sokolov was growing frustrated with the results of the excavation. He remained undeterred however—stoically convinced that there was something still waiting to be uncovered in that remote clearing hidden away in the Koptiaki Woods.

"On the other hand," he at last conceded to himself with an exhausted shrug, "if they dig any deeper, I'll have to report that the Romanovs were buried in China!"

Finally, however, he had no other choice but to pack his notebooks, box up all of the existing evidence, and return to the comparative quiet of the Ipatiev House. The truth was that he needed rest as well as time to develop a renewed plan of action. Besides, the collected evidence had to be studied and meticulously catalogued in order for any considered judgments to be made—a mundane process to be sure, but one that he knew had to be skillfully concluded before proceeding to the next stage of the investigation.

It seemed now, however, that Nicholas Sokolov's soul was wrestling with something else—some tenacious yet unseen adversary whose obstinate hold he was no longer able to deny. There was an unsettled quality about the young Investigator's physical state as well which manifested itself in several newly acquired nervous habits. During the excavation, Sokolov had grown a mustache and was now forever tugging or idly twisting the ends of it. He had also developed a curious habit of rocking back and forth whenever he sat for any length of time—a slight swaying to and fro of his upper body, as if the repetitive movement might somehow help to settle his restless thoughts.

Those troubling ruminations, hardly modified by the confines of his surroundings, tended to roam far and wide as even newer revelations surged and receded in his mind like gentle waves on some distant shore. Coming as they did in such rapid succession, they eventually overflowed into his own stream of consciousness—random scenarios and 'what if' propositions that moved through his brain without any sense of logical order.

Sokolov's only consolation was the fact that he knew this was a necessary evolution of ideas—a kind of filtering process that would eventually mold itself into a rational scenario supported by facts—facts that would be able to finally sustain a logical conclusion by the sheer weight of incontrovertible proof. Still, he had also come to accept the fact that the process was often an infuriatingly slow one.

Sometimes in the midst of her household duties, Natalya Kolya would stumble upon the Investigator sitting alone in one of the upstairs rooms of the Ipatiev House—and, as always, he would seem completely oblivious to the old woman's presence. He usually sat facing a window, arms folded over his chest in quiet contemplation. As his torso gently swayed back and forth, his gaze always seemed fixed on something beyond—something that couldn't be seen or perceived by the human eye. In a strange way, Kolya felt that Sokolov's gaze was focused more inward than on anything he could possibly see in the physical world.

Unnoticed by the preoccupied Investigator, the long Siberian winter was also facing its own unrelenting adversary. Day by day, the harsher elements of a stubborn winter were being forced to give way to an early spring. The snows were becoming less frequent and tiny, almost undetectable buds were beginning to form on branches of the linden trees. Gray days edged by chilling winds were still numerous, but as one week slowly rolled into the next, the harsh season's bleakness was finally dissipating. It was reassuring to think that the dense forests, rich soils, and fertile valleys of the region would soon transform themselves with signs of new life. This reassurance, however, belonged only to those who afforded themselves the luxury of such seasonal expectancy.

If Nicholas Sokolov anticipated anything, it was certainly nothing remotely resembling a beginning. Too immersed in his obstinate quest to arrive at some sort of conclusion, he was dismissive of anything that didn't support what had now become his underlying theory. If it was the beginning of anything, Sokolov would only concede that it might possibly be the beginning of the end.

He continued excavation work at the site, but reduced the number of workers by half. In the days that followed, he returned to the Koptiaki Woods less frequently. When he did, it was usually late in the afternoon—once the work had been completed for the day and only a few guards remained on sentry duty. Always alone in the fading twilight, he would stand a silent vigil atop that small mound of earth next to the lip of the mine shaft, gazing into its murky depths as if expecting to finally notice some definitive bit of evidence that had been carelessly overlooked the entire time.

In a perfect world, it might actually have happened in just such a way. The Investigator, however, had long ago accepted the fact that he inhabited a world that was sadly far from perfect.

Sokolov's Notes—1924
"There are no miracles in our investigative trade."

What remained most disagreeable to the Investigator was the begrudging concession that, so far, his worthiest opponent had turned out to be nothing more than a damned hole in the ground.

More often than not, Sokolov's evening hours were spent in the quiet solitude of his small room where he poured over boxes of evidence and stacks of ever accumulating dossiers. As was now the routine, Natalya Kolya would bring dinner to him each evening on a tray. Not wishing to disturb the papers which had been so painstakingly arranged on his desk, he would perch on the edge of his bed, tray on lap, and hastily devour his evening meal there. Half an hour later, Kolya would quietly return to retrieve the dinner tray and put fresh wood on the fire. Sokolov would then resume his place at the desk to submerge himself once more in what could best be described now as a continual process of elimination.

As the hours dragged by and his mental faculties depleted themselves, his weary gaze would inevitably turn to the small silver-framed photograph of Anastasia which had now become a permanent fixture on his desk. As always, the sad eyes gazing back at him from that faded photograph would draw him deeper and deeper into the hidden realms of his own imagining. It was only there in the midst of silent rumination that Sokolov was finally able to shed some of the depressing burden of his drab existence in order to be finally lifted by the shimmering wings of a dream that would gently bear him through the mists of Time—back to the lost world of the Romanovs. He savored the peace he was able to experience each time he surrendered to that dream. The effects were restorative to his mind and body, allowing him to retain the sense of forward motion he so urgently required. Otherwise, the stagnation that now defined this portion of his inquiry would have become overwhelming.

He had not wavered in the belief that members of the Imperial family could have survived the horrors of July 16–17, 1918. Aside from verbalizing this speculation in Dmitri's presence, however, he had not dared breathe the words to another living soul—nor would he until he had the indisputable proof to support any such public declaration.

Believing as he did in the possibility of survival, however slim the chances, he couldn't help but agonize over thoughts of where any of the surviving Romanovs might be at this point in time. Since the rumors primarily concerned Anastasia, his thoughts naturally centered on her. But he also had to remain as professionally oblique as possible. To do that, he decided to employ the non-specific term 'survivors'. It was a politically expedient choice, to be sure, but, if pressed, he could at least refer to the possibility of survival without being too specific.

This approach, however, did little to allay his more private anxiety. If one or more Romanov survived the slaughter in that basement room, where could they have possibly gone—and how? The Ipatiev House was under heavy guard twenty-four hours a day.

Each unanswered question led to another until Sokolov felt himself floundering in harrowing notions and growing apprehension. Nights on end, he would be jolted awake from bouts of fitful sleep, his body convulsed in throes of acute anxiety attacks. A shortness of breath alarmed him most of all—that dreadful sensation of being smothered to death by someone...some *thing*...unseen in the imperceptible darkness of his room.

He was well aware of the fact that these seemingly disjointed symptoms were also taking a toll on his personal health in more cumulative ways. Stress was robbing him of sleep, and that deprivation alone was affecting not only his mental state, but was also compounding the apparent physical problems that were undeniably beginning to surface. Aside from the bothersome tics he had developed, the occasional pains in his chest were unmistakable signals of more potentially serious problems.

Unfortunately, warning signs serve their purpose only when heeded, and Sokolov simply refused to give them any earnest attention. What consumed him now—what alone gave him reason for motion and existence—was a singular quest for tangible and irrefutable proof.

Thankfully, and as a direct result of self-imposed isolation, one particular source of stress had at least been lessened. Sequestered and predisposed as he was, Sokolov's grasp of current events had become rather outdated. Kolchak's White Army had been on the offensive when he first arrived in Ekaterinburg. Since he'd taken little time to receive any news to the contrary, he assumed they still were.

After all, the usual signs of normalcy remained apparent. Ragged troops continued to move in and out of the war weary city and the trains were as infrequent as ever. Even Admiral Kolchak still managed to make the occasional and obligatory local appearance, his heavily guarded motorcade lumbering along some muddy street, stopping at this or that building long enough for his group of bodyguards to hustle him through the nearest doorway. He never seemed to linger at any of these locations, however. Within minutes, the same entourage of burly guards, their weapons drawn, would hustle their Supreme Commander back to the safety of his armored automobile. The motorcade would then rattle to life once more and move on to the next location, finally fading altogether into the twilight of another day.

The city's inhabitants went about their own daily activities with a desensitized casualness typical of those who have grown too accustomed to the ravages of war. They had become in fact, nothing more than living casualties unaffected by the fact that, beyond the securer boundaries of Ekaterinburg, ravenous wolves still roamed the darker forests.

Sokolov knew that he had also allowed himself to be at least partially lulled into this false sense of routine as well, but wasn't overly troubled by the realization. After all, once you come to view the world as a prison, it's much easier to accept the certainty that more and more people will be selected each day for execution.

To most of Russia, in fact, it was this very sense of unalterable predestination that had at last deadened the harshness of reality, numbed the fearful mind, and finally—lethally—managed to weaken the natural instinct of self-preservation itself. Once that sacrifice had been made, life became nothing more than a downward spiral from which there was no return. The saddest epitaph of all, however, was that this national march into oblivion set its stride—as always—to the drumbeat of national pride and intellectual justification:

"A new revolution was admissible, an uprising was legitimate, the liquidation of the existing regime was indispensable."

N. N. Sukhanov

Chapter Fourteen

Alexandra — In a Letter to Nicholas II

"We understand each other perfectly without words, and I swear, upon my life, that we shall see you again on the throne, raised there once more by your people, and your army, for the glory of your reign."

Sokolov's investigation into the disappearance of the Romanovs might very well have collapsed entirely during those last dismal days of winter. The complete story of why it didn't is still something of a mystery. What is known is that one morning in mid-April, the front door of the Ipatiev House swung open and the young Investigator strode out into the brilliant sunlight of a new day, armed with a fresh sense of purpose and determination. The agonizing stalemate had been broken.

The dramatic turning point had come during one of those endless gray afternoons as Sokolov drifted through the hours, sitting alone in one of the upstairs rooms of the Ipatiev House, surveying the world through one of the frosted window panes. He often took advantage of opportunities such as this to more fully concentrate on various details of a particular interrogation—occasionally discovering, for instance, that testimony was at odds with known facts. A time consuming process to be sure, but the results always proved to be well worth the effort.

Gullibility was certainly not one of Sokolov's shortcomings. He considered himself a rather keen judge of character. He also rarely let his guard down when conducting interrogations, only permitting himself the privilege once he felt an unusual degree of reciprocal trust had been established.

The particular epiphany that rejuvenated his resolve had come to him in one of those afternoons of studied silence. It took a few moments for the realization to settle in, but once it did, his first response had been one of exasperated self-contempt at not having caught the lie the moment it had been uttered. The realization that he had missed such a glaring disparity was an undeniable blow to his ego, yet it was this single revelation that arguably became the most determining factor in the outcome of the entire inquiry. For whatever reason, it reignited a fire in Nicholas Alexeyevich Sokolov that nothing was ever able to extinguish.

#

The heavy wooden door of Anatoly Yakimov's dingy cell slammed open with such force that the sleeping prisoner, on his pile of dirty straw and blankets, was jarred instantly awake. As a prisoner of war, he knew his life was constantly hanging by a thread. Because of that, any sudden loud sound or motion was always the source of panic and reflexive action.

Yakimov immediately jerked his body into a fetal position and instinctively covered his face with crossed arms in dreadful anticipation of what he assumed would be some sort of violent physical assault. When, after a few moments, nothing happened, he slowly opened his eyes and glanced apprehensively toward the door of his dingy cell.

Nicholas Sokolov stood silhouetted in the open doorway—frozen in place, his fearsome gaze locked on the prisoner's own eyes. The only part of Sokolov's face that was visible to Yakimov was a single eye which seemed, in the dimness of the surrounding gloom, to radiate an eerie sort of luminescence all its own.

Yakimov lowered his hands from his dirty face and gazed up at the Investigator in fearful confusion. "I didn't think I'd see you again," he finally managed to softly stammer. Sokolov paused a few moments more, then stepped silently into the room, closing the heavy wooden door behind him. Yakimov pulled himself into a sitting position still defensively tugging one of the ragged blankets around his waist and legs.

The Investigator reached into one of the pockets of his military tunic and withdrew the familiar pack of cigarettes and held it towards Yakimov. The prisoner, though still utterly confused, allowed himself a slight smile.

"Thank you," he nodded while still clutching tightly to the ragged blanket that encircled his waist. Slowly he pulled himself to his knees, and extended his free hand. His eyes still returning Sokolov's silent gaze, Yakimov withdrew a single cigarette form the pack and placed it between his lips.

Sokolov produced a tiny box of matches and silently lit the prisoner's cigarette. As he did, the small blaze from the match illuminated the faces of the two men. Sokolov's eyes were still locked on Yakimov's boyish face. They seemed to blaze with such intensity that it startled the young prisoner. He blinked several times, but continued to respond with a cryptic gaze of his own. The Investigator, returning the box of matches to his pocket, allowed the prisoner to take several drags from the freshly lit cigarette.

"Good?" Sokolov gently inquired.

"Very," the prisoner replied with a slight smile.

"How good?" the Investigator asked, never once shifting his eyes from Yakimov's. The young prisoner seemed confused by the question.

"I mean," Sokolov continued, "good enough to repay me…if you had the opportunity?"

Yakimov's posture shifted slightly as he quietly considered the Investigator's curious words. All the while, his inquisitive gaze remained locked on Sokolov. Instinctively, he thought he understood the true meaning of the question, but also knew he had to be certain beyond any doubt.

"Of course I would repay you," he replied softly, "in any way I could."

Sokolov stared at Yakimov for a few more moments of silence. "The first time you were sent here," he finally replied softly, "I asked to see your hands. They're very smooth…not the hands of a laborer."

The Investigator paused and slowly lowered himself to one knee so that his face was level and close to Yakimov's.

"In prison," he went on deliberately, "a young boy like you doesn't survive for very long unless he's useful for…something. Granting certain…favors."

Sokolov paused again so that the full significance of his soft words would not be lost. There was no need. Yakimov understood exactly what was being suggested. The Investigator slowly stood again, his eyes still locked on the uplifted face of the boyish prisoner who remained kneeling before him, wrapped in that dirty blanket.

"So then," Sokolov concluded evenly, "it has occurred to me that you might already know of a way to repay me. What shall we say? A small token of your gratitude?"

For the first time since Sokolov entered the room, Yakimov let his eyes leave the Investigator's face. His gaze drifted lower…to Sokolov's chest, then his stomach. Even more slowly now, the prisoner's gaze moved further down the Investigator's torso, finally coming to rest on the crotch of Sokolov's trousers.

Instinctively, Yakimov parted his lips in mute acquiescence, finally allowing his eyes to return to the Investigator's waiting gaze.

"Yes," Yakimov obediently whispered, "I understand."

Though the young prisoner had allowed his hips to sink back onto his heels in a more relaxed posture, he now lifted himself into a more upright kneeling position, allowing the dirty blanket to fall away from his midsection. He was naked from the waist down— wearing nothing but a ragged shirt. His skin was shockingly pale...almost translucent...as he offered his nakedness to the Investigator's smoldering gaze.

Slowly and trembling slightly, Yakimov placed both hands on Sokolov's thighs. Sensing no resistance, his hands deftly slid to the crotch of the Investigator's trousers and began a soft massage.

"Shall I thank you now?" Yakimov asked in a hoarse whisper, once more lifting his gaze to Sokolov in anticipation of the expected response.

What he received instead was the back of the Investigator's hand across his face in a move so sudden and with such violent force that it bloodied his lip and sent the young prisoner sprawling.

Yakimov slammed into the ground with such impact that he slid another foot or two in the muddy straw before his body finally came to rest next to the rough wooden wall of his cell. He had only begun to shake himself free of a dazed shock, when the bellowing Sokolov rushed forward to collar him once again. Lifting the half nude prisoner from the filthy earthen floor as if he weighed nothing at all, the raging Investigator hurled the boy against the opposite wall of his cell with such force that Yakimov was literally knocked senseless. His limp body slid to the floor in a crumpled heap.

If the poor boy thought this meant a reprieve, he was mistaken. In another instant, Sokolov had once more seized Yakimov, yanking his face close to his own.

"Please," the stunned prisoner pleaded, "I... I only thought..."

"I know," Sokolov raged again, "anything I wanted."

"Yes."

"Anything!"

"YES," Yakimov screamed frantically, "I'll tell you whatever you want to hear!"

"Just as you did the last time we talked," Sokolov bellowed, "making the truth whatever you thought I wanted it to be?"

Sokolov dragged the flailing prisoner to a nearby wooden stool and forced him onto it.

"Well, citizen Yakimov," the Investigator concluded sharply, "if force and fraud are the cardinal virtues of war, you're about to be blessed by the Pope."

Sokolov snatched up the ragged blanket. Hurling it at Yakimov, the Investigator watched as the cowering prisoner fearfully covered his nakedness. Once this had been done, Yakimov turned his fearful gaze to the face of the man towering over him.

"I want you to listen very carefully," Sokolov warned with lethal deliberateness, "I'm going to ask you one question. Only one. I expect an honest answer. There's nothing at stake here but your life. Is that clear?"

Shaking with fear, Yakimov could only nod.

"Good," the Investigator snarled before allowing some bit of silence to elapse in order to be able to speak more calmly. "Now," he finally began again, "when last we talked, you told me you had seen one of the Tsar's daughters in an upstairs window of the Ipatiev House."

"The Grand Duchess, Anastasia," Yakimov nodded eagerly.

"One of the Tsar's daughters," Sokolov intoned sternly. "Interesting," he continued, "I've been there, you know? The room upstairs. Studied it in detail. Floor, ceiling, walls...windows. Everything's been scrubbed clean, of course, but I did notice something peculiar around the window sills." As he said this, Sokolov leaned forward until his face was threateningly close to Yakimov's, "I noticed bits and pieces of chipped paint."

Yakimov reacted as though he'd been hit in the chest with terrific force—as if all breath had instantly left his body.

"That's why I'm curious," Sokolov continued. "How could you have seen anyone in the upstairs window of the Ipatiev House when that window had been painted over...as were all the windows that comprised the imperial family's living quarters?"

Yakimov still blanching visibly, turned slightly and lowered his head so the Investigator could not see the tears filling his eyes. As soon as he did, it was as though all tension in the room completely dissipated. His rage spent, Sokolov sighed heavily and turned away from the prisoner for a few moments in order to give both men a chance to reclaim some sense of composure.

"I never saw her that night in the window," Yakimov finally sobbed, "as you say, I couldn't have."

"But you knew her," Sokolov interjected.

"Yes."

"You had the opportunity to observe her often in fact."

"None of the doors in the family's living quarters had doorknobs or latches," Yakimov explained through his tears. "Everything had been removed. Before the Cheka arrived...when we were part of the inner guard, we were encouraged to interrupt...to disturb their routines."

"Routines?"

"Especially the daughters," Yakimov nodded shamefully. "The others...the other soldiers in my unit...seemed to take a sort of delight in it. They'd wait and listen...and when one or more of the girls were dressing or using the lavatory, they'd burst in...suddenly. Like some kind of game. It never stopped."

"And what about you?" Sokolov asked, "Did you also take part in these...games?"

"Never!"

For the first time, there was indignation in Yakimov's eyes as he pulled himself upright on the wooden stool and glared defiantly at the Investigator. Then, as if apologizing for the reaction, he lowered his head and repeated again softly, "Never."

Sokolov, leaning against one of the walls of the room, crossed his arms over his chest and inhaled deeply.

"Go on," he sighed with the slightest hint of resignation in his voice.

"I thought it was cruel..." Yakimov continued, "a kind of torture that grew worse with time. I knew how they felt. I knew that kind of shame."

"It grew worse with time you said?"

"Yes."

"In what way?"

Yakimov shifted uncomfortably on the wooded stool. "What way do you think?" he replied curtly.

Sokolov took a small but impulsive step towards the prisoner then hesitated. "They were raped," he continued—as if answering his own unspoken question.

As if replying was physically painful, Yakimov shut his eyes tightly, winced, and nodded his head in silent affirmation. His back was to Sokolov now, but the Investigator could plainly see the sudden change in the prisoner's posture.

163

"Once? Twice? How many times?" Sokolov continued to press.

"I don't know," Yakimov suddenly sobbed loudly, burying his face in his hands. "I swear! I begged them to stop. They only laughed and said: 'No one cares what happens to the Romanovs.' But they were wrong. I cared...about her."

The Investigator took another step towards the remorseful prisoner. "Cared about whom?" he asked in a voice just loud enough to break the silence.

Even as he said the words, Sokolov's right hand was slowly unfastening the cover of his holster. In another moment, his hand had gently cupped the handle of his pistol.

"Her," Yakimov sobbed again. "Anastasia. She was so...beautiful...so sad. I often wondered how anyone could've survived something like that. How could anyone have come through what they all suffered? But they did...and with a sort of dignity I've never seen before...never thought possible."

Sokolov's pistol had silently cleared the holster and was now aimed at the back of Yakimov's head.

"Then you know," Sokolov admitted aloud—as much to himself as to the sobbing prisoner.

"Know what?" Yakimov whimpered pitifully, still unaware that the barrel of Sokolov's pistol was only inches away from the back of his head.

"You know what happened to her," Sokolov declared with soft menace.

"Yes," Yakimov confessed, breaking down once more.

Sokolov's index finger tightened on the trigger of the pistol. A few seconds more and, it would all be over.

"I told you," Yakimov suddenly sobbed aloud, "she died!"

Sokolov instantly shifted the barrel of his pistol away from the back of Yakimov's head and waited for the prisoner to continue.

"That's how I know that Death is sometimes a blessing..." the prisoner sighed tearfully, "and why, sometimes, I wish for Death to come to me. A moment ago, I would've done anything you wanted. I've already lost all that I once was...everything I used to be. There's nothing left you can take from me. I'm not as lucky as she was." Yakimov pulled the ragged blanket around his shoulders and turned to face Sokolov. "You know what I've actually heard?" he said with some degree of astonishment. "That one of them escaped...one of the daughters. I know better. God wouldn't play such a cruel joke on one of His children."

164

"You saw proof of what you believe?" Sokolov replied eagerly. "The bodies?"

Yakimov shook his head sadly. "I lied to you when I said I never saw them again after that night," he confessed softly. "I should've said, I never saw them alive. I did see the Cheka load bodies on a truck. They were covered with sheets. Blood was everywhere."

"How many bodies? Do you remember?"

"It had to be all of them. No one could've survived what happened in that place. No one."

For a few moments, the room was filled with heavy silence. The Investigator quietly slid his pistol back into its holster as Yakimov finally rose to his feet. Squaring his shoulders, the young prisoner turned his sad gaze once more to Sokolov.

"Please understand," he began simply, "in my life, I've known only war. She was someone...something...beautiful. The reason I didn't tell you everything; it was only to somehow protect the memory of her. To keep her the way she was...to me."

Sokolov took a few steps towards Yakimov. "Keep your memories, Comrade..." he said softly, "and your life. Guard both of them well."

Sokolov turned and strode to the doorway of the cell. He swung the door open but hesitated before exiting.

"One more thing," he interjected as casually as he could, "Is it snowing in Lys'va?"

"I... I don't know," Yakimov replied after a brief moment's earnest contemplation. "I'm sorry."

"Never mind," Sokolov concluded. "Thank you."

With a heavy sigh, the Investigator stepped into the musty hallway and slowly closed the cell door behind him.

From the other side of the thick wall he heard Yakimov's faint words of parting:

"Goodbye, Investigator Sokolov. Goodbye."

Chapter Fifteen

Nicholas Sokolov's Journal — 1919

I remember an evening a thousand years ago. In the dizzy hours between darkness and dawn, a full winter moon was hanging low in a clear night sky over the sleeping city of St. Petersburg. Its soft golden glow against the deep darkness of evening burnished the fresh fallen snow that stretched in a blanket of white as far as we could see. The reflected iridescence actually lit he facades of the old buildings that lined the empty square around us like so many silent sentries.

Sergé, Dmitri and myself. All three of us floundering happily about in that deep snow...drunk on vodka and youthful exuberance. Our years together as university classmates had at last come to a joyous end. I think perhaps we were as intoxicated from the newfound sense of irrepressible freedom as we were from that long night of drinking.

We were three brash young men—Children of the Light—on the brink of a thousand hopeful tomorrows...and so, with arms casually draped about each other's shoulders in happy comradeship, we stumbled along, singing to the night sky, thumbing our noses at any obstacle that might possibly await us in the years ahead, and all the while we danced the dance of joyous liberation!

Long years have come and gone since that late night of unrepentant foolishness...and sadly, all but one of those brash young men have been swallowed up by Death. The ravages of war have long since swept aside those happy memories, burying them so deep in the common grave of remembrance that they rarely surface anymore.

That is most probably the reason that what I still remember about that one drunken night so long ago is that, for one solitary evening, only Happiness existed...along with a well-intentioned but misconceived sense of invincibility. I think perhaps it was the best evening of our lives.

Dear God, how it would have changed everything—shaken loose the very stars from their fixed place in the heavens—if only

166

we had known that it was the last time we would all be alive together!

I have heard it said that the past never dies...that it still exists, somehow, in another layer of time that drifts eternally alongside the present. It is an occasional consolation, then, to imagine that Sergé, Dmitri and I are alive there...in that golden yet distant yesterday...still young, still foolish, still free...forever.

#

Suddenly aware of another presence in the room, Nicholas Sokolov glanced up from the paperwork on his desk to find Boris Gorev, leather valise in hand, posed casually in the open doorway.

"There is a window in the upstairs bedroom of this house—" Gorev smiled derisively, "the room on the top floor—once occupied by Nicholas and Alexandra. On the windowsill is a cross..."

"A reverse swastika, actually. Drawn in pencil," Sokolov interrupted, fixing his chilly gaze on the figure in his doorway. "Beneath the swastika, words and numbers '*17/30 April 1918*'. The Imperial family's first day in this house. The handwriting? Definitely feminine, most probably Alexandra's. Shall I tell you which hand she used when she wrote it?"

"Bravo, dear boy!" Gorev practically cooed as he placed his valise on the floor of the threshold and glided into the room. "Such marvelous attention to detail! Oh, they said you were good. But YOU, my dear boy, are better at it than even they suspect." Gorev paused next to one of the windows of the room to slowly remove his gloves. "However," he continued casually, "and just between the two of us—I wouldn't bedazzle them with too much brilliance, if I were you."

Sokolov's eyes were cold as ice. He seethed only two words: "Sit down."

"Ah, yes," Gorev replied with a weary sigh, "you're making a rather pointed reference to our little appointment, I should think. Well, as much as I would love to linger and bandy semantics, I'm afraid that simply won't be possible."

"Sit...down," Sokolov repeated again through clinched teeth.

"Ever been to Berlin?" Gorev continued with undeterred jauntiness, "Quite lovely this time of year."

With eyes narrowing to threatening slits, Sokolov slowly rose to his feet. "I will not ask you again."

167

"Oh yes, I know," Gorev smirked, indicating the holster hanging from the Investigator's belt. "You'll draw your revolver. I hear you're becoming quite adept at that. Of course, when all else fails, brute force is so effective. Effective, that is, only when it produces fear." Leaning towards Sokolov for emphasis, Gorev's lips curled into a twisted and defiant smile. "That is why, dear boy, your efforts are quite wasted on me."

"I wouldn't be too sure," the Investigator warned with soft menace.

"But that is your job, isn't it?" Gorev chuckled, "Not to be too sure of anything. As for me, there are several things I am quite certain of. One is this: there is a train bound for Berlin, promptly departing Ekaterinburg this afternoon at three o'clock. I am sure of that fact because it was scheduled to leave at precisely that time two days ago. I'm equally certain of one other thing: my wife, Maria, and I will be on it. I've merely come to bid you 'Au Revoir and to wish you well on whatever remains of your little...investigation."

With a slight nod of his head, Gorev then turned on his heels and headed for the open doorway.

"You go nowhere without my authority," Sokolov snapped. "Try it and you'll be shot."

Gorev halted and slowly turned to face the Investigator once more. "My, my," he sniffed disdainfully. "Violence is becoming all the rage these days, isn't it? A sure sign the good Admiral's Ship of State is listing rather decidedly to port. Can't you tell? Things are becoming rather off-balance, wouldn't you say? Precisely why I took the liberty of prevailing upon the good Admiral...before the ship does begin that last, terrifying nose-dive into oblivion...to grant me...how shall we put it? An indefinite leave of absence...which he has done and set his signature thereto...and which I now present to you."

With a click of his heels and a slight bow, the smirking Gorev withdrew a folded document from his coat pocket and formally presented it to Sokolov. "If you're smart...and I think you are..." he concluded with his patronizing air, "you'll have Kolchak make up one of these for you as well. You may need it, dear boy, sooner than you think."

"I've been given complete authority in this investigation," Sokolov shot back as he snatched the paper from Gorev's hand. "No one is exempt." Tossing the document back to Gorev without even bothering to read it, the Investigator concluded bluntly, "As far as I'm concerned that changes nothing."

Gorev's mocking laughter was girlish and shrill. "As far as you are concerned?" he derided with an expression of mock amazement. "Still haven't pieced it together, have you?" The smile vanished completely from Gorev's face. His features grew cold and his eyes were instantly glowing with undisguised contempt. "You were never concerned, dear boy, with anything. Not in the beginning and certainly not now. Shall I tell you what you are? Merely window dressing—nothing more. You have power to do only what you're told. You have permission to say only what you are allowed to say. That is all."

Gorev turned his back to Sokolov and strode to the open doorway. Pausing only long enough to retrieve his valise, he turned back to Sokolov with one last formal bow. "If it's truth you seek," he sneered with obvious relish, "let me share this revelation with you now. You are nothing. You never were."

Gorev spun smartly on his shiny heels and disappeared into the deep shadows of the hallway.

#

Admiral Kolchak, in his best dress uniform, stood before an assembled group of military officers. Cognac and cigars were being savored as military maps were shuffled and perused.

"And so you see..." Kolchak was explaining as though addressing a classroom of unseasoned cadets, "War, in the popular sense of course, is generally defined as a conflict among political groups, sufficiently equal in power to keep the outcome uncertain for a time, and involving hostilities of considerable magnitude and duration. As such, War has actually become a sort of world-wide institution, more or less, recognized both in custom and law."

Casually thumping his cigar in a nearby ashtray, the Admiral enjoyed another sip of cognac. "I want to make it clear in this case," he continued, "that I'm not referring to armed conflicts with primitive peoples. Hostilities with primitive peoples are more generally referred to as pacifications. Hostilities with small states are merely interventions or reprisals. With internal groups, they are rebellions or insurrections."

Swirling the cognac in his glass, he strolled comfortably among the assembly.

"Whatever the category of conflict," he continued, "one rule applies to all: you are at a great disadvantage when you fight with those who have nothing to lose." He took another moment to puff on his cigar before resuming, "Finally," he smiled, "any of the previously mentioned categories, assuming, of course, that the resistance was sufficiently strong or protracted, could ultimately be referred to as a 'War'."

Kolchak squared his broad shoulders and paused briefly for dramatic effect.

"Gentlemen," he announced somberly, "make no mistake. We are at war with Lenin's Bolsheviks."

The door to the smoky conference room swung open with sudden force and Nicholas Sokolov strode unannounced into the midst of the startled assembly. Totally bewildered at this unexpected intrusion, the attending officers deferentially made way for the tenacious Investigator as he plowed through their midst.

Coming to a halt in front of his superior officer, Sokolov demanded, "Why am I not allowed to question Boris Gorev?"

The attending officers, in anticipation of a reply, immediately shifted their baffled gazes to Admiral Kolchak.

"Investigator Sokolov," the Admiral beamed graciously, "do come in."

"That man has information vital to this investigation," Sokolov continued as if totally unaware of the others in the room. "Why am I not allowed to question him?"

Kolchak calmly placed his glass of cognac on the conference table and cordially nodded to the others in the room. "If you will excuse us," he announced softly.

Sokolov held his ground as the assembled military personnel obediently vacated the room, filing past the Investigator in dutiful silence.

When the door had finally closed on the last departing officer, Kolchak, languidly puffing on his cigar, leveled his stern gaze at Sokolov.

"Boris Gorev?" Admiral Kolchak began again, "But I understand you have questioned him."

"He has a great deal more to disclose," Sokolov interjected, "believe me."

"That may very well be," Kolchak demurred with a shrug, "but, whatever he has to disclose will not be disclosed to you. Sorry."

"That man is a material witness," Sokolov bristled.

"To what?" Kolchak demanded. "What has he seen? Distant glimpses of a captive Romanov in an upstairs window of the Ipatiev House? Or perhaps one of the infrequent trains leaving Tyumen station? Such vital information!"

The Admiral stepped closer to the Investigator as his voice purposefully rose in unmistakable rebuke. "And his sources; what of them?" he sneered. "A chambermaid whose closest contact with the Imperial family was their soiled bed linen? I believe, my dear Sokolov, you could do a bit better than Boris Gorev."

Sokolov recoiled slightly but kept his defiant gaze locked on the Admiral. "You're certainly well informed," he countered evenly.

"I make it a point to be," Kolchak shot back. "The general population may cling to fairy tales. Governments prefer facts! In the real world, not everyone is allowed to live happily ever after."

The Admiral paused long enough to puff once more on his cigar. "By the way," he sighed as if the information he was about to impart was only of passing importance, "one of the men you've also been questioning—prisoner by the name of Yakimov. Found this morning in his cell. Last night while he slept, someone slit his throat."

Sokolov couldn't help but recoil at the shocking news. He tried not to betray a reaction of any kind, but knew he hadn't succeeded.

"I still formally request," he began once more as if the words themselves actually helped to reinforce his determination, "to be allowed to question Boris Gorev."

"No," Kolchak replied firmly.

"Then I insist on knowing why," Sokolov demanded.

"You insist?" Kolchak repeated in mock surprise. "Really?"

Sokolov steadied himself. "How else do you expect me to bring you the truth?"

"You're an intelligent man," Kolchak shrugged, "you'll find a way."

All barriers were down now. Although these two military men were obviously granting themselves unspoken permission to dispense with the limits with which rank would have normally framed such a conversation, neither intended to give an inch.

"You, too, are an intelligent man," Sokolov challenged the Admiral, "Would you be satisfied with that answer?"

Kolchak could not disguise his regard for the question—or his begrudging respect for the determined Investigator. "You're a real pain in the ass," he finally admitted, "but, you know? I still like you!"

Kolchak leaned back against the conference table and took another unhurried puff of his cigar. He studied his stubborn adversary for a few moments more.

"Very well," he finally yielded with a dismissive wave of his hand. "No attempts to rescue the Romanovs were ever made by Boris Gorev. When the Imperial family was moved here from Tobolsk, he was conveniently arrested, held for a few days and released, providing him with a suitable alibi for doing precisely nothing."

As far as Sokolov was concerned, the implications of Kolchak's admission were earth-shattering. Having forced this insubordinate confrontation on the good Admiral with no expectation of ever succeeding, he could now only stand in mute astonishment. The truth had been unhesitatingly supplied, and in the most unadorned terms imaginable. The stunned Investigator was momentarily at a complete loss—struck dumb in the face of such unexpected frankness.

Sokolov actually had to take a step backward in order to retain his balance. "My God," he finally managed to stammer, "Gorev is a spy...for us. He's been working for the White Army all along."

"As far as that's concerned," Kolchak replied rather blandly, "I'm afraid you'll have to draw your own conclusions. I may neither confirm nor deny what you choose to believe. In point of fact, this little conversation of ours has never taken place."

"He was never intended to rescue the Romanovs at all," Sokolov blurted, still reeling under the true significance of the revelation, "he was only supposed to gain their confidence and pass information along to you. That's all he was ever meant to do, wasn't it?"

"There must be some convenient platitude about necessity and strange bedfellows," Kolchak smirked, "but I won't bore you."

The Admiral, obviously relishing the moment, retrieved his glass, lifted it to his lips and finished off the last of the cognac in silent triumph.

"One other point of interest worth mentioning in this non-existent conversation," he finally concluded smugly. "Boris Gorev is also working as a secret agent for the Germans. We've known it for some time."

The Admiral said the words as though he actually savored the way they formed themselves in his mouth. As far as Kolchak was concerned, Sokolov's stunned reaction to the news was well worth the price of Gorev's callous betrayal. The sudden pleasure the Admiral allowed himself as he confided his dark secret to the young Investigator seemed a sweeter victory than even he could have possibly imagined. Military might had triumphed over intellect as Kolchak always knew it would. The meek might indeed inherit the earth, but only when he had finished with it.

"A double agent," Sokolov had to say the words, "and you've done nothing?"

"The information Gorev receives from us," Kolchak explained with some irritation, "is naturally calculated to pass to the Germans precisely what we wish them to know. It's—what?—a productive arrangement."

"But the Romanovs?" Sokolov pressed...needing to hear Kolchak verbalize the unthinkable.

"Clearly, it is in our interest to accept the notion that all of the family died," the Admiral went on obligingly. "No survivors. However, we are aware—as you must certainly be—of one particularly tenacious rumor. It's suggested that one of the Tsar's daughters survived the evening of July 16th. Well, of course, you see the nuisance. As propaganda, the slaying of the Romanovs could certainly be used to expose Lenin's Bolsheviks as vicious murderers of helpless women and children. Unfortunately, such a move would also have the effect of elevating the Romanovs to the status of martyred saints. Not quite what we had in mind. No, Investigator Sokolov; if murder has been committed, then quite obviously there has to be a murderer."

"And how fortunate for our side if the evidence should point to Lenin," the Investigator concluded aloud.

"My dear Nicholas," the Admiral grinned in mock surprise, "what an absolutely novel idea!"

Kolchak's grin vanished instantly. "What is needed," he advised Sokolov, "is a public inquiry with a private premise."

"That all of the Romanovs are dead."

"Not one survived."

"And if one did?"

"In that case," Kolchak replied evenly, "we would very much like to know where *she* is. But...there are no survivors, are there? Proof of that fact is essential. Yes? The Romanovs are worth more to us dead than alive. All of them."

"What is it you really want from me?" Sokolov demanded more out of mounting frustration than anger.

"Why, Investigator Sokolov," the Admiral gasped sarcastically, "the truth, of course. After all, your truth is Truth Eternal."

"How will you know it is the truth," Sokolov demanded, "because I say so?"

"Because you *have* to say so!" Kolchak exploded triumphantly. "I know you, Investigator Sokolov. You'll bring me the truth for two reasons. First, you're too proud of your precious reputation not to. Secondly, you'd like nothing more than to beat me at my own game. Intellect over military might! What an opportunity for someone like you. This is the most important assignment of your career. One of the greatest mysteries of the century! And you know what? I don't believe you could bear the thought that history might possibly remember you as a failure. No. You couldn't walk away from this assignment if you wanted to! So—it finally comes down to a question of trust. Wouldn't you say? Between the two of us."

"Trust?" Sokolov blurted angrily. "There's no such thing! Not anymore. Trust was one of the first casualties of the revolution!"

"Warfare is based on deception," Kolchak fired back, "and moderation of any kind in warfare is imbecility. We used what was necessary to win!"

"Have you never stopped to consider the price?" Sokolov implored.

"For what purpose?" Kolchak roared, slamming his fist on the conference table. "We're fighting a war...for our lives! Face to face with your enemy on a battlefield is hardly the time or place to debate the morality of your actions. You either kill your enemy or your enemy kills you! And to do that, you will use any weapon at your disposal. You'd better be willing to, because your enemy certainly will. That's why, if you do find the Grand Duchess, you'll only finish what the Cheka executioners began. If the real truth is what you seek, let me give you a bit of it. If you find Anastasia alive, you'll kill her yourself...with your bare hands if you have to. You will have no choice. Do you know why? Because as long as one member of the Imperial family lives, there will always be a chance that Russia might once again belong to the Romanovs. And as much as you hate me, I believe you loathe that possibility even more."

"Then we've become no better than they were," Sokolov cried out in agony, "What difference does it make who wins anymore?"

"The winners get to live," Kolchak thundered. "That's the difference! Win or lose. Live or die. Stop to think and you're a dead man. Instinct, Nicholas Sokolov, is the only thing that keeps you alive!"

"And honest, rational thought?" Sokolov bellowed back. "Where does that fit into your very unique concept of moral judgment?"

"Wars live on lies!" Kolchak roared. "Do you think Lenin cares that he just might offend the world's concept of wartime morality? 'Cancel the revolution, Comrades! I have two tickets to the Bolshoi!'"

Kolchak was now nose to nose with Sokolov. "Let me tell you something, my dear idealistic friend," the Admiral laughed incredulously, "Lenin doesn't give a shit! And the only person who cares less about wartime morality than he does is standing here in front of you!"

"Your truth!" Sokolov erupted. "Your truth; not mine!"

"Men grow tired of sleep. They grow tired of music and dancing," Kolchak sneered. "Men can even grow tired of making love! But if history has taught us anything, it is that Mankind will never in a million years grow tired of war!"

"No," Sokolov bellowed back, both of his fists raised heavenward in a frozen stance of utter defiance.

"Then show me a better way," Kolchak furiously dared the Investigator. "I'm waiting. Tell me something I don't already know."

Sokolov, still trembling with barely contained rage, considered his reply for only a moment.

"They could've sunk the Titanic under the weight of what you don't know," Sokolov replied with sudden and softer emphasis. "Sergé Tegleva, Vladimir Karlovna, and Paul Eugenivitch," he continued evenly, "are those names familiar to you?"

"They mean nothing to me," Kolchak snorted.

"All three were loyal monarchist officers. Our men! They secretly traveled to Tobolsk during the Tsar's detainment to gather information for us. All three were subsequently caught and executed by the Bolsheviks."

"So?" Kolchak shrugged. "This is war. Russians die every day."

"Do all of them die after secret meetings with Boris Gorev?" Sokolov seethed in utter contempt. "Because these three men did."

Reaching into his jacket, Sokolov withdrew a thick envelope. Offering it to Kolchak, the Investigator went on. "I cabled for their dossiers. It won't mean anything to you, but I used to know one of those men. An absolutely brilliant mind. He was sent to Tobolsk with two other undercover operatives in October a little over a year ago. Their contact was Boris Gorev. He turned them over to the Bolsheviks!"

Sokolov slammed the envelope onto Kolchak's desk. "It's all there," he continued fiercely.

The Admiral merely glowered at the seething Investigator.

Suddenly, Sokolov's anger gave way to a quieter resolve. "The first day I arrived here," he softly admonished Kolchak, "you touched a book and asked me to tell you its title. Do you remember?"

"As a matter of fact, I do," Kolchak replied icily. "You said it was *The Art of War*. How's that?"

"You should've read it," Sokolov advised sternly, "because it argues that the highest form of warfare is winning without fighting a single armed battle. It says you can achieve victory by exhausting an adversary's resources, dividing the loyalty of its people, demoralizing its leadership, and ultimately 'breaking the enemy's resistance'. Sound familiar?"

Kolchak snickered incredulously. "The original Bolshevik strategy? Is that what you mean? Lenin's master plan? Brilliant deduction, Investigator! So what?"

"So," Sokolov replied, "you burn books. Lenin reads them! He reads…and he learns."

The Investigator glanced at the thick envelope lying on the Admiral's desk then shifted his accusatory gaze once more to Kolchak.

"Boris Gorev already works for you and Germany," Sokolov affirmed. "What you never stopped to consider was the possibility that he's also been working for the Bolsheviks as well."

Sokolov paused in order for the full import of his words to strike Admiral Kolchak broadside with the greatest force possible.

"Boris Gorev is a triple agent," he concluded as if twisting a serrated knife's blade in Kolchak's gut. "He has been all this time."

The Investigator couldn't help punctuating his next words with a lethal smile. "Do you know what Lenin's most probably doing right now?" he asked pointedly. "My guess is that he's sitting at a desk in some warm room of the Kremlin, going over every one of your secret maps and war plans. He knows your strengths and your weaknesses, and he'll use every bit of what he knows to bring you to your knees."

The Investigator spun on his heels, strode to the door of Kolchak's office and swung it open. He paused briefly and turned back to once more face the stunned Admiral who now seemed frozen in place with absolute shock.

"Russians die every day?" Sokolov concluded bitterly, "At least now you know why."

With unconcealed satisfaction, the Investigator turned his back on the staggered Admiral and strode out of the room.

Chapter Sixteen

Sokolov's Journal—1919

May I tell you something? Occasionally I am haunted...for lack of a better word, let us say by a reoccurring dream. In this dream, God reveals Himself to me. Not only does He manifest Himself in such majesty as to render description impossible, He also, for some unknown reason, actually confides in me. The two of us sit in comfortable chairs before some friendly fire and talk together.

Suddenly, God becomes amused by something. He smiles.

I say, "What is it that amuses you so?"

In the subsequent hush that abruptly engulfs an endless universe, God softly tells me of a marvelous joke He has played...is playing...on all mankind.

It is this: for some reason, known only to Him, He has led humanity to believe that their dreams are but fantasy; their waking hours real.

But you see, God then whispers to me that exactly the opposite is true. What we believe to be our dreams, those inconstant and unexplained fragments of our imaginings are actually reality, and what we so earnestly believe to be reality is nothing more than the sum total of our disjointed fantasies—our dreams—that drift like clouds through our empty minds as we sleep.

I awake from this revelation in a cold sweat, trembling...with God's mocking laughter still echoing in my ears.

Totally spent and dispirited, Nicholas Sokolov stood alone in the empty upstairs room of the Ipatiev House—the corner bedroom once occupied by Nicholas and Alexandra. His face was a mask of undisguised anguish as he quietly regarded the sparse furnishings.

The oppressive stillness of the heavy air seemed almost suffocating. The familiar pungent mustiness that had once only haunted the darkest recesses of the house now seemed to suffuse everything, so much so that it was even causing a burning sensation in his lungs. But this was precisely why he had returned to this particular room. He wanted to banish the numbness that had so overtaken his being. He stood there laboring to sear the profound remorse he was experiencing into the very core of his soul.

The confrontation with Admiral Kolchak had been an emotionally draining affair. And yet, Sokolov was still struggling in silent torment to dredge up whatever remaining emotions he could possibly muster. He wanted to know and feel it all. The humiliation and terrible sorrow, the guilt and pain—he wanted not only to experience it, but to assume the full burden of its emotional weight…to finally take upon himself the collected sins of Mother Russia. He wanted to somehow believe that this solitary act of penance might somehow appease the restless spirits of the Romanovs, and that they, in turn, might finally see fit to consecrate his effort by affording him some sense of forgiveness and peace.

It was false hope, and ultimately he knew it. The sad truth was that even as his tormented soul struggled so desperately to find some degree of exoneration, his heart was already accepting the sinking realization that he would most probably never know true peace again. From this moment until the end of his life, he knew that absolution was destined to be nothing more than the fleeting shadow of an unattainable dream.

Suddenly, in the distance, Sokolov heard the shrill sound of a locomotive whistle slicing the air. A train was pulling into the Ekaterinburg station.

Sokolov's eyes widened with the instant realization that this was the train Boris Gorev had so smugly referred to…the train that would take Gorev and his wife away from Ekaterinburg and beyond the reach of Sokolov's legal jurisdiction. Within a matter of minutes, the whistle would sound again and the train would leave the depot.

A fit of rage instantly overtook Sokolov's entire being, filling him with terrible resolve. Madly pivoting from where he stood, the furious Investigator bellowed his defiance into the empty air and dashed out of the silent room.

#

The sleepy Ekaterinburg train depot was teaming with feverish activity. A black locomotive, belched clouds of steam, was clanking to a stop as soldiers from the White Army, hurriedly collecting knapsacks, weapons and various pieces of equipment, darted to and fro like bees protecting a busy hive. Horses were being herded up ramps and into waiting cattle cars as machine gun placements on several flat-bed train cars were also being quickly assembled, sand-bagged and manned by anxious soldiers. A few civilian passengers, waiting to board, were presenting necessary papers to the supervising military personnel. A handful of uniformed officers were barking orders and directing the hurried activity as best they could. Minutes were precious, and they were quickly ticking by.

Into the din of this frenetic commotion, Boris Gorev's automobile rattled into view and chugged to a stop near the depot's wooden platform. Gorev and his wife promptly disembarked and, carrying a few valises and bundles, began to make their way towards one of the waiting train cars.

As all of this was taking place, Nicholas Sokolov was dashing like a madman through the empty Voznesensky Prospekt in a desperate race to reach the depot before the train pulled out. He was being propelled by nothing more than sheer determination—prodded on by the single thought of confronting Boris Gorev once more before he and his wife, Maria, left Ekaterinburg forever. Nothing else mattered.

His lungs almost bursting now, Sokolov finally raced into the railway yard and continued his mad sprint toward the waiting train. His aching legs churned...fighting the physical exhaustion that was beginning to overtake him.

It was at that moment...just as Boris Gorev was hoisting himself onto the steps of the train car, that he caught sight of Sokolov, angrily pushing his way through luggage carts and shoving people aside as he came. Gorev, held fast by the sight, had no time to escape the approaching storm. He remained haplessly frozen on the steps of the train car, watching in stunned disbelief as the furious Investigator continued to close the distance between them.

In only several moments more, Nicholas Sokolov arrived, heaving for labored breath, at the foot of Gorev's train car. Skidding to a stop and pulling himself into a threateningly upright posture, he focused the full force of his terrible gaze on his strangely ambivalent adversary.

"Do you know," Boris Gorev began with a voice rising just above the din of the loading platform, "even during the coldest days of winter, there are actually men who swim in the Moscow River?"

Sokolov, still desperately struggling for breath, could merely glare at the blasé passenger now perched only a few feet above him.

"Of course," Gorev continued, foolishly taking several steps downward, "I've never witnessed this bizarre ceremony personally, and therefore couldn't tell you precisely what those gentlemen resemble when they emerge from their icy aberrations. But I imagine they must look rather like you…just now. Reality can often have an equally chilling effect."

The next move was Sokolov's, and was executed with such amazing swiftness that Boris Gorev had no time to think, much less react. In one fearsome lunge, the outraged Investigator grabbed Gorev by the lapels of his morning coat and violently yanked him from his perch on the steps of the train car. Sokolov's fist then caught the reeling Gorev with a savage uppercut to the chin. The impact lifted Gorev completely off the wooden floor of the platform and propelled his body backward with such force that it slammed into a waiting luggage cart, scattering suitcases and hat boxes onto the deck of the depot. Gorev, his arms and legs splayed like a downed scarecrow, lay sprawled on the muddy platform in a disheveled heap.

Sokolov, his fist still tightly clinched in silent readiness, towered threateningly over his fallen adversary as if daring him to rise.

Blood trickled from Gorev's bottom lip as his eyelids finally fluttered open and his body twitched back into consciousness. Still reeling from the ferocity of the attack, it took a few moments more for him to focus completely on the silent figure looming over him. Trembling slightly, Gorev pulled a silk handkerchief from the breast pocket of his morning coat and dabbed at his bloodied lip.

"And I was so hoping we would be able to part in more amicable fashion," Gorev finally coughed nervously as if to clear his throat.

"Were you?"

"At least, I'd hoped," Gorev replied as, with some difficulty, he struggled to his feet. "You see, unlike the others you've encountered here, I was the only one who never lied to you."

"You heartless son-of-a-bitch," Sokolov snarled as he took another threatening step toward Gorev.

"I swear," Gorev protested defensively, covering his face with upraised arms. "Oh, I may not have volunteered the complete truth on my own. But I always answered honestly whenever you asked a question. A son of a bitch? Perhaps. But heartless? Never."

Steadying himself as much as he could, Gorev concluded with reclaimed haughtiness, "That's why, when I leave today, I will do so with my dignity intact. I only hope the same for you."

Sokolov squared his shoulders and leaned into Gorev as closely as possible. "Whatever dignity you take from this place when you leave today, has been stolen off the bodies of the Romanovs."

The train whistle shrieked its second blast. Gorev hurriedly dusted off his coat and pulled his body upright as best he could. "My dignity, Sir, has been purchased," he hissed, "and for a price no one will ever know."

"Not exactly true," the Investigator replied with lethal directness, "Sergé Tegleva knew. So did Vladimir Karlovna and Paul Eugenivitch. And now… I know as well. You may leave this place with something, Comrade, but it will most assuredly not be dignity. Take that thought to your grave."

Gorev's eyes were instantly alive with silent fury. Sokolov anticipated an outburst, but received instead only a muted reply.

"In that case," Gorev whispered contemptuously, "allow me to leave you with something I do possess: '*It never snows in Lys'va this time of year.*' That was the correct response to Strovka's question."

The import of that single statement hit the Investigator like a thunderbolt. Still, his hands responded instinctively, again collaring Boris Gorev by the lapels and jerking him close.

"You really expect me to believe you?"

"Dear boy," Gorev managed with an all-too-familiar sneer, "I wouldn't waste a moment like this on a lie."

Pulling himself free from the stunned Investigator's grasp, Gorev made his way back up the narrow steps of the train car. Pausing on the small landing, he turned once more to Sokolov with a formal bow and one last mocking admonition: "You may take that thought with you to your grave as well."

In the next instant, Boris Gorev—along with whatever secrets he still possessed—disappeared with his wife into the shadows of the train car. The two men would never meet again. Nicholas Sokolov, speechless and transfixed, heard the third shrill whistle of the locomotive as its wheels began to grind away in billowing clouds of steam.

Slowly at first, then gradually picking up speed, the train, along with its occupants, finally began to fade into the misty distance of an empty Siberian landscape.

Chapter Seventeen

"You do not know, anymore,
what there is to hope for
and what there is to await.
And so there is no one but God.
Let it be as He wills it."

Nicholas II

It was mid-afternoon when Sokolov, sitting alone in his room, wearily glanced up from the latest stack of files he'd been reviewing since early morning. Still haunted by Boris Gorev's parting words, the Investigator had poured himself into his work for the past several days, spending long and tedious hours digging through boxes of collected evidence and once more scouring endless stacks of thick files. This was partially done to distract himself from the unspent anger he still harbored, but for the most part, it was an attempt to revitalize his focus on the investigation itself. He still lived in the hope of finally uncovering that one hidden clue that would at last solve the nagging mystery.

He knew the answer was there somewhere...like his story of the two fish who had failed to comprehend what water was. The thought that he had possibly already stumbled over the answer without realizing it spurred him ever onward in what often seemed an endlessly frustrating search.

The afternoon sun, creeping lower now in the azure sky over Ekaterinburg, was already burnishing the trees, rooftops, and surrounding hills with a soft, golden glaze. Sliding his chair back from the table, the Investigator slowly rose to his feet and arched his back only to wince at the dull ache brought on by too many hours spent in a sitting position. Strolling idly to the window, he let his hands hang limply by his sides and then shook them several times to stimulate increased blood flow.

Pausing a few moments more to take in the familiar sights beyond his window, he watched as a gentle gust of wind tumbled a few scattered leaves from one end of the empty courtyard to the other.

"How like our lives on this earth," he softly whispered to himself as he leaned forward to gently rest his brow on the cold windowpane.

Closing his eyes, he strained to hear any noise that might be coming from the street, but as usual, the wooden stockade fence muffled or totally blocked out most of the sounds of life emanating from the world beyond its formidable perimeter. As always, since the first day of his arrival, there was only the sound of distant wind ...mournful and ever present.

Returning at last to his cluttered table, Sokolov reached for the first thing his hand happened to find. As fate decreed, it was a worn photograph that had been attached to one of the many dossiers he had reviewed earlier that day. The Investigator rubbed his good eye and brought the photo a bit nearer to his face for better focus.

A familiar pair of cold, unblinking eyes stared back at him from the photograph while the thin lips below an aquiline nose had shaped themselves into what could only be described as a sinister smile.

Sokolov knew only too well the gaunt and haunting face that glared back at him. It belonged to Jacob Yurovsky, the former Commandant of the Ipatiev House...the man who, by all accounts, had planned and carried out the systematic execution of the Imperial family.

As Sokolov quietly studied the photograph in more detail, he began to review a few of the things he had learned about this methodical executioner.

Jacob Mikhailovich Yurovsky was something of a political enigma. He had been born on June 19, 1878, in the Siberian City of Tomsk, the eighth of ten children. His father, who was very strict and deeply religious, had worked as a glazer. His mother had been a seamstress. With ten children to care for, both mother and father often worked to the point of exhaustion.

"From the time of my birth," Yurovsky had written, *"my place in life was settled as a worker, just as it had been for my father. There was no escape. I would often sit in the doorway of our apartment thinking what a difficult life we lived. At the time I thought it possible that one could go to the Emperor and tell him how hard our lives were. But of course we would then have been told that such hardships were sent from Heaven."*

In 1891, by a strange twist of fate, Nicholas II, then the future Tsar of Russia, arrived in Tomsk from a tour of the Far East.

Yurovsky, only thirteen years old at the time, actually got to see him in person. As church bells pealed and crowds of people cheered, the teenager had watched in silent awe from the doorway of the watch shop where he worked as Nicholas Romanov passed by in a brightly painted troika. Yurovsky had then happily followed the jubilant crowd to the Governor's house where Nicholas finally appeared on a high balcony.

"*I remember how handsome the heir was*," Yurovsky had written, "*with his little, neat brown beard. I cheered loudly as he nodded and waved to us.*" And yet, only six years later, Jacob Yurovsky would lead a workers' strike, the first such protest Tomsk had ever witnessed, and twenty-two years after that, by his own account, he would fire a single bullet into the Tsar's chest, killing him instantly.

Letting the worn photograph slip from his hands to gently come to rest on the cluttered table and glancing again at the window of his room, Nicholas Sokolov was suddenly seized by an idea. According to the dossier, after spending some years as a watchmaker, Jacob Yurovsky had decided to become a photographer, and had actually plied his trade from a small shop in Ekaterinburg. By chance, the shop's address had been preserved on an old, hand-tinted postcard which had been included in the material Sokolov had so meticulously collected. And so, in what would prove to be a most fortuitous impulse, the Investigator decided to visit Yurovsky's photography studio that very afternoon.

In just a little over an hour, Sokolov found himself standing in front of a small, shuttered studio located on one of the city's many side streets. The golden hue that spread across Ekaterinburg and saturated everything within sight seemed deeper now. It was late afternoon and most of the shopkeepers and workers were beginning to close up for the day.

After knocking loudly on the door several times to no avail, Sokolov tried the doorknob. To his surprise, it turned and the door easily swung open.

Pausing on the threshold, the Investigator peered into the gloom and called out several times.

"Hello? Is anyone here?"

Silence was the only response, so after a brief moment's hesitation, Sokolov stepped quietly inside and gently closed the door behind him.

He found himself in a deserted room still cluttered with paraphernalia a photographer might use—a dusty backdrop curtain, several rusting light fixtures, a table, and a few wooden chairs. In a far corner, leaning against a wall, Sokolov spied an old wooden full-plate box camera, covered with cobwebs and still perched on a wooden tripod. It appeared to the Investigator that the studio had been hastily abandoned.

Sokolov strolled over to the camera for a closer look. It was an old box camera with collapsible bellows and rear focusing. Cameras of this type were usually made out of mahogany and used glass plates instead of film. Focusing was carried out by adjusting the ground glass back's position forward or backward until the image on the matte screen became sharp. The lens had no shutter; instead, the lens cap was simply removed and replaced to control the exposure time.

The Investigator carefully moved the camera and tripod to the middle of the deserted room. He then took a position behind the camera, leaned forward, and peered into the rear glass. After a few minor adjustments of the bellows, the image of the room's far wall came into focus. It was upside-down, of course, but the details were sharp and clear.

Leaving the camera, Sokolov then moved to a nearby chair and took a seat. It might have seemed foolish to some, but the Investigator wanted to quietly absorb what he could of the room's ambience in an effort to assemble a mental picture of the various activities Yurovsky would have undertaken here on a daily basis. The Investigator was of the opinion that routines tended to reveal a great deal about a person's nature and overall disposition. There was, he surmised, a certain mindset to grasping the rudiments of photography that seemed very well suited to what Sokolov knew about Yurovsky. The practical application of the craft itself tended to be very methodical, with many variants to be considered in creating a perfectly composed photograph.

As his silent gaze moved slowly around the deserted studio, Sokolov began to connect several immediate impressions with a few disjointed facts he had previously collected. In doing so, a clearer mental image of the man himself began to emerge.

At the age of twelve, Jacob Yurovsky had been taken out of grammar school by his father and apprenticed to the town's best watchmaker where he would work a grueling sixty-hour week for the next ten years in a jeweler's shop. Yet, this was precisely where his meticulous attention to the smallest of details was born and nurtured.

The tiny and exact inner workings of a watch required, among other things, a keen perception of how the many intricate pieces fitted together to form the finished timepiece. Everything had to finally come together in perfect balance and synchronicity. The very same traits that Yurovsky employed as a watchmaker would eventually serve him equally as well once he began to delve into photography.

And yet, the long hours of tedious and repetitive work in the jeweler's shop fueled a growing resentment that Yurovsky would carry for the rest of his life. After leading the ill-fated worker's strike in Tomsk, he was arrested and sent to prison. Though he served only a few months, it was enough to fan the flames of his inner rage. When Jacob Yurovsky emerged from his brief imprisonment, he did so as a full-fledged revolutionary.

Unfortunately, he was now also considered an outcast in Tomsk. No longer welcomed at his old job, Yurovsky spent the next few months wandering across Siberia—a lost man with no idealistic cause to satiate his restless hunger for a self-defining purpose. His aimless wanderings finally led him to Ekaterinburg where he found employment in another jeweler's shop and met his future wife whom he married in 1904. In short order, he also became a father of two young children. As his family grew, so did his burning sense of injustice. The Revolution that followed one year later seemed God's answer to this burgeoning revolutionary's fervent prayers.

"*My children*," he would write, "*deserved a life different from the one I was forced to live, a life of freedom and hope.*" It didn't take long for these sentiments to drive Yurovsky into the welcoming arms of the Bolsheviks. He joined the party in 1905.

In 1915 Yurovsky was drafted into the medical corps of the 198th Perm Infantry Regiment and sent to the Carpathian front. Though he would eventually desert the army, those who knew him say he came back from the war a very different man. One friend recalled that it seemed he had lost all decency.

There would be other hardships, self-imposed exiles, arrests, and fateful brushes with the cruel brutalities of war before Yurovsky reached his fortieth birthday, a mere two weeks before he became Commandant of the Ipatiev House. The watchmaker-turned-photographer had also become a dark and hardened man committed, as he later wrote—'*to settle the Revolution's score with the Imperial House for centuries of suffering'*. When he joined the Regional Cheka in the fall of 1917, his murderous sense of purpose was at last able to cloak itself with official sanction. The transformation of Jacob Mikhailovich Yurovsky was now complete.

The late afternoon was fading into another fresh evening as Sokolov, still sitting all alone in that deserted photography studio, continued to slowly piece together his collected impressions of the man who had executed the Imperial family.

One incident in particular now seemed to take on a deeper and more significant meaning. Although Yurovsky was remembered primarily for his cruelty towards the Imperial family, the Investigator recalled that one of the first things he had done as Commandant of the Ipatiev House was clearly an act of kindness. What's more, it had been directed towards the former Tsar.

The new Commandant had personally returned an item to Nicholas Romanov that had been stolen from the Imperial Family's belongings when they first arrived in Ekaterinburg. The reason he had done so now made perfect sense to Sokolov. The item Yurovsky had returned was the Tsar's own pocket watch.

Although Nicholas II may have politely welcomed this gesture for nothing more than sentimental reasons, Yurovsky must have harbored deeper and more complex feelings of familial attachment. Because the former Tsar was clearly a sort of father figure from whom Yurovsky still sought approval, the watch must have had great significance. Yurovsky, after all, knew and appreciated the inner workings of the timepiece and most probably anticipated that the former Tsar would respond accordingly.

However, considering what he had learned about Nicholas Romanov's public persona, Sokolov doubted that the Tsar had responded to Yurovsky's gesture with anything more than a brief smile and a slight nod of his head. In his diary, the Tsar had written: *"Decidedly Yurovsky pleases us less and less."*

As for Yurovsky's gesture itself, was it a way for the newly appointed Commandant to somehow atone for the brutal deed he secretly knew he had been ordered to carry out? Or was it merely a sadistic attempt to waylay the Romanov's sense of dread at his sudden arrival?

"It was impossible," Yurovsky would later write, *"not to hate what the Imperial Family represented, and have bitterness for all the blood of the people spilled on their behalf. Yet even with these feelings, it was difficult for me to view them in this way. One could*

not find such simple, unassuming, and generally pleasant people. If I hadn't been given my charge, I would have had no reason to have anything against them after I got to know them. It made my position even more difficult."

It was apparent to everyone that Yurovsky was a man of strange contradictions. For instance, when he took over command of the Ipatiev House on July 4, 1918, he immediately reduced deliveries of food and other provisions from the nuns of the nearby Convent, and yet he allowed the baskets to be handed over to the Imperial Family without first being pilfered by the guards. A small stack of mail previously confiscated by the Rural Soviet was distributed to the absolute delight of the Romanovs. Pangs of conscience? If so, Yurovsky certainly didn't allow them to interfere with the orders he had been given. As the Imperial Family eagerly poured over each letter, devouring any and all news from friends and relatives, the new Commandant was quietly installing additional guard posts around the Ipatiev House in preparation for the slaughter he knew was about to take place.

As for the former Tsar, Yurovsky thought he *'appeared to be an ordinary gentleman, simple, and I would say very much like a peasant soldier'*. He found Anastasia *'very attractive'*, and *'best adjusted to their position'*.

Was Yurovsky at all conflicted? Sokolov didn't think so. The cunning manipulation, superficial charm, criminal versatility, and his rather overblown sense of self-worth pointed to only one conclusion—Jacob Yurovsky was the textbook example of a psychopathic killer. Whatever human emotions he ever displayed were shallow indeed. With very few exceptions, his acts of kindness were finally nothing more than cunning deceptions.

Sokolov's records indicated that immediately after the murder of the Romanovs, Yurovsky, along with his wife and children, fled to Moscow, where he had been given work in the Kremlin. Ironically, his job there was to catalogue the jewels and personal possessions of the Imperial Family he had been ordered to butcher. As far as Sokolov knew, Yurovsky was still there...still alive in the world...still harboring a frightening secret.

By the time the Investigator left the deserted shop, he knew he had actually stumbled upon a startling revelation. His impulsive visit to Yurovsky's abandoned photography studio had been nothing less than a major turning point in the entire investigation.

All this time, Sokolov had considered his major adversary to be Admiral Kolchak. This, he now concluded, had been a significant error. Kolchak was a bully who tended to overcompensate with displays of false bravado. Likewise, airs of nonchalance to the contrary, Boris Gorev had been no more than an opportunistic coward.

What Nicholas Sokolov now realized was that, from the very beginning of it all, his true adversary had always been Jacob Mikhailovich Yurovsky—the man who was the dark heart and disparate soul of a twisted yet dazzling plan to murder Russia's Imperial Family. And yet, more than the horrific act of regicide itself, Yurovsky had gone much further. He had also taken great pains to devise a cunning way to cover up the entire crime…to hide it forever beneath a carefully constructed maze of false clues. Words Sokolov had spoken to Dmitri instantly flooded back into his consciousness, "It's never what it is; it's what it's made to look like." The Investigator should've paid more attention to his own admonition.

The Commandant of the Ipatiev House…former watchmaker and photographer…the frightening psychopathic killer with the slight smile tracing his thin lips…had indeed created one of the most brilliant deceptions Nicholas Sokolov had ever encountered.

What was now abundantly clear to Sokolov was the fact that Yurovsky's meticulously planned coverup was the Rosetta Stone that held the secret of what had so far been such an unfathomable mystery.

It would take more time, of course, but at least Sokolov now knew where to direct his attention for the best results. He would have to reexamine each of the clues Yurovsky left behind in order to determine which were true and which were only false leads. This meant, among other things, that he would have to revisit the infamous basement room of the Ipatiev House—the place Yurovsky had actually begun the cover-up. Every bullet hole and bayonet scar …the mysterious letters carved into one of the walls …Strovka's account of the execution …all of it would have to be reexamined, this time with a different premise in mind.

The end result would be well worth the effort. Once he had identified each layer of Yurovsky's masterful deception and carefully peeled them back like the leaves of an artichoke, Nicholas Sokolov was convinced the hidden truth would be revealed at last!

Chapter Eighteen

A Quote from Sokolov's Finished Report

"People who don't understand investigatory procedure always see things the same way—the simplest crime appears mysterious until it is solved, and the most mysterious crime seems remarkably simple after it has been solved. You always come up against the objection—how could the criminals have left such a vital piece of evidence undestroyed? Is this genuine?"

The warmer spring thaw, known in Russia as '*dacha season*', was slowly transforming daily life in and around Ekaterinburg. Milder winds, now moving across the central Asian plains, were slowly dissipating the relentless Arctic chill of the past five months. Even among the seemingly eternal patches of snow and ice, buds and blooms were beginning to appear in the Koptiaki forest—adding scattered patches of blossoming color to what had been such a drab and barren landscape. The melting ice and snow from higher elevations sent life-giving water flowing again ever downward now—swelling the Lena, Yenisey and Ob rivers to the East—as well as Ekaterinburg's own Iset River. The same was true for hundreds of smaller streams and creeks scattered throughout the local countryside.

Like the welcomed reappearance of birds and other wildlife, the human inhabitants of Ekaterinburg were also beginning to be seen more frequently. Dryer roads meant that more workers were able to make their way to the outlying factories each morning. More work meant more money. More money meant more and more women would be passing each other on the main streets of the town—making the weekly forays to local butcher shops, dry-good stores and marketplaces. Wives of the well-to-do merchants even began to organize samovar tea parties, while working class women delighted in mid-afternoon barbecue gatherings called '*shashlyk*' parties. Children happily scoured the edges of nearby forests for wild berries and mushrooms. The lilting sound of Balalaika music floated once more on soft afternoon breezes as life in general slowly began its seasonal emergence from the sheltered monotony of winter into the welcomed sunlight of a gentler springtime.

The all-too-familiar signs of an ongoing war could still be found almost everywhere, but milder weather seemed to somehow render them less ominous, which in turn made the very real danger easier to disregard. Sporadic artillery fire continued to bookcase the beginning and end of each day. Solemn formations of weary soldiers still occasionally tramped down the city streets, only now they trudged along in heavy silence—the rousing military music from once shiny marching bands having long since faded away. Only the dull tramping sound of worn boots marked the dreary cadence of their passing. Absent too were the teaming throngs of joyous onlookers who, only months before, had turned out in such impressive numbers to cheer their young army's glorious march into oblivion.

To those who were now left, life was no longer focused exclusively on the war. Nor were they concerned about having no other choice but that of surrendering to the inevitable. As miraculous as it may seem, Russian life was now about something more than mere survival. As spring began to infuse the landscape with signs of regeneration, so too did the citizens of Ekaterinburg begin to reconsider their own bleak concepts of daily existence.

As if by some unspoken desire, the people of Russia had finally reached a point where they no longer wished to merely endure; they wanted to truly live once more in some degree of peace. Perhaps that basic desire had never really deserted them at all. Perhaps it had been only temporarily swallowed by the deep despair that is always the brother of war.

Whatever the reason, the dream of redefined life was now taking on a renewed sense of urgency among the population. If the changing of one season into another was still an earthly reality, so too was the possibility of improving the quality of their daily lives. Whether or not the populace of Ekaterinburg realized it, they—as well as millions of their countrymen—had reached a critical turning point that would alter the course of their lives for decades yet to come.

Only one man seemed completely unfazed by it all. Nicholas Sokolov's daily existence continued with the same steady sense of purpose he had first adopted after blindly accepting Kolchak's seductive and ultimately daunting assignment. For him, the milder weather meant only one thing: excavation at the Four Brother's mine could once more resume in earnest. The reappearance of more people on the streets of Ekaterinburg merely offered him the opportunity to hopefully uncover fresh and potentially useful information regarding the disappearance of the Romanovs.

Increased social contact also meant that Sokolov was now beginning to receive more firsthand accounts of the White Army's progress...or lack thereof. It was a depressing but undeniable fact that good news was becoming rarer by the day. Lenin's Bolsheviks, by all accounts, were now on the offensive. But in the ongoing struggle to capture and control the minds of the masses, their military victories, while certainly significant, paled in comparison to their devious use of propaganda. It didn't matter that Lenin's grandiose promises were empty ones; the patience of the Russian people had finally worn thin. Lenin knew only too well that people who are drowning will cling to anything that floats. Russia's desperation, therefore, gave wings to his lies.

The White Army's unfortunate ties to the old monarchy, no matter how tenuous or obscure, had become a major factor in Lenin's cunning propaganda campaign to win the hearts of the populace. And where hearts lead, intellect follows. As far as the peasants were concerned, the monarchy represented the past and everything that had gone so disastrously wrong with it. Lenin's counter-offer was cunning in its vagueness. He simply offered Russians a change—the promise that their lives would be different from what they had been—and that was all that mattered.

In their eagerness to embrace the promise of change, however, the working class never stopped to consider whether or not it was going to make their lives better or worse. Time would prove this neglect a tragic blunder of unbelievable proportions, the burden of which would be borne by the Russian people for generations to come.

For Nicholas Sokolov, however, the unsettling news of the White Army's possible defeat during these first vibrant days of spring in 1919 simply meant that he had no more time to waste on listless speculation. If he was to finally solve the mystery of the Imperial family's disappearance, he would have to move quickly and decisively from this point on.

What was needed now, more than time itself, was simply a break in the case—and it didn't have to be a major one—just something solid enough to reenergize the investigation's focus and propel the remainder of his own efforts toward a definitive conclusion.

Thankfully, as Sokolov often reminded himself, "God occasionally smiles."

It was on a particularly beautiful April afternoon, as the Investigator was pouring over the usual paperwork, that Natalya Kolya shuffled into his room after a perfunctory knock on the door. A small envelope, clutched in her weathered hands, was silently deposited on the desk in front of him, after which the old woman limped to the wood stove to stoke the ever constant flame.

Opening the envelope at once, Sokolov was surprised to discover a brief note from none other than Admiral Kolchak—in his own hand no less—alerting the Investigator to the news that the White Army's Supreme Commander would be arriving in Ekaterinburg that very afternoon. What was even more startling was the Admiral's request that Sokolov dine with him that evening in a private room at Ekaterinburg's Amerikanskaya Hotel. The note also went on to inform the baffled Investigator that there would be one other guest joining them at the dinner table—a British gentleman by the name of Charles James Fox, whose presence, Kolchak's note cryptically concluded "may be of some particular interest to you".

Sokolov leaned back in his chair, silently considering the note's contents. Of course, he instinctively knew that Kolchak's polite invitation most probably cloaked some ulterior motive having to do with the aforementioned guest, but Sokolov had no immediate clue as to what that might be. The name—'Charles James Fox'—meant nothing to him. Try as he might, his usually dependable photographic memory was drawing a blank. Had he even glimpsed the name before, Sokolov concluded, he would've remembered.

The Investigator's contemplation was terminated by Kolya's soft voice.

"Beautiful day," she murmured, carefully placing the iron poker back in its usual place next to the glowing wood stove.

"Yes," Sokolov replied, pushing his chair back from the table and standing to face the old woman. "It is indeed."

Kolya hardly spoke to anyone unless she truly had something to say. This moment was no different, and Sokolov immediately understood that the old woman was not making idle conversation. She was not someone to waste aimless chatter on the weather.

"And what," the curious Investigator continued with a slight smile, "would you suggest I do with such a beautiful day?"

"Get out in it," Kolya sniffed with an air of forced indifference.

The old woman then turned to leave, but hesitated—as she so often did before exiting any room. "The Iset River is particularly lovely this time of year," she added. "Perhaps you should visit the docks this afternoon."

If there was one thing Nicholas Sokolov had learned during his stay in Ekaterinburg, it was to follow Kolya's advice whenever she felt compelled to share it. Additionally, the old woman's use of the word 'lovely' seemed so completely out of place that it instantly captured Sokolov's attention.

It's better to see once than to hear a hundred times.
(Russian proverb)

In less than an hour, therefore, the Investigator was taking a purposeful stroll along the local waterfront. The air was still cool, but the sky was clear and cloudless. Some patches of hardened snow remained caked in a few shadowy places here and there, but these few stubborn reminders of winter were already becoming outnumbered by the early buds of spring.

Hands clasped behind his back, Sokolov paused now and then to take in the sights and sounds of the riverbank, or to simply soak in the warm light of the afternoon sun. For once, at least, following Kolya's advice was actually proving to be a pleasurable experience.

Though one could hardly describe the riverside docks as bustling these days, Nicholas Sokolov could plainly observe that a few merchant ships and fishing vessels still considered Ekaterinburg a safe port-of-call.

That is why one particular ship, larger and moored away from the other vessels in the immediate vicinity, stood out from all the rest—a British gunboat, *HMS Kent*. It was also quickly apparent that there was considerable activity taking place along the dock where the Kent was moored.

The entire area was cordoned off and patrolled by armed guards. Sokolov could see that the contents of at least three military trucks were being transferred to the waiting gunboat by military personnel. A few moments more and two additional trucks chugged sluggishly into view. Though canvas tarpaulins hid whatever the trucks were transporting, Sokolov assumed that the contents of these additional vehicles were to be loaded onto the *Kent* as well.

Curious to discover more about this unusual activity, Sokolov deftly maneuvered himself as close to the site as possible. A high planked fence surrounded the dock itself and prevented undue access, but Sokolov could at least position himself to clearly observe what the five trucks were hauling—heavy steamer trunks. A preliminary count revealed there were at least twenty-five of them. The weight of each trunk was suggested by the number of men it took to lift and move it. Four men to each trunk clearly indicated that the contents were unusually heavy.

Sokolov shifted his position slightly in order to get an even better view through the open space between the planks of the high fence that barred his way. As he did, one of the trunks being carried up the gangway tilted slightly so that the lid came into view.

The breath caught in Sokolov's throat as he immediately recognized a familiar symbol on the trunk's lid—the royal crest of the Imperial family. These were the same trunks the Investigator had first seen in the locked carriage shed next to the Ipatiev House—the ones he had assumed belonged to the Ipatiev family. It was now clear to him that these same trunks, most probably filled with the Romanov's personal belongings, were being loaded under heavy guard onto a British gunboat.

Clearly, this was the reason Natalya Kolya had suggested that Sokolov should visit the waterfront on this particular afternoon. She must have witnessed the trunks being loaded onto the trucks in the courtyard of the Ipatiev House. But when? And how, Sokolov wondered, did Kolya know the trunks were being taken to the docks? Could she possibly have known they were also to be loaded onto the *Kent* as well? Did this have anything to do with Admiral Kolchak's sudden arrival in Ekaterinburg on the very day the Romanov's belongings were being taken away? Too many questions; too few answers.

Finally pulling himself away from the curious scene, Nicholas Sokolov made his way back to the Ipatiev House, all the while consoling himself with the thought that he now had at least one more piece of the mysterious puzzle within his grasp. More importantly, he was perhaps one more step closer to understanding exactly how each piece would finally be fitted together.

Sokolov strode into his room in the Ipatiev House to find Natalya Kolya carefully arranging a freshly ironed dress uniform on his bed. She immediately turned to face him.

"I thought perhaps..." the old woman began with averted eyes, "you might need this tonight."

Sokolov glanced at the uniform laid out so carefully, then once more returned his gaze to Natalya Kolya.

"Thank you," he replied. "But how did you know I had an engagement tonight?"

A slight smile traced Kolya's lips. "Everyone knows the Admiral has returned to Ekaterinburg. I only assumed you might be asked to give him a report on your progress."

Knowing that the old woman always knew a great deal more than she was ever willing to admit, Sokolov decided on a more circumspect response.

"As a matter of fact," he nodded, "you're quite right...as usual. I've actually been invited to dine with the Admiral tonight."

Kolya reacted to this announcement with only a slight nod of her head. The invitation obviously wasn't news to her.

"I'm also told there will one other person joining us," Sokolov continued. "An Englishman by the name of Charles James Fox."

Again Sokolov marked nothing more than a slight emotional response in the old woman's eyes—a mere flicker of recognition—but the nuance was enough.

Kolya tilted her head slightly while shifting her gaze about the room as if laboring in vain to somehow conjure the name of Charles James Fox It was a ruse, of course, and Sokolov recognized it immediately. Attempts to deflect significance, no matter how deftly played, always tended to communicate the exact opposite to someone like Nicholas Sokolov. That is precisely why Kolya's endeavor to underplay her reaction was, in fact, the very thing that betrayed the hollowness of her ploy and attracted Sokolov's attention. Even though the old woman seemed to be immediately aware of her fumble, she also appeared to realize the futility of any attempt to backtrack. That she had somehow managed to catch herself in her own snare, however, was a moment not to be ignored by Sokolov who purposely followed the old woman's self-conscious exit from the room with a penetrating gaze and knowing smile.

Perhaps it was his increasing familiarity with Kolya and her mannerisms that now allowed the Investigator to decipher the hidden meaning behind her slightest reactions. Whatever the reason, Sokolov instinctively grasped the significance of the moment as well as the potential dividends that were now clearly possible.

But this was to prove to be a surprising evening of many discoveries.

The Investigator peeled off his tunic and shirt in preparation for the evening's appointment with Admiral Kolchak. He needed to shave before changing into the dress uniform Kolya had so painstakingly prepared.

Bare-chested, Sokolov hurriedly gathered his shaving mug and straight razor before stepping into position before a small mirror attached to the wall just above a small table upon which rested a pitcher and shaving basin full of hot water. A moment more and he had lathered his face in preparation for a shave.

As he silently lifted the straight razor to his face, his gaze casually drifted further into the mirror's reflection of the room immediately behind him. Almost absentmindedly, his good eye began to focus on the mirror's reversed image of the room's familiar contents until his gaze finally came to rest on the desk immediately behind him, now littered with documents, stacks of paper and countless folders.

And then, for some inexplicable reason, Sokolov began to slowly ratchet focus on one particular piece of paper that happened to be lying atop the rest of the clutter.

It was a rubbing he had made of the letters that had been hurriedly carved into the wall of the Ipatiev House's basement room. Only four letters—'v s y l'—but seeing them reflected in his shaving mirror, Sokolov was now reading them in reverse order— 'l y s v'.

The sudden revelation caused his entire body to convulse in stunned disbelief. The straight razor slid from his hand and dropped noiselessly into the basin of steaming water.

Sokolov spun around and dashed to the table. Snatching the rubbing in eager hands, he held the piece of paper up to the shaving mirror for an even closer inspection.

Of course! Why hadn't he seen it before? Karl Strovka had practically handed him the solution to the riddle when he'd asked Sokolov if it was snowing in Lys'va.

The letters, which Sokolov deduced had been hastily written by someone standing with their back to the basement wall, were clearly referring to the town of Lys'va which was located northwest of Ekaterinburg—along the railway line that eventually led to the city of Perm. Written in reverse, the message had been obscured. So incredibly simple. Almost too simple. Yet there it was!

"*Is it snowing in Lys'va?*"—alluded to by both Strovka and Gorev, obviously had significant meaning—as did the expected response: "*It never snows in Lys'va.*"

There was no time to ponder this newest revelation in detail. Admiral Kolchak's dinner invitation had also stoked the Investigator's keen interest and he didn't want to be late for his evening's curious appointment.

Even as he hurriedly donned his dress uniform, Sokolov's mind was churning furiously. There were dozens of questions he wanted to put to Kolchak, though he fully expected the Admiral's usual caginess when it came to providing any sort of forthright response.

On the other hand, the Investigator had decided that courtesy and deference to rank were expendable at this point. They had to be. Time was of the essence now. News from the front was less than encouraging, and Sokolov had no idea how long he would be allowed to continue his quest.

The opportunity to unravel such an incredible mystery still presented itself. Many pieces of the puzzle were now in place. Not all, but enough to form a preliminary scenario that would account for the many inconsistencies in the story so far—explanations that would hopefully begin to satisfy even Sokolov's own private doubts. Admiral Kolchak might provide no more than a few crumbs—but to a hungry man such as Nicholas Sokolov, crumbs can often become a veritable feast…not enough to completely satisfy the insatiable hunger, but to diminish—at least in part—the vestiges of starvation that makes rational thought impossible.

When the Investigator, adjusting the freshly starched shirt cuffs of his dress uniform, at last strode through the open doorway of the Ipatiev House and into the cool twilight of early evening, he was still meticulously organizing his thoughts and prioritizing the questions he would present to the good Admiral at the first available opportunity.

In any game of Cat and Mouse, it is always the mouse who finally determines the quality of the match and its eventual outcome. Kolchak had clearly won the first round; Sokolov the second. The evening ahead was an opportunity to break the tie.

As Sokolov stepped into his waiting automobile, he was confidently determined that if it came down to the survival of the fittest, this mouse was clearly ready to teach the cat a few unexpected lessons.

Chapter Nineteen
A Letter from Empress Alexandra
March, 1918

"We live here on earth
but we are already half gone
to the next world."

To the citizens and occupiers of Ekaterinburg, the Amerikanskaya Hotel—even during the bleakest days of war—somehow managed to remain a cherished bastion of normalcy. The windows of the building always seemed to glow with friendly light—a welcomed beacon to those in need of whatever gentle reassurance its congenial atmosphere provided. Though the establishment's menu continued to fluctuate depending upon the availability of staples, customers with four rubles to spare could at least depend on something hot from the kitchen. Dark Russian tea (complete with orange rinds, sugar, cloves and cinnamon) as well as vodka always seemed to be in plentiful supply. Card games, friendly conversations and occasional balalaika music helped to pass the long evening hours. Warm fires continually blazed from the hearths of the hotel's numerous fireplaces. All available rooms were nicely furnished and the beds were comfortable.

Though few citizens realized it, the unusual prosperity enjoyed by all of Ekaterinburg's best hotels was now due in large part to the dire conditions brought on by the war itself—and, most specifically, because of the lingering questions still swirling around the fate of Russia's Imperial family. Officers of the White Army, newspaper correspondents, businessmen and international spies now made up the greater portion of the hotel's clientele. They circled the area like vultures hovering over a bit of remaining carrion.

During the previous regime's occupation, Ekateringburg's Amerikanskaya Hotel had been the chosen meeting place for members of the Bolshevik's Ural Regional Soviet and the *Chrezvychainaya Komissiya*—the local Cheka. Room Number three on the first floor—the hotel's largest and best private dining room—had been the gathering place of choice. Some said the fate of the Romanovs and their attendants had actually been decided in that very room on the evening of June 29, 1918, during an urgent meeting attended by six members of the presidium of the Ekaterinburg Soviet. Others believed it was there that Lenin's secret order of execution was passed along to local officials from his special representative, Yakov Sverdlov. Whatever the deciding factor, it was common knowledge among those who frequented the Amerikanskaya Hotel that whatever happened to the Romanovs had been the result, at least in part, of fateful decisions made during various secret meetings held in room Number Three.

The significance of this fact was certainly not lost on Nicholas Sokolov when, upon his prompt arrival at the hotel that evening, he was directed by the maître d' to the doorway of this very same room. Obligingly making his way through the warmly lit lobby, Sokolov was immediately struck by the fact that there seemed to be a singular lack of laughter or lighthearted banter emanating from any of the various groups of strangers clustered together about the room. Faces were markedly stern and the snippets of conversations that could be overheard seemed unusually grave and subdued.

While such somber behavior might naturally be expected of individuals who are so heavily engaged in the daily pressures of warfare, it was Sokolov's experience that the exact opposite was most often the case. Boisterous laughter was traditionally the bi-product of just such social gatherings—particularly when alcohol was in such plentiful supply. Humor was, after all, the easiest and most effective way to break heavy tension and dissolve the lethal stress of their lives. Not so here in the well-appointed lobby of the Amerikanskaya Hotel on this particular evening, and Sokolov could only conclude that the majority of the men assembled throughout the room were not Russians at all—but rather emissaries from other countries who had been drawn to Ekaterinburg because of their own varied interests in the ongoing conflict. It was also quickly apparent to Sokolov that each person in that room had, like him, a vested interest in knowing the ultimate fate of the Romanovs. He could, of course, only venture a guess as to the diverse reasons.

The muted conversations died away momentarily as inquisitive gazes immediately turned to follow the Investigator as he made his silent way through the lobby. His simulated nonchalance was obviously enough to satisfy any overlong curiosity and the momentarily subdued conversations quickly resumed once he passed. Still, not even the most casual visitor could have crossed that room without noting the palpable tension in the air, and it was precisely this quiet realization that refortified Sokolov's perception of the fundamental importance of his unfinished assignment. It also reconfirmed his singular resolve that regardless of any possible unpleasant consequences, tonight was a time for unfaltering confrontation.

The Investigator had to wait only a few moments after announcing himself before the door to Private Dining Room Number Three swung open. Two burly bodyguards on either side of the doorway snapped to attention as Admiral Kolchak, also in his best dress uniform, stepped into view.

Had it not been for the uniform, however, Sokolov would have been hard-pressed to recognize the former national hero. The man who stood before him now was a mere shadow of his former self—thin, graying and shockingly diminished. He held a half-finished glass of vodka in his free hand, clearly indicating that he had already availed himself of the room's bountiful amenities.

Sokolov's initial response was to mask any outward reaction to Kolchak's deteriorated appearance. Immediately squaring his shoulders, the Investigator instead pulled himself into sharp military attention. With all the formal courtesy he could muster, Sokolov clicked the heels of his polished boots, saluted and then bowed slightly from the waist. The Admiral promptly returned this gesture of kindness with his own familiar and disarming grin. It was—and Sokolov recognized it immediately—a brave charade on Kolchak's part. The aura of defeat clung to the Admiral like a heavy weight—and without a conscious thought, every shred of the Investigator's previous animosity simply dissolved on the spot and melted away into nothingness.

"Investigator Sokolov," the Admiral beamed, "punctual as ever. Do come in."

Once the Investigator crossed the threshold, the reason Dining Room Number Three had been chosen for the evening's gathering became clearly apparent. Larger than any of the other private rooms in the hotel, it was handsomely adorned. A rectangular dining table provided the room's centerpiece, over which hung an electric chandelier. It was, however, the color scheme that was so dramatic. The room's wallpaper and thick draperies were deep crimson—offset by the dark richness of the hand-carved mahogany wall paneling, table, sideboard and leather upholstered chairs. The table was splendidly set with fine china, crystal glasses, linen napkins and gleaming silverware.

The handsome sideboard was furnished with a splendid array of dishes which included generous servings of *Osetra* and *Beluga* caviar, *Seld' pod shuboy* (salted herring under a coat of boiled beets and other vegetables), *Shchi* (a traditional hot cabbage soup), *Pelmeni* (a local dumpling made with minced meat filling, wrapped in thin dough and served with butter and sour cream), boiled potatoes, *Vatrushka* (a kind of cake consisting of a ring of dough and cottage cheese in the middle), *Syrniki* (fried curd fritters garnished with sour cream, jam, honey and apple sauce), hot tea, chilled vodka and '*stavlenniy myod*'—(an alcoholic drink not unlike wine and based on large amounts of honey and berry juices.) Entirely too much food for three people, and the Investigator guessed that the good Admiral had it set out to impress.

It took only seconds for Nicholas Sokolov to complete his initial inspection of the room's furnishings and dinner buffet. He was then able to shift his complete attention to what intrigued him most of all—the silent stranger who was leaning next to a fireplace at the far end of the room, his arm resting easily on the hearth's mantelpiece.

"Investigator Sokolov," Kolchak intoned respectfully, "allow me to present Mr. Charles James Fox."

The handsome stranger acknowledged the introduction with a slight nod of his head and immediately strode the length of the room in order to face the Investigator. As he did so, it seemed to Sokolov that, as he moved through space, Charles James Fox seemed to literally split the particles of air like a sharp knife passing through warm butter. He wasted no movement, but rather invested each with a sense of purposeful grace that was impressive to behold.

Occasional moments in our lives, because of their sudden impact, brand themselves on our senses with silent but indelible intensity. Manifesting themselves as revelations, they have the ability to elevate human consciousness to levels of clarity and understanding that defy description. This was one of those instances, and the moment Charles James Fox stepped into Sokolov's life, the Investigator was immediately aware of its import.

"A great pleasure to meet you at last," Fox smiled warmly. He then extended his hand to Sokolov while concluding, "I've heard a great deal about you and your work."

"Yes," Kolchak added with a wry wink as he poured both men a chilled glass of vodka. "Most probably more than he'll ever admit to."

As they shook hands for the first time, Sokolov quietly tallied up his initial impressions of Kolchak's dinner guest. Fox was a handsome man in his mid-thirties with dirty blond hair and chiseled features tanned by the sun. His dark suit was obviously tailor-made. His demeanor, distinctly British upper class. His deep blue eyes were his most arresting feature, particularly when they occasionally seemed to betray a hint of amusement at some seemingly insignificant remark. He was obviously a man who knew secrets and took some degree of private delight in that knowledge. How much, Sokolov wondered, would he finally be willing to share?

Reaching for his own glass of vodka, the Admiral raised it in the form of a toast. "To the good days," he exclaimed before downing his drink with familiar gusto. Sokolov and Fox, their eyes still locked on each other, obediently followed their host's example.

Finishing what was to be one out of many glasses of vodka during the evening's small gathering, Kolchak took a seat at the head of the table. Sokolov and Fox moved to their respective places on the Admiral's right and left. As if on cue, the door to Room Number Three swung open and several smartly dressed waiters entered and began serving dinner—but not before promptly refilling the empty vodka glasses.

Lifting his freshly poured drink, Kolchak smiled graciously. "Well, Nicholas Sokolov," he began with a wry smile, "I'm sure I speak for Mr. Fox and myself when I suggest that we're both extremely interested in how your investigation is progressing."

Placing the linen napkin in his lap, the Investigator returned Kolchak's smile with one of his own. He replied with a slight nod of his head, "It's going very well."

Kolchak leaned close to Fox and grinned. "What did I tell you? We're going to have to pry it from him if we wish to learn anything."

Fox smiled also and took a sip of his freshly poured vodka. "I'm sure the Investigator would rather present his complete findings at the proper time," Fox politely offered in Sokolov's defense. "I assume, at this point, any conclusion would be premature and mere conjecture."

"To a degree," Sokolov replied. "I do believe I've managed to uncover a good many new and intriguing leads. At this point, it's primarily a matter of determining in what direction those leads move the investigation."

"You see what I mean," Kolchak chuckled while giving Fox a wink. "How many words did he just use in order to tell us precisely nothing at all? If you ask me, we have a natural born politician on our hands!"

"I don't mean to be evasive," Sokolov responded, "it's simply that there are still a great many loose ends that need to be more completely explored before I render any sort of conclusive theory."

"Theory?" Kolchak replied with slightly raised voice, "I hope the months you've spent nosing around Ekaterinburg will produce something more than theory. A conclusion based on facts! Indisputable facts! That's what I need. Otherwise, others will make short work of picking your collection of theories to the bone."

Charles James Fox, contentedly nursing his vodka, seemed to be quite enjoying this display of familiar bluster on the Admiral's part. He did his best to mask a smile by dabbing at the corners of his mouth with his linen napkin.

"The Investigator may find," he added softly, "that others will try to pick his final report to the bone regardless of the veracity of any supporting evidence. If I've learned anything in this particular line of work, it's that no fact is ever truly indisputable."

"Sir Isaac Newton might disagree with that opinion," Kolchak chuckled in response. "How many falling apples have to finally hit you on your head before we have enough evidence to prove that gravity exists?"

"On the other hand," Fox responded, "birds actually defy gravity each time they take flight. So do all flying insects. The law of gravity may be grounded in fact, but that doesn't mean it can't be defied and finally even overcome."

Kolchak considered Fox's statement only briefly before releasing a sudden gale of boisterous laughter. "Well, that's it then, isn't it?" he roared gleefully. "Sir Isaac Newton's apples should've had wings!"

Fox glanced at Sokolov with an expression that seemed to indicate some bit of silent encouragement. This was obviously a game of wits and Fox knew how to play it well. When Kolchak was at his boisterous best, the wisest strategy was to dodge until the target was clear and exposed. At that point, any of the Admiral's entire broadsides could be deflected with little or no intellectual effort at all. And for one brief moment, Sokolov paused to wonder how many times Admiral Kolchak had most probably heard the words 'checkmate' uttered from an opponent sitting just on the other side of a chessboard.

It was only a split-second more, therefore, before Fox and Sokolov reacted to the moment by joining the Admiral in shared laughter. Whatever tension there might have been at the outset in Room Number Three seemed to dissipate amid the congenial laughter. The attentive waiters happily completed serving plates of food to their guests.

Once the Admiral eagerly began to shovel food into his mouth, Fox took advantage of the silence in order to expand upon his previous observations.

"My point is simply this," he smiled, "facts occasionally appear to be at odds with each other. A bird lifts its wing and the law of gravity is overcome. On the surface, one fact would seem to invalidate the other. The challenge is to finally reach a point wherein you're able to accept the presence of two or more opposing facts, and to realize how they are actually able to coexist."

"Couldn't have put it better myself," Kolchak mumbled as he continued to stuff his mouth with more food. "For instance," he continued, "an entire family is supposedly executed in the basement room of some nearby house. A dozen men empty their revolvers into a small group of hapless victims. Not content with this, they decide to finish the gruesome assignment with bayonets and rifle butts. Now, who in their right mind would ever imagine that someone might've actually survived such a brutal assault? And yet...well...there are rumors suggesting that such a thing actually happened."

The Admiral spread his arms in dramatic fashion. "Two occurrences! But, if the first is true, how could it possibly co-exist with the second?"

"The same way one accepts a bird's flight," Fox replied with a disarming smile, "gravity exists and birds still fly. If a small bird is therefore able to defy the mighty law of gravity, might it not also be possible that someone in that basement room could have indeed managed to overcome the odds against survival?"

At this point, Kolchak and Fox quietly turned their gazes to Sokolov—a move, by the way, that he was fully anticipating.

"Possible?" the Investigator answered simply. "Perhaps. But probable?" Sokolov answered his own questions with an enigmatic shrug of his shoulders.

"And yet," Kolchak continued, "I'm given to understand that at least some of the facts you've uncovered might actually give a bit of credence to the rumors. Wouldn't you agree?"

Nicholas Sokolov was fully aware that he was being pressured to reveal, however prematurely, just what his true inclinations were regarding the possible survival of Anastasia—an uncomfortable position at best. His responses had to be convincing, clever and yet politely vague.

He knew that a great deal depended upon his ability to deflect and eventually redirect the good Admiral's preferred topic of conversation. His instinctive reaction was to change the subject entirely.

"Speaking of uncovered facts," Sokolov replied with convincing earnestness, " I happened to be enjoying a stroll along the banks of the Iset River earlier today and noticed a British gunboat—*HMS Kent*—anchored at the docks."

Admiral Kolchak's posture shifted slightly but noticeably and his brow furled in mute reaction to Sokolov's unexpected shift.

"Steamer trunks were being loaded onto the Kent," Sokolov continued, "more than twenty at least, and each trunk was heavy enough to require the combined effort of two strong men. I also observed that each trunk bore the insignia of the Imperial family. I assume you are aware of this?"

Sokolov had managed a rather artful dodge indeed. In one deft move, he had maneuvered Kolchak into a defensive posture—a position the Admiral always found disagreeable at best. It was Charles James Fox, however, who seemed to display a hint of honest admiration at the cleverness of Sokolov's tactic. His blue eyes were twinkling with barely concealed amusement as he shifted his gaze to the visibly uncomfortable Admiral.

"Yes," Kolchak finally managed to admit, "I do seem to recall that the Kent was in port earlier today."

"And the Imperial family's steamer trunks?" Sokolov continued to press with some degree of relish.

"I believe there were seventy in all," Kolchak replied somewhat petulantly while pouring another fresh glass of vodka. "They're being transported to England at the personal request of His Majesty King George V. He is, after all, the former Tsar's cousin. I saw no reason to deny the request."

"In that case, you must obviously have some idea as to the contents of those seventy trunks," Sokolov ventured as evenly as possible. "I may only assume that whatever the contents were, they had no bearing on my investigation."

"None whatsoever," Kolchak replied with a tinge of irritation in his voice. "I can assure you of that."

"May I also assume that a manifest was compiled?" Sokolov continued with his usual persistence. "A detailed list of the contents?"

The good Admiral, obviously flustered, seemed suddenly at a complete loss for words.

Sokolov's question, simple and direct, hardly left room for successful evasion. Kolchak's flustered gaze shifted to Fox in a silent but obvious appeal for reinforcement. Observing Fox taking another contented sip of vodka in silence, however, it was plainly obvious to the Admiral that help was not to be forthcoming.

"A list?" Kolchak finally managed to respond with some exasperation, "I'm sure there must be one somewhere. Nothing more than personal items once belonging to the Romanovs. Hardly worth the effort to retrieve such an inventory, but I'll do my best to have a copy located and sent to you."

Sokolov knew this was a blatant lie, but decided not to press further. He concluded with an appreciative nod of his head. "Thank you," he smiled. "That would be most helpful."

Buoyed by his success with Kolchak, the Investigator decided to shift the conversation to Fox.

"Speaking of King George," he began, slowly pivoting in his chair so that he could more easily face the attentive Brit. "It's always seemed strange to me that the king of England didn't do more to aid the former Tsar. As the Admiral has correctly pointed out, they were cousins after all."

"On the other hand," Fox replied solemnly, "appearances can be deceiving. For instance, I do know for a fact that Thomas Preston, our British consul here in Ekaterinburg, actually did all he could to support a rescue. He also continually requested to be granted access to the royal family while they were being held as captives here, but every entreaty was rejected. On the surface, it might indeed also appear that His Majesty attempted very little in defense of his royal cousin. I might point out, however...and I do hope you will forgive the intentional vagueness of my reply...that history may prove otherwise."

His curiosity instantly piqued, Sokolov leaned forward in his chair. "May I assume you have some specific assurance of that fact?"

It was Fox's turn to carefully weigh his response. "Yes," he finally admitted in a voice that rose just above a whisper. "You may assume precisely that."

Silence engulfed the room briefly as glances were exchanged while Kolchak hastily downed another glass of vodka.

"Well, I'll tell you this," the Admiral suddenly grinned across the table at Fox, "my own security detail couldn't have guarded those last few statements any better than you two just managed to do!"

Fox and Sokolov responded with polite laughter as Kolchak poured—rather unsteadily—another fresh round of drinks.

"You're both damned good at this," the Admiral grandly pronounced as he raised his glass in the form of a salute. "Hell, the two of you could stroll through a rainstorm without getting wet!"

The copious amount of alcohol he'd imbibed in such short order was obviously taking its toll on Kolchak's sobriety and sense of decorum. Sokolov concluded that this was most probably due to the Admiral's diminished physical state. Anyone could see that Kolchak was not in good health. His faculties, once so vital and astute, now seemed sadly depleted by illness, stress and sheer exhaustion. Whatever the reason, he was becoming more intoxicated by the minute—and it clearly showed. What's more, the good Admiral seemed absolutely aware of the fact.

"You know," he continued, "you can drink vodka all night if you know the secret. Wake up at about five in the morning, drink a beer and go back to bed. Works like a charm!" Grabbing a bottle of vodka from the table, Kolchak clumsily shoved it toward Fox. "Care to try it?" he grinned.

"*Ya propuskau,*" Fox demurred, gently covering the rim of his glass with the palm of his hand.

Rebuffed, Kolchak stiffened and leaned back in his chair. "Why is it," he huffed, "you damned English will always find some way to insult your Russian hosts? You know what I think? I think it's because you foreigners don't know how to drink...at least not like we drink here in Russia!"

The Admiral threw back his head and laughed heartily. "I never get drunk," he bellowed. "No matter how much I drink. Know why? Because I'm smart; I eat two boiled potatoes, one raw

211

egg, and take a shot glass full of sunflower oil before all social occasions!"

Kolchak's lips curled into a sneer. "But you English," he smirked at Fox, "you're very happy with your afternoon tea times and your silly little canapés!"

For additional emphasis, the Admiral suddenly slammed his fist down on the tabletop. "You English should drink more vodka," he bellowed enthusiastically. "Lots of it! You'd live a hell of a lot longer, and be a damned-sight happier too. That, I can assure you!"

Completely unruffled by the Admiral's boisterous comments, Fox merely smiled. "As everyone knows," he replied softly, "only the first three vodka shots at any Russian party are obligatory. I've had mine. Of course, I should point out that my refusal doesn't mean I intend to abstain from drinking anymore tonight. I'm merely excusing myself from this round—as a foreigner. As such, I believe I am now allowed one shot out of two that you take."

As if to prove his point, Fox politely stood and gently took the bottle of vodka from Kolchak's hand. He uncorked it and proceeded to pour his host another drink. As he did, Kolchak threw Sokolov a smirking, self-satisfied glance, as if to indicate that he had won a point in the game. In doing so, however, he missed an almost unnoticeable gesture made by Fox.

As he poured the vodka into Kolchak's glass, Fox deftly snapped open a tiny compartment hidden underneath the gem which adorned a ring on his right hand. A few grains of white powder silently fell into the Admiral's glass and immediately dissolved. The gesture was skillfully handled...and Sokolov saw it all. What's more, Fox was aware that Sokolov had witnessed the maneuver, because, as he did it, he was looking directly at the young Investigator as if to actually direct his attention to the slight-of-hand.

Admiral Kolchak regarded the freshly poured vodka with satisfaction. His irritation smartly deflected by Fox, he lifted the drink in the form of another toast.

"Ah, what the hell!" he grinned with a conciliatory shrug. "Here's to English tea and Russian vodka! May they always live at peace with one another!"

With that, the Admiral crowned his expressed desire with a hearty laugh, and downed the drugged vodka in a one joyous gulp.

"I'll tell you this," he went on happily, "two boiled potatoes, one raw egg, and a shot of sunflower oil have done nothing to whet my appetite! I don't know about you two, but I'm still famished!"

Pushing his chair back from the table, the Admiral struggled to his feet with some bit of sudden difficulty. Grabbing his empty dinner plate, he made his way back to the sideboard for another helping of food. As he ladled a second generous serving onto his plate, Kolchak suddenly dropped a bombshell.

"You believe she's alive, don't you?" he said flatly—and more as a statement than a question.

There was no need to mention a name. Each man in the room knew exactly to whom Kolchak was referring. His back was to Sokolov and Fox, so he didn't see their reactions. He didn't need to.

Hardly anticipating a reply, he snickered to himself and went on with one of his now familiar diatribes. "Impossible? Improbable? Doesn't matter a tinker's damn either way, does it? Not a tinker's damn! Because what it finally comes down to—when all your clever dodging is over and done—what it comes down to is nothing more than what you believe did happen. That's all it ever is anyway...that gnawing bit of honesty...hiding deep inside your gut...that won't allow you to rest until you know the truth. So, you search for proof to back up what you believe. In which case, how can you say it's an unbiased investigation?"

His plate now piled with more food, Kolchak wheeled around to face the two men seated at the table. "Look at you!" he growled with ever-slurring speech. "Guarding your precious little secrets like children hoarding candy!"

The Admiral staggered back to the table and slumped into his chair. Pouring more vodka into his empty glass, Kolchak laughed again to himself and shook his head. "You know what I think?" he finally sneered. "I think the two of you couldn't exist without your damned secrets."

The Admiral raised his glass and downed the freshly poured vodka in one gulp. He then slammed the empty glass onto the table and sighed audibly. In another moment, and with a more subdued voice, he turned his blurry gaze to Sokolov.

"Whether she's alive or dead...whatever you know...whatever you believe...set it all down on paper, and soon. We'll be abandoning Ekaterinburg in a matter of weeks at most. Weeks! Goddamned Bolsheviks! May they all burn in hell!"

The news of an impending retreat did not come as a total surprise to Sokolov. He'd been vaguely aware of the fact that

Kolchak's White Army was faring badly. It was still something of a jolt, however, to hear the Admiral's dire prediction stated so bluntly—and from his own lips. The obvious ramifications of such an admission were indeed dreadful to contemplate—and did much to explain Admiral Kolchak's obvious physical and mental decline. The White Army's ship of state was floundering beneath his feet, and he was obviously grappling with the stark realization that there was little he could do to delay the inevitable.

White-knuckled and ashen-faced, the drugged Kolchak suddenly gripped the edge of the dining table with both hands in a vain attempt to steady himself.

"Here's what I believe," he blurted with dreadful, if unsteady, conviction. "The Romanovs are still alive! All of them!" Sokolov and Fox briefly turned to each other in mute reaction. Interpreting their silence as an invitation to expound, Admiral Kolchak began to nod his head emphatically as if such a gesture might somehow verify the profound depth of his belief in such a shocking statement. "It's true," he intoned ruefully, fixing an increasingly apprehensive gaze on something in the room—something that remained unseen to all eyes but his. "They gather each night beside my bed…there, in that dreadful darkness," he moaned with an expression of painful agony that was twisting the gaunt features of his face into a frightful mask of dread. "The Romanovs," he bellowed again with even more chilling intensity. "I hear them breathing! I can feel the heat of that putrid breath on my neck and smell the ungodly stench of their rotting bodies. That's how I know they're still there in the darkness…hovering close to me." Kolchak's wide eyes darted about the room in frantic desperation. "They'll always be there…" he cried, "watching…waiting…the bloody Romanovs…haunting my waking hours…stalking my dreams…always…until the day I die."

Having finished this terrified confession, Admiral Kolchak sighed heavily, closed his eyes and, as the drug-induced stupor finally—gratefully—overtook him completely, slipped into a state of vacuous semi-consciousness. His inglorious presence at the evening's gathering was thus concluded.

The next few moments of silence that engulfed Room Number Three in the Amerikanskaya Hotel were clearly understandable. Sokolov and Fox had been totally unprepared for the Admiral's emotional confession, and took advantage of the momentary lull in order to process the outburst they had just witnessed.

Fox finally arose from his chair, moved to the head of the table and gently checked the Admiral's pulse. In a moment, he nodded silent assurance to Sokolov and strode to the door. Opening it, he beckoned the two guards to enter. Indicating the White Army's slumbering leader was all that was required. The two guards, one on either side of Kolchak, lifted him from his chair and half dragged, half walked the staggering Admiral out of the room. This ceremony, obviously familiar to the guards, was dutifully completed in stoic silence, after which Fox gently closed the door before turning back to Sokolov.

"Each generation will carry the burden of its own wars," Fox sighed. "Unfortunately, the merciless weight of memory is too often underestimated."

"Thankfully for some," the Investigator replied, "memory can be selective."

"For some," Fox nodded. "I would suggest, however, that Admiral Kolchak is not among the lucky few."

Fox strode to the sideboard and poured two glasses of the Admiral's expensive brandy which he then transported to the table. Placing one of the glasses in front of Sokolov, he lowered himself into Kolchak's empty chair.

"Circumstances aside," Fox began again, "I actually wanted us to have a bit of time to ourselves."

"In that case," Sokolov smiled cryptically, "it was fortunate indeed that Admiral Kolchak proved to be so obliging."

Fox returned Sokolov's smile. "The Admiral will have a bit of a headache in the morning, but will most probably be very grateful for a night of undisturbed slumber."

Fox then lifted his glass of brandy in the form of a toast. "To crooked paths," he smiled again, "may they all become straighter as we approach the end of our journey."

Sokolov lifted his own glass and touched the tip of Fox's glass with a soft, agreeable clink. "Kolchak was correct about one thing," Fox continued in a more serious tone, "you don't have much time left here. Ekaterinburg will fall to the Reds again. It's only a matter of days now."

Sokolov swirled the brandy in his glass as he silently considered Fox's somber prediction.

"With that in mind," Fox went on, "may I speak frankly with you?"

"By all means," the Investigator responded.

"Is it indeed your belief that one or more of the Romanovs survived?"

"Yes."

"But you have no proof...nothing more than your own private convictions?"

Sokolov considered for a moment, then nodded in silent agreement.

Fox took a sip of his brandy before speaking again. It seemed to the Investigator that he was very conscious of trying to carefully select his next words.

"If there were survivors," Fox began again, "where do you believe they were taken?"

"Survivors?" Sokolov repeated deliberately. "Your question implies that there could have been more than one."

Fox did not reply. Sokolov paused to sip his brandy before continuing, "Your statement would also seem to imply that the survivors—if indeed there were any—were in someone's custody."

"Well," Fox smiled, "if there were survivors, I seriously doubt they managed an escape on their own. I'd be more inclined to believe they had some form of assistance. Wouldn't you agree?"

"I suppose," Sokolov replied as obscurely as possible.

"On the other hand," Fox continued, also with purposeful vagueness, "there is always the possibility that an escape could have occurred after rescue."

Sokolov was becoming quite intrigued by this discussion. Fox was obviously in possession of crucial information and, for the moment at least, seemed willing to share what he knew—if only obliquely at first. Sokolov decided to take the risk.

"When you say 'after rescue'," he began. "I assume you are referring to the survivors being taken to Lys'va. Am I correct?"

Fox showed practically no reaction to such a deliberately leading question. He did, however, push his chair back from the dining table. Rising to his full height, he withdrew a thin silver cigarette case from his inside coat pocket.

"Do you smoke?" he asked Sokolov.

"Occasionally," the Investigator nodded.

"In that case," Fox smiled, "and because I'm given to understand that walls do occasionally have ears, may I suggest that we take our drinks and adjourn to the hotel's front porch?"

#

The evening air was fresh and delightfully cool as the two men, brandies in hand, stepped through the open doorway of the hotel and onto the front porch. Leaning against a wooden railing, Fox withdrew a slim brown cigarette from his small silver case and lit it. Noticing that the Investigator was observing him, Fox extended the cigarette case toward Sokolov.

"Try one," he indicated with a nod of his head. "They're imported and quite good."

Accepting the offer, Sokolov withdrew one of Fox's slim brown cigarettes from the small silver case and lit it.

"Do you happen to know of a Count Alvensleben?" Fox inquired as he exhaled a small cloud of cigarette smoke and sent it curling into the cool night air.

"One of Berlin's chief diplomats in the Ukraine," Sokolov replied. "Age thirty-five. Count Hans Bodo van Alvensleben. Yes?"

"Yes," Fox concurred after taking another sip of his brandy. "He was undoubtedly a major component of the German's intelligence network set up over a year ago here in the Urals. Thankfully for all concerned, Hans favored a Romanov restoration."

"To what end?" Sokolov shrugged. "A year ago? Wasn't it too late by then?"

"You tell me," Fox smiled wryly. "It so happens that on July 5th of last year, Count Hans Alvensleben warned us that between July 16th and 20th rumors would be spread regarding news of the death of the Tsar. He then added that this news shouldn't alarm us unduly. Like previous rumors of the impending murder of the Tsar, which were rather prevalent in June of last year, he advised that these particular reports would be admittedly false, but would also be necessary for certain reasons, specifically to help implement the Tsar's rescue."

Sokolov couldn't resist a dubious smile of his own. "One more rescue plot?" he inquired somewhat cynically. "Do you think there was anything to it?"

Exhaling another small trail of smoke from his brown cigarette, Fox ventured softly, "Count Alvensleben was personally entrusted by Germany's Kaiser to ensure the absolute safety of Alexandra and her children. Their absolute safety, mind you. In retrospect, the fact that Count Alvensleben just happened to know that the Tsar's death would be announced ten days before the event allegedly took place becomes rather significant. Wouldn't you agree?"

"Quite significant, yes…" Sokolov concurred, "if you are able to substantiate what you're telling me now."

"If I couldn't," Fox chuckled, "I assure you that I wouldn't be wasting your time…or mine."

Gazing thoughtfully into the night sky filled with glittering stars, Fox continued smoothly. "There are those who will tell you that the German government was actually fostering Bolshevism all along in order to finally defeat Imperial Russia from within…to remove her as a military threat on the Eastern front."

"Is that what you believe?" Sokolov pressed once more.

"It would've been the smart thing to do," Fox ventured with a slight shrug of his shoulders. "Rather interesting, though, that everything happened just as the Count predicted."

Fox, turning to face the deepening darkness, extended his hand beyond the front porch railing and deftly flicked away a few glowing ashes from the tip of his slim brown cigarette. Taking another drag, he paused briefly before exhaling and appeared to be thoroughly savoring the moment.

Turning his discerning gaze again to Sokolov, he softly continued his intriguing observation. "It's quite obvious that a good many people—along with their respective governments—had advance knowledge that the Romanovs were going to be executed by the Bolsheviks sometime in July. Once that knowledge was shared with the various factions who had a stake in the game, I venture to suppose that anyone with plans for intercession would have redoubled their efforts."

"What else do you venture to suppose?" Sokolov asked pointedly.

"Simply this," Fox replied, "the rumors that one of the Tsar's daughters managed to escape are credible."

"Credible."

There it was at last! The long-awaited admission from someone who could certainly be considered a reliable source. There was indeed a possibility—however slim—that one of the Tsar's daughters could have avoided her family's tragic fate! If true, and if he could prove it beyond a doubt, Nicholas Sokolov would rewrite the pages of recorded history after all—his legacy, intact; his greatest quest, completed at last. Even this, the merest suggestion of vindication, was water in the desert to the single-minded Investigator who remained determined to accomplish what Admiral Kolchak believed he never could. For a fleeting moment, Sokolov even considered trying to explain to Fox exactly how much the statement had meant, but instinctively knew there was no need.

"Let's walk," Fox suggested with an easy smile. "It's a pleasant evening for a stroll."

The two men, brandies in hand, sauntered down the front steps of the hotel and strolled off together into the evening's dim stillness.

Fox, lost in contemplative thought for a few moments more, continued to puff contentedly on his brown cigarette before eventually flicking the butt into the surrounding darkness. Finally, he broke the silence with another soft revelation.

"The Roman emperor, Marcus Aurelius, once said *'life is a warfare and a stranger's sojourn, and after fame is oblivion'*." Fox actually smiled at this and then went on to elaborate, "Some of us would be quite happy with an outcome like that."

"Satisfied with oblivion?" Sokolov countered.

"As if we never existed." Fox replied, "For a certain few of us, that would work out quite nicely, I should think."

Sokolov understood the statement. Spies, undercover agents, provocateurs—all of whom strive to remain undiscovered, also ultimately hope to be unremembered. In the game of espionage, a player's ultimate goal is to complete the mission as expeditiously as possible and then to simply fade into the background as though he or she had never existed.

"When you're young," Fox continued, "and the need to prove yourself is greatest, you tend to generate a great deal of furious heat and impatient energy. But with the addition of a few years and a bit of experience under your belt, you begin to move through life a bit more decisively. An abundance of options may seem quite nice to begin with, but my experience is that it rarely accomplishes a great deal. It's only when you're able to observe events with a detached objectivity that the wheat begins to separate itself from the chaff and the real truths are finally revealed."

Fox turned his soft gaze to Sokolov and held it for a moment or two before offering another observation.

"You have ambitious goals," he smiled. "I don't. Not anymore. Unless, of course, you consider survival itself to be ambitious...and perhaps, in days such as these, the benefits of perseverance are substantial indeed."

"I'm curious," Sokolov replied. "You've obviously lived a very extraordinary life, taken a great many risks, and most probably faced death more than once. Considering all of that, what is left for you to fear in this life?"

"Not much," Fox answered without the slightest hesitation. "I put fear aside a long time ago. Something of a requirement in my occupation, I suppose."

"Every man is afraid of something," Sokolov insisted. "No one is ever completely without fear."

Fox, quietly considering his answer, withdrew another brown cigarette from the small silver case, placed it between his lips and lit it. Inhaling the first draught, he held it in his lungs for a moment before exhaling thoughtfully.

"I suppose," Fox began again, "that what I fear most is to eventually fade away into old age and uselessness. I would much prefer to leave the world long before that happens."

If espionage could ever be considered a game, Sokolov was clearly in the presence of a master player. The more they talked, the more the Investigator became aware of that fact. What he was still left to determine, however, was just how much of this intellectual tête-à-tête was for show and how much was substantial truth. As desperate as he was for reinforcement, Sokolov continued to hold himself at bay, wanting instead to extract as much useful information as possible...especially where Anastasia's arguable survival was concerned. Time was fleeting and speculation was cheap. Separating fact from fiction was paramount now.

As the evening stroll continued, Sokolov quietly nursed his brandy in hopes that his prolonged silence might entice Fox to dispense more intriguing information. He didn't have to wait long at all.

"What do you make of all the train nonsense?" Fox finally inquired.

"I'm afraid I don't understand the question," Sokolov replied, genuinely confused for the moment.

"The mysterious train with its windows painted black," Fox responded. "A bit theatrical, wouldn't you say? As if the apparent attempt to disguise the railway car was actually a very clever way of calling it to everyone's attention...to make certain that it would be remembered...as though the Reds wanted everyone to reach an obvious conclusion."

"That the assassins were being secretly taken out of Ekaterinburg?" Sokolov asked in only partial seriousness.

Fox was not so easily baited. "You don't believe that for a moment," he grinned before taking another sip of his brandy.

Sokolov smiled too, in spite of himself. Fox was not letting him get by with very much at all.

"If there were assassins on that train," Fox interjected, "it would necessarily imply that there had actually been an assassination."

"Excuse me," Sokolov interrupted, "are you saying that you doubt an execution actually took place in the basement room of the Ipatiev House?"

"Well, put another way," Fox elaborated, "in order to prove that someone had survived an execution, wouldn't you first have to be assured, beyond all doubt, that there had indeed been an execution to survive? And if so, were the Romanovs actually among the victims?"

"Do you doubt it?" Sokolov asked.

"Nothing is a fact," Fox replied, "until it's backed up by substantiated proof."

"Yes," the Investigator nodded, "my approach exactly."

"And yet," Fox smiled, "you must admit that the thrust of your investigation has been based entirely upon one unsubstantiated rumor."

"I'd rather say," Sokolov countered evenly, "that my investigation rests on evidence suggesting that a crime was indeed committed. The crime appears to have been that of regicide. I was assigned to prove it."

"More truthfully," Fox added, "you were ordered to prove that the entire Romanov family was murdered by the Bolsheviks...that not one survived. You were, in fact, handed a public investigation based on a private premise. We both know the conclusion you're expected to reach. So, the tantalizing question of the evening appears to be: will you do what they expect?"

Sokolov considered Fox's last statement to be particularly intriguing. There were only two people present in the upper room of the Ipatiev House when Admiral Kolchak had first presented the young Investigator with the assignment; and yet, Fox was quoting that private discussion almost verbatim. The walls of the Ipatiev House obviously had many hidden ears.

"You seem quite familiar with a great many details of this case," Sokolov responded. "Do you believe the Imperial family died in the basement of the Ipatiev House?"

"What I believe," Fox sighed, "is hardly the question. You are the one who now holds Russia's future in your hands...or in your heart, as the case may be. Your final report to Admiral Kolchak may very well prove to be one of the most significant documents in Russian history."

Another clever sidestep by Fox. Sokolov downed the remainder of his brandy and paused on the dimly lit sidewalk. Fox paused as well, and turned to face the determined Investigator.

"After fame comes oblivion," he repeated with a slight shrug of his broad shoulders. "Dark truths will always be hidden away for the sake of brighter legends. Our reality...tomorrow's history...is already being reinterpreted...becoming something it never was. A rather relentless transformation is taking place this very moment...inextricably...even as we speak...out there...in the darkness beyond...shaping a legend from a lie. The way it's always done. But if the truth is what you seek, then know this: no one survived the evening of July 16th. Not the Romanovs. Not Lenin. Not Mother Russia. Not even you or I."

For a moment, a heavy silence seemed to wrap the entire star-filled universe in a blanket of world-weary melancholy. Fox's words, too wise to remain earthbound, drifted upward in the night sky to finally melt away into the ether.

And then suddenly, as if pronouncing a mutinous benediction on all that had gone before, Fox spun on his heels and playfully hurled his empty brandy glass into the darkness. Finding some unseen target a short distance away, the sound of shattering glass broke the reverent stillness. Grinning ear to ear like a mischievous boy who had just risked doing some forbidden thing, Fox wheeled back around, hands proudly on hips, to face Sokolov.

The Investigator, hesitating only a second or two before accepting the unspoken challenge, turned on his heels and in one carefree act of adolescent abandon, hurled his own empty glass into the darkness as well. At the euphoric sound of more shattering glass, both men broke into gales of happy laughter.

It was impossible to tell in that moment whose soul had received the most benefit from that one giddy act of juvenile misbehavior, but there was no mistaking the fact that the gesture was a most welcomed release for both men. Their shared laughter mingled with the distant barking of a startled dog, sustained itself in the lighthearted release of the moment, and then comfortably faded away. As if in mutual acquiescence to the more somber realities of adulthood, both men then grew silent, allowing the night and the heaviness of the world to settle back around them once more.

The occasional warm pools of friendly light from the street lamps lit the winding way ahead, but neither man felt especially pressed to hurry the stroll.

The evening, at least in Sokolov's opinion, was becoming a most agreeable one. He hadn't enjoyed such an intellectual exchange in quite some time and was in no apparent hurry to see it end. Fox didn't seem particularly ready to conclude the conversation either—so, as if on some unspoken cue—the two men resumed their evening ramble.

"What, I wonder, will history say about all of this?" Sokolov suddenly mused aloud.

"History," Fox grinned broadly, "will do what it always does; it will look the world squarely in the eye and commit perjury."

Chapter Twenty

"I've made my peace. What about you?"

Karl Strovka

Nicholas Sokolov was up and dressed for the day even before the sun had dared to break through the heavy predawn clouds over Ekaterinburg. He greeted the few remaining hours between darkness and dawn with only one burning desire: to meet again with Charles James Fox as soon as possible in order to continue their intriguing conversation. The thought that he could finally discuss the investigation with someone so thoroughly versed in the complicated and often conflicting details of his case...someone who additionally seemed to agree with many of his own observations...had seemed almost too much to hope for. Yet, he had found just such a man in Fox. Indeed, Sokolov felt there was so much more still left to debate that he truly wondered if a single day would be enough time to cover everything sufficiently. One thing was quite clear to the young Investigator, however; every additional moment he could possibly spend with Charles James Fox was going to be vital to the successful conclusion of his assignment.

For the few chilly predawn hours left to him, Sokolov had to content himself by anxiously pacing back and forth in his own silent room. Too nervous to eat and too distracted to know if he even had an appetite, he would only occasionally pause mid-stride for a hurried sip of strong Russian tea. He kept going over and over various discussion topics in his mind, trying as best he could to arrange them into some kind of proper order. It was extremely important to him that he should be able to express his observations as clearly and logically as possible. In order to accomplish this, he had to mentally go back and force himself to recall as much of the specific pieces of evidence as possible. His anxiety was due to the fact that, out of necessity, this predawn mental review was going to be a hurried job at best, and that always increased the possibility of error. He never liked to feel rushed. Still it was a challenge he had no choice but to accept. Wanting to be able to competently follow up on each specific point Fox had made during the previous night's discussion, Sokolov therefore pushed himself into this exercise with as much mental clarity and attention to detail as his photographic memory could systematically produce under such pressure.

Once sunrise began to finally tinge the cloudy sky with the first light of day, the nervous Investigator couldn't help but increase his fretful pacing. Proper etiquette dictated that he had to wait until an acceptable hour to pay a visit to the British Consulate which was just across the street from the Ipatiev House. The British were strict adherents to custom after all, and business hours did not begin until all of the proper morning routines had been completed.

Another glance from his window at first light revealed a cold gray sky slowly filling with heavy clouds that were drifting in from the far horizon. It was very evident, however, that the approaching rain storm was about to dampen everything but Sokolov's eager anticipation. The Investigator was, in fact, completely oblivious to the morning's weather.

Finally, seeing lights go on in the Consulate windows across the street, Sokolov decided that he had waited long enough. The staff should certainly be up and bustling by now. The Brits were not late sleepers.

Snatching his overcoat and fur cap from a nearby chair, Sokolov dashed out of the room, down the adjoining corridor and through the front door of the Ipatiev House. As he did, he almost collided with Natalya Kolya and her daughter who were just arriving for another day of chores. He paused long enough to nod to the two women as he slipped into his overcoat and then brushed by them to hurriedly make his way across the courtyard.

He sprinted across the street and bounded up the steps of the British Consulate. Coming to a halt in front of the door, he quickly adjusted his coat before knocking. When a few moments passed with no answer from within, he knocked again.

This time, the door slowly opened and an elderly gentleman with neatly combed white hair, wire-rimmed spectacles, and a rather large mustache appeared in the doorway. He was dressed in a starched white shirt, gray trousers, tie and black topcoat.

"May I help you?" he inquired with just the proper air of British aloofness.

"Yes, thank you," Sokolov replied. "I would like very much to speak to Mr. Charles James Fox if it's convenient."

"I'm terribly sorry," the elderly Englishman sniffed, "but Mr. Fox left Ekaterinburg early this morning...before sunrise, I believe."

Nicholas Sokolov actually staggered backward at this totally unexpected news. His jaw sagged and, for a moment, he couldn't muster his ability to speak.

"Is there someone else on the Consulate staff who might be of assistance?" the haughty doorman inquired.

Still dazed, Sokolov could only shake his head.

"In that case," the doorman continued, "is there anything else I might assist you with this morning?"

Partially regaining his speech, Sokolov managed to stammer, "Did Mr. Fox leave a forwarding address?"

"I'm afraid not," was the flat reply.

For a moment neither man spoke, each seemingly waiting on the other to either prolong or conclude the conversation.

Finally, it was the elderly doorman who broke the stalemate with the only logical rejoinder left to him. "Well, if there's nothing else you require..." His voice trailed off and he briefly paused once more for a possible response from the Russian Investigator. When none was forthcoming, he nodded with perfunctory politeness and slowly closed the door.

Nicholas Sokolov, ramrod straight in confused disbelief, remained frozen in place for a few seconds more simply staring at the door which had just closed in his face. It took that long for the unexpected news to truly begin to sink in. The one person in possession of decisive information had suddenly and inexplicably disappeared! All of the Investigator's nervous anticipation had finally counted for nothing. The questions he had spent all night and most of the early morning formulating would now be left unanswered. The proverbial rug had just been pulled from underneath Sokolov's feet and he found himself so completely unprepared for the overwhelming sense of bewilderment that he even considered knocking once more on the door in order to ask the elderly doorman if he was absolutely certain that his information was correct. It was simply inconceivable to Sokolov that Charles James Fox had left without a word of parting. Of course they had only met the night before, but the Investigator still felt he had established an almost instantaneous bond of friendship and mutual respect with the dashing British agent. Perhaps it was because of Sokolov's own insatiable appetite for intelligent conversation or the fact that he had put so much stock in Fox's validation of his theories. Whatever the reason, he was now suddenly bereft of any optimistic response or conciliatory thought. His hopes had been dashed and for the moment at least his brain continued to reel in utter disbelief.

Fumbling to adjust his overcoat more out of habit than need, Sokolov slowly pivoted on the porch of the Consulate to gaze in mute despair at the scene before him. Across the street, he could see the tall stockade and the top story of the Ipatiev House just behind it. The sun was up now, though partially hidden behind heavy clouds.

Another day was beginning for the population of Ekaterinburg. Horse drawn carts and carriages were starting to appear in the streets. A few rumbling trucks, carrying men to work in the nearby factories, were already starting to turn onto the main thoroughfare. It was going to be another day like any other for everyone but Nicholas Sokolov.

Still dazed, the despondent Investigator shoved his hands into the deep pockets of his overcoat and started down the front steps of the British Consulate. He strode into the street without so much as a cursory glance to gage the possible traffic. In his current state of agitation, being run down by a lorry would've most probably been something of a relief. On this particular morning, however, it was apparent that Fate was not in an overly generous mood.

Sokolov passed through the open gates of the high wooden palisade surrounding the Ipatiev House and into the empty courtyard. He paused once more in an attempt to more fully regain his senses. He inhaled a deep breath of the chilly morning air, held it in his lungs for a few seconds, and then exhaled slowly. Not wanting to reenter the house without first feeling a bit more in control of his emotions, he simply stood silently in the empty courtyard for a few moments more, still struggling to process the somber news in its entirety.

What could have been the cause of Fox's abrupt departure? Unexpected orders regarding some other assignment? Is it possible that he knew all along that he would be leaving? And if so, did the knowledge of his impending departure serve as the catalyst for his unusual willingness to disclose so much information during the previous evening's stroll?

These were nagging questions that would have to remain unanswered…at least for the immediate future. For the present, Sokolov needed find a way to more fully regain his focus. He had to propel himself back into the final stages of his work in order conclude the investigation as proficiently as possible. To accomplish this, he was going to have to rely on the evidence he'd managed to collect as well as his ability to process all of it in a very short period of time. For the remaining hours that were left to him in Ekaterinburg, this single challenge would be the unrelenting focus of all his considerable skills and mental acumen. If there was a way to wring victory from such an exasperating setback, he was determined to find it. Sheer determination may have been all that was left to him—but for Nicholas Sokolov, that stubborn resoluteness had always been a major deciding factor in his struggles both private and professional. Those close to him knew that his ability to persevere against all odds was not to be underestimated.

Back in his room, the dejected Investigator shed his overcoat and hat. As he did, he heard the first distant rumble of thunder. A dreary rainstorm, rolling in from the far horizon, was about to settle itself over the sleepy city of Ekaterinburg, shading the daily routines of its inhabitants with an unshakable sense of melancholy. Sokolov certainly felt it. With most of his papers packed away, he had nothing easily available to occupy his time. He briefly considered penning another entry in his journal but quickly dismissed the idea. A disconcerting sense of emptiness stemming from Fox's sudden departure had left him strangely listless and suddenly bereft of words to adequately describe what he was feeling. No, he would have to occupy his time with some other activity.

As he stood crestfallen in the middle of his room, taking full measure of the morning's disclosure as well as an unshakable sense of despondency, he began to hear the first soft sounds of cold rain on the roof of the Ipatiev House. The steady pelting of raindrops began gently enough, but eventually grew louder as the storm settled over the city, its dark and heavy clouds blotting out any cheerful morning light that might have otherwise signified the fresh beginning of a new day.

It was in that moment that the thought occurred to Sokolov that it was not just his investigation that would soon be taken from him; his time in the Ipatiev House would also be coming to an abrupt and untimely end. The last remnants of Admiral Kolchak's White Army were already abandoning the city in ragged droves, and the Investigator knew that it was now only a matter of hours before he would be forced to become yet one more weary member of that desolate retreat.

In a rather unexpected way, the young Investigator had become oddly attached to the old house and its grounds. Having spent some crucial time within its walls, Nicholas Sokolov had grown to feel an undeniable connection to the momentous events of its recent history. It was this inexplicable bond that had actually come to redefine him. It had certainly given his life a welcomed sense of accomplishment. Whatever the reason, he was loath to see it all come to an end.

Though there was no question that he would have to relinquish everything, it also suddenly occurred to Sokolov that he still had enough time to manage it by degrees. As long as it was such a rainy day, why not take an hour or so to walk through the Ipatiev House one last time. It was an activity to occupy his time at least, much better than lingering morosely in an empty room, listening for the distant wail of a locomotive's whistle.

And so, with renewed purpose, the intrepid Investigator squared his shoulders and strode out of the room. The only sounds that accompanied him were the steady pelting of raindrops on the roof above and his soft but resolute footsteps echoing in the empty rooms and hallways.

These were to be Nicholas Sokolov's final hours in the Ipatiev House...one last opportunity to carefully file away precise mental images of a place that was certain to become for the Russian people a stark but necessary reminder of the seismic political upheaval that had taken place so violently within its walls.

This last solitary stroll through the premises would be undertaken in a determined effort to view each room as it appeared at that moment in time—without embellishment—and to then permanently commit the details of all he observed to the innermost recesses of his remarkable memory.

At the same time, he couldn't help but try to imagine how these same rooms would appear in the years ahead...his imagination stretching far away into an unknowable future. There was, of course, no way for him to know that the Ipatiev House would stand for only fifty-eight more years before being demolished on orders from the Kremlin. And yet, despite Lenin's most treacherous efforts, Yurovsky's cunning, and the Bolshevik's continued deceit, the mystifying disappearance of the Imperial family was to remain a particularly bothersome thorn in Russia's side for decades yet to come.

Inside the House of Special Purpose on this particular morning, however, complete with the sound of pelting rain and the rumbling of distant thunder, the future and all it held for Mother Russia was unknowable and still years away.

For the present, Nicholas Sokolov was taking his final tour of the infamous Ipatiev House—a place he had called 'home' for a period of some months and which he was now being forced to abandon.

As he walked, he recalled his first few days in the house along with the sights and smells that were to become all too familiar. The odors were still present—the pungent and combined scent of oil cloths, sweet soap, lye, kerosene, terpin-hydrate mixed with codeine, cod liver oil, paregoric, bees wax from melted candles, camphor, dying flowers mixed with barely detectable medicinal odors including cloves, cinnamon, lavender, bay rum, rosemary and peppermint.

The Investigator passed through the dining room, where he had held his first interrogation with Boris Gorev and the smaller adjoining room where he had questioned Anatoly Yakimov—two people who had provided a great deal of information—some of it unintentional. Their testimony would most certainly find its way into Sokolov's final report.

The door to the kitchen was open. As the Investigator passed it he glanced inside to find Natalya Kolya and her daughter going about their daily routines. As always, they worked side by side in what appeared to be comfortable silence.

Sokolov paused briefly to consider who the occupants of this room might have been on the day of the planned execution. Jacob Yurovsky would have most certainly been one of them. Leonid Sednev, the kitchen boy, would have been the other. Yurovsky had summoned the boy early on the morning of July 16th to tell him that he would have to leave the Ipatiev House. According to Yurovsky, the boy's uncle Ivan had returned to Ekaterinburg and wanted to see his nephew. It was a lie, of course. The uncle had been murdered days before by the Cheka. Sokolov had initially wondered about this seeming act of kindness on Yurovsky's part, but after learning more about the commandant of the House of Special Purpose, the Investigator had come to attribute the episode to nothing more than expediency.

Jacob Yurovsky was a sociopath who would have had no qualms at all about adding the boy's name to his list of intended victims. But the basement room was going to have to accommodate almost too many people that night as it was, and the kitchen boy would've been one more additional headache in the larger scheme of things. Better to send him away, save a few more bullets, and be done with it.

Nicholas Sokolov took some consolation in the idea that perhaps Leonid Sednev would go on to live a long life, eventually becoming an old man sitting before the evening fire, retelling the haunting story of a twist of fate that would forever connect him to one of Russia's most tragic events.

At the northwestern end of the central corridor on the main floor Sokolov passed the lavatory, its linoleum covered floor still stained and cracked from the constant drip of the exposed pipes. On the walls of this room, the guards had drawn their filthy pictures of Rasputin and Empress Alexandra. Yurovsky had the door knob removed so that anyone was able to barge in on the room's occupant at any time and for any reason. Even though he was most certainly aware of their inevitable fate, he was still determined that the most rudimentary forms of common decency would continue to be denied to 'Citizen Romanov' and his family while they lived.

Climbing the stairs that led to the upper floor Sokolov made his way down the upstairs corridor until he reached the empty room at the southeastern corner of the house—Nicholas and Alexandra's bedroom. Pelting rain blurred the view from the four windowpanes. It was difficult to even make out Ascension Lane, the dirt road that accessed the house—the same road that had brought the Romanovs to the Ipatiev House. The pale yellow wallpaper that covered the wall of this bedroom seemed more faded in the dim light that filtered in through the rain streaked windows. Sokolov's gaze took in the room's furnishings—a rug, two beds, couch, the baize-covered table, the bronze lamp complete with a handmade lamp shade, the single empty bookcase between the two sets of windows, card table, armoire, and the washbasin still sitting on the cracked marble counter.

Just after midnight on July 17, 1918, the Romanovs' physician, Dr. Eugene Botkin, had been sent to this same room on orders to awaken the sleeping family and to request that they put on their clothes. Yurovsky had just informed the doctor that the family would have to be moved to a safe location due to impending chaos in Ekaterinburg. Under this false pretext, the family was to have then been taken to the basement room of the house where they would be informed that Yurovsky needed to take a photograph of them as proof that they were still alive and unharmed. This additional lie had been concocted so that

Yurovsky would be able to arrange the hapless victims in a formation that would make them easy targets for the executioners. Everything had been planned to the smallest detail...everything but one.

As he stood in the doorway, Nicholas Sokolov was most aware of the fact that he always felt a sense of heaviness sweep over him whenever he entered the room—something he would do only on the rarest of occasions. It was one place in the House of Special Purpose, other than the basement room, where the silence seemed almost deafening. Additionally, the Investigator could never shake the feeling that his presence seemed an intrusion of sorts—as if the familial love that had once filled the room and still seemed to linger in the atmosphere like some invisible spirit, deserved to remain forever undisturbed by the invasive presence of others.

As Sokolov finally turned to leave the bedroom, he suddenly remembered the dim hallway on the ground floor that he had always hurried though.... the one place he had so often felt a supernatural presence especially late at night when spirits roamed and he was the only living person inside the house. Unlike the more peaceful spirits that inhabited the upstairs bedroom, however, the invisible phantoms that lurked in the lower hallway seemed to him more restless and sinister. At least that is what the constant temperature drop in that one specific place in the downstairs hallway always indicated to Sokolov. Since the day he had first become aware of its disturbing aura, the Investigator had harbored an unshakable feeling that something sinister had taken place in that one particular section of hallway, and whatever it was had charged the very air itself with the haunting chill of death. Sokolov had always avoided lingering there, but today he was filled with a sudden sense of resolve. Before he left the House of Special Purpose forever, he was determined to at least try and decipher this one additional mystery.

A moment later and the emboldened Investigator had descended the flight of stairs that brought him into the downstairs hallway. It loomed ahead of him in the faint light like a mocking apparition daring him to proceed. In the past, he would have most likely succumbed to the conjured threat. Not today. This time Nicholas Sokolov took a deep breath, and proceeded down the dim hallway—straight to the spot where he had always felt that unworldly presence.

As he entered that familiar area, his steps slowed down. He had to pause only a second before he felt once more that unmistakable drop in temperature. It was definitely cooler in that once spot than anywhere else in the dim corridor. But why? Was there something more than a supernatural reason?

He remained anchored to his place in the center of the hallway for a few moments more…long enough to begin to become truly cognizant of the surroundings. The chill in the air where he stood seemed damp and for the first time, Sokolov could detect a faint odor. Dark wooden panels lined each side of the hall. They were approximately five feet in height and three feet wide. There was no artificial light in the hallway. The only illumination filtered in from the rooms that joined both ends of the corridor. Small pieces of furniture may have once been placed here or there but they had long since disappeared. The hallway was empty except for the Investigator who still held his place amid the chilly air that engulfed him.

Slowly, Sokolov spread his arms wide and held his hands outstretched in order to try and take some measure of the temperature. Once he did, he was immediately aware of a soft almost imperceptible movement of air on his left outstretched hand. He turned to face the wall to his left and extended both hands towards the wooden panel directly in front of him. Once both of his palms were several inches from the surface of the wooden panel, he began to move them slowly from right to left.

As he did so, he could feel a faint but definite flow of air come and go depending upon the placement of his hands over the edge of the wall panel. Ever so slowly, he allowed his hands to come to rest lightly on the wooden surface itself so that his fingers could begin to gently trace the thin molding that framed the panel.

The tips of his fingers slowly inched along the top of the molding and then further down the right side. Suddenly, his index finger came to rest on a small raised lever that protruded only slightly from the outer edge on the molding strip. Sokolov held his breath and increased the pressure of his touch ever so slightly.

He instantly heard a barely audible click much like the sound tumblers make when a key is turned in a lock.

In another instant, one of the wall panels, released itself from hidden restraints, slid back several inches and slowly swung open, revealing a vertical shaft that appeared to descend to a depth of at least twenty feet or more.

233

With a soft gasp, Sokolov staggered several steps backwards in shock. When he was immediately engulfed by a cold updraft of air rising with some force from the depths of the shaft, he realized at once how foolish he had been to so hastily ascribe the hallway's changes in temperature to supernatural forces. This cleverly hidden space was certainly not the work of ghostly apparitions. Sokolov's immediate guess was that the shaft and hidden doorway had been someone's clever idea when the house was originally constructed. The Investigator also understood that the discovery, in and of itself, might not prove to be particularly unusual. Underground root cellars were quite popular and useful conveniences in many of Ekateringburg's homes. In most cases, these cellars were nothing more than deep earthen pits where vegetables, wine and cheese could be safely stored and kept fresh for prolonged periods of time.

Sokolov stepped forward and peered into the vertical shaft for a better view. A wooden ladder resting against one side of the shaft was mute testimony to its extended depth, and though he didn't think he'd be greatly surprised by what he might find, Sokolov knew he had to explore this most unusual discovery.

Dashing back to his room, the Investigator grabbed the kerosene lamp from his table and hurried back down the musty hallway. Pausing in front of the secret opening long enough to light the lamp, he clutched one side of the ladder with his free hand and began a careful descent into the darkness below. It took a bit of concentration to keep the lamp steady while safely descending the ladder at the same time, but Sokolov got the hang of it rather quickly.

A few steps more downward and he reached the bottom of the vertical shaft. As his eye grew more accustomed to the darkness, he began to inspect the small earthen chamber in which he found himself. This was clearly no root cellar. He raised the kerosene lamp and extended it for some length in front of his chest only to gasp softly at what the light instantly revealed.

The opening of an underground tunnel, large enough to easily enter without even having to stoop, materialized from the gloom directly in front of him. Pausing momentarily, Sokolov glanced around to get his bearings. It was instantly evident to him that the position of the opening meant that the tunnel snaked underneath the street above him in the direction of the British Consulate. The realization was staggering, so much so that the Investigator stood anchored to his spot in that tiny earthen chamber to simply gaze in utter astonishment at the tunnel's gaping entranceway that seemed to somehow beckon him to enter.

Reclaiming his composure after a few awkward moments, Nicholas Sokolov steadied himself before continuing. As the flickering light of the kerosene lamp cut through the thick darkness ahead of him, the Investigator took a deep breath, stepped into the tunnel's opening and began to cautiously inch his way along the passageway. His fear was that there might yet be another vertical shaft hidden somewhere in the gloom ahead, obscured from sight by the distracting shadows created by the lamp's flickering glow. For his own safety, all forward movement was intentionally slow and carefully measured. Besides, this gradual but steady progress afforded him time to give some additional attention to the passageway itself.

It was obvious to Sokolov that the tunnel's design had been diligently planned, its construction also appeared to have been carried out by experienced laborers who knew what they were doing.

Thick wooden columns lined each of the tunnel's side walls at regular intervals, connected to heavy joists that supported the weight of the damp earthen ceiling. Flat wooden planks laid end to end lined the floor of the tunnel, stretching into the darkness beyond his sight.

The light from his lantern continued to cast flickering shadows that appeared to dance along the earthen walls of the tunnel as Sokolov continued to inch his way forward. Every few feet, the lantern's light illuminated a bit more of the passageway. By his reckoning, Sokolov surmised that the British Consulate was almost directly overhead.

Suddenly, a solid wall of mud, rock and charred wood loomed into view from the darkness in front of him. The passageway ahead was completely sealed off! Sokolov raised the lantern and leaned closer to examine the wall of debris. The pungent smell of sulfur immediately filled his nostrils. The odor of sulfur and the jagged bits of charred wood protruding from the wall of debris pointed to only one conclusion. The tunnel's collapse had been caused by the detonation of explosives. Someone had deliberately sealed off the passageway!

Sokolov raised the lantern higher and stepped back to further consider the situation. The flickering light illuminated enough of the debris to make one thing very clear. The explosion had dangerously weakened the remaining wooden support beams. Any attempt to clear the wall of debris would most certainly cause even further collapse—possibly even loss of life. There was nothing left for Sokolov to do but turn around and retrace his steps back to the tunnel's entrance. The exasperation he felt as he did so was understandable. Sokolov was certain that had it not been for the deliberate collapse of the tunnel at that very spot, the passageway would've led him up and into the British Consulate.

The obvious question was whether the collapse had been caused before or after the evening of July 16, 1918. Had the Bolsheviks set off the explosion to prevent escape or had the tunnel been used during an attempted rescue? Sokolov's heart was pounding. This was, without doubt, an extraordinary discovery that had the potential to decide the final verdict of the entire investigation. Everything depended on the date and time of the tunnel's collapse.

Sokolov's heartbeat increased and his footsteps also quickened as he made his way back through the underground passageway. His brain was reeling. How could he possibly determine when the explosives were detonated? Were there witnesses in the British Consulate who might be able to tell him? Were the Ipatiev guards aware of this potential escape route? And if the Bolsheviks had known in advance about the tunnel, is it possible they even allowed the Romanovs to initiate an escape attempt in order to be able to justify the brutal execution?

Sokolov was almost sprinting through the passageway now. He could see the faint light of the opening that led into the vertical shaft which would take him back into the Ipatiev House. Using the light ahead as a reference point, he allowed the lantern he was carrying to drop slightly at his side so that it was a bit closer to the earthen floor of the passageway. That's when the lantern's flickering light caused Sokolov to notice something on the dirt floor only a few feet ahead. He came to a full stop just in front of the vertical shaft's opening and fixed his gaze toward the mud-packed floor of the passageway. He carefully knelt on one knee and held the lantern just over that one particular spot directly in front of him.

There, pressed down into the hardened mud floor by the weight of one or more people who had obviously been wearing boots, Sokolov could still clearly see the half-smoked remnants of six or eight brown cigarettes!

Chapter Twenty-One

"I think about a hall in semi-darkness,
About the velvet, into lace inclined,
About the poems we would have told each other,
You—yours, I—mine.
I also think about the remaining
From your lips and your eyes handfuls of dust...
About all eyes, that are now in the graveyard
About them and us..."

Marina Tsvetaeva

The late afternoon sky over Ekaterinburg, still laced with a few remaining storm clouds, was fading into hues of deep amber, laced by thin streaks of scarlet red. Nicholas Sokolov sat alone in his silent room, trying to take full measure of the transformation that had so quickly taken place. The once-familiar stacks of paper, dossiers, envelopes and containers of evidence—now catalogued and boxed—had all been hastily removed by two of Kolchak's burly Ipatiev guards earlier that afternoon and loaded into a truck waiting in the rain soaked courtyard. The photographs, drawings and charts that had once filled almost every square inch of the walls in his room had all been taken as well. Aside from his meager personal belongings, the young Investigator had been left with nothing more than his customary evening thoughts, the small silver framed photograph of Anastasia, a single kerosene lamp that still glowed reassuringly from the tabletop before him, a dying fire in the nearby wood stove, a half-empty bottle of vodka, and several drinking glasses.

On the table top in front of him was also one salvaged sheet of writing paper upon which he had hurriedly jotted down a few passionate observations:

Regardless of my official conclusions, they will hardly be the final words of the Romanov's story. The curtain has only been temporarily rung down on the first act of an ongoing theatrical saga. One group of players now leaves the stage while yet another group prepares to enter. But to what end? The curtain will rise again on another freshly assembled cast of characters who will resume playing so earnestly at waging war—just as each assembly before them has done. The play grinds on, you see. No ending. No applause. Never victory—only the perpetual attrition of manpower and material. And finally, no survival...for anyone. That is a rather closely kept secret, of course. Not even Lenin has learned it yet. He still believes that he's achieved victory on his own terms. For the moment, the knowledge that some form of warfare will always be allowed to continue doesn't seem too high a price to pay. A fatal misstep, of course, never fully realized until it's much too late. When his time on the stage has run its course, the preordained truth is that Lenin won't be treated any differently than Nicholas Romanov. After all, when the game is finally over, as they say, the king and pawn will go back into the same box together. All matinee idols finally outlive their youthful appeal...and the world will always be so full of eager understudies willing to pay any price for their own brief turn under the lights. One may only hope that they will learn what those who went before came to know in their turn; it isn't merely about winning the role, it's also about being able to sustain it. The easiest way to accomplish that, of course, has always been to simply eliminate the competition. We once gave that particular act of madness a certain gravitas by calling it patricide, regicide, genocide—simple assassination. Generations to come, of course, will see it as nothing more than a logical progression—the shortest distance between two points—hardly worth a moment's hesitation, regret or second thought. And God help us if they ever invent killing machines capable of replacing the human connection to it all. At least when you wield the bayonet yourself or are forced to pull the trigger of your own weapon, conscience has a fighting chance. Mechanization, on the other hand, provides distance. And distance is rather sanitizing. It makes it so much easier to kill—because those you're killing have no faces or families. They don't celebrate birthdays or gather together for holiday dinners. Distance makes them merely things—unknown and unknowable. Unfortunately, in the process, we become things as well. For, you see, by the time responsibility has been successfully avoided, we will have become as faceless, mindless and anonymous as the things we kill. That is why I wonder if it will finally come to mean anything at all to future generations. Once the music fades and the houselights rise...once they step forward to take their bows...will they feel even the slightest tinge of communal loss or regret when, in the ensuing silence, they sadly realize that, all this time, they were only playing to an empty theatre? The audience, having long since lost interest, will have deserted them, and their well-intended performance—full of sound and fury—will finally have been for no one but themselves. The message of the play and any difference it might have made to the plight of Mankind will be lost forever.

Nicholas Sokolov gazed for a moment at the prophetic words he had just scrawled on that single sheet of writing paper. Then, with only a soft and fatalistic sigh, he gathered it into his hands, crumpled it into a tight ball and tossed it aside.

The time for pretty words had come to an undeniable end. It was simply that, despite the recent discovery of the underground tunnel, Sokolov still couldn't shake the damnable sense of failure. The assignment he was now being forced to abandon had completely driven his life and ruled his soul for the past few months. In its sudden absence, he was floundering in the unfamiliar void of inadequacy. There was little consolation to be found in the knowledge that he had given the challenge all of his considerable professional skills. Because, beneath it all, he knew that this time, albeit reluctantly, he had committed the unforgivable sin. He had allowed himself to become emotionally involved. It was this private acknowledgement that was proving to be the last nagging entanglement…the one unshakable link that would not allow him to completely sever the tenacious connection that had been forged. And now, despite his past avoidance of that truth, everything suddenly seemed to be crashing in on him…fracturing his heart under the weight of what he knew would be nothing more than a hurried and incomplete resolution. Like the underground tunnel so recently discovered, the path which might have led him to some kind of irrefutable conclusion remained blocked and impassable.

The abrupt decision to terminate the investigation had not been his, of course, nor even Kolchak's. Fate had decreed it. The White Army's war with Lenin's Bolsheviks was lost. Of course, the wholesale slaughter would continue to grind on for a few more bloody months, but defeat was inevitable. So, too, would be Lenin's savage retribution. Years of unimaginable suffering were soon to be the White Army's only reparation for all their selfless valor, vainglorious hopes and shattered dreams. In the last days that remained to them, the depressing gloom of predestined defeat would hang shroud-like over everything, draining all energy, optimism and devotion from the brave cause to which they had once so valiantly rallied. In the end, most would even be denied the final dignity of walking from the battlefield; they would be carried. The bodies of the rest would be left to finally melt back into the blood-soaked earth along with the long winter's last frost.

None of that mattered now to Sokolov. Failure was his only concern. He did not bear it willingly or well. What made it all the more insufferable was the vexing and yet unrelenting feeling that he was actually quite close to solving the mystery.

Leaning back in his chair, the Investigator sighed deeply and closed his eyes for a moment. This was an oft repeated ritual whenever he wanted to try and clear his mind. Almost unconsciously, his hand moved to the breast pocket of his tunic to withdraw the single yellowed cigarette he always kept there. Why deny a nasty habit now? What, after all, did he have to lose?

Placing the cigarette between his lips, he retrieved a small matchbox from his trousers' pocket and struck a match. As he did so, the flickering light from that small single flame briefly illuminated the vodka bottle sitting on the table before him, behind which rested the small silver-framed photograph of the Grand Duchess. For an instant, he caught a glimpse of Anastasia's face through the clear but slightly distorting liquid in the bottle—a face he must have studied a thousand times before—and yet, in that split second, there was something that caught his attention and held it fast. Before he could decide what seemed so suddenly unusual about the face in that faded photograph, the match he held between his fingers flickered and went out.

Sokolov quickly lit another, and this time leaned closer to the bottle of vodka which was once more illuminated by the light of that single small flame. He peered intensely through the clear shimmering liquid in the bottle to more closely examine the lovely but slightly distorted face that gazed back at him from the faded photograph. His gaze moved from the eyes to the nose, the cheeks, the chin, the forehead, the lips and mouth.

As he continued to study the photograph, his jaw began to sag ever so slightly in growing realization. He snuffed the match and quickly tossed it away. In one rapid move, he swept up the photograph in one hand and the bottle of vodka in the other. Leaning closer to the more revealing glow of the kerosene lamp, he held the bottle of vodka closer to his good eye while positioning Anastasia's photograph directly behind it.

It was as though he was seeing her face for the first time; and yet, as he peered even more closely, it was becoming increasingly apparent to him that it was not the face of the Grand Duchess at all. The slight distortion created by viewing her photograph through the clear liquid seemed to transform the Grand Duchess's features in such a way as to make her seem to become someone else entirely. Someone…

As the audible gasp caught fast in Sokolov's throat, his head jerked backwards in such reflexive shock that he lost his grip on the small framed photograph. Slipping from his hand, it fell to the tabletop with an abrupt clattering sound that broke the silence of the room and jolted him out of his momentary paralysis. As conscious control of his senses flooded back to him, so did the shattering realization that he had accidentally uncovered an astounding secret. In that one extraordinary moment, the bewildering mystery of Grand Duchess Anastasia Nikolaevna had been solved!

Sokolov hardly had time to regain his composure when the door to his room swung open, revealing Natalya Kolya in the doorway, holding a small tray containing a single cup of hot tea.

"I beg your pardon," she began tentatively. Indicating the cup of tea, she continued—"I thought perhaps…" and then her voice trailed away.

Sokolov pulled himself upright in the chair. "Thank you, yes," he replied with sudden warmth and, with a slight nod of his head, indicated the table in front of him.

Lifting the cup of steaming tea from the small tray, Kolya approached and silently placed it on the table in front of the Investigator. She then turned to leave the room.

"Must you go just yet?"

Sokolov's soft voice stopped the old woman in her tracks. She turned back to face him in quizzical silence.

"I was merely hoping you might sit here with me for a while," Sokolov continued, indicating the empty chair across the table from where he sat. "I'll be leaving Ekaterinburg soon."

A slight smile traced the old woman's lips at the news. "You have finished what you came here to do?" she inquired.

"Yes," the Investigator answered evenly, "I believe I have."

Sokolov pointed to the half empty bottle of vodka and the two empty glasses on the table in front of him.

"I was hoping you might join me," he smiled. "A small celebration."

Noticing that Kolya's anxious gaze quickly darted to the hot cup of tea, the Investigator smiled reassuringly. "I'll have the tea later."

The old woman silently considered the unusual invitation for a moment, then with a slight nod of her head, slowly pulled the chair back from its place across the table from Sokolov and sat down.

"Thank you," she managed softly.

Sokolov immediately stood to pour two glasses of vodka. "To be quite honest," he explained, "Ekaterinburg has become a rather desolate place. Your company is much appreciated."

He handed one glass of vodka to Kolya, then poured another for himself. Having done so, he once more took his seat across the table from her. Raising his glass, he smiled once more and nodded as if to offer Kolya the chance to speak.

"To what shall we drink?" the old woman inquired.

"To the truth," Sokolov replied. "Why not!"

Kolya studied his face with passing interest, then downed her vodka in a single swallow.

"Tell me," he continued as he poured more vodka into the old woman's glass, "your daughter, is she still with you?"

"My daughter-in-law," Kolya corrected him. "No, she isn't."

"You have a son then?"

"Had a son," the old woman answered softly. "He was killed in the war."

"I'm very sorry. So—you and his wife are together now.

"Yes."

"In that case," Sokolov smiled as he lifted his glass, "why not drink to her?"

Kolya once more took a moment to study the Investigator's face as if trying to decipher what possible agenda might be hidden behind this peculiar gesture of kindness. Finding none, the old woman concluded the moment's silence.

"If you wish."

Kolya then obediently raised her glass and downed the vodka. Sokolov did not.

"You know," he began again deliberately, "they tell me I have an incredible recollection of details. Photographic memory, if you can believe that. One reason I've had some bit of success at what I do. For instance…an off-hand remark from a prisoner referring to the fact that the Imperial family's hair had been cut only a few days before they were shot. Or Gorev mentioning a train car, its windows painted black, mysteriously appearing at the

Ekaterinburg station several days before the execution. Enough collected peasant clothing to fit every member of the Imperial family. Peasant clothing. Intriguing details...at least to me."

"Intriguing details," the old woman agreed. "But what do they finally prove?"

"Not a thing," Sokolov sighed. "That's the irony of it all. It's only what I believe."

The old woman leaned back from the table and crossed her arms over her chest.

"And what is that?" she asked with a half-smile.

"That nothing is what it seems," the Investigator replied. "I'm afraid there will be a great many questions left unanswered by this investigation."

"What do you believe happened to Nicholas Alexandrovich Romanov," Kolya asked pointedly. "What was the fate of Russia's last Tsar?"

"The world outgrew its need of him," Sokolov shrugged. "And so, they decided that he had to die. Politically, there was no other choice. I don't think he was to die here in Ekaterinburg, however, I believe Nicholas Romanov was to have been executed in Lys'va. Nothing personal. Politics."

"And what of the women?" Kolya asked in a voice just above a whisper.

"Ah, yes." Sokolov replied. "The women. Well, we know for a fact that several days before the alleged execution, the Reds cut their hair...in this very room, in fact, and disguised them as peasants."

"For what reason?" Kolya asked.

"A single train car, windows painted black, stood waiting, for all appearances, to secretly evacuate the executioners once the bloody work was done. I think it was meant to carry the women instead. At least that was the Bolshevik's original plan."

"You say the train was meant to carry the women," Kolya concluded. "Are you inferring that it didn't?"

"By that time," Sokolov smiled, "there were no Romanov women left to put on that train. No men either, for that matter."

"I don't understand," Kolya said with an expression of puzzlement on her face.

"Of course you do," Sokolov corrected the old woman softly. "You and I both know that not one Romanov died in the basement of this house."

Kolya could only stare in silent shock at Sokolov from across the table. The Investigator let the silence linger for a moment longer before continuing.

"I believe Dr. Botkin, Trupp, Kharitonov, and the servant girl Demidova are the ones who died downstairs in that basement room. They were executed in a desperate panic."

Kolya could only stammer one word, "Why?"

"Because," Sokolov explained, "the Romanovs had disappeared. Imagine that! They had vanished completely...all of them...prisoners in a heavily guarded Siberian fortress...and right under the noses of the ever-vigilant Bolsheviks. Shortly after midnight on that fateful day, Yurovsky told Dr. Botkin to awaken the Imperial family and tell them to get dressed. When the good doctor didn't return promptly, however, Yurovsky most probably climbed the stairs himself and entered the Tsar's bedroom. Imagine the look on his face when the royal family's servants were the only ones quietly waiting for him there!"

Sokolov leaned toward Kolya. "I know about the tunnel," he admitted softly. "That's how Charles James Fox was actually able to manage the impossible—and within an hour...perhaps even within minutes...of the scheduled execution of the menials. Impeccable timing to say the least."

"But how was it possible?" the old woman replied. "How could six people simply leave the house when the place was filled with Cheka guards?"

"Yurovsky ordered all of the interior guards into one of the downstairs rooms." Sokolov explained. "They drank vodka and prepared their weapons for the execution which was to take place sometime after midnight. Yurovsky had specific orders he also wanted to communicate."

"But," Kolya interrupted, "that still doesn't explain how the Imperial family managed to escape without being overheard."

Sokolov smiled again and reached inside his tunic. Slowly withdrawing a folded photograph, he placed it on the table in front of the old woman. With trembling fingers, Kolya unfolded the photograph and found herself gazing at the faces of the squad of Cheka henchmen who supposedly carried out the execution of the Romanovs. The faces were familiar to her—Yurovsky, Nikulin, Medvedev, Kudrin, Kabanov, Netrebin, Tselms, Yermakov, Strekotin, Vaganov and Strovka.

Nicholas Sokolov then silently pointed to another man in the photograph who was standing slightly behind the Cheka killers.

His image was slightly blurred, and yet, one could tell that he was blond-headed and sported a large mustache.

Kolya glanced up at Sokolov with a look of confusion on her face.

"I retrieved this photograph from my files after having dinner with Admiral Kolchak." Sokolov explained. "There was something about the blond man in the picture that seemed familiar."

Kolya leaned closer to the wrinkled photograph and squinted her eyes in an attempt to see the blurred man more clearly.

"If the image was sharper," Sokolov began again, "and you removed the mustache, the blond man bears a striking resemblance to Charles James Fox."

Kolya glanced up at Sokolov then back at the photograph. She seemed genuinely astonished at the revelation.

"I believe," Sokolov went on, "that Fox may have been the reason the Ipatiev guards weren't as alert as usual on the evening of the supposed execution. He does have a degree of familiarity with certain drugs—and since this photograph seems to be proof that he managed to gain access to the Ipatiev House at some point prior to the execution, I believe Fox could've easily laced the bottles of vodka in Yurovsky's room with a sedative of some kind—just potent enough to render the guards a bit more thick-headed than usual. After all, Fox only needed a moment or two to get the Imperial family safely into the tunnel. The truck Yurovsky had positioned outside, revving its engines in order to prevent anyone from hearing the execution squad's gunshots, most probably also helped to cover any possible sound of the Romanov's escape."

Natalya Kolya leaned back in her chair and shook her head in amazement. "Your attention to detail is quite impressive."

The Investigator accepted the compliment with only a slight smile before continuing.

"Unfortunately," he began again, "the Tsar once stubbornly swore that he'd never abandon his retinue of faithful menials, and there's absolutely no doubt that he meant it. Such a scene, however, would most certainly have imperiled the success of any escape plan that depended, as this one did, on such precise timing; and Fox may very well have had to physically subdue Nicholas in order to finally force him into leaving without his servants. Both men must have known what the ultimate cost of that abandonment would mean to those left behind. On the other hand, once Nicholas and his son were on their way to Lys'va and the women had been loaded onto the train, the servants were slated to be exterminated in any case. Whatever took place, however, during the brilliantly timed rescue of the Romanovs, and for whatever inexplicable reason, the Grand Duchess Anastasia became somehow separated from the rest of the group...another potentially disastrous delay that would've posed a serious threat to the success of the entire plan. Conscious choice or tragic mistake? We may never know. For whatever reason, it was now Anastasia's dreadful fate to have to fend for herself...to hide away, struggle to survive...and if at all possible, to somehow finally rejoin the rest of her family in exile. I can't imagine how frightfully impossible the odds must have seemed to her at the time."

"But the Bolsheviks," Kolya interrupted. "The Ural Regional Soviet. The Cheka. Yurovsky. How would they possibly explain something like that to Lenin?"

Sokolov rose from his chair and strolled over to one of the windows in the dim and barren room. Gazing out into the deepening darkness that was slowly enveloping Ekaterinburg, he softly continued his amazing story.

"The truth is, you wouldn't explain something like that to Lenin. You'd cover it up...as quickly as possible...or suffer the same brutal fate he had decreed for the Romanovs. And that's exactly what I believe happened. In order to save their necks, Yurovsky and his men managed to create a masterful and intricately detailed charade. Sheer panic and self-preservation can become a very effective muse."

Sokolov turned from the window to glance back at Kolya. She remained sitting in stoic silence, her clasped hands resting on the tabletop and her gaze riveted on the young Investigator.

Sokolov turned back to face the window once more. "Since the Ural Regional Soviet was well aware of the fact that Lenin wanted the Imperial family to eventually be executed," he went on, "Yurovsky knew that he had to produce the correct number of bullet-ridden bodies in order to prove that Lenin's directive had indeed been carried out, albeit sooner than he may have wished. The murder of the Romanov's servants partially served that purpose. As for the additional corpses that were needed, we know that at least seventeen other members of the Imperial House of Russia—of varying ages and gender—were also murdered by the Bolsheviks during that same time period; so royal bodies were not all that difficult to come by. Besides that, the Koptiaki forest is so full of hastily buried victims of the Revolution that every Birch

246

tree might as well be considered a tombstone. Regardless of who they really were or where they finally came from, once the required number of corpses had been hurriedly collected, Yurovsky had them driven to the Four Brothers mine, deep in the Koptiaki woods. There, under cover of darkness, the bodies were partially destroyed by hand grenades, acid, fire and dismemberment before being buried—but not in the mine shaft itself. As the pièce de résistance, Yurovsky had his men partially burn some of the Romanov's clothing and belongings and dumped them all into the mine shaft—where they were sure to be found by someone with a curious memory for details. Of course, the search of the mine shaft was eventually abandoned because it became obvious that the bodies weren't there. Like a magician's parlor trick, it had all been a simple case of intended misdirection."

"But the Bolsheviks didn't count on you discovering the mine shaft, did they?"

"Of course they did," Sokolov grinned. "In fact, Yurovsky's plan depended upon that very discovery. A prisoner I interrogated actually gave me the idea. He said Yurovsky seemed overly fixated on the appearance of the mine and its surrounding area. He was a photographer, after all, and had a very keen sense of a picture's proper composition. He wanted to be absolutely certain that the mine would be the immediate focus of our attention. If the object of the search was a mine shaft, it would seem all the more convincing later on when we finally discovered the doppelgänger—a mound of freshly dug earth next to the shaft's rim. A mound of earth that hid a shallow grave filled with the partial remains of the substituted bodies…all waiting to be uncovered by someone like me."

Sokolov paused in his remarkable story long enough to return to his chair at the table. Once more seating himself, he downed his full glass of vodka with some satisfaction. He then leaned back in his chair and crossed his arms over his chest.

"An amazing tale," the old woman nodded. "But what finally happened to the Imperial family? You said they escaped Russia. How?"

"By boat, of course." Sokolov smiled. "Traveling by train would've been much too risky. Trains can be easily stopped and searched. A British warship, on the other hand, would have commanded a certain degree of deference from the Bolsheviks. It would've been allowed to proceed unimpeded."

Sokolov cocked his head slightly and grinned at Kolya. "But then you know all of this. You were, after all, the person who suggested that I take a rather fateful stroll along the river. You knew very well what I would find there."

This time, Kolya returned the Investigator's smile with a slight nod of her head.

"So the Romanovs were taken out of Russia by boat," she repeated. "But to where?"

"There is a window in the upstairs bedroom of this house," Sokolov replied, "the room once occupied by Nicholas and Alexandra. A cross has been drawn on the window sill...a reverse swastika, actually—literally meaning 'well-being'. I'm sure you must've seen it."

Kolya nodded in silence.

"In Christianity," Sokolov continued, "the swastika is used as a hooked version of the Christian Cross, the symbol of Christ's victory over death...a rather fitting analogy in this particular case. But, in answer to your question, there happens to be a country where the reverse swastika is actually revered as a symbol of good fortune. You wouldn't happen to know what country that might be, would you?"

The old woman shook her head, but her eyes told a different story.

Sokolov leaned closer to her face and softly offered one word, "Tibet."

The old woman's gloved hand betrayed her with one simple gesture—it moved reflexively to cover her mouth as she gasped softly but audibly. As far as Sokolov was concerned, however, that one gesture confirmed everything he'd just said. His steady gaze locked on the old woman's face, Sokolov poured himself another vodka. In a silent attempt to reduce the old woman's obvious nervousness, the young Investigator also slid an empty glass toward her and filled it with vodka as well. Kolya picked the glass up with both of her trembling hands and readily downed its contents. She then returned the empty glass to the table.

"During all that befell him and his family, do you know when I think the Tsar was happiest?" Sokolov asked.

Speechless, the old woman once more shook her head.

"In my opinion," the Investigator mused softly," Nicholas Romanov was happiest chopping firewood while a prisoner in Tobolsk. There are photographs of him there. I've seen them. His face is all aglow...smiling...contented. And there is such an incredible light in his eyes—something you don't see in earlier photographs. He never really wanted to be a monarch, you know. He said so himself. 'I'm not prepared to be Tsar. I know nothing of the business of ruling.' Those were his own words. I believe the simple life appealed to him more than all the trappings of his royal heritage."

Sokolov once more let his gaze drift to the window of the dim room and into the dark Siberian landscape that now stretched somewhere beyond sight.

"Tibet declared its independence six years ago," he continued. "One year after that, the Tibetan government signed the Simla Accord with Britain which ceded the South Tibet region to British India. My guess is that the Tsar is there somewhere…caretaker of some nondescript little farm tucked away in some secluded mountain glade…all under the vigilant surveillance and very quiet protection of King George and the British Empire. I'd like very much to think that Nicholas Romanov is more content there than he's ever been—still chopping firewood, tending to a garden perhaps, and enjoying quiet evenings by the fireside with his beloved family gathered close by. All but one anyway."

The young Investigator let his gaze drift back to Kolya.

"Do you know about the incredible jeweled eggs the House of Fabergé made for the tsars of Russia?"

The old woman nodded her head.

"In that case," continued Sokolov, "you must also know that they are some of the most unbelievable feats of craftsmanship the world has ever seen. After the fall of the Romanovs, the Bolsheviks naturally ransacked the House of Fabergé and all of the eggs were confiscated. They made, however, one rather unpleasant discovery: eight of the eggs from that priceless collection were missing…each one valued in the millions. Now, I imagine it would've been next to impossible for the Romanovs to have smuggled gold or silver out of the country. But eight eggs?"

Sokolov chuckled softly and then once more leaned close to the old woman as if about to share a secret in confidence.

"Can you imagine what that little Tibetan farm finally cost Nicholas Romanov?" Sokolov smiled wryly. "Untold wealth. The inconceivable riches of an empire. The shimmering and distant world that was once Imperial Russia. That was the going price for his life and the lives of his family. The offer was most probably tendered by King George himself—proving, in this case, that royal blood is sometimes actually thicker than water…for a price at least. But, you know? I think the Tsar must've given it all away quite happily. It never meant that much to him anyway. I believe he knew all along, more than anyone else, what his genuine treasure was...the only wealth that ever truly matters to a husband and father."

"So," the young Investigator finally concluded, leaning back in his chair with a slight shrug, "there you are."

Kolya gazed at Sokolov for a moment in complete silence, then a slight smile began to trace her pale lips.

"Well," she replied, lightly tapping the table top with her finger for emphasis, "that is quite a story."

"Yes," Sokolov continued, "and as I said, it's only what I believe. Merely a theory strung together from a curious collection of small, seemingly unrelated details. Like your daughter-in-law for instance. You see, I keep being drawn back to her. My first night here, when you both brought my luggage into this room—she placed the bags on the floor, stood up, and very gently brushed back a lock of stray hair from her forehead. I remember the gesture particularly because of the way in which it was done—very daintily and with the little finger of her hand. May I know her name?"

"Anya," the old woman answered in a voice just above a whisper.

"Yes," the young Investigator replied as he raised his glass of vodka once more in the form of a salute. "I drink to her—to her beauty—her silence—her sadness. I drink to Grand Duchess Anastasia Nikolaevna."

Sokolov downed the vodka and gently placed the empty glass back on the table before continuing.

"It was brilliant," he smiled. "All this time I was searching for a Grand Duchess. Not once did it ever occur to me that I might find her behind the dirty face of a peasant girl...someone who has come and gone in this house since the day I first arrived. But then...where else would you hide something or someone so completely but in the very midst of the searchers?"

Again leaning closer to Kolya, he added another question.

"It was your son who helped her?"

"No," the old woman replied. "Not at first. There was another man who helped her. One of the guards here, inside this house. He and my son had known each other, so he brought the girl to us. She owes her life to him."

"One of the guards here?" Sokolov asked. "In this house? Do you know his name?"

"You met him, Inspector," the old woman answered drily. "Karl Strovka, the man you shot. He was the one who saved the life of Anastasia. As you say, things are not always what they seem to be. Admiral Kolchak obviously believes the Grand Duchess is alive. Your job is to lead him to her. After which, you are to disappear as well. As you say: nothing personal. Politics."

This time it was Kolya who leaned toward the stunned Sokolov for quiet emphasis.

"On the last night in this house," she continued, "the Empress Alexandra read to her daughter from the Bible. The words were from the Prophet Obadiah. '*Though thou exalt thyself as the eagle, and set thy nest among the stars, thence will I bring thee down...*'"

The old woman's voice, choked with emotion, trailed away into silence as she gazed mournfully at the young Investigator for several moments before feeling composed enough to continue.

"How many more lives must we lose?" she finally pleaded with trembling lips. "How much more Russian blood is left to spill? When does it become enough to satisfy Lenin's ambition...or Admiral Kolchak's...or, yes, even yours? I tell you this: you have the power to help make an end here and now. The life of Anastasia Nikolaevna for the price of your signature on a piece of paper."

Natalya Kolya, her lips trembling and her cheeks fresh wet with tears, still kept her defiant gaze locked on the young investigator.

"I am an old woman," she stated evenly. "I haven't much time left on this earth. But I swear to you that I will use every moment I do have to keep that child safe from further harm. Where we go from here is up to you."

With a deep and thoughtful sigh, Sokolov leaned back in his chair and paused to consider Kolya's words. He knew very well how much depended upon his answer.

"Herodotus," he finally began slowly, "once wrote that Xerxes, the Persian king, wept on the eve of his invasion of Greece because he knew that every soldier in his enormous army would someday be dead. I doubt that Nicholas Romanov ever shared such sentiments. He was much too committed to the one thing that mattered most to him—his own family. If the Tsar ever wept, it would most certainly have been for them. And, God knows, there was finally great cause for weeping. The Romanovs were always so much larger than life—distant—aloof. They lived in a world that was theirs alone. I suppose...in a very real way...all of them, along with the world they inhabited, did die here in the early morning hours of July 17, 1918."

Sokolov paused briefly before concluding, "At any rate, that's what I intend to say in my report."

For a moment, neither person in that room moved or attempted to cut through the emotional silence that lingered for a while after Sokolov's astounding statement. Her greatest fear dispelled, Kolya, with a deep sigh, seemed to sink slightly in her chair as though her tired body had suddenly been freed from some enormous burden. Her shoulders sagged with relief and she lowered her head for a moment in what appeared to be prayerful gratitude. Then, lifting her penetrating gaze to Sokolov, she once more addressed the young Investigator.

"The Whites are going to lose this war. You know that, too, don't you?"

"Yes."

"What do you plan to do?"

It suddenly occurred to Sokolov that he hadn't given a single thought to what his immediate plans might possibly be. He hesitated for a moment and then smiled.

"I believe I'll take one last walk in the garden outside and then...go home."

Kolya considered the reply briefly before nodding her head. With some bit of effort, she then slid her chair back from the table and stood. Sokolov, observing her limp to the door of his room, suddenly remembered the cup of still steaming tea the old woman had been kind enough to bring him.

"Tell me something," the Investigator mused aloud as he lifted the cup from its saucer. "I'm curious about one thing. Suppose, a moment ago, I had told you that I intended to tell the world the truth...all of it. What could you have possibly done to stop me?"

The old woman paused in the doorway and turned back to face Sokolov with a wry smile.

"Very simple really," she answered. "I would've let you drink that cup of tea."

Sokolov froze in shock, as his mouth sagged open. Gingerly, he lifted the cup of tea closer to his nose and sniffed. The scent of bitter almonds was faintly discernible. Turning his stunned gaze to the old woman in the doorway, Sokolov managed only three whispered words in response: "I'll be damned."

Kolya turned again to go, but before she exited the room and disappeared from Sokolov's life forever, she shared one last parting wish with the man who was only just beginning to realize the full import of her gratitude.

"Have a good life, Nicholas Sokolov," the old woman concluded with a slight wave of her gloved hand...and then, in another moment, she was gone.

Chapter Twenty-Two

"Nicholas Sokolov was relentless, tireless, full of resource in the pursuit alike of murders and beasts of prey. The Tsar case called for the exercise of all the skill that the most genial and courageous of magistrates could display. Sokolov never faltered."

Robert Wilton

The sun, as though offering a closing benediction, was finally setting on Nicholas Sokolov's last day in Ekaterinburg. It was a time he had so often dreaded, but given the tumultuous events of the day, whatever residual anxiety he might have been harboring had happily given way to a more liberating sense of accomplishment and successful resolution. The mystery had at last been solved. All that remained for Sokolov to do now was to make his way out of Ekaterinburg, write the report and submit his conclusion to Admiral Kolchak. Before he was to begin his journey, however, he would keep his word to Natalya Kolya and make one last visit to the Ipatiev garden.

The early evening's stillness was broken only by the occasional sounds of artillery fire rumbling ominously in the surrounding hills. The Bolsheviks, now on the outskirts of Ekaterinburg, were beginning their final push to retake the city. Knowing that the minutes that now remained to him were few, Sokolov hurriedly exited the House of Special Purpose for the last time, his knapsack slung over his left shoulder and the handle of his valise gripped firmly in his right hand. One last glance at the garden and he would be on his way.

All available motor vehicles had been confiscated by the evacuating White Army, or what was left of them. Sokolov would have to make his way to safety on foot, a challenge that didn't trouble him overmuch. His pistol was holstered at his side for protection should he encounter a need for it. He had also carefully planned his escape route knowing that the approaching darkness would provide useful cover. In a matter of a few hours, he would be sufficiently out of harm's way, and therefore able to continue his journey to safe harbor at a more measured pace.

Sokolov hastily descended the front steps of the Ipatiev House and made his way into the deserted courtyard. A few steps more and he rounded the corner of the house that led to the neglected little garden...the one place that had provided the Imperial family with brief but welcomed relief from their otherwise claustrophobic day-to-day existence in Ekaterinburg.

Entering the garden, Sokolov paused under the fragile ruins of the wooden trellis. He was taking one last look at the surroundings when he became suddenly aware of another presence. Apprehensively, he placed a hand on his holstered pistol and quickly shifted his gaze to the far side of the garden. A soft gasp rose in his throat at the sight that greeted him.

There, only a breathless distance away, stood Anastasia Nikolaevna Romanova, the Grand Duchess of Russia. She was gazing back at Sokolov with an expression that seemed a combination of shyness, gratitude, and even a bit of childlike curiosity. Still dressed in her familiar peasant garb—kerchief, fingerless gloves, long overcoat and boots—she carried a small bundle of meager belongings slung over one shoulder. She, like Nicholas Sokolov, was obviously prepared to depart Ekaterinburg forever. For whatever reason, she had also found herself drawn one last time into that little garden so full of memories.

Sokolov could only stand in breathless awe, returning her soft gaze in the sacred silence of that beautiful twilight. There were no words to describe what he felt in his heart at that moment...no sentiment that could possibly express the profound emotional impact of this completely unexpected encounter. They faced each other from either side of that forsaken little garden with the gentle knowledge that words were finally useless to them both. And so, they would say it all with nothing. Only later would Sokolov begin the struggle to describe what he believed had taken place during those few transforming moments of heartfelt redemption and staggering revelation.

Nicholas Sokolov's Journal
Hotel du Bon Lafontaine—Paris, 1921

She was standing a short distance away, gazing off into the deep crimson horizon as though she could see not only her destination, but her future as well, whatever the inconstant gods now deemed it to be. She seemed somehow resolved and strangely at peace with it all—perhaps because she could, at least for the moment, cast off what must have been such an agonizing charade and step once more into the vindicating light of day, clothed in her own identity. Perhaps the serenity I read in her face was also because of my own hopeful wish that she might now be able to reunite with the distant ones she loved most in this world.

But I will never know.

What I did finally understand in the sweet reverence of that golden moment so long ago, was that Dmitri had been right after all—I was completely captivated by her, and had been since Kolchak first placed that tiny, silver-framed photograph into my hands. But what I still had not admitted to myself, at least up to that moment, was that I had also fallen deeply in love. It was truly one of the most bittersweet realizations of my life.

Since my first years after completing my studies at the university, the possibility of love had always tended to paralyze me with a terrible sense of dread because love, you see, has everything to do with vulnerability, and I had always considered that kind of emotional commitment to be not only a loathsome human weakness, but also the certain pathway to professional ruin.

That is not to say that I have lived my life completely without loving, nor am I totally devoid of human emotion. I have known, if only fleetingly, the beautiful whisper of a woman's sweet favor. It's simply that, as time passed, I made a conscious decision to focus my love entirely on my work ...on my stubborn dream of a better world ...and on a deep longing for that world to finally know peace. My search for Anastasia became, at least for me, a way to transform that dream into reality.

And now she stood before me as the physical embodiment of all that had once been so fleetingly pure and beautiful about the Past ...as well as a living testament to the resilience of unsullied youth. She had seen and lived the worst of a world at war ...suffered unimaginable loss ...endured enough tragedy for several lifetimes. And why? Because it had been her fate to have been born of royal blood—the same blood that had flowed through the veins of her legendary ancestors, sustaining the Romanov dynasty for over three hundred years.

As I continued to stand there, drinking in the sight of her and the magnificent backdrop against which she stood—a landscape saturated with all of the deepening colors of a dying day—the blood-red hues that tinged the endless Siberian sky as if paying homage to the ghosts of so many lost lives, the soft wind on my *face like a remembered melody from a distant childhood lullaby, the golden shoreline of the shimmering Iset River that stretched far into the horizon of a thousand tomorrows that still lay beyond knowing, the distant hills of Ekaterinburg that surrounded a now empty place that had only recently been the very center of my universe—all of it was suddenly swept up in one single, heartbreaking breath, and held before my unbelieving eyes. Everything was suspended in time, infinite space, and all-consuming silence.*

And then I noticed them...even from that distance ...tears...streaming down her pale cheeks as she silently returned my gaze. And I knew, beyond all doubt, that she somehow understood everything I ached to say...every secret longing I wanted with all my heart to share.

As the reverent silence continued to fill the world around us, I watched as she briefly knelt and placed the bundle on the ground next to her. I then saw her slowly rise again...but as she did, something absolutely miraculous occurred. As her body continued to straighten to its full height, it seemed as though all layers of her burdensome masquerade simply began to fall away. Her stooped shoulders slowly squared themselves, and she lifted her face ever so slightly until one side of it caught the amber light of the setting sun just so. And then, as if to crown the amazing transfiguration, with a simple movement of her hand she slid back the kerchief from her head so that it fell away and her hidden hair was freed. Beautiful auburn locks instantly fell about her shoulders, practically shimmering in the alabaster light.

How can I possibly convey the searing glory of those next few moments? For, even more than the simple physical adjustments to her posture, something else began to happen ...something internal and astounding was also taking place ...transforming her entire being before my disbelieving eyes. The result was an almost indescribable metamorphosis. In a matter of only several seconds, the timid and shabby peasant girl I had known as 'Anya' had disappeared completely. In her place, bathed in the shimmering light of a time that would never come again, stood Grand Duchess Anastasia Nikolaevna Romanova, caught for one brief moment in all of her former glory.

For the rest of my life, that image of her bathed in the setting sun's radiant afterglow will forever seem to be her parting gift to a sad and weary world. It was, I believe, her way of bearing living testimony to the fact that some bit of innocence and beauty had indeed survived the savage cruelty of the time.

And when she at last stooped to once more take up her ragged bundle of earthly belongings, I knew that she was also reassuming the burden of an incredible secret...one that would hopefully shield her from the dangers that most certainly lay ahead.

At least for the two of us, our moment of parting unfolded with a sense of unspoken grace—a knowing that would forever bind us together in mutual respect and loving remembrance. What mattered most was that Anastasia now had a second chance to experience every precious moment of life that was left to her. With time, she might even find a way to free herself from any lingering nightmares of the Past. The heart never forgets, of course—but perhaps the horror would at least recede enough for her to regain some sense of normalcy. The hopeful possibilities stretched as far as the open vista that now lay before her.

And so, as the Unknown between us at last began to widen, I stood at mute attention and slowly raised my hand to my cap in the best military salute of which I was still capable. I am so thankful that was the last image she had of me—a silent sentry formally acknowledging her departure. My final display of emotion, however, was withheld until she had turned her back to me. Only then could I truly bless the heartbreak of her leaving with my tears.

As Anastasia walked out of my life forever, an era unlike any other also passed from the pages of Russian history. The story of the Romanovs, as far as the world would ever know, had come to an end. They were, when given full measure of the time in which they lived, a truly remarkable family whose like we shall not soon see again.

I wish them well.

Nicholas Sokolov continued to watch in tearful silence as Anastasia faded into the distance ...until the pale mists that filled the far horizon finally swallowed her up and she was gone. Even then, he lingered, holding his salute and gazing sadly into a landscape that would somehow never seem complete again. As the sun slipped behind the distant hills, transforming the world into evening, he still remained, gazing into the empty horizon where he had last seen her disappear, until with one last sigh, he beheld the enveloping darkness take it all from his sight. Only then did he lower his hand from his cap in silent testimony that his official duties had come to an end. He turned and walked slowly away, shouldering his melancholy like a heavy weight from which he would never be totally free. It was a private sadness beyond description...one that would echo in his soul for the remainder of his days on earth. And yet, to him, it would always seem such an exquisite burden.

> I yield my place to you: it's time
> For me to decay and you to blossom.
> I say goodbye to each day,
> Trying to guess
> Which among them will be the anniversary of my death.
> And how and where shall I die?
> Fighting, traveling, in the waves?
> Or will the neighboring valley receive my cold dust?
> And though it's all the same
> To the feelingless body,
> I should like to rest
> Closer to the places I love.
> And at the grave's entrance
> Let young life play,
> And the beauty of indifferent nature
> Never cease to shine.

Alexandr Pushkin

Epilogue

"After fame is oblivion."

Marcus Aurelius

Three months later, Kolchak's Military Command called off the investigation. Nicholas Sokolov wrote down precisely what 'they' wanted to hear and dutifully served it up in triplicate.

"No survivors—not one."

In issuing that final report, Sokolov knew he had repaid Anastasia's sacrifice with one of his own. Her secret was now his, and he would guard it with lasting devotion for the rest of his life.

Five years later, when his findings were initially released, they began with a rather cryptic declaration:

"I here set forth the results of a successful judicial investigation. At its basis lies the law, the conscience of a judge, and the demands of the search for the truth."

The real ending wasn't quite so tidy however. Lenin's Bolsheviks won their Civil War. All it cost was the total collapse of Russia's standard of living—an economic loss amounting to 50 billion rubles ($35,000,000,000.00 in current U.S. Dollars).

In the end, war had also cost an estimated 15 million lives. Widespread starvation, epidemics, and wholesale slaughter by both sides took the lives of millions more.

By 1920, famine had claimed three million more souls. Children roamed city streets, many of them surviving on human flesh. The terrible droughts of 1920-21 only intensified the disaster. Another one million people fled the country. In 1924, Ekaterinburg was renamed Sverdlovsk in honor of one of the Bolshevik leaders in charge of the Romanovs' execution. The United States would not recognize the Soviet Government until the beginning of the Roosevelt administration in 1933.

Lenin's newly established state ultimately proved unable to run the economy on any competent scale. The peasants, who had borne so much of the unimaginable suffering, finally responded to Lenin's continuous requisitions by refusing to work their fields. By 1921, the harvest yield was only about 37% of normal.

The combined effect of so many wars coming in such quick succession was to prove insurmountable for Russia. Decades of bellicose delusion would come and go, but the implosion of Lenin's grandiose dream was, from the outset, a historic inevitability. The 'iron curtain' which eventually descended upon Eastern Europe was also destined to be rent asunder, and its prodigy—the infamous Berlin Wall, built on so weak a foundation to begin with, had no other option but to finally come crashing down.

As for the Romanovs, a small wooden chest supposedly containing the family's mortal remains was passed from palace to palace in Europe, among the few surviving relatives. Never officially claimed, it eventually vanished forever.

Of the remaining fifty-two members of the Imperial House of Russia, seventeen were murdered by the Bolsheviks. Thirty-five members of the family managed to escape.

The Ipatiev House in Ekaterinburg was finally converted into a museum where, for a few coins, you could visit the scene of the murder. Under cover of darkness on July 27, 1977, however, it was finally demolished. The man in charge of the demolition was the first Secretary of the Sverdlovsk Region. His name was Boris Yeltsin.

So much for Justice.

Admiral Alexander Kolchak once said that Lenin didn't care what he had to do in order to win, but he must have cared very much, one year later, when he captured the good Admiral—and had him shot. Three years after that, Lenin was dead as well. Some say poisoned. (He was quite fond of hot tea.)

So much for Survival.

Boris Gorev made his way to Berlin where he was hailed by many as the man who had so valiantly tried to save the Imperial family. His wife, Maria, became a lion tamer. He managed a restaurant.

So much for Dignity.

Sokolov never saw 'Anya' again. He preferred to cling to the hope that she eventually found happiness with her family. In truth, he harbored his doubts. In the years that followed, there were more than a few who publicly claimed to be the Grand Duchess Anastasia—and each of them had an amazing story to tell. Only one was ever true.

So much for Dreams.

As for Nicholas Sokolov, he made his way out of Russia and eventually settled in France where he finally rented rooms in the Hotel du Bon Lafontaine, on the Rue des St. Peres, in Paris.

It was there that he met Prince Nicholas Orlov, another dedicated monarchist emigre. Of Nicholas Alexeievich Sokolov, Prince Orlov wrote:

"Alone, supported by no one... Nicholas Alexeievich [Sokolov] did not falter...He guarded the truth for future generations, guarding it from every encroachment of personal intrigue. He determined to proclaim that truth himself—on his own, and not under the banner of any political party whatsoever."

On his way through Petrograd for the last time in 1920, Sokolov did make one happy discovery. They hadn't burned all of the books. Some things managed to survive after all. He wasn't one of them. The sad eyes from that faded photograph haunted him for the rest of his days. He died in 1924 at the age of forty-two and was buried in a small country churchyard in Salbris, south of Paris. It ended as he said it would. Nicholas Sokolov was no one's special memory. Hardly anyone was left to grieve his passing.

The epitaph, carved on his tombstone reads: *"Your Truth is Truth Eternal."* You can barely make out the words now. They've almost faded away completely.

Last Entry in Sokolov's Journal—Paris, 1924

So much for me.

To this day, the fate of the Russian imperial family remains shrouded in continuing mystery. Perhaps because the case was always based on circumstantial evidence, remarkable stories have continued to thrive.

Of the three completed and identical sets of sworn testimony, each of them signed by Investigator Sokolov, two copies, including the Investigator's own, disappeared. The third was finally rediscovered in Harvard University's Houghton Library where, for years, it had gone almost completely unnoticed.

In 1976—the same year that America celebrated its own proud bicentennial—and less than twenty years before the collapse of the Soviet Union—the official conclusions of Investigator Nicholas Alexeyevich Sokolov were finally made public.

"We must tell the truth—the massacre has become one of the most shameful pages of our history."

Boris Yeltsin

On July 17, 1998, eighty years after the alleged execution, the world was told that the remains of the imperial family (minus two bodies) and those who died with them were buried in the St. Catherine Chapel of St. Peter and Paul Cathedral in St. Petersburg. Senior church officials refused to attend, however, and the head of the Russian Orthodox Church ordered the officiating priest not to refer to the remains as '*Romanovs*' but as '*Christian victims of the Revolution*'.

On August 23, 2007, a Russian archaeologist announced the startling discovery of two burned, partial skeletons at a site near Ekaterinburg. The bones were reportedly those of a boy between the ages of ten and thirteen years, and of a young woman between the ages of eighteen and twenty-three years. (Anastasia was seventeen years and one month old at the time of the alleged execution.) Along with the remains of these two bodies, archaeologists also unearthed 'shards of a container of sulfuric acid, nails, metal strips from a wooden box, and bullets of various caliber'.

Subsequent DNA testing by multiple international laboratories including the Innsbruck Medical University and the Armed Forces DNA Identification Laboratory confirmed that the remains are those of the Tsarevich Alexei and one of his sisters. However, a group of experts affixed their names to a written report stating that 'the identification of either Maria or Anastasia was not possible by DNA analysis alone'. They further concluded that 'A well-publicized debate over which daughter, Maria (according to Russian experts) or Anastasia (according to US experts), has been recovered from the second grave cannot be settled based upon the DNA results reported here'.

As if to even further confirm the tenacity of this lingering mystery, on August 26, 2010, a Russian court ordered prosecutors to reopen an investigation into the murder of the Romanovs.

And so it continues.

Admiral Kolchak once warned Sokolov: "*Nothing will be what it seems. Never believe what you hear. Believe only half of what you see. Suspect even what you absolutely hold to be fundamentally true.*"

There was more wisdom in those words than perhaps he ever imagined.

A Scribbled Note
Found in Nicholas Sokolov's Paris apartment after his death

From a distance I have seen you
In the warm sweet summer's air
Playing with the pretty flowers,
Tying roses in your hair.

From a distance I have loved you.
Though you've never seen my face.
Someday, I will meet you.
Another time. Another place.

From a distance I will leave you.
I shall always call you 'friend'.
I know I could never love you.
I could never catch the wind.

The public still clings to fairy tales, and governments continue to prefer their own manufactured 'facts'. Whatever the obstacles, Russia's *Children of the Light* are at last free to tell the ages what they were.

—Finish—